DESIRING
LADY CARO

Books by Ella Quinn

The Marriage Game
THE SEDUCTION OF LADY PHOEBE
THE SECRET LIFE OF MISS ANNA MARSH
THE TEMPTATION OF LADY SERENA
DESIRING LADY CARO
ENTICING MISS EUGENIE VILLARET
A KISS FOR LADY MARY
LADY BERESFORD'S LOVER
MISS FEATHERTON'S CHRISTMAS PRINCE
THE MARQUIS SHE'S BEEN WAITING FOR

The Worthingtons
THREE WEEKS TO WED
WHEN A MARQUIS CHOOSES A BRIDE
IT STARTED WITH A KISS
THE MARQUIS AND I
YOU NEVER FORGET YOUR FIRST EARL
BELIEVE IN ME

The Lords of London
THE MOST ELIGIBLE LORD IN LONDON
THE MOST ELIGIBLE VISCOUNT IN LONDON
THE MOST ELIGIBLE BRIDE IN LONDON

Novellas
MADELEINE'S CHRISTMAS WISH
THE SECOND TIME AROUND
I'LL ALWAYS LOVE YOU

Published by Kensington Publishing Corp.

ELLA QUINN

DESIRING LADY CARO

ZEBRA BOOKS
Kensington Publishing Corp.
www.kensingtonbooks.com

ZEBRA BOOKS are published by

Kensington Publishing Corp.
119 West 40th Street
New York, NY 10018

All Kensington titles, imprints, and distributed lines are available at special quantity discounts for bulk purchases for sales promotion, premiums, fund-raising, and educational or institutional use.

If you purchased this book without a cover you should be aware that this book is stolen property. It was reported as "unsold and destroyed" to the Publisher and neither the Author nor the Publisher has received any payment for this "stripped book."

Special book excerpts or customized printings can also be created to fit specific needs. For details, write or phone the office of the Kensington Sales Manager: Kensington Publishing Corp., 119 West 40th Street, New York, NY 10018. Attn. Sales Department. Phone: 1-800-221-2647.

Zebra and the Z logo Reg. U.S. Pat. & TM Office.

First *Desiring Lady Caro* eBook and POD edition: April 2014
First *I'll Always Love You* eBook: December 2018

First Zebra paperback printing: September 2022

ISBN-13: 978-1-4201-5370-5
ISBN-13: 978-1-60183-254-2 (eBook)

10 9 8 7 6 5 4 3 2 1

Printed in the United States of America

Chapter 1

*End of June 1816, on the road back to London
from Yorkshire*

Gervais, Earl of Huntley, heir to the Marquis of Huntingdon, leaned back against the soft leather squabs of his traveling coach as it made its way along the Great North Road toward London. The previous day, he'd attended the wedding of his friend, Robert Beaumont. Huntley couldn't believe that Beaumont, one of London's foremost rakes, had fallen in love. If it could happen to him, no one was safe. In fact, Huntley's friends were being caught in the parson's mousetrap much too frequently for comfort.

Evesham, Rutherford, Marsh, and Worthington? All married. There must be some way to avoid their fate. Marriage meant dancing attendance on one's wife, children demanding one's attention, and getting into all sorts of trouble, not to mention the estate, a great rambling place, his father would foist on him, in Suffolk of all places. He shuddered.

No, marriage was not to be thought of, not until it was necessary for him to produce an heir. His stomach tightened at the thought of being caught in the quagmire of so-called "wedded bliss." What was worse, married men thought others should join their club. He needed to get away from his friends and their influence immediately.

Tapping on the roof of the coach, he called to the coachman. "Spring 'em."

The carriage moved faster, and the scene outside his window passed by swiftly but didn't change over-much. Hedgerows and fields led to more hedgerows and fields.

He turned his attention to his friend William, Viscount Wivenly. "I'll tell you, Will, my mother and older sister, Maud, are going to be impossible to live with now that Beaumont's been riveted."

Wivenly heaved a sigh and slouched down in the seat as if to hide. "I know what you mean. Mine won't be any better. I think I'll leave for a while."

Huntley raised a brow. "Where? It's too early for hunting."

His friend's lips pursed in concentration. "No, I mean, leave England. I've always wanted to travel, and now that the war's over, that's just what I'll do."

Travel was a good idea. He nodded. "Europe?"

Wivenly's brow creased, and he got a faraway look in his eyes. "I think I'll go to the West Indies. After listening to Marcus's and Lady Marsh's stories, I've a hankering to see turquoise water and half-dressed native women."

Huntley straightened and uncrossed his legs. "The West Indies?"

If he mentioned going to the West Indies to his father, the old man would re-open the dungeon and have him chained there. That was a damnable part about being the heir; even at three and thirty, the old gentleman still had too much control over him. "Will your father let you?"

Rubbing his chin, Wively replied hopefully, "I think he might. We have some family there, and he's still young enough not to worry about dying while I'm away. Always going on about me not having a Grand Tour."

Huntley leaned back against the dark brown squabs. "I think I'll go to the Continent. Germany, Austria, Italy. Practice some of the languages I learned. Italy's got to be a damned sight warmer than it's been here this year." The thought percolated in his mind. "Got an aunt in Venice I haven't seen for years. I hear Italian women are passionate."

Will, who'd been looking out the window as if he could already see the ocean, turned back around. "Isn't that Lady Horatia?"

Huntley glanced at his friend and frowned. "How the devil do you know that?"

Wively shrugged. "M'mother's bosom friend. Heard your aunt caused your grandfather to have apoplexy."

"Something was bound to, the way he went on about everything." Huntley lapsed into silence, until Wively took out a deck of cards.

"Penny a suit?" Wively asked. "Don't care to be fleeced by you before quarter day."

Smiling, Huntley put down the folding table and picked up the cards Wively dealt. "I'd let you win some of it back."

End of July 1816. Huntingdon Abbey.

As the last trunk was strapped to Huntley's coach, his twelve-year-old sister, Ophelia, clasped her hands together.

"Oh, Huntley!" she cried. "Bandits will attack you, and you will be lost to us forever."

"Good Lord, Lia, this isn't Drury Lane."

She dropped her arms. "I'd make a *wonderful* actress, just like Mrs. Siddons."

"Huntley"—his mother's mouth was set in a line, but her eyes danced—"watch your language. Lia, young ladies do not become actresses."

Not willing to surrender, Lia retorted, "But I'd make our fortune."

"Then marry a wealthy man," Huntley retorted dryly, then added before that idea could take root, "We are sufficiently well off that you have no need to worry."

He had no idea from whom his sister inherited her excess of emotion. His mother was steady as a rock. This needed to be nipped in the bud. The actresses he was acquainted with might earn a great deal, but not on the stage.

Mama embraced him, kissed him lightly on the cheek, and smiled. "Have a good trip. I suppose we will not see you until spring."

He jumped up into the coach. "Probably not. I'll send word when I start my way back."

Several days later he and Will had met up in London to make the trip to Dover together. Now, after a neat dinner, they sat in a private parlor with a decanter of brandy. Though he'd never admit it, he hadn't been so excited about anything since he'd gone to Oxford. He'd finally get to see all the places he'd only read and heard about.

Wively dealt the cards. "What did your father say?"

Huntley grinned. "Made me promise not to bring back a wife."

Giving a bark of laughter, Wively picked up his cards. "No chance of that. But I suppose you didn't tell him."

Huntley picked out a card and discarded it. "No. I just said I'd not think of marriage until I returned home. Unfortunately, he's got it in his head I must marry then. I take it your father didn't raise a fuss?"

Wivenly grinned. "Winked at me and told me he had a spare." He scowled at his cards for a moment. "Appears we've got some problems concerning my great-uncle's family, therefore it's a good thing I'm going."

Early the next morning, Huntley clasped his friend's hand before Wivenly walked up the gangplank to the large merchant vessel bound for Jamaica. "Safe trip, Will. Don't forget to come back."

Wivenly laughed. "Good luck to you, my friend. Enjoy the Continent and all it has to offer. I hear the Italian ladies are particularly lovely."

Grinning, Huntley retorted, "I'll let you know."

He strode farther down the dock to his packet bound for Calais, looking forward to months of unfettered freedom.

Huntley knocked on the large, ornately carved door of his aunt's *palazzo*. At last, two months of travel through France, Germany, and Austria—some of it tedious, most luxurious—were over. He looked forward to staying in Venice for an extended visit, provided the women of Venice proved as warm and welcoming as the Italian weather. The door was answered by a tall, somber servant just past middle age.

A low, musical voice floated down. "La Valle, who is here?"

At the top of the marble stairs stood the most beautiful creature Huntley had ever beheld. At first, he thought she was a figment of his imagination. Shaking his head, he blinked before gazing at her again. No, he was right the first time. Fair, flaxen hair curled around her face. The eyes fixed on him were wide and set under perfectly arched brows.

And, Lord, her lips. There was only one good use for them. Kissing. More specifically, kissing him.

His body hardened as if he hadn't had a woman in months, which was certainly not the case. She was so exquisite, even the heavy frown marring her countenance couldn't make her less than beautiful. Only his old nurse had frowned at him like that, but it hadn't made him want to . . .

Pulling himself together, he bowed. "Lord Huntley, at your service."

"You are early." She pressed her lips together. "We did not expect you for another few days."

As the seraphic creature turned on her heel, the costly silk of her light turquoise gown swished around her. Who the deuce was she? He'd never heard of Horatia having any children. He grinned to himself. A widow perhaps?

She walked away, stopped and turned, brows furrowing. "Don't just stand there, follow me. Lady Horatia will want to see you."

Huntley checked to ensure his mouth wasn't hanging open and started up the stairs. "Yes, of course. I would like to refresh myself first. I'm in no fit condition to meet my aunt."

Though her frown deepened, it had no power to distract him from rosy lips. "You may bathe and change later."

"If you wish." He remembered his mother telling him that if he scowled, his lips would grow that way. "I'll wager you are much prettier when you don't glower."

She speared him with a glare. "Why, my lord, should I wish to be pretty for you?"

He could think of a number of reasons, but in her current mood, she'd probably not be receptive. "Very well then, take me to my aunt."

She glanced at the ceiling with a look of long suffering. "*That* is what I've been trying to do."

Hmm. Prickly. That wasn't an attitude that was generally directed toward him. Picking up his pace, he followed the mystery woman.

Turning once more, she led him into a large, magnificent, pale blue room trimmed with gilt. Brightly colored tiles paved the floor and louvered doors led to a bálcony overlooking the Grand Canal.

"Godmamma," his nemesis said, "here is Lord Huntley. *Early.*"

She infused the word with so much disapproval, he was again forcibly reminded of his old nurse.

His lips twitched, but he managed to keep his expression grave as he bowed. "Aunt Horatia, I am sorry to have inconvenienced you. It was not my intent."

A woman just a few years older than he, whom he recognized from her portrait in the gallery at his ancestral home, Huntingdon Abbey, sat at a table sipping white wine. Her bright green eyes peeked up through dark lashes. She was still a beauty. Her hair was dark brown, but her eyebrows and eyelashes were much darker, almost black.

His aunt's laugh reminded him of tinkling bells. "You silly boy, you've not put me out at all." She glanced at the younger woman. "Did Caro berate you?"

Ah, she had a name. A lovely one at that, but who was she?

Horatia turned to Caro. "You know you should not, my dear. A guest should always be made to feel welcome."

Caro's face turned a deep rose. "I am sorry, my lord."

Wanting to ease her discomfort, he gave a slight bow. "I did not feel unwelcomed. Merely that my aunt was anxious to see me." Huntley gave her his most charming smile. "I'm sure that was all you wished to convey, miss?"

She curtseyed and in a cool tone said, "Lady Caroline Martindale."

Martindale. She must be one of the Marquis of Broadhurst's daughters. The eldest. Huntley'd heard she'd married; apparently not. What was she doing here? "Lady Caroline, my pleasure."

His aunt waived her hand airily. "We are not at all formal at home. Call her Caro, and do not allow her to make you feel six again."

He hadn't thought it was possible, but her blush deepened.

"*Godmamma.*"

At least one of his questions was answered.

"You may address me as Horatia." She took another sip of wine. "*Aunt* Horatia is sure to make me feel much older than I am."

He tore his gaze from Lady Caro to his aunt. "We couldn't have that."

"Well then, Huntley." Horatia smiled slowly, and he got the distinct impression she'd noticed his interest in Lady Caro. "I'm sure you'd like to bathe and change. You're fortunate we are dining in this evening, for I shall tell you, we are a couple of gadabouts."

Lady Caro pulled a bell and a footman entered. "Please escort Lord Huntley to his room."

Huntley followed the man out of the parlor and up the wide marble stairs to another large room overlooking the canal. The chamber he was given was almost directly above the drawing room he'd been in. A shallow balcony drew his attention and he walked out on to it to watch the activity on the canal below.

"My lord," the footman said in Italian, "I shall have water sent to you directly."

Huntley turned. A metal tub stood before the unlit fireplace. "*Grazie mille.*"

His valet, Maufe, poked his head in from what must be

the dressing room. "I'll be with you in a moment, my lord. Just putting your kit away."

"No hurry." Huntley turned back to the balcony, taking in the view. Gondolas jockeyed for position in the canal, and people walked with an unhurried pace over the nearby bridge. His mind wandered away from the scene below and back to Lady Caro. He puzzled over what it was, beyond her beauty, that attracted him in spite of her obvious disinterest. It was almost as if she was being purposely rude. Perhaps it was a certain vulnerability that lurked beneath her prickly exterior. Much like a hedgehog, or the thorns on a rose. Yes, a rose was a much better analogy than a small, silly-looking animal.

Water being poured in the tub and his valet's voice intruded on Huntley's thoughts. "Yes, Maufe?"

"My lord, your bath is ready."

Huntley undressed and climbed into the tub. Leaning back, he soaked in the warm water, and closed his eyes, enjoying the various calls from the canal. A vision of kissing Caro's delightful lips floated in his mind. A pleasure he had every intention of enjoying. He jerked his thoughts away from his nether regions. That way led to marriage. A state he wanted to avoid. Yet Lady Caro was certainly a temptation.

Caro repaired to her chamber to change for dinner. They ate unfashionably early, but Godmamma claimed it was the only way for her to avoid becoming fat. Caro splashed her face with water and, after drying her hands, held her arms up as the pale green gown her dresser, Nugent, held slipped over her. After it was laced, she sat at the dressing table.

What was it about Huntley that disturbed her so? Though she'd been tempted, she'd never allowed herself to be intentionally rude to a gentleman before. What was worse, he was

Horatia's nephew, and he'd be living with them. She gave herself a little shake. She would treat him like a brother. That would dampen any interest he might have in her.

"My lady, sit still," her dresser said. Nugent had been Caro's nursery maid and, before her come out, had trained as a lady's maid, though that didn't stop Nugent from chastising Caro as if she were still a child. "What's got you so fidgety?"

She was tempted to raise her chin, but that would only earn her another rebuke. "I am not fidgety."

Nugent twisted Caro's hair into a top-knot. "I hear Lord Huntley is a handsome young man."

"It doesn't matter if he is." Caro resisted huffing. "I'm not interested."

"Harrumph. Time you started."

A thought occurred to her, and she narrowed her eyes. "My mother hasn't written to you, has she?"

"No, my lady." Nugent concentrated on her work. "What business would her ladyship have writing me?"

"Well," she mumbled, "someone did."

"Did you say something, my lady?"

"No."

Nugent nodded, and Caro thought she heard her maid say, "Good."

She should let the whole topic drop. "I do not understand why you are suddenly so interested in men."

"I'm not, but you should be."

"Good heavens, why?" Before her maid could answer, the tines of a hair comb scraped her scalp. "Ow, that hurt."

"I told you to stay still."

Caro took a breath. She was going to end this conversation once and for all. "I'm perfectly happy as I am."

"You're not."

Why did she have to have a dresser who had been with her since the nursery? "What makes you say that?"

"You deserve the life you were born to lead," Nugent said in an uncompromising tone.

Caro ground her teeth. "You know very well all chances of that ended years ago."

"The right gentleman wouldn't think so."

She took the strand of pearls from her dresser, wrapping them around her neck twice and allowing one loop to hang down, then added the matching earbobs. "I'm not talking about this any more."

Nugent gave a wry look before busying herself picking up clothing. How maddening. Caro picked up her fan and reticule, and strode out the door. Running straight into the person in question.

His hands reached out to steady her.

"I'm sorry." She kept her gaze averted from him. "I should have watched where I was going."

He chuckled. A deep, soothing sound. Caro made the mistake of looking up. A smile lurked in his eyes, which hovered between green and blue. One dark brown lock of hair fell over his brow, and she itched to push it back into place.

Caro stepped sharply back. She wasn't interested in Lord Huntley, she wasn't. Men were not to be trusted. She had made that mistake before.

Huntley dropped his hands as anger flared in Lady Caro's eyes, and she quickly retreated against the wall. What the devil had he done? "The mistake is mine."

She dropped her gaze and shook out her skirts. "Perhaps we should both be more careful."

He offered his arm. "Please accept my escort."

Lady Caro nodded but didn't place her hand on his arm

as he'd expected. Instead, she made for the stairs, her back as straight as a poker. There was some mystery about Lady Caro, and he intended to discover what it was.

Horatia glanced at Huntley and Caro as they walked onto the balcony. A small smile played on her lips, and she lifted her wine glass, motioning him toward a long, narrow cabinet set against the wall.

He poured glasses of chilled white wine for himself and Lady Caro. She took a seat next to Horatia on the small sofa. He chose a chair on the side nearest to her.

"Huntley," Horatia said, "there are quite a few English gentlemen in Venice this year. Shall I give you the directions to the clubs they frequent?"

He grinned. "Thank you, Horatia."

Her green eyes twinkled with mischief. "I know how you gentlemen like to get away from the ladies on occasion."

He gave a bark of laughter. "Would all women were so understanding. You'd make an excellent wife."

She tilted her head and smiled. "I did make an excellent wife, and now I choose to please myself."

Huntley sat forward a bit, bringing himself closer to Lady Caro. She took a sip of wine, but her breathing quickened. "Why is it you never remarried?" he asked his aunt. "Weren't you quite young when Laughton died?"

Horatia chuckled lightly. "I was, indeed. Barely two and twenty. Yet I'd been married for five years to a man older than my father." Her smile thinned. "I was fortunate. He was still well-looking and very kind. We had a happy and full marriage. If I'd gone back to England and allowed my father to marry me off again, I would have had no guarantee of the same treatment."

Huntley saluted her. "I heard Grandfather wasn't happy about that."

"Was he happy about anything?" She glanced down and

smoothed her skirts. "That was the reason I remained here. My husband left me a considerable independence and taught me how to handle my funds, so I did not have to marry again unless I wished to. So far, no man has captured my interest, and I doubt if I could bring myself to wed again now. I would lose too much freedom."

Lady Caro drew his attention. Her face was serene, but nothing else about her was. He could almost feel the effort she made to remain still. "And what about you, Lady Caro? Are you waiting for a gentleman to sweep you off your feet?"

Lady Caro took another drink of wine. "I am not interested in marrying." She glanced at him with her chin raised. "Anyone."

"Indeed?" Keeping his gaze on her, Huntley sat back, toying with the stem of his glass. She'd included him in a broad swath that included all men, and he didn't like it.

"Huntley," Horatia said, breaking the silence, "to-night Caro and I are attending the opera. You may join us or find some male company. Though you might find the clubs a little thin of guests. Unlike in London, most of the gentlemen will be at the performance and the rout party afterwards."

"I'd be happy to accompany you." Perhaps then he'd discover how Lady Caro came to be in Venice and what she had against men.

Caro wished Godmamma had not invited Lord Huntley to accompany them to the opera, though there was really no way to avoid it. The way he stared at her was disconcerting, and she sincerely hoped he didn't see her as a challenge. She'd spent the last five years making her life over and finding a quiet happiness. She'd not allow him to come along and upset all her plans.

Once they arrived at the *teatro* La Fenice, Caro spent a moment taking in the atmosphere. La Fenice was the first public opera house in Europe and no matter how many times she visited, it never failed to impress her. The *teatro* was much grander than the opera house in London. The interior had five rows of private boxes on each side, with seating in the gallery below as well, for those who could not afford a private box or chose not to sit in one. The whole place glowed with candles in crystal chandeliers suspended from the ceiling and in wall sconces. Paintings adorned each row of boxes, and gilt-covered plaster accented it all. The effect was magnificent.

Horatia's box was located in the middle of the second row. Once they'd settled themselves and been served glasses of champagne, Lord Huntley raised his quizzing glass and surveyed the theater.

Not long afterwards, Mr. Throughgood, a good-natured young man who never bothered her, joined them.

"Huntley! I didn't know you were here. Welcome to Venice."

The two men clasped hands. "Chuffy, good to see you. I'd heard you were on your Grand Tour as well."

"You'll like it here." A jovial man, he grinned broadly and bowed to Horatia and Lady Caro before addressing Huntley again. "How long do you plan to stay?"

"Several weeks at least."

While they talked, Caro plied her fan. It was amazing how small and close the box became with two large men in it, particularly when one was Huntley.

"Huntley, Mr. Throughgood," Godmamma said. "I'm happy for you to renew your acquaintance, but please do it in the corridor so some of my other friends can visit as well."

The two men moved to the other side of the doorway. Caro took a sip of champagne and visited with some of the ladies who'd arrived. When she glanced back at Lord Huntley, Mr. Throughgood was introducing the Marchese di Venier. *Damn*. Caro moved farther away from the entrance. For some reason, the marchese refused to believe he irritated her, or any other woman for that matter. Hopefully, Huntley and Mr. Throughgood would keep the man occupied.

The marchese was a few inches shorter than Lord Huntley and more slightly built. The Venetian's black hair shone with pomade in contrast to Lord Huntley's more natural Brutus, which became his dark brown waves.

The marchese entered the box, swaggering toward her. Really, she'd made it clear enough, she did not wish him to court her. If he got too close, she had her hat pin. Fortunately, Lady Haversham, a friend of Horatia's and Caro's, caught the man by the arm and kept him in conversation until it was time for the performance to begin. Di Venier was becoming much too assiduous in his attentions.

Standing next to Chuffy, Huntley studied the Venetian and Lady Caro's scowl as he entered the box. "Who exactly is di Venier?"

"His grandfather's a duke," Chuffy responded. "He's descended from the Doges of Venice. Very powerful family even with the Austrians in control of the whole area."

Huntley took a drink of champagne. The marchese glanced several times at Caro, but she studiously ignored the Venetian's presence.

"We appear to be overrun with English," the marchese drawled as he walked out of the box. "You are staying with Lady Horatia, are you not?"

Lady Haversham must have been gossiping. Huntley raised a brow. "She *is* my aunt."

"Yes, of course." Di Venier's dark eyes became cold. "I will caution you not to indulge in any fantasies about Lady Caroline. I have other plans for her."

"Indeed?" By the set of Lady Caro's chin and the exasperated look she'd given di Venier when he left, it appeared she didn't want anything to do with the man. "I hadn't heard the lady was interested in any one in particular."

Di Venier stiffened. "If she is not now, she will be."

Not if Lady Caro objected to di Venier, and he was sure she did. Huntley lifted his quizzing glass and studied the Venetian, then, without glancing into the box, said, "You must excuse me. My aunt requires my presence."

Di Venier scowled. "Remember what I said."

This was like a bad play. Only a rogue would force his attentions on a lady after she'd made clear she had no interest. Tension thrummed through Huntley's veins. Someone had to watch out for Lady Caro. She *was* under his aunt's care, and he was the only gentleman in the house. In fact, considering she was Horatia's goddaughter, she was practically family. One could argue it was his duty. Not to mention foiling the marchese might be good sport.

Once Huntley had taken his seat, he noticed that di Venier sat in a box located across and up one level from Horatia's. His attention focused on Caro, his gaze like that of a hawk before it swoops down for the kill. An older gentleman next to di Venier held up a lorgnette, pointed it at Caro, and grinned. For her part, Caro kept her face averted, all her attention focused on the performance. If she was aware of di Venier's interest, she gave no sign.

Huntley attended the opera in London a few times each Season, but he was not prepared for the exuberance of the Venetian opera. Once the performance began, the energy in the theater rose, as if the audience was part of the drama, cheering on the heroine and hissing at the villain.

Horatia leaned closer to him. "Very different to London, wouldn't you say?"

"I would indeed. It almost seems as if the crowd will tear the scoundrel apart. Lady Caro, how do you find the opera here?"

Her face glowed with pleasure, though it was clearly only for the performance. "I enjoy it very much."

Once again, she took his breath away. He wished she'd smile more often.

During the intermission, Caro moved easily among their visitors, conversing with gentlemen and ladies alike. However, when di Venier arrived, she once more ensconced herself in a group of ladies.

Huntley moved inconspicuously to hinder the marchese's access to Caro. "Good evening, my lord. I must say, I've never enjoyed the opera as much."

"Lord Huntley." The Venetian inclined his head before taking a step forward.

Huntley didn't move.

Di Venier's jaw clenched. "I would like to speak with Lady Caroline."

"You don't want to go in there." Huntley tilted his head toward the box. "It looks like a hen party. Not to mention there's no room to move."

In a low, rough voice, di Venier said, "Do not attempt to thwart me."

"Then don't do anything that would require me to step in." Huntley waited until the marchese left before returning to his seat. He didn't like the man's attitude. The marchese acted as if Lady Caro were a piece of property to be fought over.

After the performance, the jockeying for position among the long narrow boats called *gondolas* was nothing remotely akin to the orderly departure of carriages in England. Horatia's servants escorted them from the door to the docks. Once in the *gondola*, the ladies resumed their places in the *felze*, a small cabin in the middle of the boat. They arrived at the venue for the party, and as Horatia had said, it appeared as if most of the opera attendees were present. He escorted his aunt and Caro to nearby chairs, and Horatia was once more in a circle of friends. Chuffy found him, and he joined his friend's group, a little apart from his aunt.

This time di Venier was able to make his way through to his quarry, but when the marchese asked Caro to promenade, she raised an imperious brow and refused, going back to her conversation. Not long afterward, he apparently received the same answer. He headed toward the card room, but not before a calculating leer entered his eyes.

The marchese reminded Huntley strongly of another man who thought all women were his for the taking. It might be helpful to try to find out a little more information about di Venier. "Chuffy, I don't suppose you have anyone like a Bow Street Runner here who could be hired for a private investigation?"

His friend rubbed his chin for a moment. "No, though I believe I can put you in touch with a man. More of a thief-taker, but very effective."

"That will do."

Chuffy ambled off to the card room and Huntley walked out onto the terrace, drawn once again by the Grand Canal. His curiosity was starting to get the better of him, and he could not stop wondering why Caro was so against men. His hands, braced on the railing, tightened into fists as he watched the moonlight play on the rippling water.

"My lord, how wonderful to see you here."

Glancing to his side, he was not particularly pleased to see Lady Darling. They'd had an affair for a few months, but they'd parted company more than a year ago. Her fan waved languidly, drawing attention to her barely contained breasts. Her skirts clung to her form. She must have taken to dampening her petticoats. He was much more interested in what Caro's shape would look like under her demure silk gown.

Bowing, he took the hand Lady Darling offered and raised it to his lips. "My lady," he murmured. "I didn't know you'd left England."

They stood at an angle to the terrace doors, facing the canal. Her eyes fixed on his face before dropping to his lips and then lower, stripping him with her gaze. Despite her ladyship's abundant charms, his body failed to respond to what was a clear invitation.

"London was becoming a dead bore. But"—she stepped so close to him, her ample bosom pressed into his chest—"it is always nice to see old friends."

Keeping a polite smile on his face, he took a step back. "Indeed."

She leaned into him, and tapped the now furled fan on his chest while moving her other hand down his jacket and over his breeches. Whispering huskily, she said, "Come see me some afternoon, Huntley. I am much better company than the Ice Maiden." Lady Darling pouted. "I do not understand why she attracts so much male attention."

He glanced in the direction her head was turned and saw Caro staring at them. Their eyes met for a brief moment before she looked away, and he turned back to Lady Darling. In stark contrast to Caro's restrained beauty, Lady Darling's obvious sensuality appeared tawdry.

Angling herself so that one hand was hidden from the room, she stroked between his legs. He grabbed her hand, pulling it away from him. Breathing in sharply, her lips parted, waiting for him to kiss her.

God, if he were so inclined, he could probably push her into the shadows and take her. Huntley kept his voice low. "Try not to be so easy, m'dear. Gentlemen like a challenge."

Opening her eyes wide, she purred, "Don't you remember how good it was?"

"I remember how expensive it was. You'll have to find someone else to fill your jewel box and plow your field." He dropped his hand, stepped back, and bowed. "If you'll excuse me, my lady?"

Striding back inside, he joined his aunt and Caro. Caro widened her eyes. "I'm surprised Lady Darling let you go so soon."

"Are you indeed?" Huntley resisted smiling and wondered what prompted that remark. "I dance to no woman's tune."

"Then we have at least one thing in common," Caro said. "I dance to no man's."

Ah, back to prickly. Yet the look she'd given him while he was with Lady Darling was not disinterested. What would it take to bring her round?

Chapter 2

Caro struggled not to frown at Huntley as he lounged against the ancient stone wall surrounding one of the many gardens of the church of Santa Maria dei Penitenti, a hospice for fallen women. She visited the hospice at least a couple of times a week to help out with the children abandoned by the war. A small, dark-haired boy sat on her lap as she read to him, as a hen leading her chicks bustled by.

She glanced up as Huntley turned. Ever since his contretemps with the Marchese di Venier, Huntley had taken to accompanying her to her various activities. She wished he would not insist on going almost everywhere with her. Both men needed to stop acting like dogs over a bone. Though she had to admit, Huntley was helpful in keeping the marchese away from her.

The problem was, his very presence disturbed her. It was as if her nerves were on edge whenever he was near her. Just now, for instance, she had been engrossed in reading to the child; then he moved, drawing her attention away. Drat the man. Huntley had told Godmamma that he would leave in a few weeks to travel to Florence. Well, good. Then he wouldn't be around to bother her anymore.

She'd received letters from both Phoebe, now the Countess of Evesham, and Grace, Countess of Worthington, asking if he'd arrived. Huntley was apparently a good friend of their husbands. Both her friends had families, husbands, and children. Almost everyone Caro knew was married. Her throat tightened. Just as she should be. If only it was possible.

She kissed the little boy and put him down, holding her arms out to a small girl. This was the closest Caro would ever get to having children.

She glanced at Huntley and frowned. Why did he just stand there doing nothing? Probably because he'd never entertained children before. She grinned to herself, and said in her sweetest voice, "Lord Huntley, would you not like to read to some of the children?"

He looked around at her, his gaze steady. A slow smile touched his lips. "Of course, I would love to read to them."

Caro signaled to a groundskeeper for another chair and gave him a book. One of the little girls climbed up into his lap. Caro bent her head and returned to the story, waiting to see how Huntley enjoyed reading. To her surprise, he used different voices for each of the characters. A rich timbre for the hero and a low, gravelly voice for the giant; his tone rose higher for the heroine. Other children gathered around as he stamped his feet on the ground. So much for trying to put him out. Let that be a lesson to her for making assumptions.

"You've had practice."

He smiled. "I have younger brothers and sisters."

"It shows." She returned his smile. "You're very good."

Her heart thumped hard when he broadened his grin. She shook her head and went back to the book. There was no point in even thinking of Huntley.

Huntley studied Caro as she held the child on her lap. He'd used all his skill, and it was finally paying off. She was softening toward him, but it hadn't been easy. Maybe that was part of her allure. Though aside from that, her blood-lines were excellent. God, he sounded like his grandfather. The plain fact was he didn't know why he was so attracted to her. Though with any luck, in a few more weeks he'd start courting her in earnest. Well hell. His friends had been right. Running away hadn't helped at all. Fate was bound to catch a man out.

His aunt hadn't joked when she said they were gadabouts. Balls, drums, soirées, as well as picnics occupied their time. On the evenings Huntley wasn't escorting his aunt and Caro to one entertainment or another, he normally met with a group of men his age. As in London, there were usually several events each evening.

It seemed uncanny how di Venier appeared at each one Caro attended, until, as he, Horatia, and Caro were leaving one evening, Huntley noticed men watching the house. What was worse, the marchese, rather than taking the hint, became more assiduous in pressing his attentions on Caro, thus hindering Huntley's own efforts. He frequently stood with his aunt and Caro, trying to lend what support he could as she determinedly refused di Venier's invitations time and time again.

Though di Venier accepted Caro's latest rebuffs with a smile, the black look on his countenance when he turned away concerned Huntley. The man was up to something, and Huntley needed to discover what it was. With any luck, the thief-taker he'd hired to investigate the marchese would send a report soon.

"You needn't hover over me, Huntley." Frustration was evident in Caro's tone. "I am capable of taking care of myself."

Resisting the urge to smile, he glanced down at her. "I am not hovering."

"Well, it feels as if you are." She pressed her lips together. "You'll cause a scene if you continue to look at the Marchese di Venier as if you'd like to run him through."

That was exactly what Huntley would like to do—skewer the man on his blade, or put a hole in him, but he'd probably have to settle for drawing his cork. All his instincts told him the marchese was a danger to Caro.

He flicked a piece of dust from his coat. "I don't trust him."

She rubbed her temple. "No, but what can di Venier do, after all?" Her lovely turquoise eyes met his gaze. "I shall continue declining his invitations and he will eventually go away. All men do. You do not need to feel responsible for me."

That's where she was mistaken. "Humph."

Caro sighed and glanced around. "Here is Godmamma with Mrs. Stringer. Please, go talk to your friends."

She plastered a smile on her face and turned to welcome the two ladies.

Though he did as she requested, he positioned himself to keep an eye on whoever approached her.

* * ~*

The next night they entered the ballroom of a *palazzo* overlooking the other end of the Grand Canal from his aunt's house. The rooms were alight with chandeliers of crystal and gold. Wall sconces and gilded mirrors made the room brighter and appear larger. The ornate plaster ceiling was decorated with paintings extolling the family's history, the scenes separated by gold-adorned plaster reliefs. A series of doors led to the deep balcony overlooking the canal.

Though Huntley once again saw men watching Horatia's *palazzo*, di Venier was not yet present. After waiting until the ladies were settled, Huntley approached a group of gentlemen.

"Huntley, welcome," Chuffy said. "We haven't seen you much."

He shook his friend's hand and greeted the other gentlemen. Two of the men were discussing their plans to leave Venice and travel to Florence, when Chuffy tapped his arm and motioned him away from the group. "Di Venier is after Lady Caro again."

Huntley turned to see di Venier grab Caro's arm. She jerked it away, anger infusing her countenance.

Rage at di Venier coursed through him. "Excuse me."

The devil with diplomatic relations. No man treated a lady—especially Caro—like that. With a few long strides, he reached her side. The marchese gripped her arm again, and she struggled to free it. Horatia said something to di Venier. Whatever it was, wasn't working.

Caro jerked her arm again, her voice icy. "I do not wish to stroll with you, my lord. A *gentleman* would have accepted my answer the first time."

Before di Venier could respond, Huntley hit the marchese's elbow, breaking the man's hold on Caro's arm. He glowered down on the marchese. "I think it's time we had a talk, my lord."

Di Venier glared but followed Huntley out to the terrace, scowling. "This is none of your affair. You are no relation to her. You have *no right* to interfere with me."

The blood in Huntley's veins heated to boiling and his muscles clenched, ready to do battle, but he tried to keep his temper under control. "Lady Caro resides with my aunt and is under her protection. That gives me the right."

Di Venier sneered and turned to go back inside. "I do not recognize your claim."

Huntley latched on to di Venier's shoulder and growled. "I don't care whether you recognize it or not. She is mine to protect. Don't push me, di Venier. Leave Lady Caroline alone, or your life will become extremely unpleasant."

Shaking Huntley's hand off, the man turned. "I will have her one way or another. Stay out of my business." Di Venier's lips curled. "You are nothing here, *Englishman*."

That was all the reason Huntley needed. He drove his fist into the marchese's jaw. Di Venier fell back against the rail, then slumped to the floor.

Huntley shook out his hand, entered the ballroom and glanced around, relieved to find Horatia and Caro gone.

Almost immediately, Chuffy came up to him. "The man's mad. I'm glad you planted him a facer."

Huntley smiled grimly. "He's not going to give up, and even with the Austrians in charge, his family has too much wealth and power. There must be some way to find out what he's planning."

Chuffy furrowed his brow. "Have you received a report yet?"

"No. I'll send a message that I need something immediately."

Slapping Huntley's back, Chuffy nodded. "Good idea. Try to keep the ladies close to the *palazzo* for a few days if you can. Our marchese is not going to be happy about what happened to-night."

"I'll do what I can." It was mid-October, and he'd originally planned to leave for Florence in another week. Yet even if his interest hadn't turned to Caro, his duty was clear. He could not leave his aunt and Lady Caro without his protection. "What a nuisance it is to have to guard a female who doesn't appreciate it."

Yet that was a lie. He'd do anything to protect Caro, no matter her reaction.

He left the ball and took a *gondola* directly to his aunt's *palazzo*. He was in his chamber when voices from the balcony below floated up.

"Oooh," Caro ground out. "I should have punched him myself."

Horatia laughed. "I'm sure that would have made you feel much better."

"It would have caused a scandal," Caro said in a rueful voice.

"That too. Maybe it was better Huntley did it."

"It is not fair. Gentlemen have all the fun."

Caro moved to the balustrade, giving him a good view of her rosy lips pursed into a pout.

His lips twitched as he held back a shout of laughter. "I know of at least one lady who would have planted him a facer."

She glanced up and crossed her arms across her chest, which had the effect of enhancing her already generous bosom. "Eavesdropping, Huntley?"

He grinned. "I couldn't help it." He climbed over his rail and dropped down to the balcony below. "Do you wish me to show you how to knock him down?"

Caro slid him a sidelong gaze. "Would you really?"

"Only if you promise not to use your new-found knowledge on me."

She narrowed her eyes. "What if you do something that would cause me to hit you?"

"In that case, you have my permission." He studied Caro for a moment. Her eyes had a warlike sparkle he didn't usually see. "I have one more stipulation."

Her chin rose. "And that is?"

"You must promise to allow me to hit him if I'm present."

"*Men*." She hugged Horatia. "I'm for my bed."

Once Caro was gone, he poured a glass of wine. "Is Caro all right?"

"Caro is shaken but determined to hide it. It is a pity di Venier has fixed his attention on her. I wish we'd gone to Lake Garda after all."

Huntley took a swig of the chilled, dry white wine. His jaw clenched. "He's up to something. I've no proof, but I can feel it in my bones."

He finished the glass and poured another. What he wanted was brandy. He'd have to send Maufe out to find some. "I have a man investigating him. I should hear from him soon."

Horatia sipped her wine quietly for a few moments. "I shall do so as well. This is a small and normally safe city. If he plans something nefarious, surely word will leak out."

"But will we discover it in time?"

His aunt sighed and shook her head. "Perhaps we'll stay home for a few nights."

"I think that would be best."

* * *

Early the next morning, Huntley finally received the information he had been waiting for. He stared down at the documents, almost unable to credit the report. Di Venier had murdered a girl ready to take her vows as a nun. Damn. This was worse than any of them could have guessed. The man had no honor at all.

"Maufe, please tell Lady Horatia I need to speak with her immediately."

Ten minutes later, as he sat on the balcony drinking coffee, she joined him. "Have you heard anything?"

"Yes." He handed her the report.

After reading it, her lips formed a thin line. "That poor woman. I wish I could say I'm surprised. Some men hold the lives of those beneath them cheaply. Particularly a woman's life. It says here, di Venier thought she was a prostitute. He'd have seen her as the dirt under his feet. I've received news as well. There has been some chatter concerning the marchese leaving Venice." His aunt's brows drew together. "That to me is very strange, and I do not believe it. I think we shall go to my villa at Lake Garda for a few weeks. Perhaps by the time we return, his attention will be diverted to a more suitable lady."

Huntley leaned against a support column, sipped his coffee, and watched the *gondolas* plying their trade along the side of the canal. The water sparkled blue and fresh in the morning sun. Women never seemed to understand men. Di Venier was not only determined but obsessed. Removing to a location within two days of Venice wouldn't help. In fact, the more rural area might even help the scoundrel. "He'll follow."

Sighing, Horatia set her cup on the table. "If you are sure . . . Bother. We will have to come up with something. Oh, why did the dratted man have to return to Venice? We all went on perfectly well without him."

Huntley turned from the view and leaned back against the balustrade. "There must be someplace we can take her . . ."

"I'll not leave Venice." Caro stood in the doorway to the balcony. One hand held a cup, and the other curled into a tight fist. "This is my home. I'll not run away again."

Her face was militant, and Huntley admired her spirit. Venice had been Caro's refuge for five years, and she loved the city. Of course she wouldn't want to leave, but this place was no longer safe for her. Hell, the country wasn't safe. "A few weeks ago, di Venier killed a thirteen-year-old girl because she wouldn't service him. A novice who was ready to take her vows. He may be planning to abduct you."

Her eyes few wide. "Oh God, no." China tinkled as the cup and saucer in her hand shook. "How could anyone do such a thing? We'll tell the local authorities."

Huntley shook his head slowly. "You're a foreigner, and his family is extremely powerful."

She placed the thin china cup down on a table. When she spoke, the faintest thread of fear could be heard through her defiance. "But the Austrians, surely they will do something. The man cannot go around accosting ladies and there not be consequences."

Huntley started to rise to go to her, then sat back down. She wouldn't welcome his touch, and all he wanted to do was take her in his arms to comfort her. Rarely had he felt so helpless. "They will agree his manners toward you are poor, but we have no proof of anything else." Why was she being so difficult? "Don't you understand how vulnerable you are if you stay?"

She remained standing, staring out through the doors as if she couldn't believe what he'd told her. "I'm not a victim. I won't be."

He ran a hand through his hair, a habit that he'd developed since meeting Caro. "Sit down, please. We must decide what to do."

"My lady." His aunt's majordomo, La Valle, bowed. "The Duca di Venier is here to see you."

Horatia took a breath. "Did he say what it was about?"

"No, my lady."

Rising, she shook out her skirts. "Very well, show him into my study and tell him I shall be with him directly. Place two footmen inside the door."

He bowed again. "Yes, my lady."

Horatia turned to them, her face tight with worry. "This cannot be good. The duke has never come here before. Caro, my dear, you may have run out of time. Make your plans."

Back straight, Horatia went to meet the duke.

When Huntley turned back to Caro, her countenance was alive with tension. She glanced at him. "What could he want?"

Rapidly reviewing their options, Huntley said, "Let me take you back to England."

Her eyes flew open like a wild animal ready to flee, yet her voice was firm. "No."

That was obviously not a good suggestion. Very well, then, not England. He rapidly reviewed the places he could escort her to and not cause a scandal or have them be forced into marriage. Caro wouldn't appreciate that at all. Where? "Paris is an option."

Caro strode the length of the balcony and back, skirts snapping around her ankles. After a few moments she stopped. Her lips set into a line. "I don't have a choice, do I?"

He kept his voice even. "Not one I can see."

She blinked rapidly, then picked up her cup and sipped. "Very well. When would you like to depart?"

Horatia returned to the balcony. Small lines bracketed her

lips as she tightened them. Her fine eyes flashed in anger. "You'd better leave as soon as possible. The duke was here to make a formal offer for your hand on the behalf of his grandson, the Marchese di Venier. It was not an offer he was prepared to see refused." She took a breath and continued, her voice grave. "I told the duke it was impossible for you to marry the marchese as you were already betrothed to Huntley."

Chapter 3

"*You told him what?*" What in God's name was God-mamma thinking? She knew Caro couldn't marry. She rubbed her forehead and couldn't bring herself to meet Huntley's steady gaze. "Surely there was another way."

Her godmother picked up a cup, then frowned at the now cold pot of tea. "Well, my love, he was insistent that you marry his grandson, and you are two and twenty."

"What," Caro asked, though not sure she wanted to hear the answer, "does my age have to do with it?"

"The duke would not have believed you have no wish to marry." Her godmother fiddled with a bangle on her arm. "Add to that what Huntley told us about the young man's temperament."

"*Temperament!*" Caro clenched her fists. "The man is a beast."

Horatia nodded. "Indeed, so it just"—she took a breath—"well, it seemed the prudent thing to do at the time."

"Prudent?" Caro resisted the urge to roll her eyes and instead tilted her head back to gaze at the ornately painted ceiling. The happy, frolicking cherubs weren't helping.

"Yes, of course." Her godmother smiled as if it all made sense. "You must see how fortuitous having Huntley here is. He was the perfect excuse."

Why did this have to happen now? Her life had been going so well. Caro drew a breath and glanced at him. His countenance showed not even a hint of what he was thinking. It didn't matter. An engagement to Huntley was impossible. He'd discover her secret, and it would be a disaster.

"Don't you have anything to say?" she demanded, trying to get a rise from him. "Godmamma committed you as well."

He raised a calm, aristocratic brow. *Drat the man. He cannot want this.* If half the talk she'd heard was true, he didn't wish to marry yet. How could he be so composed?

He leaned back in his chair and crossed his arms over his chest, a sardonic smile on his face. "You may jilt me when you're safely in Paris."

Caro threw up her hands. "Why do I have to be the one to do the jilting?" Her voice cracked. "I already have a reputation as a jilt. This isn't going to help. I just want to live alone, in peace."

"You know perfectly well," Horatia said tartly, "Huntley cannot end the engagement."

Caro passed a hand over her forehead. She needed to get herself under control. "You're right, of course."

Huntley drank the rest of his coffee and stood. "We should leave this evening at the beginning of the normal dinner hour." He looked at her. "Before the men di Venier has watching the house arrive."

"He's doing what?" Caro gasped. "How dare he?"

"He apparently dares quite a bit," Huntley drawled. "If we depart to-night, we won't be missed until to-morrow. We'd nothing planned for this evening, did we?"

Her godmother shook her head. "No, nothing. How far do you think you will be able to travel?"

"I—we," he amended, "will try to make Padua."

"I know an inn there," Horatia said. "Caro knows it as well."

Caro bit her lip. This was no time to fall apart. "Very well." Traveling alone with Huntley? *No, it was not possible.* "But, Godmamma. I—I cannot."

"Caro, my love, there is no choice. We cannot all leave at once. I have to make arrangements for the house and a number of other things."

"What," he asked, frowning at Horatia, "will you do after we're gone?"

Horatia was quiet for a moment. "I shall travel to Genova and take a packet to Marseille. It will probably take a full week for me to arrive at the port. You must be in Austria by then."

"Horatia," Huntley said, "are you sure you'll be all right?"

"Yes, of course." She gave them a tight smile. "We shall meet in Nancy at the main inn that I've heard of, on the Rue de Guise. It's time I visited France."

Caro took a deep breath. This was really happening. They were leaving Venice, and she would be alone with Huntley. She wasn't ready to accept defeat yet. "We can travel faster and go with you."

Her godmother smiled gently. "I shall try to cover your absence and leave in no more than two days time with great pomp. I have no doubt I will be stopped by someone in the duke's employ."

She took Caro's hands and met her gaze. She had never looked more serious and, for the first time, Caro knew her godmother was afraid for her.

"The two of you must be as close to the Brenner Pass as possible by then."

Biting her lip again, Caro nodded. If di Venier followed, perhaps her betrothal to Huntley truly was the least of her worries. After all, not many of her countrymen would be traveling at this time of year. They'd want to be home at Christmas. No one would even know about the engagement. "I'll have Nugent pack."

Horatia went to a small marble side table and poured a glass of wine. "I've already given orders to your maid. You may take only a small valise with you. The rest of your baggage will meet you in Padua."

To her disgust, Caro began to weep. It was all too much. Once again, her life was being ruined by a man. She searched in her pocket for a handkerchief and found one being pressed into her hand. She glanced up. "I don't usually cry."

Huntley's eyes held a compassion she'd not seen there before. "If this is the worst that happens, I daresay we'll muddle along well on this trip. If it makes you feel any better, I'd rather not go back either."

When she tried to return his handkerchief, he motioned for her to keep it. There was so much to do, and she was having such a difficult time thinking. "I need to go to the orphanage and tell the children I'm leaving. I cannot just disappear."

Huntley shook his head. "It may not be safe. Neither the duke nor his grandson will be happy about our betrothal. After what Horatia said and the plan . . ."

She closed her eyes. "The plan to abduct me."

"Write them a letter. It is the best you can do at the present."

"Yes." As much as she hated to admit it, he was right. The thought of being snatched by di Venier, having him touch her—her skin crawled in disgust. "I suppose you're correct."

Her godmother squeezed Caro's hand and kissed her cheek. "Try to rest as well, my dear."

"Yes, that will probably help." Caro left with what dignity she could muster and strode swiftly to her apartment. She penned her notes, holding her tears at bay until the last one was sealed, before she threw herself on the bed and wept.

Her dresser, Nugent, stopped packing and handed her a cool, wet cloth. "Put that on your eyes or they'll be all puffy." When Caro had taken the cloth, her dresser continued. "It's not what you wanted, but you mark my words, it will all turn out the way it's supposed to."

The aggravating part was she was almost always right.

"Thank you, Nugent."

Nugent continued to pack. "He's not a bad-looking gentleman."

Caro hugged a large pillow. "Lord Huntley? No, I suppose not."

Her dresser closed the last trunk and turned. "Got nice brown hair."

"Whatever you're thinking, cease. It wouldn't matter if he looked like Adonis. I'm not going to marry him."

He was well-looking. Not that it mattered. Just the idea of a man touching her made her feel dirty, like the marsh water in the fens.

Once they met up with Godmamma, Caro and Huntley could say they found they didn't suit. Then it wouldn't be anyone's fault. They were not going to marry. "Nugent, give me something to do."

Huntley and Horatia sat at the balcony table. Sun glinted off the water, and a woman on the bridge, selling her wares, called out. He pinched his nose. The news of their betrothal was not nearly as unwelcome to him as it was to Caro. Fortunately for him, she did not seem to understand at all how easily they could be forced into marriage; especially traveling alone with only her maid to lend them countenance. If anyone either of them knew saw them, the game would be up.

"Any idea on making her more malleable?"

His aunt smiled wearily. "Share the planning with her. She likes to keep busy." Horatia was silent for a few moments. "Huntley, you're taking this very well. Many gentlemen would not. Could it be you have intentions toward Caro?"

He had the odd sensation of wanting to run a finger under his neckcloth. Any thoughts he had must be put on hold for the time being. "I am merely looking at this as an adventure. Rescuing a fair damsel from an evil marchese."

God, he sounded like his sister Ophelia.

Horatia raised a brow and stared at him consideringly before shaking her head. "It is not my story to tell."

The cravat loosened. "About Caro?"

His aunt furrowed her brows and nodded. "Um."

He held his breath for a moment, waiting for her to go on; when she didn't, he asked, "How bad was it?"

"Very." Pouring another glass of the chilled white wine, she gazed out at the canal. "I hope Caro learns to trust you enough to tell you."

He hoped so as well. He looked around the large drawing room. He'd miss the view and the bustle of the gondolas. He'd miss Venice, but duty called, and he had to help the most recalcitrant member of the female sex he'd ever met escape a blackguard. "Well then, I'll go see how my valet is coming along and visit the bank. If you get the note from Caro, I'll stop by the orphanage as well."

He left his aunt sitting at the table and wondered how long she'd have to stay away from Venice. When he entered his chamber, his valet, Maufe, was folding the last of his jackets. "How much more is there to do?"

"Almost finished, my lord. I've been informed the baggage shall precede us."

Huntley gazed around the room. "Yes. I want you and Collins to travel ahead with the trunks."

"Yes, my lord."

Maufe spoke Italian, and Huntley's groom, Collins, knew how to use a coaching pistol. "Do you know how to use a gun?"

His valet's eyes opened wide. "I was taught, my lord, though it's been many years since I've fired a weapon. Do we plan to be in danger?"

Huntley cracked a laugh. "I don't plan to be, no. But I would like to be ready."

Maufe stopped what he was doing. "To the point of marriage, my lord?"

"There's no point in trying to bamboozle me. I know you've heard all the gossip. Nothing's a secret in this house."

"As you say, my lord. You do seem to have a partiality toward the lady."

Not Maufe too? So much for hiding his interest in Caro. "Right now I just want to get the lady and me out of this with both our reputations intact. It's getting to be late in the year. I trust we won't run across anyone we know between here and there."

Maufe's answering grunt wasn't comforting. If Caro agreed to marry him, he wanted it to be of her own free will. He had the distinct impression a forced marriage would be disastrous.

"Will Lady Caroline's dresser and her groom travel with you, my lord?"

Huntley faced his valet. "Yes, I suppose they must. Her maid, at any rate. Please ask her groom to attend me."

Maufe closed the last trunk and left the room.

A quarter hour later, an imperious knocking sounded on his door. Who the devil was that? "Come in and stop making that infernal noise."

The door crashed against the wall and Lady Caro stood in the doorway, her chest heaving with indignation. "My servants are not yours to command."

Damn. He should have known she wouldn't take any perceived high-handedness well. Huntley rubbed the back of his neck. "I'm sorry. I wasn't thinking."

He kept himself from smiling as she opened her lips and closed them again, stunned. She'd been preparing for battle, but he didn't want to fight with her, at least not now, before they could make up properly. "Can you tell me if your groom knows how to shoot?"

"Yes, of course he does, as do I," she replied haughtily. "Why?"

"I'm sending my valet and groom ahead with the baggage. I don't want to leave us unprotected."

She blinked and her eyes narrowed. "Don't *you* know how to shoot?"

"Of course I do." He gave her a disgusted look. What gentleman didn't know how to handle a gun? "But if they come after us, I want to have more than just me to defend us. I'll guarantee you there will be more than one of them."

"Oh, of course, I understand. He is well versed in weapons, as are my maid and I." She gave him a rueful look. "Please, in the future, if you have need to speak to one of my servants, ask me."

"I will." What else could he say to put her mind at ease? "You should have your maid sleep in the room with you."

She'd turned to go and stopped. "Thank you. Your suggestion is very considerate."

After she left, Huntley sank into a chair on the small balcony. *Damnation.* This was going to be a very long journey if she fought him every step of the way. There must be some way to come to an accord with her.

Later that afternoon, with the luggage on its way and his errands accomplished, the only thing to do was wait until it was dark enough to depart.

Horatia had ordered antipasti, breads, and cheeses to be served on the drawing-room balcony. After the meal, Caro left. Horatia sighed. "I shall miss this."

She was giving up her life for Caro, but he would not have expected anything less from his father's sister. Caro was the closest thing to a child Horatia had. "How long must you remain gone?"

Her eyes swam in tears when she glanced at him, but she

smiled. "For a couple of years, probably. Though I do not know if I shall ever return. I had never seen this nastiness before, and I am not sure once one does see that, one can return."

He was quiet for a few moments. "What will happen to your house?"

Her smile broadened. "Thinking of everything? You are my brother's son. I have an agent. He'll take care of it. I might lease it."

Horatia straightened and gave his hand a pat. "It's too soon to make any permanent decisions."

Church bells struck the hour. Huntley wished she was coming with them. "We must go."

"Yes, dear, send me letters to the hotel in Nancy with your progress, and I shall do the same. Though I expect I'll arrive before you."

Caro entered wearing a dark blue traveling cloak and a hat that covered her fair curls. She held out her hands. "Godmamma."

Horatia went to her. "How many times have I told you to call me Horatia?" She dabbed Caro's eyes with her lace-trimmed handkerchief. "Silly child. We shall all be fine. Think of this as an adventure."

Caro nodded several times as she blinked back her tears and hugged Horatia. "I'll try."

Horatia patted her cheek. "Trust Huntley, my love. He won't hurt you."

He stopped a frown. Not just a bad experience then. Someone had hurt Caro before, but what had happened?

A tall, thin woman who he could only guess was Caro's dresser, Nugent, stood in the door. "Come, my lady. We need to be off."

Horatia and Caro gave each other one last embrace before Caro turned to leave.

Huntley closed his arms around Horatia. His throat was tighter than he'd wished. "We'll see you in Nancy."

"Godspeed."

"To you as well." Huntley strode quickly out of the room and down the corridor to the stairs leading to the gondola dock.

La Valle had sent servants to act as lookouts in the event the house was being watched. So far, they'd seen nothing out of the ordinary. Still, rather than riding in the small cabin called a *felze*, where a lady would normally sit, Caro and her maid sat on the wood benches.

Because sound carries on the water, and none of them wanted their English voices to be heard, the trip to the coach waiting on the mainland was quiet. Caro kept the hood of her cloak up to disguise herself even more as the boat sailed through the canals to the dock, where Huntley's coach stood waiting on what the Venetians called *terraferma*.

Once they arrived, Horatia's groom, Dalle, grinned as he lifted a large basket from the seat next to him. "Provisions. Her ladyship thought we might need them."

Huntley smiled. His aunt really did know how to keep men fed. "We might indeed."

He glanced around and grimly wondered how long it would be before they were pursued. Di Venier was not the type of man to allow Caro to easily slip through his fingers.

Dalle took a place on the box next to the coachman, Raphael, and the horses were put to, leaving Venice and, he hoped, the marchese behind.

Huntley gazed out as they sped along the road toward Padua. Trees rose like specters against the inky night sky. Fields and the occasional house were depicted in varying shades of black. The last time he'd come this way it had been light.

His little coterie were all so still, so quiet. Almost as if they were afraid to make a noise.

Finally Caro broke the silence. "I know the inn where we'll spend the night. The couple who own it are very good people."

His stomach gave a loud grumble.

"After all, you ate earlier." Caro chuckled. "How can you be hungry?"

He shrugged. "Will they feed us, do you suppose?"

The coach lantern limned her face as she smiled. "We'll have to see what arrangements your valet made."

"I might have done a better job," he said ruefully, "to ask you to accompany my valet. Maufe's Italian is good but not colloquial."

"Yet he has such presence, it may not matter."

The banter seemed to lighten her mood. Maybe this would work in his favor after all. Huntley grinned. "Indeed, he does have that. Maufe should be in service to a duke."

"Well, the heir to a marquisate is not far off."

"Don't"—he gave a mock gasp of horror—"let a duke hear you say that."

Finally she laughed. "Oh dear. I suppose you are right."

Four hours later, they arrived at the inn to find the landlord and his wife waiting for them. Huntley followed Lady Caroline Martindale up the narrow stairs of the inn. Unable to resist, he struggled to keep a smile off his face as he enjoyed the view of her lush derrière and reflected on how nicely it would fit in his hands.

She glanced back over her shoulder and glared. He widened his eyes, giving her the most innocent look he possessed. The stairs were narrow and steep. She stopped, causing him to almost, but not quite, make contact with the object in question. So close.

Caro closed her eyes briefly, clenching her jaw. "My lord, perhaps I should follow *you* up the stairs."

He started to bow, then realized that if he did, he'd be so close his lips could brush against her bottom. She must have had the same thought as she hastily backed against the wall, thus removing the tempting sight.

He stifled a sigh and climbed past her. "Thank you, my lady."

She inclined her head stiffly. "My lord."

Caro wondered what, if anything, Huntley had been up to on the stairs. She gave herself a little shake. It was probably only her imagination. He'd been nice to her, but nothing more. She had to keep in mind he was just as trapped as she. Neither of them wanted marriage.

Caro's chamber was already warm, and a pitcher of hot water sat by a basin containing a few sprigs of lavender. She glanced around again. There was a homely feel to the room, but she was unable to put her finger on anything specific.

She raised a brow and glanced at Nugent. "Quite comfortable."

"Yes, my lady. Mr. Maufe has done an excellent job. You'd think we were staying here more than just a night. Couldn't have done better myself."

She poured water into the basin and waited with a linen towel until Caro had refreshed herself.

"Mr. Maufe had your gown for this evening out and ready as well. Very good of him, it was, to have done all this. I won't at all mind following in his wake."

"No indeed." Caro changed for dinner into a gray silk evening gown with long fitted sleeves and point lace at the bodice. Taking the Norwich shawl from her dresser, she wrapped it around her shoulders. "I won't be late. I'm quite sure we will want to leave as early in the morning as possible."

When she entered the private parlor, Huntley was standing hunched over a table upon which a large map was anchored down on the corners by glasses and bottles.

He straightened. "Good evening. Do you want to take a look at this?"

"Yes, I would. Thank you." At least he was making a show of involving her. Yet Caro wondered how much he would actually take her opinions into consideration.

He placed a long, tanned finger on Verona. "I've been informed I can hire a good horse at the posting house on the main road to Milan, not far from the town center. We've been assuming di Venier won't know we've gone for another day or so." He glanced at her, lines bracketing his mouth. "We'd be less than clever if we depended on it. I'd like to travel as quickly as we are able."

Caro nodded tightly. Why the marchese would follow after having been told she was betrothed, she didn't know. Unfortunately, she'd never been good at judging the male of the species. "May I suggest you allow my coachman to make the arrangements, thus there will be no trace of an Englishman hiring a horse to go north?"

"That's a good idea. If possible, I'd like to make Verona to-morrow evening." He considered her for a moment. "It will be a long day."

That far. She needn't have worried that he would travel slowly. "It will be a hard day, at least nine or ten hours in the coach."

His gaze was steady on her face, as if he expected an argument. "We'll stop only to change the horses."

The faster the better. "Very well. Let's do it."

A knock sounded on the door.

"We should keep this among ourselves," he said. "Let the innkeeper, his wife, and their servants think we're going to Lake Garda as Maufe told them."

Of course, they owed it to the innkeeper to not put him and his family in a position of trying to protect her little group from any of the duke's men. She glanced at Huntley. He really was thinking of everything. "You're right. If we're followed early, they can't reveal what they don't know."

The knock came again as Huntley rolled up the map. "Pinch your cheeks and lips."

Caro's jaw dropped and she quickly shut it. "Whatever for?"

"We're supposed to be betrothed." Smiling slowly, a twinkle entered his eyes. "And we are taking a long time answering the door."

Heat infused her face, but she did as he asked while he strode to the door and opened it.

"Ah, milord." The innkeeper glanced at her with an interested stare.

Oh my. Huntley was right. Her neck and face grew hot.

Once the table was set, the dishes placed on small side tables, and the wine poured, the innkeeper and his son left.

Huntley held her chair. After taking his own seat, he inspected the offerings with his quizzing glass. "This appears to be risotto with mushrooms. Would you like to try it?"

She picked up the glass of wine and took a sip. "Yes, thank you. It is one of my favorites."

For a few minutes, they ate in companionable silence as she searched for something to say. "It's a good thing Godmamma thought to provide us with food and drink for tomorrow."

Huntley glanced up from his plate. "Yes, and that her baggage carriage isn't marked in any way."

This was not working. Why was she even trying to talk to

him? She huffed. "I suppose we can go through a list of the obvious, looking for conversation, but I'm really rather tired."

"Don't feel as if you must talk. Let's finish our dinner and retire. I'd like to start by six in the morning, if you agree."

What a relief. She was in no mood to entertain a gentleman. "Very well. Have you ordered breakfast?"

He took a large sip of wine. "No. I wanted to consult with you first."

His expression was uninformative, and, not for the first time, she didn't know quite what to make of him. "Thank you. I'll order it."

He dabbed his mouth with the serviette. "Or you can leave it to Maufe. He'll be on the road at least an hour before we are."

Caro placed her knife and fork on the plate to indicate she was finished eating. "He's very capable. Nugent is impressed."

"I'll tell him you said so. Shall we finish our wine and seek our chambers?"

Huntley escorted Caro to her room. When she would have opened the door, he took her hand. He'd never done that before. She looked at their fingers and couldn't decide whether to pull back or not. In the end, she left her hand in his much larger one.

"You did well to-night with the innkeeper." He grinned. "The next time you won't have to pinch your cheeks. You blush charmingly."

Caro bit her lip and felt the warmth rise in her face. "Is that meant to be a compliment?"

"Something like that. You did well."

"Then I suppose I should thank you, my lord."

He bowed. "My lady, sleep well. I'll see you in the morning."

He left her, walked to his chamber down the corridor, and waited until she entered her room. Caro closed the door and leaned against it, frowning.

She would have stayed where she was, but Nugent hustled her to the dressing table and took her hair down to comb it. "I've had a nice cup of herb tea made for you. Drink it before you go to sleep. We've an early morning ahead of us."

"Lord Huntley and I agreed to a six o'clock start."

"So I've been told. Up you go."

Caro stood while her maid unfastened her gown and stays. She had her arms through her nightgown and stopped. "When were you told?"

Her maid pulled the soft muslin down. "Before I went to dinner. Mr. Maufe didn't want to discuss our arrangements in front of the innkeeper."

Caro's jaw dropped then snapped shut again. *That—that sneak*. He'd already made all the arrangements before he spoke to her. He hadn't listened to her at all. It was pure fortune that made her agree to six o'clock. He had already made the arrangements. Well, he'd soon learn she was not to be trifled with. "Please send a message to his lordship that I would like to leave at six thirty."

Nugent put Caro in bed and made her drink the tisane. "If you want to tell him that, you may dress yourself and walk to his bedchamber. I'll not be a part of such foolishness."

"Are you disobeying my order?" Caro asked in an imperious tone.

"I don't know what's got into you." Nugent snorted. "I've never known you to be pettish, and I don't mean to let you start now."

"I'm not in the schoolroom any more."

"Then don't act like it." Taking the cup, Nugent pulled the bed-hangings closed. "Of all people, you should know how important it is to leave early."

"You're right." Caro sighed. "I don't know why I'm acting this way either."

Nugent huffed. "Go to sleep now, my little lady. You've a long day come morning."

"Good night, Nugent." Caro pushed her pillow around. She had every intention of confronting Lord Huntley over his high-handed behavior. She would not be bullied or have her opinion ignored.

Chapter 4

A summons from his grandfather awaited Antonio, Marchese di Venier, when he arrived home. A few minutes later, when he entered his grandfather's salon, Nonno stood staring out over the lagoon. Past eighty years old and shrunken in the manner of an old man, he appeared frail, yet he still wielded enormous power in Venice and beyond.

Kneeling, Antonio took the old man's hand and kissed it. He hoped his grandfather was successful in arranging his marriage to Lady Caroline. He'd wanted her ever since he'd first seen her. She was so different from any other lady of his acquaintance, so reserved, so beautiful. A treasure that should, by right, belong to him. Just like this house, which would one day be his, along with his grandfather's wealth. In his haste to add Lady Caroline to his collection, he'd gone about it the wrong way, but his grandfather would have smoothed everything over.

She would be his wife, and he would be the envy of every

gentleman in Venice. No one refused the powerful Duca di
Venier. His grandfather remained silent for a few minutes.
Finally Antonio could wait no longer. "You sent for me,
Nonno?"

A frown formed on his grandfather's normally calm face.
"Antonio, I have bad news. Lady Horatia informed me that
Lady Caroline is to marry the Earl of Huntley. According to
Lady Horatia, they have had an understanding for quite a
while. However, Lord Huntley has only recently proposed."

Antonio stared at his grandfather for a moment, unable to
believe what he'd said. How could that be? He'd been refused? Antonio clenched his fists and tried not to growl. "It
is impossible. There is nothing in his actions toward her to
show he has claimed her. He does not even stay by her side
or dance with her. I refuse to believe it."

She belongs to me.

The *duca* raised a brow. "Would you have had me call
Lady Horatia a liar?"

Antonio snorted. "I shall see for myself. I will go to the
palazzo to-morrow. Lady Caroline will listen to me. This
Huntley, he shall not have her."

His grandfather smiled slowly, his old eyes flickering
with excitement. "A di Venier takes what he wants. She
would provide a welcome connection to a wealthy and powerful English family, as well as an elegant wife for you. As
she is only betrothed, I see no problem in you *convincing*
her to have you for a husband rather than the Englishman. I
am sure Lady Caroline would appreciate the opportunity to
become a duchess and acquire a more robust lover. The English gentlemen do not have the reputations that we Venetians
have."

"I shall approach her to-morrow." Antonio bowed. "*Con
permesso, Nonno?*"

His grandfather waived a hand in dismissal.

Rising early the next morning, Antonio fussed over his dress, wanting it to be perfect for his interview with Lady Caroline. He wore a dark blue jacket with bright gold buttons, breeches that matched his jacket, and the orders he received upon his birth and his father's death, so that his future wife would understand how powerful he was.

Small feet pattered down the corridor and stopped outside his door. Antonio smiled and hid against the wall as a small boy peeked inside. "Papa?"

He swooped his son up in his arms and turned him upside down.

"*Papa!*" Geno shrieked, laughing.

Antonio turned his son right side up and planted a kiss on his dark curly hair. "What have you been doing this morning? Where is your tutor?"

His son clasped his hands behind Antonio's neck. "One of the servants said you were awake, and I wanted to see you." Geno focused on Antonio's neckcloth. "You're going somewhere. You're not leaving me, are you?"

If only the child's mother had been as faithful. He breathed in the sweet, milky scent of his son. "No, Geno. I would never leave you. I am going to bring you a new mother. One who will never go away."

After playing with his son and breaking his fast, Antonio waited until the tall gilded clock against the wall struck nine. He wished he could go earlier, but under the circumstances, he dare not anger Lady Caroline by arriving too early. By the time he departed, he'd gone over all the reasons she should marry him rather than Lord Huntley, chief of which was the power his family wielded, despite the Austrians, and her opportunity to become a duchess. Calling for his gondola, he descended to the dock.

As he traveled from the lagoon and up the Grand Canal, he was convinced he would be met with acceptance on her part. He'd rather have her come to him willingly, but if she didn't, there was always the abduction he had ready to set in motion. One way or the other, she would be his.

When Antonio presented himself at Lady Horatia's *palazzo* and asked to speak to Lady Caroline, he was ushered into her godmother's drawing room.

Lady Horatia smiled graciously and curtseyed. "Good morning, my lord."

As he thought, her ladyship was happy to see him. She would be pleased that he was not giving up so easily. He bowed. "Good morning, my lady."

"Please." She motioned him to join her at the table on the balcony.

He took a seat and waited impatiently for the formalities to be over.

Lady Horatia lifted a pot. "Coffee, my lord?"

"Thank you, my lady." After she'd set the cup before him, he picked up the tongs and placed two lumps of sugar in the dark, fragrant brew, and forced himself to take a sip. It was time and more to turn to the subject of marriage. He did not wish to wait longer. "My lady, I wish to have a private speech with Lady Caroline."

Lady Horatia's eyes opened wide in surprise. "I'm terribly sorry, my lord," she said in stricken accents. "Lady Caroline is on her way to Lake Garda with Lord Huntley."

Antonio's fists clenched. He took a deep breath and forced his hands to relax. It was most important to remain calm. The watchers he had placed on the house last night and early this morning had only seen two male servants leave and return. "And when was this, my lady? I did not know she planned to leave Venice."

Lady Horatia took a sip of her coffee. "We had been awaiting my nephew's arrival and had no opportunity to visit my villa this summer. Of course, with the weather being so much cooler, it was not a hardship to remain in Venice, but Lord Huntley wished to see the lake. He and Lady Caroline decided to travel ahead of me. I shall leave tomorrow to join them."

Suppressed anger infused him. It was a lie, he knew it. "But why is she traveling with him? They are not yet married."

"Oh, but, my lord"—her ladyship made an airy gesture with her hand—"they are betrothed, and she has her maid with her."

The woman was so calm, he almost believed her. But, no, even *Englishmen* had some passion in them, and Huntley hadn't even danced with Lady Caroline. Aside from warning Antonio off Lady Caro, Huntley had given no sign he was interested in her. For them to be betrothed . . . it was not possible. Unless it was arranged, but the English, Antonio had been told, favored love matches.

He was wasting his time here. He would find Lady Caroline and take her from Lord Huntley. He stood and bowed. "Thank you, my lady. I shall take my leave now."

After descending the stairs to the dock, he strode to his gondola. "*Rapidamente!* We must return home."

As his boat eased into the other traffic, his blood coursed faster through his veins. A hunt. It had been a long time since he'd had a worthy quarry.

He jumped onto the dock before the gondola was secured and called for his *maggiordomo*. "Send a message to the stables. I want ten men, horses, and a traveling coach readied immediately."

Lord Huntley and Lady Caroline could not be that far, and, with the coach empty, Antonio could travel much faster than Lord Huntley. Not to mention, they were not expecting him to follow them. Yet wherever they were, he would find them and bring her back. If Huntley disagreed, well, he could go the way of others who had tried to deny Antonio.

He hoped the Englishman would fight. Antonio was an excellent swordsman and "crack shot," as the English would say. He'd like to stick his sword in Huntley and watch the life ebb out of him. Besides, who would care what happened to him any way? The lady would be happy to have Antonio, and, if she wasn't, there were ways to persuade her. His grandfather's priest would marry him and Lady Caroline as soon as they returned to Venice. By then, she would be in no position to refuse.

Huntley awoke betimes and went over the plans for the day again with his valet.

Maufe shook his head. "I don't like it, my lord. I'll be too far ahead of you. What would you do if something were to occur?"

"I have done for myself before, you know."

Maufe pursed his lips. A sure sign he was digging in his heels.

"I am well aware that, on occasion, you've looked after yourself." He sniffed. "I shall not comment as to the state of your wardrobe when you returned. I shall say only that it is not fair to Lady Caroline. I'm quite sure she is not accustomed to your rough-and-ready mode of travel. And what if you—"

This would get them nowhere, and Maufe did have a point about Caro. Huntley shook his head. "Very well. Meet us in Verona."

His valet bowed. "As you wish, my lord."

Huntley was in the parlor discussing breakfast when Caro entered, dressed in a very fetching, pale lemon twill carriage gown. Even though her lips were pressed into a thin line, she took his breath away.

In his rush to stand and greet her, he almost tipped over the chair. "Good morning. You're looking well to-day."

She inclined her head frostily. If she were any colder, icicles would drip from her lips. "Good morning, my lord."

What the hell had he done now? Why was it men were always the last to know?

Caro went to the sideboard to make her selection from the meats, cheeses, breads, and fruit, before taking a seat and relieving him of his ignorance.

"I discovered from my maid that before we spoke last evening, you'd already given orders we were to leave at six o'clock." Caro's hand shook, apparently with anger, as she took the tea-pot, then set it back down. "What would you have done had I disagreed?"

So that was it. He should have realized she'd find out. He picked up the pot and poured her a cup. "I would have tried to talk you around to my way of thinking, and if that didn't work, I'd have tried to come to an agreement with you."

Caro glanced down at the cup and added milk and sugar; when she looked up again, the lines around her mouth had softened. "Thank you for not lying to me."

His brows shot up. *Lie?* "What reason would I have to lie to you?"

She took so much time spreading cheese on a piece of bread, he was uncertain if she would answer him.

Still attending to her bread, she replied, "In my experience, men lie."

For at least the tenth time since they'd started on this journey, Huntley wished he knew what had happened to her. The only thing he was sure of was that a man was involved. She was two and twenty, and she'd been with his aunt for five years. She must have been just out when it happened.

"You're welcome. I should've told you last night. But when you agreed with me, I didn't think it necessary." He peeled a boiled egg. "If you wish to leave later, I am happy to accommodate you. Though I would like to be as far away from Venice as possible when di Venier discovers we've gone."

She nodded tightly. "No, we shall leave as soon as we may."

Willing himself to remain in his seat and not go to her, he pretended not to notice how pale she'd become when he mentioned the marchese, and went back to the egg. "As soon as I finish this, I'll ensure the coach is ready."

"Thank you."

A few minutes later, he walked out to the inn's yard to see the bags being strapped on to the coach. "Is that all of it?"

Caro's groom, Dalle, an older, wiry man, pulled a strap. "That's everythin' going on the outside. Miss Nugent has her ladyship's jewel box and another bag."

"Very well, as soon as Lady Caro is ready, we'll leave."

Dalle closed one eye and stared at him. "Suits me jus' fine. Sooner we get her away from here the better."

Huntley nodded and turned back to the inn, then stopped. "What was your mistress like before she left England?"

The groom rubbed his chin, clearly thinking over how much about Caro he should tell Huntley. "Full of fun and gig she was." The groom gave him a hard stare. "Wouldn't like to see her hurt again. If you know what I mean."

Huntley felt like grinding his teeth. He wished to hell he did know. "Then let's get her out of here before anyone catches up with us."

He'd not long to wait before Caro and her maid came down the stairs.

Nugent curtseyed. "My lord. We're ready to go."

Dalle came around to help Nugent into the coach and put

the two bags she carried under the seat. Huntley handed Caro in. He climbed up after she'd settled her skirts. As soon as the door was closed, the coach lurched to a start, and the coachman kept the team well up to their bits.

Huntley lounged on the seat, with his back to the front, and watched Caro while she slept. She seemed so peaceful in repose, like an angel. His heart ached for her and maybe for himself as well. What a fix to be in, having to leave her home in the company of a man she could barely tolerate. Never mind the marchesc, Huntley didn't want to consider what would happen if they ran in to anyone they knew.

Nugent sat upright, holding what he assumed to be the jewel box. Occasionally her eyes closed and she jerked awake again. She'd have made a decent picket.

Two days later, Caro peeped out from beneath her lashes and found the source of the warmth that had awoken her. Huntley's steady gaze was on her. His eyes changed from green to blue. To-day, they were bluer. She wondered what the different colors meant. He'd deflected her anger quite easily yesterday morning, and had quelled her angst about all the problems they'd had yesterday with the horses and baggage coach, which surprised her. Most men wouldn't have bothered explaining themselves to a mere woman. At least in her experience, most gentlemen wouldn't find it necessary. Unfortunately they had still not made Verona.

Nevertheless, if she had to be stuck with him for the journey to France—she would not go farther than that—maybe he wouldn't be so bad to travel with. If they were lucky, news of their "betrothal" would not become widely known, and she wouldn't have to jilt him.

Five years ago, while traveling to Venice, Caro had decided she'd never marry, not for any reason. Nothing had happened in the intervening years to change her mind. She couldn't bear the thought of a man's hands on her again.

She was becoming uncomfortable under his scrutiny, but kept her eyes mostly closed so that he would not know she was awake. She speculated about where they were. As if he heard her, he shifted his gaze outside.

"We should be past Vicenza." He reached under his seat. "Would you like to play chess or continue sleeping?"

Caro started to stretch and stopped. She glanced at him sharply. He'd known she was awake. Huntley focused on the box he'd taken out.

"I'll play chess."

The corners of his lips lifted. "Good."

He was an excellent player, but so was she. Caro was ahead by one game when the coach stopped abruptly, tumbling the chess pieces to the floor.

She glanced out the window but could see nothing. "What is it?"

Huntley frowned, but his voice remained composed. "Let's find out."

He knocked on the roof.

Dalle answered. "It's just traffic, my lord. We've entered Verona."

She remembered the chess pieces and bent down to help retrieve them at the same moment as did Huntley. Their heads bumped. "*Ow*. You have a hard head."

He rubbed his forehead. "So do you."

Caro grinned. "So I've been told. You are now forewarned, my lord."

He returned some of the pieces to the box. "Indeed." He pointed to her hat on a shelf above the seat. "At least I didn't get poked in the eye by a feather."

She gazed at the chip hat with the large plumed feather that caressed her cheek when she wore it. It was nice he was able to joke at a time like this. She was surprised she could feel . . . comfortable with him, even in a closed carriage. She grinned. "I doubt that could poke anything."

His eyes twinkled and were suddenly green. "No, probably not."

Some few minutes later, they turned into a large coaching inn and came to a stop. Huntley jumped out before the steps could be let down, and strode into the building.

Caro started to rise, but Nugent placed a restraining hand on her arm. "Wait until he gets back, my lady. Dalle and the coachman haven't got down yet, and his lordship wouldn't have left like that if he wasn't checking on something."

Caro bit her lip. "Yes, of course, you're right."

She had experience running and should have thought of it. What would Huntley do if the marchese were to find them? Probably something stupid, such as fight a duel with di Venier without a thought of what would happen to her if he died.

Huntley returned and signaled to one of the inn's ostlers to let down the steps of the coach. He took Caro's hand as she stepped down. "I hope you don't mind, I've made arrangements for your servants to have refreshment and a private parlor for us."

Nugent poked her head out of the carriage. "Very kind of you, my lord."

Caro glanced up at him. "Thank you, your preparations suit."

Huntley bowed slightly. "Maufe is here and has organized a chamber for you to refresh yourself. He has also ordered a meal."

She grinned. "It was actually Maufe that thought of it all?"

A smile played around his lips. "Under my direction, of course."

Suddenly all the tension drained from her. Caro would have laughed, but she didn't want to encourage him. "Naturally."

He took her arm. "Would you like to take a stroll before we resume our journey?"

She glanced up. "Yes, if you wouldn't mind."

"Well," he said confidingly, "since Maufe insisted on staying only a little ahead of us, I'm not as concerned we'll be separated from the other carriage." A rueful look came into his eyes. "I've also forgotten how hard it is to be cooped up for long stretches. I don't think I could do the next leg without a good walk."

Caro agreed wholeheartedly. The last four hours had passed pleasantly enough, but if she were to withstand another four, she'd need the exercise as well. Perhaps they could find some indication of Shakespeare's play *Romeo and Juliet* that had purportedly taken place in Verona. "We can take in a few of the sights. Not for long, but just to see them."

He glanced briefly at her. "*Romeo and Juliet?*"

How did he guess? She tried to tamp down the blush that was rising. "I doubt there is any evidence they were real, though I understand the cathedral is beautiful."

He'd escorted her through the entrance and they'd reached the top of the broad staircase. Nugent waited at a door down the corridor and Caro turned to Huntley. "I won't be long."

"Take as much time as you like."

"Thank you." She joined Nugent and rushed through her ablutions. If they were to eat and take in any of the sights, she'd need to hurry. Gentlemen were as fickle as spring weather. She had no dependence he wouldn't change his mind and want to start again soon.

Huntley waited in the corridor for her and escorted her back down the stairs to a small parlor at the front of the inn.

Maufe bowed. "My lady, my lord, I shall have you served directly."

Caro inclined her head. "Thank you, Maufe. I don't know what we would do without you."

He bowed again, with a pleased expression. "My lady, Miss Nugent asked that your jewel box remain in here. I will watch over it when you take your walk."

Caro gave him a small smile. "You are worth your weight in gold."

"He'll be asking for a raise next." Huntley's brows drew together. "I already pay him more than I should."

At first she thought he was serious, then his eyes twinkled. "You, my lord, are a fraud."

"Yes." His lips tilted up. "Don't tell Maufe."

After a large meal, Huntley and Caro spent an hour or so walking through the ancient city and touring the Basilica di San Zeno. As they were admiring the church's ornate black ceiling, a familiar English voice intruded. Huntley turned and stifled a curse. The prelate, bear-leading a young man around the church, was his cousin.

Before he could find a place to hide, the prelate turned. "Huntley, is that you?"

He was in the process of drawing Caro back behind him when he realized how odd it would look. Instead he kept her close to his side. The closest she'd ever been to him. He held out his hand. "Everard, you're the last person I expected to see here."

His cousin glanced at Caro.

Huntley patted her hand, now clutched so tightly to his jacket sleeve that his valet would never get the wrinkles out. "Lady Caroline Martindale, may I present the Right Reverend Bishop Everard Wingate, my cousin?"

Caroline smiled politely and curtseyed.

Her grip, however, tightened even more.

He smiled at his cousin. "Everard, what are you doing here? Shouldn't you be in Canterbury or someplace?"

His inquisitive round face split into a broad smile. "I decided I needed to travel, and Jonathan, here . . . Oh, this is Lord Jonathan Bearing, the Duke of Northly's second son. In any event, he needed someone to take him on a Grand Tour. The family has him pegged for a job in the foreign office."

"Well, we're glad to have run into you." He took a breath. "Where are you staying?"

Everard joined them as they continued their tour. "At the posting house near the old south gate. We only have a day here, after which we'll go to Venice." He turned to Caro. "Are you enjoying yourself, my dear?"

Ever since Everard had greeted them, her face had been steadily losing color and she was leaning more heavily on his arm. This was disastrous. He should have known better than to walk with her around the town.

Caro blinked. "Yes, indeed I am. Lord Huntley, we should probably be getting back."

He calculated the odds of his cousin allowing them to walk off without him. They weren't good. "Everard, we'd love to stay and visit, but we are traveling north and must be going."

Everard beamed. "It has been a long time since we've had a chance to catch up. Lord Jonathan and I shall be happy to escort you back to your inn."

Huntley stifled a groan and smiled politely. "Thank you. We'd be pleased for your company."

Caro threw him an anguished look, but there was nothing they could do. The worst of it was that Everard would have to be told the reason for their flight. He kept his voice to a whisper. "Do you want to be there when I tell him?"

She closed her eyes for a moment before answering. "Yes, I'm fine now. I'm not a coward."

"I never thought you were." He was so close he could smell her hair. Sunlight and fresh air. Unhelpfully, his body hardened.

Maufe was in the parlor with Nugent when the four of them entered the inn. Both servants turned startled faces toward Huntley. "Prepare to get under way. We'll be ready to leave soon."

Everard patted Lord Jonathan on the back. "Why don't you go into the tap for a bit? I'll come to get you when we're done."

The young man glanced at them curiously but bowed and did as he was told.

Maufe halted for a second as he passed by Huntley. "We won't be far, my lord. Everything else is arranged."

Nugent followed in his wake, closing the door behind her.

Before turning to his cousin, Huntley led Caro to a chair and took up his place behind it. "Everard, I imagine you'd like to know just what is going on."

Chapter 5

Everard glanced at Caro, then back to Huntley. "I don't wish to intrude, but there are several English visitors here at the moment. It would be helpful if I were told the truth, or whatever story you've set about."

Huntley gritted his teeth. If that was the case, they needed to leave as soon as possible.

Caro dropped her head into her hands. "I knew we'd never get away with it. My luck isn't that good."

"No one has seen us yet." Huntley placed a hand on her shoulder, hard as rock with the tension, and addressed his cousin. "What do you know about my trip here?"

Frowning slightly, Everard dropped into a chair. "Just that you were to have visited Lady Horatia for a while before traveling on."

"Yes—well, my plans have undergone a slight change." Huntley rubbed his cheek. When it came to the foibles of his fellow man, his cousin had always been the most understanding of his relatives. "Lady Caroline has been living with my aunt Horatia for several years. Lately, the grandson of Duca di Venier returned to Venice and has been trying to—" Huntley glanced down at her. "The marchese decided he wanted to marry her. Whether she wanted him or not."

As succinctly as possible, Huntley recounted the events that caused Caro and him to flee Venice. He'd never seen Everard's eyes flash with anger as they did when Huntley told his cousin about the murder of the young novice. Caro sat quietly with her hands folded in her lap while Huntley recounted the duke's offer of marriage to his grandson, and Horatia's desperate attempt to keep Caro out of the marchese's hands by declaring that Huntley and Caro were betrothed.

His cousin remained silent for several moments. "I'd advise you to leave here immediately. Lady Bentley is staying at this inn. A bigger gossip I've yet to meet and, to make it worse, she seems to be everywhere I am." He grimaced. "I've been attempting to avoid her as she's made it clear she has a wish to re-marry."

The idea of the woman bearing tales about Huntley and Caro caused him no little concern, but the vision of his discreet cousin being hunted by a tattling widow made Huntley give a short laugh. "You?"

Everard's already pink complexion deepened to a rich red. "It's not a matter for humor."

The situation gave Huntley an idea. "If Caro and I leave immediately, perhaps your presence will distract her from us."

Under his hand, Caro's shoulders dropped as her tension eased.

Yet the next moment, pounding hooves and shouts from the carriage yard destroyed the relative silence of the room.

"Oh no." She grabbed his hand. "Di Venier is here. I recognize his voice."

The devil must have set out early and on horseback.

Huntley brought her to her feet, holding her tightly against him. "Caro, you are safe. Di Venier cannot hurt you while I'm here. I won't let him."

"Nor will I, my dear," Everard said as he patted her back.

"Follow my lead and try to calm yourself. I will not allow him to harm you. Look at me." Caro trembled like a blancmange, but her color was still good. He hoped she wouldn't swoon.

She glanced up, and he captured her gaze. "I'm here to protect you. Tell me you understand."

Caro swallowed. "Yes, I understand. I'm not afraid."

He shifted slightly so his back was to the door and she was shielded from sight. Bending toward her, he tilted her chin up, forcing her to once more meet his gaze. Di Venier's angry voice echoed down the corridor.

Huntley whispered, "The marchese will be here in a moment. I'm going to place my lips very close to yours, but I won't kiss you. Ready?"

"Yes," she said, so quietly he may not have actually heard it.

The door swung open, crashing against the wall before bouncing back. Di Venier's voice was full of rage. "Where is Lady Caroline?"

Huntley turned. Before he could open his mouth to reply, his cousin drew himself up and, with all the authority of a bishop of the English church, said, "I suppose you are referring to the Countess of Huntley."

Caro's knees buckled. Huntley grabbed her waist. Everard sidled close to them and pressed a ring against Huntley's hand.

Huntley took Caro's left hand, sliding the ring on her finger. "I'm sorry."

"*Contessa?*" di Venier roared. "What do you mean? When?"

Everard's usually jovial countenance maintained the haughty dignity of his ecclesiastic rank. "I completed the ceremony not long before you came so rudely through the door." He flicked a hand in dismissal. "Now, sir, you may leave us."

Di Venier's face blackened. "*You?* Who are *you* to tell *me* what to do?"

Everard was giving the Marchese di Venier his full title and honors when a well-bred English female voice intruded and said sweetly, "Oh, there you are, Bishop. I've been looking for you."

Everard smiled and bowed. "Lady Bentley, how are you today?"

"Quite well, thank you." She craned her short neck for a better look into the room. "If you don't mind my asking, what is going on? Your voices can be heard all over the building."

Di Venier turned and stared at Lady Bentley. "This man is truly a bishop?"

Her eyes widened in surprise. "Oh my, yes. Of course he is. Why in the world would I address him as such, if he were not?" She squinted and once more gave the room her attention. "Who has got married?"

The marchese swung back around and glared at Caro. "You could have lived the life of a princess. I would have worshiped you. Enjoy your *Englishman* . . . while you can." With lowered brows, he flashed an angry look at Huntley and growled, "This is not over."

Lady Bentley's mouth gaped open as di Venier stalked out of the room.

Everard hurried to her and, in a soft voice, said, "My lady, excuse us. I'll see you later perhaps."

Shutting her mouth, she curtseyed. "Yes, yes, of course. *Countess of Huntley*. Who is . . . ? Oh yes, Huntingdon's eldest son."

Before Everard closed the door, he called to Maufe and spoke in low tones.

Huntley turned back to Caro and urged her to sit, pressing a glass of wine into her hands.

She stared up at him, eyes wide and her lush lips slightly parted. "This goes from bad to worse. The scandal . . ."

"Here, drink some of this."

When Caro had taken a few sips, he took the glass, and she hid her face in her hands again.

A short while later, Maufe returned with a small book and a long shawl. He handed them to Everard and left.

Everard joined them at the table. "I'm sorry, my child," he said, his tone low and calm. "It was, I believed, necessary to protect you from that violent young man."

Taking in the prayer book, Huntley closed his eyes for a moment. Any hope he'd retained that he and Caro would not be forced into a marriage died. "I take it you mean to perform the ceremony?"

His cousin nodded. "I must. There's no choice. Lady Bentley heard what I told your marchese, and she'll spread it to all her friends. Some of them are bound to have seen Lady Caro, and the news will quickly make its way back to England."

"Give us a few minutes, if you would." Myriad thoughts ran through Huntley's mind, chief of which was what his father would say about this harum-scarum marriage, but the shock in Caro's eyes trumped all concerns about the old gentleman.

Everard went to the door. "I'll be right outside. Huntley, I need to have a few words in private with you before we begin."

When Caro gazed up at him, her face was still pale. Tears glistened, and her beautiful turquoise eyes darkened in despair.

She shook her head. "You can't marry me. It would be a disaster for you."

His jaw clenched. Now was not the time for her to turn missish. "I must. It's the only way I can protect you, your reputation and mine."

"Huntley, you don't understand." She closed her eyes and her voice shook. "You'll need an heir, and I—I can't do . . ."

He dropped to one knee next to her, taking her cold, fluttering fingers in his. "Other than wed me, you don't have to do anything you don't want to. I will never, *never* force you."

Lord, he wanted to take her in his arms, but he made himself be content with holding her hands. He prayed silently she could see the truth in his eyes.

She shook her head slowly. "You need an heir."

He forced himself to smile. "I have a younger brother."

"Oh, it's impossible." Caro stared at a place beyond his shoulder, ignoring the tears rolling down her cheeks. "I have no reputation to protect. I'm—I'm not a virgin."

He took out his handkerchief and dabbed her eyes. "But no one knows, so you do have a name to worry about."

"What about you?"

"That's not important to me. Caro, please, look at me." Now he knew what had happened, and it all made sense. Her anger and unwillingness to allow a man to touch her, her determination not to marry. Some blackguard had raped her. Rage for her burbled up inside, and he pushed it back down. The time to avenge her was later. Now he needed to safeguard her as best he could. When she met his gaze, the pain in her eyes broke his heart. "The only thing that matters is to keep you safe, from Venetian marcheses and from Polite Society. We'll work the rest out in our own way."

"But you don't want to marry."

Huntley gave thanks he hadn't made his intentions known and tried to keep his countenance neutral. "It wasn't what I'd planned, but must needs."

She closed her eyes. "I really have no choice, do I?"

Her voice was so small his throat ached.

"No. Neither of us does." He firmed his voice and prayed a reminder of her breeding would overcome her dread. "We were both raised to do what is necessary, my lady."

Caro swallowed and nodded.

Once she had herself under control, he stood. "Give me a moment. There is one last thing I must attend to."

He went to a small desk situated between the windows. Pulling out a drawer, he found paper, ink, and a pen that needed sharpening. After he'd trimmed the nib, Huntley sat down and started to write.

Caro came up behind him. "What are you doing?"

"Drafting our marriage settlements. I have some funds of my own and a house. I cannot, of course, commit my father, but I can make provisions for you from what I have and enable you to keep your property."

"You'd do that?" Her tone reflected the shock in her countenance. "Without even knowing what I possess?"

He grinned ruefully. "I know you have an independence and a fair amount of jewelry."

"Most men would never . . ."

He glanced over his shoulder at her. "I strive not to be accused of being old-fashioned."

By the time he'd finished with the document and stood, Caro had turned away and was standing by the window. "Come read this. If you agree with it, we'll have it witnessed."

He left her reviewing the document and went into the corridor. "Everard, we'll be ready in a few minutes. What did you wish to speak with me about?"

"I am truly sorry," Everard said. "I just couldn't think of anything else to say."

Huntley stifled a groan. The devil take all well-meaning people, his aunt and cousin included. Yet what was done was done, and there was no undoing it. "I understand. If that is all?"

He turned to go. Everard's hand stayed him. "No, what I want to say is that even if this is not what you wanted, you must try to make it work. You seem comfortable in each other's company. Many marriages do not even start with that. There is nothing stopping you from having a full and possibly loving life."

A loving marriage with a woman who wouldn't allow him to touch her except in the most cursory fashion? Not likely. Yet she'd begun to trust him. Putting a smile on his face, Huntley nodded. "Thank you for your words of wisdom. We'll do our best. Right now, we need to proceed on our journey. I don't trust the marchese. He's bound to return."

"I don't suppose you have a ring handy?"

He didn't have time to buy one now. "No."

"No matter." Everard smiled. "Use the one I gave her. I can always buy my sister another one."

Huntley squeezed his cousin's arm. "Thank you."

He called to Nugent and Maufe, who were speaking in low tones down the corridor. Huntley waited until they were next to him and spoke quietly. "Lady Caro and I shall marry in a few minutes. You must both act as witnesses."

The servants were too well trained to betray their surprise, but Nugent studied him for a few moments as if trying to decide whether he was worthy of her mistress. At last, she gave a brisk nod. "I'll get her ready."

He and Maufe reentered the room with Everard, and a short time later, Nugent returned carrying a bowl of water and a cloth.

"Come, my lady, we can't have you looking so down in the mouth." Nugent dipped the linen in water. "Let's clean up your face."

Caro's maid pressed the cloth to his bride's red eyes. It would take more than cold water to make Caro feel better. Wouldn't Huntley's friends laugh to see him now? On second thought, they'd not. Every last one of them would help him hunt down and kill di Venier.

He touched the paper on the desk. "Do you agree to this?"

Dry-eyed and resolute, she responded, "Yes, it's very generous."

He reached out to touch her cheek. She flinched, and he dropped his hand. *Damn*. Unfortunately, there was no time to deal with her fears now.

He tried to keep his tone even. "Sign it, and we'll have it witnessed. Everard, I want to do all I can to make sure my father adheres to this contract."

His cousin nodded. "I will do everything I am able to ensure your father accepts the settlements."

Once the document was signed, Maufe and Nugent worked on making copies.

Huntley gave one to Everard. "I assume you will go to the embassy in Venice. Please have this sent by courier to my father. I've included a note about my wedding."

Everard patted Huntley on the back. "You can be sure I will. I know how difficult Huntingdon can be, and I'll write him a stern missive as well, telling him he must abide by your decision. Indeed, I can see no reason why he should not. It is not as if the match is a *misalliance*."

The wedding ceremony was short. Huntley held Caro's trembling hands in his.

"Church law requires a ring," Everard said. "This"—he held up a wide gold band with a large opal in the center— "shall be my bride present to you, but if you don't like it, my dear, Huntley can get you another later."

Caro recited her vows but could not bring herself to glance at Huntley. Everard handed Huntley the ring, and he slid it onto her finger. It fit her perfectly. Caro stared at her hand. The ring was indeed beautiful. Just the kind of thing she'd wanted before . . . well . . . before she decided not to marry.

Forcing herself to respond politely, Caro took Everard's hand. "Thank you, it is lovely."

"I am sorry, my dear child," he said in a voice full of sympathy. "Make it work. It would be a great tragedy if you did not."

Tears burned her eyes again, and she blinked them back. She wouldn't weep again. It was unworthy of her and Huntley. Suddenly, her chest contracted as if she'd been hit. *Married*. Huntley, her husband, was talking to the bishop about the letters for their families. Nugent and Maufe were making everything ready to leave. They were all acting so normal, as if nothing unusual had occurred. Her head swam and she grabbed onto a chair to keep from falling.

How could this have happened? Worst of all, she'd had to tell Huntley she was not an innocent. He'd said he didn't care, but he would, and he'd come to hate her for this marriage. She had to think, but her mind was jumbled. Someone helped her into the chair and pressed a glass into her hand.

"Drink this." Huntley kept a grip on the glass and helped her take a sip. "You've had a shockingly bad day."

She wanted to laugh like a lunatic or a drunken person. What an understatement. She wasn't the only one who'd had a *shockingly bad day*. Opening her eyes, Caro stared at him. Lines of concern etched his strong, aristocratic face. He was doing everything, taking care of everyone, while she fell apart.

It was Huntley, not her, who'd remembered the marriage settlements, insuring she'd have some degree of freedom. Caro wanted to do something to show him she was not a weak woman, but a wave of despair washed over her again, and she struggled to hold back her tears. A watering pot of a wife—not a great compliment to him, considering what he had given up for her. Someday she'd find a way to repay him.

A maid brought refreshments, and Nugent, once more, pressed a cold, damp cloth on her eyes. It was important none of the other guests see Caro had been crying. Their hour's respite had turned into three.

"Caro, we won't get as far as we'd wished," Huntley said. "Do you have any objection to allowing Maufe to leave and choose the next inn?"

She shook her head. "None at all."

"Thank you, my lady." The valet bowed and left the room.

Dalle knocked on the door. "My lady, we're ready when you are."

Taking a breath, she answered, "I am ready now."

Huntley helped her rise, and she plastered a smile on her face as they walked to the coach. He had apparently abandoned his plans to ride and joined her and Nugent in the coach. As before, he took the seat facing the rear of the coach. Caro pretended to doze for a while but decided that was the coward's way out, and she'd taken that road enough lately. Still, she could do nothing but gaze out at the old stone homes and terraced gardens. Mountains rose on either side of them as they sped on their way north into the Alps. She supposed she and Huntley, her husband, needed to discuss how they would go on, but with Nugent present, any conversation would have to wait.

Caro glanced at him, but he appeared to be sleeping. Would he ever truly understand why she could never allow him to touch her? No good could come of this marriage. Desolation overcame her again, and she closed her eyes.

Later, Caro woke sharply as Huntley tried to stretch and his foot hit hers, but really there was no place for his legs to go. Why had she not noticed before how much room he took up?

He pulled his leg back. "Sorry, I should have had the coach made a bit larger."

Of course, when he'd ordered it, he would not have imagined he'd have two women with him. Caro was a little surprised his presence in the close space didn't bother her more. "It's no trouble."

They pulled into the yard of a posting house. Their coachman yelled an order for a new team, and Huntley jumped out during the few minutes it would take the inn's ostlers to hitch them up. This was the third change they'd made since leaving Verona.

Fortunately, unlike yesterday, they'd not had to wait for fresh horses. She closed her eyes again before he got back into the coach.

Next to her, Nugent shifted in her seat and sat up straight, as if she was ready to take some sort of action. If Caro chanced a look, she knew she would see her dresser's eyes staring, fixed on something as she made a decision.

Huntley must have noticed it as well. His tone indicated his curiosity. "Yes?"

"She wasn't always like this," her maid said.

Caro forced herself to relax and listen.

Boots scraped the floor. He must be leaning forward, probably determined to learn more about her. Now that she and Huntley were wed, Caro supposed she should have expected that. Luckily, Nugent was circumspect.

"So I'd gathered," Huntley replied. "Will you tell me what exactly happened?"

Oh God. Nugent couldn't tell him. She'd promised.

Caro's dresser replied in a vague manner, "I think you've figured that out."

"I've got a good notion, but I don't know how it came about."

For a few moments they stopped talking, and Caro's skin prickled as if she was under scrutiny, then the feeling left her.

"That large building over there," her maid asked, "what is it?"

Finally, Caro couldn't stand it. Cracking open her eyes, she saw Huntley glance out at a huge gray stone building with a wall that seemed to be built into the side of the mountain. "It appears to be a monastery."

Nugent nodded. "All men."

Caro wondered where their conversation was going.

"Yes, no women allowed," Huntley said. "Not much of an existence, unless you're pious."

Nugent turned to him. "I heard tell that they castrate the monks."

Huntley choked. "I really don't know. Why would they?"

Caro didn't know a lot about monks, but she knew they didn't do that.

Nugent shrugged. "To keep them from getting on each other."

"You have a point," he replied slowly. "Men have done stranger things. Does this have anything to do with Caro?"

Her maid sniffed. "Fitting punishment for those who hurt innocent girls."

Caro wished she could kick Nugent. What did she think she was doing?

Huntley was quiet for a few minutes. When he finally spoke, his voice was hard and angry. "I have thought for a long time that the punishment for rape is too lenient. When I was seventeen, home for half-term break, I found our tweenie, Ruth, crying in the garden. Her gown was torn and her hair half down. She was from the village, and I'd known her for years. Yet she recoiled from me and started to scream when I reached down to help her."

Nugent went very still.

"I called the housekeeper to assist. But she wasn't any help at all. She took Ruth back to the house, had her cleaned up, and then blamed Ruth for what had happened. My mother intervened, but in the end Ruth killed herself."

Nugent cleared her throat. "Did you ever find out who did it?"

Huntley ground his teeth. "Yes, but not until a year later. I was attending a party at a neighboring estate, and one of the guests told another gentleman what a good time he'd had a year ago with a girl named Ruth."

"I guess, under the circumstance, there wasn't much you could do."

He gave a short, humorless laugh. "I picked a fight with him and punched the blackguard in the nose. He struck back but couldn't get beneath my guard. The man was older, but I was heavier and stronger." His hand clenched. "By the time they pulled me off him, I'd blackened both his eyes and broken his nose. I tried to get him to call me out, but the coward wouldn't meet me."

Nugent nodded in that brisk way she had when she approved of one.

Caro closed her eyes again before anyone noticed she was awake. Huntley really wouldn't harm her. Not when he still had so much anger for a tweenie who had died over fifteen years ago. She'd never had a gentleman protector. Caro allowed herself to relax.

They changed teams twice more. The sun was sinking lower into the mountains when they slowed to a stop. Dalle jerked open the door.

Huntley climbed down and turned to hand Caro out of the coach. "My lady."

Caro allowed him to take her hand and place it on his arm. He turned to his valet. "Maufe, what are the arrangements?"

Maufe bowed to Caro. "Her ladyship and Miss Nugent have rooms down the corridor, overlooking the meadow at the back. Our chambers are near the stairs."

"Perfect. Caro?"

She smiled wanly at Maufe. "Yes, I quite agree."

Huntley led her into the inn and stopped at the stairs. "I'll meet you for dinner. Send word when you'll be down."

Caro put one foot on the bottom tread. "I shan't be long."

Once she'd splashed water on her face and washed her hands, Caro descended to the tap. Only Huntley, Dalle, and Collins were there, all three drinking ale from the looks of the tall tankards. She hovered by the door, trying to decide whether to enter.

"My lady, please join us." Huntley rose and held a chair for her, his countenance grim. "We are reviewing the routes from here to Nancy."

She accepted the glass of red wine that a servant set before her. "Is there a problem?"

Huntley sat. "We are past mid-October. The Brenner Pass and other roads should be clear for another few weeks. My main concern is that we reach the other side of the pass before it snows."

Dalle set his stein down. "My lord, do ye think that marchese will come after us again?"

"I don't know." Huntley took a long draught. "If he's thinking straight, he won't, but he doesn't appear to be the most rational being."

Collins leaned over and looked from Caro to Huntley. "We hid the coaches. I reckon we'd better stay closer together now."

Huntley finished his beer, looking tired. The thought occurred to Caro that this was their wedding night, and he was voluntarily sleeping alone. When she'd mentioned it earlier, he shrugged it off. But what man could wait forever? How long would it be before he stopped being a monk and took her or another woman? Yet what right would she have to complain when she couldn't bring herself to let him touch her?

Chapter 6

Huntley finished his ale and held out his hand to Caro. "Let's go for a short walk until we have to change for dinner. There is a garden to the side of the building."

Perhaps now they'd talk of their marriage. Caro placed her hand on his arm. "A stroll is just what I need."

He led her out the front door and around to the hotel's walled kitchen garden. Vegetables grew with herbs whose scents wrapped around her. It reminded her of home in England. Paths separated the beds and a bench stood next to the back wall. "Should we speak now?"

"About us?"

"Yes." She nodded. "How we will go on."

He glanced at her. "It has been a . . . difficult day. I would prefer we each take time to consider. Once you are out of danger, we will make plans."

Caro searched his face and could see nothing but sincerity. If di Venier was to be believed, Huntley was also in peril, and he would need to concentrate on their journey. Maybe it was best for both of them to wait. "If you wish."

Huntley smiled. "I do. Right now, I'd like to enjoy a peaceful evening."

They strolled and looked at the plants and herbs still thriving in the walled garden before making their way back to the inn. He covered her fingers, briefly, with his. She hoped he would not expect more of her than she could give.

He escorted her to her chamber. "Dinner in an hour?"

Caro had trouble meeting his gaze, afraid he would want her or be angry that he would spend their wedding night alone. But when she raised her eyes, only a smile lurked in his. "I'll meet you then."

"I shall do myself the honor of escorting you."

She nodded. "Very well."

He reached around her and knocked on the door. Her dresser opened it. He bowed. "Until then, my lady."

Caro sat on a hard wooden chair that she'd moved next to the window. They were still in the foothills of the Alps, and yet the mountains rose almost straight up from the valley floor. Rows of houses abutted the base, as if they had nowhere else to go, just like her.

Countless women, she was sure, would give their teeth to be the Countess of Huntley, the future Marchioness of Huntingdon, yet it had been forced upon her. Caro couldn't think ahead even to the dinner she would share with Huntley this evening, much less to the rest of their journey, or their lives.

The snapping of Nugent shaking out a lustring silk gown drew Caro's attention away from the houses. "Yes, Nugent?"

Her dresser hung the gown on a peg, then took out a pretty paisley shawl and placed it on the bed. "I didn't say anything, *but* if I was to do so, I'd say you could've done worse than to marry his lordship."

Caro turned back to the view and gazed up to the top of the hills.

The door to the wardrobe closed. When she didn't turn, Nugent came to stand next to Caro. "Did you hear what he said to me today?"

She sighed. "Yes. I only dozed some of the way."

She and her dresser had been together so long, she didn't even have to turn to know Nugent's face had a disapproving look on it.

Her dresser put a hand on Caro's shoulder and squeezed lightly. "Let's have less of this moping and sighing and a little more starch from you, my lady. You're made of sterner stuff."

Caro took a breath and stood. "It's time I dress for dinner."

Yet when she saw the apricot silk gown Nugent held out, Caro raised a brow. "Don't you think that is a little daring for dinner at an inn?"

"It's your wedding dinner." Nugent sniffed. "You should wear something nice."

Caro didn't want to argue. She'd just have to pin her shawl together to hide the low bodice. Even though Huntley was her husband, it wouldn't do to give him ideas that were unlikely to be fulfilled.

By the time she was ready, her hair had been dressed in a loose knot from which Nugent had teased out long tendrils. A necklace of perfectly matched pearls was looped around Caro's neck, and matching earrings dangled on gold wires. She frowned at her reflection, unsure what Huntley would see, then turned away. Perhaps if she were not pretty, *the rape* wouldn't have happened. She shoved the thought back into the recesses of her memory. She had no intention of ever discussing the attack with anyone, her husband included.

A knock came at the door, and she rose. Huntley stood in the corridor, waiting. She curtseyed. "Good evening, my lord."

His eyes widened, he smiled and bowed. "You look charmingly, my lady. May I escort you to the parlor?"

Caro forced herself to smile. "I'd be delighted."

So far, they were both playing their parts—polite indifference. Except that she did think she looked well, and it was nice to be with a gentleman and not have to worry about him trying to do anything she did not want.

When they entered the parlor—a pretty room on the same floor as their chambers, with a balcony overlooking the river—Huntley led her to the table. Dishes with various foods were under covers on a sideboard. That was strange. "Why do they have all the dishes out?"

He pushed in her chair after she sat, and took his place across the small table. "With the exception of the pasta, which I was assured must be served fresh, I thought a selection of the region's foods might be nice. After the soup and the pasta, do you mind if we serve ourselves, or would you rather Maufe serve us?"

"I've no objection to serving myself. It will be a little like breakfast."

Huntley signaled the servant, and the potage of vegetables with rice was served. The pasta consisted of small dumplings stuffed with spinach and ricotta cheese. Once the dishes were removed and fresh plates brought, Caro and Huntley looked over the other dishes, which included vegetables, fish, and meats.

Caro discovered that what Huntley meant when he said they would serve themselves, was that she would make her selections and he would place them on her plate. He hovered closely, offering suggestions, helping her identify some dish or another and bravely testing a suspicious-looking item before offering it to her.

The rest of the tension in Caro's shoulders eased. She, Huntley, and their servants were safe, at least for the time being, and he was doing his best to entertain her. For the first time in days, she laughed. "How did you come up with this idea, or was it Maufe?"

He looked down his aquiline nose at her, as if affronted. "It was my suggestion, of course. I enjoy trying new foods, and the cook had so many to offer, I decided we'd sample as many as possible."

As if neither of them was ready to discuss what had occurred earlier to-day, their conversation centered mainly around what they were eating. This dinner had been a good idea, and Huntley was proving to be easy to get along with, so far. When Caro had finished eating, she placed her serviette on the table and started to rise. "I have enjoyed myself very much, my lord. Thank you."

He glanced at her. "You do not want to leave so soon. There is a special dessert."

She stared at him. What could he have in mind? Surely he couldn't be expecting them to . . . "Indeed, and what might that be?"

His eyes danced, not in a seductive manner, but playfully. "Chocolate tiramisu."

She plopped back in her chair. "I *love* chocolate."

Huntley grinned. So he'd been told. Earlier, he'd done his research and discovered from Nugent that Caro was much addicted to chocolate. When the inn's cook recommended chocolate tiramisu for dessert, he'd not hesitated ordering it. Perhaps, once they were settled, he'd write a gentleman's guide to keeping one's wife happy with chocolate.

After the dessert was served, he sat back, extremely pleased with himself, and watched Caro's small pink tongue lick the last of the chocolate and cream off her spoon. When she glanced up and smiled at him, every muscle in his body tightened, and his increasing desire for her coursed through his veins. *The devil*, this was not a good thing to happen now. First, he needed to ensure she was safe and spend time courting her.

She gave a sigh. "Thank you again. That was lovely." A few minutes later, she rose again. "I think I shall retire. We do have an early day to-morrow."

He stood. "I'll escort you to your room."

Caro waved him back down. "Really, there's no need. You stay and have your port."

Huntley came around the table. "It is my pleasure." He did his best to look innocent as he searched her face for any sign she was softening toward him. "Please?"

She glanced up, peeping uncertainly through her long, curling lashes, apparently still shy of him and their situation. He knew it would take her time, and he was willing to give it to her. After all, they only had the rest of their lives.

"Very well."

He opened the door and stood back to allow her to pass before joining her and placing her hand on his arm. "Do you mind if we break our fast at six o'clock?"

"Not at all. When do you wish to leave?"

They strolled down the corridor. "As soon thereafter as possible. If you agree, I'd like to continue to stop in smaller towns, where we are less likely to meet other travelers."

Caro turned to him, and the fear he was determined to vanquish crept into her eyes. "Do you think he'll follow?"

He stopped at her door and knocked. "I don't know. We'd be wise to assume he will. Better safe than sorry, but try not to worry."

She nodded. "I suppose you're right. Thank you again for dinner. I had a lovely time."

When Nugent opened the door, Caro turned and entered her chamber.

He stood for a few moments staring at the door, wondering when he'd finally be allowed in her bed. He sighed and ambled slowly back to the parlor, where he poured a glass of local red wine—port would only give him a bad head in the morning. The lack of sleep and events of the day were finally catching up with him. The thought occurred that this was his wedding night, and he wouldn't be spending it with his wife.

He shrugged it off. Perhaps he was too optimistic, but there was always hope that somehow they'd work it out. The only thing he knew right now was that he'd not dishonor her by taking another woman.

He could take small steps to convince Caro to be a real wife to him and protect her at the same time. To-night was the warmest she'd ever been toward him, and he wanted it to continue. Yet if he went even a little too quickly, she would draw back like a scared animal in fear for its life. He wondered if they could ever grow to love one another. Strange how he looked forward to having a real marriage when he'd been so set against it only a few months earlier. This must be what Beaumont and Rutherford had gone through for their wives.

Huntley sipped his wine. It would be largely up to him whether they did or not make it work. He must craft a plan to woo her: feeding her, which included finding chocolate, keeping her busy and engaged, and showing her how safe he could make her feel. He'd not take any steps toward physical intimacy until she was ready, but little by little, he would convince her to be a wife and make her his, body and mind. By the time they got to Nancy, she would be his countess and his lover.

Movement on the street below caused him to look down.

A man on horseback stopped and spoke with their coach-man, Raphael. Once Raphael stepped back from the horse, the man turned around and cantered back in the direction he'd come. The marchese must be closer behind them than Huntley had thought.

He started for the door when it opened, admitting Collins and Dalle, with identical looks of worry mixed with humor.

Huntley motioned them in and shut the door. "Was he looking for her ladyship?"

Dalle bowed. "Yes, my lord. Raphael told him he saw a fair-haired woman and a man in one of the towns we passed early this afternoon. It'll take him a good long time to chase that hare."

The rider would need to find a place to stay this evening and have a look around before returning here to-morrow. By then, his little party would be well on their way north. "Dalle, ask her ladyship to join me. Collins, I need the map."

A few minutes later, Caro entered the room dressed in a morning gown. A frown marred her lovely countenance. "Dalle told me about the marchese's man."

Huntley spread the map out and put his finger down on the town of Ala. "This is where we are. If we change every time the horses tire, we could make forty or fifty miles a day on a good road. But we're going uphill, and it's going to get steeper the farther north we go. I suggest that to-morrow we try for Bolzano, and if we make it that far, spend the night in Frangarto. It's off the main road by a few miles."

Caro leaned over the chart. She was close enough he could smell her light, lemony scent, mixed with chocolate. He breathed in and was distracted by the thought of running his tongue over her ear and down her neck to her . . . Good God, the woman was temptation incarnate.

"We'll have to leave even earlier than we'd anticipated," she said.

He bent over her, lightly caging Caro in his arms. "To ensure we make it, yes."

Rather than moving away as he thought she would, she measured off the miles with her fingers. "See here, if we stay in Frangarto to-morrow night, we might be able to reach Vipiteno or Brennero the next night. Though I don't think we want to cross the pass in the evening."

Exactly what he'd been thinking, when he wasn't engrossed in her. Nothing could convince him to start across the pass after noon. "I agree."

He straightened when Caro started to stand. Little by little he was making progress. Her hair was pulled back into one long, thick braid; tiny curls escaped around her face, and he longed to caress the wispy ones on her neck.

She glanced at him with a strange look on her face, as if she didn't quite know what he was thinking. All things considered, that was a damn good thing.

"Well then, my lord"—Caro's brows came together just the slightest bit—"I shall see you in the morning. If you will let Dalle and Raphael know our plans?"

Huntley walked her to the door. "Certainly." Keeping his desire from her was becoming more and more difficult. She was so close it was all he could do to stop from kissing her. "Until then. Five o'clock?"

"If you wish. I can always sleep in the coach."

He accompanied her to her chamber, then returned to the parlor and called for Collins, Dalle, and Raphael. When the men arrived, he explained the plan. Huntley glanced from one to the other. "Do any of you have a comment to make?"

Raphael and Dalle spoke in a rapid colloquial Italian that Huntley had trouble following. Dalle looked at Collins and Huntley before saying, "If we stop just long enough to change horses, and if we don't have to wait for them, we can do it, my lord."

He stared at the map and nodded. "Which means we'll have to bring provisions with us."

"Yes, my lord," Collins said.

"Very well. We still have some of what Lady Horatia gave us. I'll have Maufe speak with the innkeeper and the cook."

Raphael spoke quickly to Dalle, who frowned. "Raphael says that it'd be better if we were to even out the loads. The coaches would be able to travel closer to the same speed, and that would make it easier to keep everyone together."

Under the circumstances, that was an excellent idea. "Very well, distribute the baggage between the carriages."

Dalle glanced down and shuffled his feet before saying, "Raphael says it would be better to move . . . The thing is, he wants Miss Nugent to ride with Maufe."

The devil! Were they trying to get him murdered? Huntley took a large breath and tried not to think about Caro's reaction to that suggestion. "I could ride with Maufe."

"No, my lord. That won't work," Dalle said. "We need to keep the weight the same."

Huntley dragged his fingers through his hair. "Perhaps it would be better if I hired a horse."

Collins shook his head. "No, my lord. The marchese and his men know what you look like. You'd be right noticeable on a horse."

Damnation. If they thought he was going to tell Caro, they deserved to be in Bedlam. Extensive experience with angry women told him he'd be better off playing least in sight until the fracas was over.

Huntley raised a brow and fixed Dalle and Raphael with a firm gaze. "Which one of *you* is going to explain this to her ladyship?"

Dalle gave him an innocent look. "We thought you'd do it, your lordship."

Ha. They were delusional. Huntley looked down his nose. "Then you thought wrong. I have a better sense of self-preservation than that."

"You sure, my lord?" Caro's groom grinned knowingly.

"Very."

Dalle screwed his face up as if he were in pain. "I reckon it'll take both me and Raphael to explain."

"I wish you joy of it." Huntley took a swig of wine. "Collins, you can tell me when it's safe to make an appearance."

Huntley held Collins back when the other two left. Once the door was closed, he asked, "How are we fixed for weapons and ammunition?"

Collins scratched his cheek. "Pretty well, my lord. I'm told both her ladyship and Miss Nugent are good shots." He paused for a few moments. "You want me to make sure everyone's armed to-morrow?"

"Yes. I want to be prepared for whatever happens." Huntley would like nothing more than to grind the marchese under his boot, but he had the feeling his wife wouldn't appreciate such a primitive display of masculine power. He grinned. He'd let the marchese make the first move. "We will not start the fight."

"No, my lord."

After his groom left, Huntley poured another glass of wine. At least they'd eat and drink well on this trip. Huntley's muscles hurt just thinking about how stiff he'd be to-morrow evening after another full day in the coach. He tossed off his wine. It was time to go to bed. He'd have an irate wife in the morning; he didn't need a headache as well.

He went to his chamber and gave Maufe his orders.

"Just what I suspected would happen, my lord." He helped Huntley out of his jacket and hung up the clothes. "I'll go down now so that the landlord has some warning."

Huntley climbed into his cold bed and pulled up the cover. *His wedding night. Damn.* One day he'd have one, but it wouldn't be to-night. He prayed that one day his wife would look forward to time alone with him in a coach, but it wouldn't be to-morrow. What would it be like to have Caro, warm and lush, next to him? His body sprang to readiness with arousal, and he punched the pillow. One day couldn't come soon enough for him.

Chapter 7

Antonio was almost half-way back to Venice before he'd recognized his mistake, leaving the inn in Verona. After stopping at a posting house and arranging for new horses, he'd sent messengers out in all directions. One by one, his servants returned with no news of where Lady Caroline might be. Only the rider he'd sent north had not yet arrived or sent a message.

Waiting for news, Antonio paced the large chamber he'd demanded from the innkeeper. He'd been so shocked at the announcement of Lady Caroline's—no, the Countess of Huntley's—wedding, that he had not thought it through properly. Antonio punched the wall next to him. He should have dragged her out of the room. What did it matter that she and Lord Huntley were wed? Many men had married women for mistresses, and Lady Caroline would be his. *Diavolo*. If he'd taken her to-day, she would still have been a virgin for him. An image of her spread beneath Huntley as he pounded into her raged in him. He ground his teeth. Antonio refused to be cast down. He would keep Lady Caroline as his mistress, until the Englishman died. If Huntley remained alive Antonio would have to marry another woman, but that was no trouble. His grandfather would arrange for a suitable match, and after his wife had given him a son, she could go her own way.

Of course, if Lady Caroline's husband should die, Antonio could marry her. He rubbed his chin. He'd made the threat to-day out of anger, but truly, that was the answer. Kill the Englishman and take Lady Caroline to wife. He poured a glass of brandy and tossed it off. She'd be under him soon. All white skin, shimmering blond hair, and blue eyes. Soon the most beautiful woman in Venice would be Antonio's, and his life would be perfect.

The next morning, Huntley decided to assist Maufe in the kitchen as he arranged the provisioning. The noise level in the carriage yard, where the coaches stood ready to depart, rose. Swift, light steps ascended the stairs; something hard hitting a door echoed down to the kitchen. Whatever Caro was using to hit the door was probably meant to be used on him as well. Soon her steps returned rapidly back down the stairs again.

Maufe opened his mouth. Huntley held up a hand, silencing him, until the outside door to the inn closed. "I'll tell you, Maufe, I know why my father makes himself scarce when m'mother is on a rampage. There are few things worse than having an irate wife looking for one."

"Yes, my lord." Maufe's lips twitched. "Especially if the wife in question is one's own."

And unbedded, Huntley thought ruefully. All his tricks to calm a woman involved touching of some sort.

A few minutes later, Nugent's voice climbed above Caro's. "*My lady*, they have already explained it to you twice. This is the best distribution of the weight, so that the coaches can travel quickly and remain together."

The voices lowered, and Huntley studied the kitchen's dull white ceiling, waiting until it was safe to go outside. He'd no doubt be treated like a pariah for at least several hours, but even if nothing more interesting than a game of chess occurred, at least he'd have Caro to himself for the rest of the day.

The shouting stopped, and Maufe touched Huntley's sleeve. "I think it's all right to go out now, my lord."

"I suppose so." He ran his hand over his face. "We must leave sometime."

The cook's mustache twitched and he gave Huntley a sympathetic look. "Sometimes the ladies, they are difficult, no?"

If only he knew. "There's no understanding them."

The cook smiled and made a drawing with his hands of a woman's shape. "But, with such perfection." He shrugged. "We do not need to understand. Only *amore* is needed."

Huntley stared, stunned, at the cook for a few moments before grabbing his hand and shaking it. That was the answer Huntley had been searching for. "Thank you. You're absolutely right. Only love"—*or something damned close to it*—"is needed. Come, Maufe, we have a full day ahead of us."

"Ah, milord, perhaps I have something that will help put your lady in a better mood. A moment, please." The cook went into his larder and came out with a package. "For the contessa."

Huntley held the parcel to his nose and breathed in deeply. *The chocolate tiramisu.* That would go a long way to getting him back in Caro's good graces. "I cannot thank you enough, signore. This is exactly what I need."

"We husbands, we must support each other." The cook pointed toward the yard. "Our lives are not always easy."

"How true." Huntley strode out the door, plan literally in hand. The coaches were ready to go. Maufe distributed the bundles of food between them.

Huntley climbed into his carriage, glanced at his wife's frowning countenance, and handed her the package. "This is for you."

Her expression changed from angry to curious. "What is it?"

He leaned against the plush squabs and grinned. "Smell."

Caro lifted it to her nose, her bad mood disappeared, and a beatific smile appeared on her face. "*Chocolate*."

"The rest of the tiramisu." Huntley hid his sigh of relief. That was easier than he'd thought it would be.

She held the package close to her generous breasts for a few moments before giving it back to him. "Keep it from me until after luncheon. Otherwise, I shall eat it all now."

He raised a brow in inquiry.

"Even if I *beg* for it," she said, "*do not* give me the parcel until after luncheon."

He leaned his head back again and regarded her for a few moments. Her turquoise eyes sparkled with joy, and it occurred to him that there was very little he'd withhold from her, and she didn't even need to beg. "Very well, but you must remember, this was your decision, not mine."

She made a shooing motion. "Put it away where I can't see it."

"Very well, close your eyes."

Instead Caro's eyes narrowed. "Why?"

Damn. He hated to see the mistrust. He gave what he

hoped was a reassuring look. "Trust me," he said teasingly, "only for a moment. I promise not to try to steal a kiss."

Her body seemed to hum with palpable tension, but her sable brown lashes fluttered down.

Huntley quickly placed the tiramisu under the seat behind her bag. "There. You can open them now."

She stared at him in surprise. "What did you do?"

"I hid the package," he said calmly. "What did you think I was going to do?"

Caro blushed. "I—I don't know."

He tried to keep his face relaxed. "Caro, you have nothing to fear from me."

"I'm sorry. I am not used to trusting." She rubbed her forehead. "May we discuss something else?"

"Anything you wish." He had a long road ahead of him before she'd allow herself to have enough faith in him to discuss the most crucial topic, the rape. Yet if he and Caro were to have any kind of marriage at all, they must talk about it, though now was obviously not the right time. One step at a time. After she was safe, he would broach the subject with her. "Would you care for a game of chess?"

She let out a breath and smiled. "Yes, the same rules as yesterday?"

"No, a bit different, I think."

They whiled away the hours making extravagant bets. Caro moved her queen. "Checkmate," she crowed happily. "I believe I now own your castle, my lord."

Huntley gazed down at the board. She had him dead to rights. "I think you do. I've nothing more to wager." The coach slowed. "Aha! My fortunes have turned."

Caro laughed. "You're lucky it's time for new horses."

They'd agreed that all their imaginary property would return to its owner and the slate would be wiped clean at each change.

"I wouldn't gloat overmuch," he retorted. "I seem to remember you were down to your last chicken the last time we stopped."

He placed the game board on the seat beside him and, after jumping down, held out his hand.

Caro took it and, still unused to the travel, climbed stiffly out of the coach. "So I was. How quickly one forgets near poverty."

They strode briskly back and forth for the few minutes it took to hitch up the new team.

"In you go." Huntley glanced up at the sun and calculated how long it would be before it started to sink behind the mountains. "We should have just one more change." He turned and called out to Dalle. "How much farther?"

"Another ten or twelve miles, my lord."

Holding up her skirts, Caro started to climb the carriage steps, then fell back. Huntley caught her. His every nerve awakened when his arms went around her warm body. His senses clamored for him to continue to hold her as her soft feminine form pressed against his chest. She tensed and remained silent. Sucking in a breath, he brought his errant body under control.

"Careful," he said, not knowing if he spoke to himself or her.

He slowly released his arms from around Caro and grasped her elbow, steadying her as she stepped in and took a seat.

Huntley folded the stairs and hopped in as the coach lurched forward.

"You aren't hurt, are you?" he asked solicitously.

"No." Caro hesitated. Her arms and back still tingled from where Huntley had touched her. That had certainly never happened before. She was even more surprised that she hadn't wanted to struggle away from him. "No, I'm fine.

Thank you for keeping me from falling," she said. "I don't know what is the matter. I am not usually so clumsy."

He stretched his neck from side to side. "It is really not very surprising. You're stiff from sitting for such long stretches in a confined space. When we get to our inn, would you like to take a walk before dinner?"

In an attempt to ease the ache in the small of her back, she leaned forward and rubbed it. "You must be right. I am feeling cramped. A walk will be just the thing."

He was much stronger than he looked. When she'd slipped, he had caught her and lifted her upright as if she were a feather, and his arms when they went around her were much more muscular than she'd thought they would be.

"Would you like your tiramisu now?" he asked.

"Oh, you kept me so busy, even during luncheon, I forgot about it." Her mouth watered. "Perhaps I should wait until we reach the inn."

He shrugged, and the corners of his lips tilted up. "You could, but the chef might have something else to tempt your appetite."

Caro found herself grinning. "Very well, but you must eat some as well."

Huntley had a very charming smile. How straight his teeth were, and his face was strong. That was a strange thought for her. Other women talked about such things, but Caro didn't think she had ever noticed a man's teeth before, not unless there was something wrong with them, that is. Reaching under the seat, he brought out the box and utensils, placing them on the fold-down table they'd played chess on. He handed her a spoon and opened the container. Oh, it smelled heavenly. If she ever returned to Italy, she would make a point to stop at that inn again.

Before she could dip her spoon in to take a scoop, Huntley's spoon touched her lips. Caro opened her mouth and tasted. "Oh, that is so good. But you cannot feed me all of yours."

She took some on her spoon and stuck it out at him. Her spoon wavered. Just reaching out to his lips, even if only to feed him, seemed so very intimate. He, of course, would have engaged in this sort of conduct with other women. Caro tried to ignore the irritation pricking her over Huntley being with other females.

"Here," she said, jabbing the spoon at him again.

He guided it to his mouth and closed his eyes as he tasted the tiramisu. "That is every bit as good as it was last night."

Caro's mouth dried as she watched him lick the spoon, taking the last little bit. He held a dollop of the confection to her lips again. What had she gotten herself into? She opened her mouth, and he grazed the spoon over her lips. She wanted to sigh as the smooth metal slid into her mouth. Each time she held her spoon out to Huntley, he took her hand and prompted her to lean closer to him. She searched his face for any sign that he may try to touch her in another way, but could only see his enjoyment of the tiramisu.

A few minutes later, she sighed as she glanced down at the empty dish. "There's no more."

He gave a short laugh. "No, my lady, there is no more. We can only pray that the chef in the next inn is as good."

Leaning back against the squabs, she watched while he put the utensils and dish away before setting up the chess-board again. Spending the day alone with him had not been nearly as horrifying as she'd originally thought. Other than catching her when she started to topple or helping her from the coach, he'd not attempted to touch her and, under the law, he had every right. Perhaps he really had meant what he'd said, that he'd not force his attentions on her.

She sat up. "Are you black or white this time?"

"I'm white." Huntley's eyes sparkled bluer than yesterday. "What have you to lose?"

"Let me think." Caro tapped her nose. "I have an old castle on the Rhine, and hills of vineyards."

He stared at her for a moment, and she stopped. "What is it?"

Shaking his head, he responded, "Go on. I'll ask later."

"Well, a castle and vineyards, and a village, I think."

Smiling, he said, "I have a chateau on a river . . ."

Close to an hour later, Huntley was just about to put her queen in jeopardy with his rook when they pulled up at an inn.

Caro laughed. "Ah, saved in the nick of time."

He gathered up the game pieces again. "You're very lucky, my lady."

Caro was impressed; he really was an excellent strategic player. "You play to win, my lord."

"I didn't think you'd want me to *allow* you to prevail."

"No indeed." She had always been proud of her abilities, and anyone letting her win was the last thing she wished, but, other than her father, she'd never before played against a man. She'd enjoyed it more than she thought she would.

He'd descended first and held out his hand to her. To her surprise, Caro found herself glancing shyly at him and smiling. Even considering she was on the run from the marchese and had spent the better part of three days in a carriage, she had to acknowledge she'd been having . . . fun. Even eating the dessert had been enjoyable, albeit a little disturbing. Her whole life was literally in his hands, and she wanted to trust him. If only she could. Placing her hand in his, she said, "Thank you, my lord."

Huntley bowed. "It is my pleasure. Do you still desire a walk?" He glanced around. "It appears there are paths through the vineyards."

For the first time, Caro gazed around her. The inn of unpainted gray-and-white flecked stone, with a wide, steep slate roof, was situated with the vineyard on three sides. "Yes."

As they approached the front door, it swung open, and Maufe bowed. "My lady, my lord, dinner will be served in about an hour, if that is acceptable."

"Thank you, Maufe," she replied, as if Huntley's servants were hers. She paused for a moment, confused by her behavior. Yet this was what she had been brought up to be. The wife of a wealthy, titled gentleman. It was almost as if Huntley and she were living in a dreamland. She knew it would end by the time they arrived in Nancy, but resolved to enjoy it while it lasted. There would be no running around smashing the fragile bubbles of which this world consisted. She'd pretend it was all real, as she had as a child, and be happy for a while.

"Her ladyship and I shall take a stroll," Huntley told his valet, then turned to her. "I'll ask about the paths. Meet me down here when you've refreshed yourself."

She glanced up at Huntley to find his kind eyes gazing at her. "Thank you, I shall."

As Caro made her way toward her chamber, she marveled at how comfortable she was becoming with her husband. Even when he'd caught her to-day, it was the first time in years she hadn't been revolted by a man's touch, and the warmth she'd experienced afterwards was vaguely pleasant. If they could learn to be friends, that would be something wonderful indeed.

When they'd married, she had resolved to give him the freedom to take whatever mistresses he wanted. Though now, for some reason, she hoped he would not, yet that was a silly girlish dream. Most men, even those with willing wives, took other women; and she was definitely not willing.

Huntley would be required to return to England, but Caro could not, not while her attacker was still moving freely about Polite Society. Perhaps she could remain in France and her husband could visit occasionally. Though why he would want to remain was a question for which she had no answer.

There was still the problem of an heir. Even though he had a younger brother, it bothered her that he wouldn't have an heir because he'd been forced to marry her. She shook her head, trying to clear it of their problems.

She reached the head of the stairs and saw Nugent standing next to a chamber door. As Caro entered the room, she said, "Lord Huntley and I are going to take some exercise."

"Very well, my lady," her maid responded and removed Caro's cloak.

She started to take off her hat and realized it wasn't on her head. "I must have left my bonnet in the coach."

Nugent took out the chipped-straw hat Caro had worn the night they'd left Venice. "I'll ask Dalle to bring it to me. In the meantime, you can wear this one."

Caro splashed her face and washed her hands, drying them well before taking a fresh pair of gloves from her maid and entering the corridor, where Huntley waited. For some reason, she couldn't yet think of him as her husband. She'd have to at some point. She glanced up. He had a smile on his face and nice, even features. *Handsome* was the word that came to mind. He was extremely handsome, and he'd been very kind to her. Yes, there was no reason at all they could not be friends.

Caro wondered if she would miss Huntley when he finally left her, and her throat tightened painfully. Yet she could not imagine a time when she could allow him to touch her more intimately. No man could live with a wife like her. She tried to push the thoughts out of her mind, but her chest started to ache. It was much too soon to think about any of that.

After Caro went to her chamber, Huntley went to find the chef. Surely they must have something chocolate for Caro. If the shy smile she'd given him was any indication, it appeared that his plan to woo her slowly was working.

She'd laughed, in almost childlike delight, as she'd won and lost her imaginary holdings. Her turquoise eyes had sparkled when he'd brought out the tiramisu and warmed to a deeper blue just before she closed her eyes, savoring the taste. Huntley's initial attraction to her had deepened over the past few days, and now it was all he could do to keep from kissing Caro when she'd peeped at him from beneath her long lashes.

He'd made the right decision when he decided not to take what was his by law. He'd wait until his wife was ready to come to him of her own free will. In many ways, it was as if she'd been trapped by her suffering, and he vowed to find a way to release her. After what she'd been through and the number of years the effects of the abuse had been allowed to fester and harden, that would take time and patience. He groaned. Lots of patience.

Thinking about how unjust society was when it came to women who'd been raped made his jaw clench. They had so few choices. It didn't matter whether they were well-bred virgins or tweenies. Huntley had known husbands who had turned their wives out, blaming the women for being attacked.

He tracked the cook down in the kitchen garden, where the man was cutting spinach. Thank God they spoke German here, one of the three languages in which he was most fluent. "*Guten Abend, mein Herr.*"

The older man stood. "*Guten Abend, Herr Graf.* I understand from your servant that you would like to speak with me about the menu?"

Huntley grinned. "Indeed I would. My countess and I would like to sample your special recipes."

The chef was about Huntley's height, but rounder. A smile showed under his large mustache. "May I suggest for the soup *minestra di farina scottata* and for the pasta, *Schlutzkrapfen.*"

The soup he knew to be of vegetables with beans, but the second dish, he didn't recognize at all. "*Schlutzkrapfen?*"

The man grinned. "Small pockets of dough stuffed with spinach."

Huntley nodded. "Very well. What about the rest?"

In the end, they decided on polenta with venison, local fish sautéed in butter with almonds, and a variety of vegetables. He held his breath before asking, "Do you have anything with chocolate in it?"

The chef smiled broadly. "I have a wonderful chocolate torte with ground almonds."

"Perfect."

He went back inside and had only to wait a few moments for Caro to appear outside her chamber.

They strolled through the vineyards, now bare of fruit, until the sun started to sink very low over the mountains, and then they turned back. The inn was ablaze with lights, making it appear warm and cozy.

"It is very nice here."

"It is." He pointed toward the horizon. "Look how blue the twilight is against the snow on the mountaintops, and you can see lights from some of the houses on the hills."

She gazed up and sighed. "It all looks so peaceful."

"*Tranquil* is the word that comes to mind." Just like the life he desired for her. He wanted to give her children to love and homes of her own to manage. He pictured playing with little girls who looked like her. Tossing them in the air and then holding them close, and breathing in their soft, sweet scents. In the evenings, he'd read to her. Even Suffolk wouldn't be so bad if he had Caro with him.

He led her back inside the inn and up the stairs to her door. "Can you be ready in half an hour?"

"Yes, I think so."

When he knocked on her door thirty minutes later, she emerged dressed in a turquoise silk gown that matched her eyes and caressed her body when she walked toward him.

Relief and happiness coursed through him when she smiled and allowed him to twine her arm with his. He had touched her more in the past two days than he'd done in the weeks he'd been in Venice. Perhaps, just perhaps, she was finally beginning to warm to him.

Their dining parlor was on the ground floor. He led her to the stairs. "Tell me about your family."

Glancing at him, she smiled, and a longing entered her eyes. "I'm the eldest daughter. I have one brother, only two years older than I, and three younger. For a long time, my mother despaired of having any more girls, but then she had two in a row. They still have a few years before they make their come outs."

"Do you miss them?"

Her lips quivered as her voice hitched. "Yes. But they write me all the time. Barely a week goes by that I don't receive a packet of mail."

He forced himself to remain composed, when all he wanted to do was drag her to him and comfort her. *His wife*.

Whom he was not allowed to soothe. "When we reach Innsbruck, we'll send a letter to them asking them to write to the hotel in Nancy. Perhaps someday we can visit your family."

Caro's eyes flew to him, and she tensed like a skittish colt about to bolt. "I—I cannot return to England."

That wouldn't work. He'd have to find a way of dealing with her intractability concerning England. They could not live forever on the Continent, and he would not live apart from her. "I'm sorry to have mentioned it. We can discuss where we'll live later. Let's talk of something else."

Gradually, her arm relaxed. "I told you about my family, now tell me about yours."

They had reached the parlor and entered. Huntley held a chair for her and smiled as he thought of his younger sisters and brothers.

"As you know, I am the eldest male. My older sister, Maud is married, after me there are two younger brothers and four sisters. The oldest of my sisters at home, Dorie, will make her come out next Season. I already feel sorry for her future husband. Dorie is very firm in her beliefs and will at least try to rule the roost. Ophelia should have been born into a theatrical family. One would think she spent her life acting out a play. Louisa is the most normal one in the family, but she's only ten. Too early to know how she'll be yet. The two youngest are twins, a boy and a girl."

He grinned at her. "They manage to get into an extraordinary amount of trouble. Once they decided to feel sorry for my father's hunting hounds and let them all out for a walk. That in itself wouldn't have been much of a problem, but they chose the pasture where the mares were foaling."

Putting a hand to her lips, Caro giggled. "I can see how that might cause some trouble."

If only he could coax more laughter from her. He reached out to touch her and stopped. "My father wasn't happy at all.

I think it was a week before they could take their meals sitting down."

"Is he a hard man? Your father?"

"I wouldn't say he is unreasonable." Huntley drew his brows together as he thought. "Though he's very fond of getting his way. The only one who will gainsay him is my mother, and Everard, of course. Even my father does not argue with his cousin."

Caro glanced up at him, her eyes searching his. "What will they say about your marriage?"

The urge to draw her into his arms grew stronger. "They'll be happy I had the sense to marry someone as intelligent, strong, and beautiful as you."

She bit her lip and opened her lips as if she was going to say something, then the servants entered with their dinner. Why was it waiters had such bad timing? Caro had been so happy earlier and was now distraught; but why, and what could he do to fix it?

Chapter 8

After the landlord entered and informed Huntley and Caro dinner would be a while yet, Caro moved to the doors leading to the terrace. Huntley joined her. She gazed through the heavy glass at the stars. He admired the curve of her jaw and how it flowed gracefully into her neck and down to her breasts. If only he could. . . .

"It's beautiful," she said, interrupting his thoughts.

"I agree."

When he discovered there was a local sparkling wine, he decided it would be the perfect accompaniment to the chocolate torte and ordered it to be served both before dinner and after.

He handed her a glass. "This is from the region. Try it and tell me what you think."

After taking a sip, she grinned. "Extremely nice."

He tasted it as well. Perhaps someday the wine could be

put to even better use. "I agree. I wonder if there's a way to take some with us."

"I could consult with Dalle," she said. "He should know. He is very good at packing."

"A wonderful idea." Huntley filled their glasses again. "Caro, were you about to tell me something before we were interrupted?"

She took a breath and glanced at him almost hopefully, and then the moment was gone and her eyes dulled. "No, it was nothing really."

Holding her gaze, he said, "Don't ever be afraid of telling me *anything*."

She gave a curt little nod. "I won't."

But she was, and he didn't know what to do about it. His fingers clenched. Not being able to touch her was going to kill him. Fortunately, the waiters came in with the soup before he did something guaranteed to set him back.

He took her hand. "Come, it's time to dine."

Huntley held Caro's chair as she sat. Lowering her lashes as she took a sip of her soup, Caro wished she could tell him, but only her mother, father, and Nugent knew. Maybe Huntley had figured it out from what Nugent told him, and that was the reason he was being so good to her. She'd sworn to herself she would forget the attack, but even after all this time, it still came back to haunt her dreams. Not as often as it used to, but enough to keep her fear and anger alive.

Huntley was being so kind. Treating her as if she was a real wife to him. Truth be told, he had the worst part of this marriage. Any other man would have forced her by now, but he was too honorable.

His soft, deep voice intruded on her thoughts. "Now for the question I had earlier. Tell me about your trip from England to Venice."

She was glad he picked a topic that she enjoyed discussing. "It was interesting. We sailed to Rotterdam, took a barge to Stuttgart, and a coach to Ulm, where we found another boat to take us to Buda and then over to Venice."

"That was in 1811, wasn't it?"

"Yes." They were now on the pasta course, and she took a taste of the spinach-filled ravioli. The flavors of garlic, the nuttiness of the cheese, burst into her mouth. "Um, this is excellent. You should eat some of yours."

She waited until he'd taken a few bites.

He chewed and swallowed. "Yes, it is very tasty. Go on with your story."

"Well, then I left in late spring of that year. I could have taken a ship but . . ." But there were too many men on board, and she couldn't stand to be around them. "I thought it would be more interesting to travel through Europe. There was no fighting at the time."

Huntley grinned. "I'm sure it was. Did you experience any problems?"

Shaking her head, she responded, "Not really. Papa had taught Nugent and me how to shoot before I came out. We dyed Dalle's hair a little grayer so he didn't look young enough to be conscripted, and made arrangements to hire an older coachman and outriders. The French weren't drafting older men. I loved traveling down the rivers. It was so peaceful, and such a lot to see." Not for the first time, she noticed what a lovely smile he had.

Eyes twinkling, he asked, "Such as castles with vineyards?"

Caro couldn't help smiling. "Yes, old castles, vineyards, and towns. Maybe someday I shall do it again."

He nodded. "Perhaps, one day, we can make a boat trip."

She bent her head. Why did he have to talk as if they'd be

together for more than a few months? This time was almost magical, but it couldn't last.

She tried to keep her tone light and reminded herself that she was not going to ruin this dream world, but then, unable to help herself, she said, "You do not have to stay with me, you know." Suddenly her throat was sore. Yet she had to tell him. "I'll understand if you need a mistress."

Huntley scowled. It was the first time he'd frowned so seriously at her. When he spoke, his tone was harsh. "No."

"You needn't be angry with me." What right did he have to be incensed with her when she was giving him the freedom to be with other women that most men wanted?

"I have no intention of being unfaithful. No good ever comes of it. This will all work itself out," he growled, and went back to his pasta.

For some ridiculous reason, her heart lightened, and it shouldn't have. This marriage was so unfair to him. The waiters returned with trays of other foods. Huntley must have planned another dinner like the one last night. She smiled. "Thank you."

Shedding his frown, his lips tilted up. "I hope you like what the chef and I have selected. The dishes here are much more Austrian than Italian."

As before, they inspected the offerings on the sideboard. He hovered over her and helped her choose the dishes to try first. She turned her head toward him and, for a moment, their faces were close together. His gaze dropped to her mouth and rose, almost at once, back to her eyes. Her heart had stopped when she'd thought he was going to kiss her. Thankfully, he didn't, but he was still too close. "I think I have enough food for now."

He held out her chair and, after filling his plate, joined her. Once Caro had finished the last piece of venison, she leaned back in her chair. "All of it was wonderful. I don't think I could eat another bite."

A wicked smile appeared on his lips. "Oh, I think you might eat just a little more, my lady."

He stood and walked to the bell-pull. After giving it a short tug, he sat back down. The door opened and a waiter entered the room carrying a large platter. She sniffed and sat up, then looked. "*A chocolate torte?* Oh, Huntley, thank you!"

The waiter placed the plate on the table and cut them both slices of the cake. She took a forkful of the piece Huntley offered, and sighed. "It has fruit in it as well." Caro held out the next bite to him. "Here, have a taste."

Leaning over the table, Huntley touched her hand as he guided the fork to his lips and opened them. She drew a sharp breath as warmth infused her fingers. What on earth was that tingling, and why was it suddenly so hard to draw a breath?

Chewing slowly, Huntley realized the game had just changed. If he played his cards correctly, the spark they'd both just experienced would help him kindle a fire, and their marriage would be real.

After dinner, Caro called for her book to be brought to her, and settled in a large, overstuffed chair as Huntley partook of a glass of brandy. For the first time ever, they sat companionably together after dinner. It may not have been romantic, but it couldn't have been more domestic, and he found himself longing for more times like this.

"I've noticed we've been slowing down. Do you still think we'll reach Brennerbad by to-morrow evening?" she asked.

"If we keep to the same schedule and only stop for changes, yes." He and his wife had covered almost two hundred miles in the last five days, almost all of it steadily up-hill. One more day would see them to the Brenner Pass.

There had been no sign of di Venier, and Huntley prayed that the marchese had given up the chase. Still, to be sure, he'd sent Raphael and Dalle into the nearby town to scout for information.

An hour later, Dalle knocked on the door and entered. The grim look on his face told Huntley all he needed to know. They had not yet escaped.

Caro glanced up as well. Her lips tightened. "The march-ese is still chasing us, isn't he?"

Her groom nodded. "Aren't that many Italian speakers hereabouts. His people sort o' stood out."

"Dalle, are they only searching the larger towns?"

"Seems so, my lord. They're getting pretty frustrated going from one inn to t'other, and that marchese has even more men looking along the coast, and at the pass through Turin."

Huntley nodded and turned to Caro. "Let's leave even earlier in the morning than usual. The moon is full and has not been setting until after sunrise. We should have enough light to travel by."

She drew her full lower lip between her teeth. "When will he stop?"

"I don't know, my dear, but we cannot go farther than Brennerbad to-morrow. It wouldn't be safe to cross the pass near dark."

"Of course, I understand." Putting on a smile, she quipped, "Better safe than sorry."

Their moment of homely bliss was over. He tossed back the rest of the brandy as she stood and waited for him. "Come, my lady. We've a hard day of travel come morning."

* * *

Two days after Huntley and Caro had departed Venice, Horatia sat on her balcony overlooking the Grand Canal, drinking wine. Even if he did have a reputation as a bit of a rake, her nephew was a good, kind man. He'd take care of her goddaughter. She sent out some of her servants and discovered the marchese departed Venice yesterday after he'd left her house, presumably to follow Caro and Huntley.

Horatia's glass shook, and she took another large sip. Whatever happened, she must keep to her plan. To do anything else would cause suspicion.

The knocker echoed through the house. She'd miss it here. It was the only house she had ever owned, and she'd made it hers. For the past ten years, she'd been happy here. Horatia's heart ripped apart, as if she was leaving a loving friend.

La Valle appeared before her and bowed. "My lady."

"Yes?"

"The Duca di Venier is here."

"Again?"

Her major-domo nodded.

"Very well, show him into my study. The same arrangements as the last time."

"Yes, my lady."

She'd be damned if she would rush. It was his grandson's fault her peaceful life was being destroyed. Savoring the last of the wine, she swallowed and stood.

When Horatia entered her study, two large footmen were in place and the duke was pacing. Curtseying, she greeted him. "To what do I owe this pleasure, Your Grace?"

"The Lady Caroline and Lord Huntley, are they still here?"

Opening her eyes wide, she replied, "Good gracious, no. Huntley volunteered to ensure all was ready at my villa, and

Lady Caroline decided to go with him. They left yesterday morning, as I told your grandson."

The duke scowled. "She went with him alone?"

Horatia shrugged, trying to keep the gesture carefree. "Surely there is nothing wrong with that? She has her maid and groom with her, and they are betrothed, after all."

His bushy eyebrows drew together. "You English have a different way of thinking about this."

Tilting her head, she gave a small smile. "Yes, well, we can be a little different from the Venetians. And they *are* both English."

He stepped back and bowed. "Yes, in that you are correct." Turning on his heel, he left the room.

He was going to do something. If only she could figure out what it was. She sank into a chair and prayed Huntley and Caro hadn't killed each other.

La Valle knocked and entered. "My lady, most of your clothing has been packed. I will have it sent to Genova early in the morning."

Rising, she turned to him. "Thank you. Are you sure you want to go with me? I may never return."

He bowed again. "My lady, I promised your husband I would never leave your employ."

Tears threatened to choke her. "Thank you. Another bottle of wine, I think. I'll be in the drawing room."

"My lady, with your permission?"

"Yes, what is it?"

"Several others of the staff would like to accompany you as well. It matters not to them if they come back."

"Very well." She grinned. "I hope the ship will have room for them all." If she took most of her staff, it would support her story that she was going to Lake Garda, and save her the problem of hiring new servants when she got to wherever she was going. Most importantly, it would keep her from worrying about them. Most of her servants had been with her for so long, it would have been hard to leave them. She would have missed them all so much.

La Valle's lips inched only slightly upward. "I have made the arrangements. You need worry about nothing, my lady. We will take good care of you."

"You always have." Before George died, he'd made sure she had reliable servants. She could never complain that her husband had not always looked out for her. It was a shame she'd never found another man who could be so good to her. Then again, what man would want a woman who was barren, other than for a mistress? Now it was too late.

La Valle bowed and left. Horatia made her way back to the drawing room with mixed feelings concerning her departure from Venice. One more day to get through. Only one more day to sit on her balcony. She was loath to leave, yet she could no longer remain here. She stayed until late in the evening and, perhaps, drank a little too much before making her way to her chambers.

When she awoke the next morning, her maid, Risher, was packing sheets. Horatia rubbed her eyes. "What are you doing?"

"Well, my lady," she said, "if anyone were to check the trunks you have with you, they'd find out pretty quickly there's nothing in them. Therefore, I'm packing other stuff and putting a gown or two on the top."

"I'm glad you thought of it," Horatia said. "I never would have."

Her maid grinned. "No, my lady."

Horatia was at breakfast when someone started beating on the door so hard, she thought it would break.

La Valle strode swiftly into the room. "My lady . . ."

"The duke?" she asked.

He nodded.

"Now what? Please show him in."

Instead of rising, she motioned the duke to the table and called for tea. "Your Grace. What brings you here at such an early hour?"

Rather than sitting, he paced. "I am here to inform you that Lady Caroline is now the Contessa of Huntley."

This *was* news. Horatia did not even have to feign her surprise. "Indeed? And how do you know this?"

"My grandson went after her, and when he found them, the English bishop told him they'd just been married."

"How precipitant of them." She took a sip of tea, wondering if the news was good or bad. "You know how it is when two young people are in love."

He stopped and turned on her. "Are you not upset?"

On the contrary, she was enormously relieved and could have collapsed at his feet and kissed them for bringing her the news. Perhaps now his grandson would give up on Caro. "How should I be? They are both of age and betrothed. I would have expected them to marry, though I had hoped for a large wedding with both families in attendance."

He seemed a bit taken aback. "*Sì, sì,* of course. I understand you depart Venice soon. I shall wish you a good journey to the lake."

After he left, Horatia heaved a sigh of relief. What bishop could Huntley and Caro have got to marry them? And why did they marry? They hadn't been getting along at all when they'd left. She frowned. If it was true. She rang for La Valle. "We leave within the hour. Lady Caro and Lord Huntley are apparently wed. I do not think it will appear at all strange if I leave immediately."

He bowed. "That is not a problem, my lady. I've already sent word to the stables to have the coaches readied."

"La Valle, I want to travel as quickly as possible. Can we reach Genova in five days?"

He raised a brow. "If you wish it, my lady, I will make it happen."

An hour later, Horatia and her servants, other than an older couple who would act as caretakers, took gondolas to the mainland, where she found the vehicles already packed.

Two hours into her journey, Horatia's carriages were stopped by the marchese. With exquisite politeness, he bowed. "My lady, I thought you were not traveling until the morning."

She raised an imperious brow. Now was not the time to kowtow to a spoiled aristocrat. "Having been informed by your grandfather that my nephew and goddaughter were married, I decided to leave early. Now, remove your men from the road."

"Perhaps you would like an escort to the lake, my lady," di Venier said. "The roads are not always so safe."

How dare that loose fish threaten her. She smiled politely. "I would not wish to take so much of your time, my lord. My journey will not be swift, as I plan to visit friends along the way and cannot disappoint them."

"As you wish, my lady." The marchese sketched a bow and took off in the opposite direction from Venice with his band of riders following. Now where was that stupid man going? Drat, she should have discovered what his plans were.

"La Valle."

"My lady?"

"Have one coach travel to the lake and then take another road back to meet us," Horatia said. "I do not think di Venier would accost us at the villa, but if he is intent on finding Lord Huntley and Lady Caro, he may well look to see if there are people in residence."

"May they be informed of the threat?"

Horatia nodded. "Of course." She tapped her chin. "Bring me the maps this evening when we stop. I think I shall plan a route that will leave the marchese guessing if he tries to pursue us."

Chapter 9

Huntley escorted Caro to her chamber. "If you agree, I'd like to leave even earlier than usual to-morrow."

Though her heart was in her throat, she refused to allow her fear to show. Raising her chin, she asked calmly, "Because of the marchese's men?"

"Yes," he replied. "With any luck at all, they'll decide they've lost us, but I don't want to drive through Bolzano when it's light and take the chance of being seen."

"We may leave as early as you wish." Caro considered how far they'd come since she first thought he would try to take complete charge of their escape. Other than the surprises at dinner, which she enjoyed more than she could have imagined, Huntley had willingly included her in all the plans for their journey.

He grinned slightly. "Thank you. If five o'clock is agreeable to you, I'll tell the others."

She nodded and went to open the door, but his arm reached around and, without touching her, opened it for her.

If only she'd met him before she'd been raped. How different everything would have been. Her voice was not quite steady. "I'll see you in the morning."

"Caro."

She turned back to him and gazed into his steady blue-green eyes. "Yes?"

His voice was deep and comforting. "I won't let him touch you."

Her throat became so tight, water couldn't pass. She had never been so afraid and yet felt so safe at the same time. The idea of what di Venier could do terrified her. Yet Huntley made it seem almost as if the marchese was a child's bogeyman. Like the monster who, as a child, she'd thought lived under her bed. If only she could bring herself to believe her husband could in truth protect her. She knew he'd try, of course. Not trusting herself to speak, she merely nodded.

When she entered her chamber, Nugent was ready to prepare Caro for bed. "Nugent, we'll leave at five in the morning."

"Yes, my lady. I spoke with Mr. Maufe, and he told me they'd run into the marchese's men, so I thought we'd be making an early start. Let's get you ready for bed."

After Caro's gown and under-garments were removed, she lifted her arms for her nightgown, Caro waited until it had slid down her body before responding. "The news that we are still being hounded means we'll not be able to slow down. Someday, I'm going to visit the region again."

"That would be pleasant," Nugent said as she combed out Caro's hair. "I'm glad his lordship has matters well in hand. He's not a man to be trifled with."

She met her dresser's gaze in the mirror. "He is much more competent than I expected."

Snorting, Nugent continued to comb Caro's hair and then braid it. That they were still being followed bothered Caro greatly. Yet her dresser noticed the same thing she had: Huntley was proving to be much more of a man than she'd previously thought. The rage on the marchese's face when the prelate told him she and Huntley were married still caused her heart to pound in fear. She'd seen that expression on a man's face previously, right before his fist slammed into her face, knocking her to the floor.

She slipped onto the cool bed. Nugent pulled the feather-bed up over Caro and blew out the candle on her night-table.

Caro tossed and turned before finally slipping into a rest-less sleep.

Hands grabbed her roughly and soft, wet lips pressed hard to her face. Her stomach revolted and she thought she'd be sick. She moved her head from side to side in a fruitless attempt to avoid the wetness. She tried to push him off, but he grabbed the bodice and ripped her gown, shoving her against the wall. Biting down hard on his lips, she tasted the sharp tang of blood. He muffled an oath, and his fist came at her. When she fell, her head hit the floor. She tasted more blood—hers. He got between her legs and she was still struggling when there was a sharp pain. She screamed, and screamed, and screamed.

Caro bolted up and cried out as Nugent reached her. "There, there, my little lady. It's not but a bad dream. He can't hurt you anymore."

Her maid cradled Caro and rocked her back and forth, as

she'd done all Caro's life. Sobs mingled with mewing sounds. "Nugent, when will it stop?"

She gently stroked Caro's head. "I don't know, my lady, but the dreams will go away in time."

Finally, Caro's heart stopped beating so quickly and she was able to calm herself. A knock came on the door, and Maufe said, "I have warm milk for her ladyship."

"I'm coming." Nugent tucked Caro back under the cover called a featherbed. "I'm just going to the door, and I'll be right back."

Caro nodded and lay staring up at the overhead bed hangings.

Her dresser returned and handed her the milk. "From his lordship. It has honey and cinnamon, like he used to have."

"Please thank him for me."

Nugent looked as if she would say something, and then shook her head. "I will."

When Caro was finished, her dresser took the empty cup and set it on the small table by the bed. "You sleep now."

She did. And this time, she dreamt of a kind man with brown hair, who made her laugh and fed her chocolate.

It was still pitch-dark when Nugent woke her. "Come, my lady."

Swinging her legs over the side of the bed, Caro stood and went to the basin where the warm water awaited her.

After quickly washing and dressing, she met Huntley in their parlor. *Their parlor*. Even after a few days, it seemed so natural to take her meals with him. "Thank you for the milk last night. I slept peacefully after that."

He held the plate for her as she made her selections. "It used to help me when I had bad dreams as a child."

He poured her tea, as he had since the first morning.

When they were safe, she'd have to think about their marriage and what they would do. Maybe he'd want to divorce her. Come to think of it, what were the grounds for divorce? "I'll eat quickly."

Huntley nodded and applied himself to his food, while surreptitiously studying Caro. She'd scared him to death last night when she'd screamed. He had only just remembered to grab his dressing gown before he opened the connecting door to her chamber.

Nugent had held Caro as she cried and gulped for air. As if sensing him, her maid had glanced up and shook her head. He might not be able to comfort his wife, but there had to be something he could do. Then he'd remembered what his nurse used to do when he had a bad dream.

Maufe had been behind Huntley when he'd turned back into his room. Huntley put a finger over his lips and closed the door. "She'll be fine. Get some warm milk infused with a bit of valerian, add honey and cinnamon, and take it to her."

His valet left the room and, in a surprisingly short time, was knocking on Caro's door. Huntley had made his way to the connecting door, opening it to watch as Nugent gave the cup to his wife and nodded to him.

He stayed until Caro's breathing calmed enough to assure him she was asleep, and he had racked his brain for something else he could do to help her. There was nothing, but if he ever found the man who'd hurt her, he'd make him pay with his life.

When she'd come down for breakfast, she had dark smudges under her eyes and yawned. She finished her cup of tea and took a bite of bread with cheese.

"How are you doing?" he asked as he poured her more tea.

Smiling brightly at him, she replied, "I'm much better."

"Caro, if the dreams happen again, if there is anything else I can do, please feel free to command me."

Caro gazed steadily back at him. "You are very kind."

Stabbing a piece of ham, he stifled a growl. *Kind*. Kind was not how he wanted her to see him, except maybe some of the time. He struggled to hold back the primitive warrior who wanted to kill to protect her, and confront di Venier instead of playing this cat and mouse game. Yet going after the marchese would only put Caro in danger. At every turn, Huntley's need to defend his lady was being stymied. He wasn't allowed to fight the marchese, he didn't know who the blackguard was who'd hurt Caro, and he couldn't even kiss his wife.

Huntley's voice was huskier than he'd wanted it to be. "Caro."

Her eyes flew to his. "What is it? Not more bad news?"

"No." How could he tell her she was his, his to care for, his to protect, and she need never worry about her safety again? "We need to leave soon."

"Do you think we'll run into them again? The men looking for us?"

Huntley searched her face. Her expression was calm, but her eyes reflected her fear. He wouldn't lie to her. "I don't know. Eat and we'll go."

He felt the need to stay close to her and escorted Caro to her chamber. "I'll see you shortly."

She gave him a small smile. "We won't be long."

Once the door closed, he returned to his room to find Maufe already packed. Only one bag was left to take to the coach. "My lord, is her ladyship better?"

"Yes. She needs some more sleep, but she'll be fine. I want to get out of the marchese's reach as soon as possible. The closer we get to the pass, the less influence he has. Tell everyone to keep their eyes and ears open."

"Yes, my lord," Maufe said and left the room.

When Huntley arrived in the yard, the coaches were loaded and ready. The morning was much cooler than the previous one had been, and he expected the weather would become colder still as they climbed high into the mountains. They'd been traveling for almost a week, and he'd wanted to be in Austria by now. "Maufe, make sure the fur rugs are in the carriage and there are hot bricks below. I don't want Lady Huntley catching a chill."

Maufe bowed and his lips twitched. "No, my lord. Every provision for her ladyship's comfort shall be made."

"I know. I'm like a nervous cat." He rubbed his chin. "Bear with me, and I'll try to get us all out of this without any of our people being killed or injured."

When Caro came down, he handed her into the coach. The floor was already warm from the hot bricks under them, and he tucked the fur around her.

Her lips curved up as he stepped back to survey his handiwork. "Huntley, thank you, but it's not that frosty. I am perfectly fine."

He resisted an urge to growl. "It is getting late in the season and will become colder as we travel farther into the Alps."

She gave him a curious look. "Of course, I didn't consider. Thank you for thinking of it."

The coach lurched forward as he tried to relax. It was still full dark, the stars and moon bright in the sky. The vineyards surrounding the inn took on the appearance of a dark maze. Several minutes later, when they reached the main road, Huntley reached under the seat to retrieve the chess box. There was just enough light from the inside coach lanterns to see, but when he glanced at Caro, her long brown lashes rested on her cheeks, and her breathing was deep and steady. Quietly, he placed the box on the seat next to him and, once again, took in the view. Mountains rose up from the narrow valley floor, casting dark, uneven shadows around them.

In the antelucan light, his two carriages sped through the ancient Roman town of Bolzano. Fortunately, the only traffic they encountered were farmers bringing in their wares. It must be market day. For Caro's sake, Huntley fervently prayed any other travelers, most particularly the marchese's men, were still abed. He glanced at her again and hoped she wouldn't have another nightmare. He doubted she'd respond well to him trying to calm her.

They were pulling into a coaching inn to make a change when Caro finally woke.

She covered her mouth with a small gloved hand and yawned. "Where are we?"

Grinning, he opened the door as the coach stopped. "Brixen. We're half-way to Brennerbad, but the steep road has slowed us down."

Caro glanced around. "It must be almost noon. I can't believe I slept so long."

"You must have been tired." He held out his hand. "We'll stop here for a while."

She gave him a wry look. "The last time we did that we ended up having to marry."

Huntley laughed. "Yes, well, we don't have to worry about *that* anymore."

Smiling ruefully, she shrugged. "No, it's already done."

Yes, for better or worse, it was done, and she was his, for the rest of their lives. Although outwardly his wife seemed to accept that fact, he wondered if her appearance of acquiescence was caused by the danger she was in. He had the feeling it was. There must be a way for him to tie her to him, and the sooner he found it, the better.

He and Caro were walking into the inn in Brixen when

Dalle, who'd been on horseback as an out-rider, rode up. "My lord, get you inside. I'll have the coaches hidden."

Caro started to whirl around, her lips open to question Dalle. Huntley grabbed her arm and dragged her into the inn. "There's no time. Pull your hood up. We're going to find a table in the corner of the common room. Whoever it is, they are less likely to look for us there."

"I'm sorry. It was just such a shock."

He placed his hand over hers. "I understand. Will you do as I say?"

"Yes." She settled her hood over her hair and followed him toward the back of the large room filled with tables and crowded with midday customers. Servers carrying large trays laden with plates dodged them. The ceiling was low, and there was only one fireplace. Each time the door opened, cold air blew into the room. The other diners, a mix of locals and travelers, were too busy eating to give Huntley and Caro more than a glance.

He found a table behind one of the large square support posts away from the windows, which were the only source of light for the room. "Stay here. I'll get a wine for you."

A serving girl hurried toward them. He ordered, and had just taken a seat next to Caro when shouting erupted from the corridor.

Di Venier.

The marchese was demanding to see who was in the inn's private parlors.

Caro's face tightened.

Huntley took one of her small hands in his and kept his voice low. "He won't look in here. Remember my promise to you. Trust me. I'll keep you safe."

She stared down at his large hand and wondered why she did not have the urge to pull hers away as she always had before. She glanced up. "You do that well. Take care of me."

He'd been watching the door to the main hall but turned briefly to her and smiled. "It is my pleasure, my lady."

She jumped when a door slammed suddenly. A woman screamed and several deep voices were raised in anger, then the uproar moved to the outside.

At the sound of horses riding off, Caro remembered to breathe again. "Thank you."

Huntley's hand tightened on hers. He didn't answer for a few moments, then his watchful expression cleared, and he nodded to someone she couldn't see. "You don't have to thank me. You're my wife, and, as I've said before, I'm not going to allow anyone to hurt you."

His jaw hardened in anger. She thought it was due to her doubting him, until he said through clenched teeth, "If I could dispatch di Venier without putting you in danger, I would."

Thank the Lord for a reasonable man. "I am very glad you have decided not to fight him."

His sharp glance pierced her.

"Not," she added quickly, "that I think you would lose, but it would complicate our lives tremendously."

He had still not released her. She wondered if his protection extended to the harm he could cause her if he wanted her to be his wife in truth, but then dismissed the thought as unworthy. They'd been together for six days now, four of them as a married couple, and he'd not once attempted to take what was his to demand. Perhaps he wasn't interested in her. For some reason, that thought didn't comfort her at all. Yet was that the explanation for why he didn't care if she could never perform her intimate marital duties? No, she was forgetting the reputation he had among women. Then what could it be?

"A penny for your thoughts," he said.

The touch of his warm breath caressed her ear.

"It was nothing."

A line formed between his brows. He didn't let go of her until their meal arrived.

Caro pushed back her hood but kept her cloak wrapped around her as she tucked into the savory slices of roasted pork covered with a light sauce and accompanied by round dumplings and red cabbage. Once again, Huntley had found something she would enjoy eating. Nugent and their other servants sat farther down the long table in a way that made certain no one else would join them.

After she'd finished her meal, Caro surveyed the room. This was the first time she'd been in a common room, and would probably be the last. She took the opportunity to study those who seemed to be locals. The men wore leather breeches held up by colorful suspenders with a strap across the front, thick woolen stockings, and heavy leather shoes. The women wore gowns of stuff or heavier wool, and aprons. Most of them spoke in a guttural language she recognized as a type of German, but it seemed to have Italian overtones.

Next to her, Huntley stretched out his legs and held a huge, heavy pottery stein from which he sipped. She took a sip of the excellent, hot, spiced red wine he'd ordered for her, which was served in a much smaller version of his mug.

Feeling his gaze on her, Caro turned to him. "I like it here. It's fascinating. There are so many people from different stations of life."

After taking another draught of the beer, he replied, "You've never been in a common room before, have you?"

"No, I wish we could always dine in this sort of place."

He sat up, and a smile tugged at his lips. "It's enjoyable now, but you wouldn't like it in the evening. There are not many women, and the men frequently drink too much. Still,

I understand the draw." Huntley paused. "If you'd like, we'll do it again."

"Thank you. If you don't see a problem, I would enjoy it." He'd given her a wonderful adventure that she was willing to repeat. Ladies missed so much by not being able to experience a common room. Of course, some would not like it at all, considering it vulgar, but Caro loved watching different sorts of people. She'd miss Huntley when he left. He said that he wouldn't, but no man could live celibate. She'd go back to the boring routine of a spinster.

"After what happened earlier," he replied grimly, "we might be safer to avoid private parlors, at least during the day." He seemed to study the room again before adding, "As long as I'm with you, there can be no impropriety. It wouldn't do if we were in England, of course."

"I understand." One benefit of being a married lady was being allowed so many more freedoms. She glanced at him as he watched the others in the room and drank his beer. Somehow she'd have to find a way to repay him for his sacrifice.

Huntley took another sip of the ale, relishing the slightly bitter taste on his tongue. Caro's eyes were wide and her face alight with curiosity as she continued to observe their fellow guests.

He still wasn't quite sure what his feelings for her were. That he'd been attracted to her from the first was clear, and he didn't mind at all being married to Caro, except for the lack of intimacy. Though, if he had any thought that their forced marriage would relieve him of courting her, he'd be mistaken.

If anything, given what she'd endured, a courtship was absolutely necessary to ensure a happy marriage. At least that part was progressing satisfactorily. His parents' marriage had been arranged and turned out well. He had no doubt that once she got to know him better, they could make a go of it and have a happy life. The only question was how long it would take.

"My lord?"

He glanced up to see Dalle addressing him. "Yes."

"If we want to get there before dark, we should be going soon."

"How long before you're ready?"

"Raphael and Collins are getting the horses hitched up now."

"We'll be right out." After the groom left, Huntley addressed his wife. "Caro, if you need to do anything before we leave . . ."

He stood as she rose, and he nodded at Nugent to accompany her. He escorted Caro and her dresser to the hall, where the staircase to the first floor was located.

Glancing over her shoulder, Caro said, "I'll meet you outside?"

Damned if he'd let her go outside accompanied only by her maid, with all the traffic in this inn. Smiling, he replied, "I'll wait for you here."

Nugent got the attention of one of the serving maids, who led Caro and her dresser up the stairs.

Maufe came looking for him. "Oh, there you are, my lord. Dalle asked me to tell you we're ready."

"I'll be out as soon as her ladyship returns. Tell me what happened with our marchese."

His valet's eyes lit with amusement. "He pushed his way into all the private parlors and disturbed several people, including one of the high-ranking members of the Hapsburg family, a *Graf* from Bavaria and his wife. The Hapsburg gentleman threatened to inform the emperor and told our marchese to go back to Venice. Then the landlord had his lordship escorted out."

Huntley chuckled. The Hapsburgs now owned all of Northern Italy, including Venice. "Which way did he go?"

"Back south. Dalle heard one of his riders say that he was crazy, and the general consensus was that they'd missed the lady somewhere along the way."

Huntley only had to wait for a few minutes before Caro returned. "I think we're ready."

Maufe bowed before going to the inn's yard and telling the others. Huntley took his lady's arm and led her through the milling people and vehicles to their coaches, with Nugent following close behind.

He settled Caro in the coach, with more hot bricks loaded in the space below the floor to keep her warm.

"*Lord Huntley.*"

Damnation. How the hell had the marchese found them?

Di Venier dismounted a black horse and was striding toward the coach.

Quickly sliding a sidelong glance into the carriage, Huntley saw Caro's lovely face turn deathly white and knew he must find some way, short of killing di Venier, to get rid of him once and for all.

Huntley turned back to the other man. "What do you want?"

Di Venier's obsidian eyes glittered with malice. "Your wife."

"Not in this lifetime." Huntley fingered the pistol in his greatcoat pocket. "Go find your own."

He turned to step into the coach and di Venier grabbed Huntley's shoulder.

"I want satisfaction, Lord Huntley." The lines of the

Venetian's face had hardened. "Lady Caro was mine, and you stole her."

Huntley shook off the marchese's hand and stepped back, putting enough space between them that he wouldn't be tempted to drive his fist into the other man's face. His jaw clenched. If only he hadn't vowed not to fight di Venier. Schooling his countenance into a polite mask, he said, "You are mad, and a gentleman does not meet a Bedlamite."

The flash of steel glinted in the sun. Di Venier rushed toward him. Before the marchese got within arm's reach, Huntley drew the gun from his pocket and shot di Venier in the shoulder.

The Venetian's scream rent the air as he grabbed his arm and sank to the ground. His men surrounded him, and a mass of people rushed out from the inn.

A neatly dressed, middle-aged man cut through the milling crowd and asked in German, "What is going on here?"

Caro's firm, self-possessed voice came from the carriage. "The Marchese di Venier threatened my husband and then tried to kill him."

"My lady," the man said in lightly accented English, and bowed. "Allow me to introduce myself. I am Graf Rudolf of Bavaria, a member of the Hapsburg family and the emperor's envoy to Venice."

Caro inclined her head slightly in acknowledgment. "I trust you will be able to stop the marchese's persecution of my husband and me and allow us to continue our journey."

The Austrian glanced at di Venier and smiled coldly in his direction. "You again. I ordered you to leave once already." He bowed to Caro. "My lady, it will be my great pleasure to escort the marchese to his grandfather and suggest he make immediate arrangements for the young man's marriage. Perhaps then, the marchese will cease to chase married women." The *Graf* nodded to Huntley. "You may be on your way, my lord. Please accept my apologies that this unfortunate incident occurred in my family's territory."

Huntley bowed to the Austrian. "Thank you, my lord."

Caro glanced at the dirty and bleeding di Venier, her gaze piercing him with disdain. This was the first glimpse Huntley had had of the woman Caro was meant to be. Not one jumping at shadows and suffering from bad dreams, but strong and commanding. A perfect countess and future marchioness. "Come, my dear. Let us be on our way."

Caro gathered her skirts as she took her seat in the coach. "Thank you, my lord. An excellent idea."

Once she was settled, he closed the door and pounded on the roof of the coach. It started forward with a lurch. Raphael must be as eager to leave as Huntley was.

This had been a good day. Putting a ball in the marchese satisfied the part of Huntley that had been spoiling for a fight, and that he managed it without breaking his promise to Caro made it even better.

A sound between a hiccup and a cry escaped his wife's lips.

"Caro, are you all right?"

She held her gloved hand to her lips. "*He almost killed you!*"

Huntley leaned forward, wanting to touch her. "No, my dear," he said in a soothing tone. "Di Venier never had a chance to hurt me. The only reason I didn't fire sooner was that I did not want to put a hole in my coat pocket. Besides, Dalle and Collins had their weapons pointed at di Venier."

Caro gave him a strange look but didn't respond.

He pulled out the hot chocolate from this morning. "Would you like a drink of the chocolate? It is no longer very warm."

She glanced up and smiled at him. "Yes, thank you. That would be just the thing."

He passed the flagon to her. After a while, the color returned to her cheeks and he asked, "Chess, my lady?"

"Certainly, my lord."

He set up the board, and Caro and he played as they'd done for the past several days. With the problem of the marchese taken care of, Huntley was free to focus his efforts on her and their marriage. From her reaction, she must care for him at least a little. Keeping his mind on the game became more difficult as he thought about wooing her. Teasing her rosy lips with kisses, and running his hands through the long, silky curls of her hair, and over the creamy mounds of her breasts. Taking the hard pink bud in his mouth . . . His member stiffened, and he stifled a groan. Soon, it had to be soon.

Chapter 10

Venice, Italy

Several days later, Antonio arrived back at his grandfather's *palazzo* under an armed escort. He was ready to murder someone. The Austrian envoy had treated him like a common criminal. He hadn't even been allowed to bathe and change his clothing while the Austrian talked with the duke.

Finally, he was summoned to his grandfather. Going down on one knee, he took the old man's hand. "Nonno."

"My grandson, I am greatly disturbed by some of the stories I've been hearing about you lately."

The duke's hand settled upon Antonio's head and he knew he was in trouble. Never in his life had Antonio heard his grandfather raise his voice, but the softer his tone, the stronger the steel.

"But, Nonno, you told me to take what is mine."

"*Sì, sì*, but the emissary said you created a great scene, which you know I cannot allow. We have the dignity of centuries to uphold. And that is not all. A rumor has reached the ears of my priest. Antonio, is it true you killed a novice?"

No, he'd done many things, but not that. "Someone is lying. She was a whore, pretending to be an innocent to get more money."

"My priest has seen the headdress and the torn clothing, and he spoke with the Mother Superior." His grandfather's voice was soft but disapproving. "The girl's mother is a prostitute, the girl was not. You will go to confession and make a large donation to the convent. That will put it right in the eyes of God."

Antonio had no remorse. A holy woman had no business in a brothel. She would have made a bad nun. "Yes, Nonno. I will do it immediately. Then I must find Lady Caroline . . ."

"No. That is over. She is married."

"What if it was a farce?" It did not matter one way or the other to Antonio, but he must convince his grandfather.

The old man's lips tightened. "Yet another scene you made over this woman."

Antonio couldn't stop from flinching.

"How do you think I enjoyed being lectured to by an English bishop over your behavior? She and her husband come from influential families. Do I need to remind you that Austria is aligned with England? Your actions could harm us politically. I will arrange a match for you. It is past time for you to be married."

His grandfather lifted his hand from Antonio's head and he stood.

"You need a legitimate son to follow you."

Antonio's jaw clenched. "She must promise to treat Geno as her own."

The duke shook his head. "I have received a messenger from the baron. He wants Geno back."

This couldn't be happening. Geno belonged to him, not

the baron. No man should have to give up his son. "But he is my son. From my loins."

His grandfather nodded. "He is your natural son. He is the baron's legitimate one, and his only heir. Think of the boy. What is best for him?"

Antonio's chest hurt as if his heart was being ripped out. "Her father should never have given her to him. She should have married me."

His grandfather stood firm, but there was compassion in his gaze. "There was a contract. She could not disgrace her family. If she had survived childbirth, perhaps the baron would have had the marriage annulled, yet that was not her fate."

Tears stung Antonio's eyes. "The baron will mistreat Geno."

"He will not. I will send servants with the child, who answer only to me. I know you love him, but you cannot deny the boy his birthright."

There was no point arguing with Nonno when he used that tone. Antonio would do as he said, except for the part about Lady Caroline. He'd not give up everything. Though he must get her back before she was with the Englishman's child.

The next day, he called his head groom to him. "Find someone to track the lady."

"*Sì*, milord. Do you wish her to be kidnapped?"

"No. No other man will touch her. I must remain in Venice for a short while, but when I am ready, I want to know where she is."

"I will see it done." The groom bowed and left.

She wanted him, he knew it. He would have his heir with her.

* * *

By the time Huntley and Caro reached the town of Campo di Trens, he'd lost his racing stables to his wife. Always a good chess player, she'd improved remarkably over the course of the past week.

"Well, my lord." She sat back with a smug smile. "I'm very happy you decided to allow me to keep my property when we married. Else you might have lost it all in some game of chance."

He scowled. "You, my lady, are a Captain Sharp. I would think you'd feel some remorse for leading your innocent husband to ruin."

Caro's turquoise eyes sparkled as she let out a peal of laughter. He'd never seen her so happy, almost carefree.

She asked coyly, "Are you innocent, my lord?"

The coach pulled to a stop. He resisted the urge to tease and risk her pulling back from him. "Innocent enough. Come, let's stretch our legs for a bit."

The day had definitely cooled. After about five minutes, he took out his pocket watch. It confirmed what the sun hanging lower in the sky told him. "Collins."

"Yes, my lord."

"Will we make it to Brennerbad before dark?"

"We believe so. Mr. Maufe's gone ahead to procure lodging."

Glancing around, Huntley realized the second coach wasn't with them. "When did they leave?"

Collins made a noise suspiciously like a laugh, then turned it into a cough. "They've been ahead of us since luncheon, my lord."

With his free hand, Huntley rubbed his chin. "I didn't even notice."

"No, my lord." Collins ducked his head. "We're ready to go when you are."

As Caro climbed the steps to the carriage, she glanced

back over her shoulder at Huntley. "It is strange, but I didn't notice either."

He hoped that meant she was enjoying his company. After they were back on the main road, he set up the game again. This time, he was determined not to let his wife fleece him. He played ruthlessly and, by the time they'd rolled into the outskirts of Brennerbad, Caro was down to the clothes on her back and her wedding ring.

Grinning wickedly, he moved his queen into place. "Checkmate, my lady."

"I can't believe I lost everything." Caro looked at the game board with dismay before narrowing her eyes at him. "You haven't been letting me win, have you?"

"Not at all," he replied. "But I couldn't allow you to think you'd married an incompetent gamester. I do have my pride."

"You will see." She raised her head haughtily. "I shall come about."

He grinned. "That's what all hardened gamblers say."

Caro gasped. "I am not."

He gave a bark of laughter at his wife's outraged face. "Don't eat me. I have no doubt the next time you'll show me the way."

The coach drove into the yard of the inn at the northern end of the town of Brennerbad and stopped. Thankful that he wouldn't have to get back in it again until morning, Huntley jumped down and held out his hand to Caro. "Come, my lady."

Maufe and the landlord met them at the arched entrance to the inn. "My lord," Maufe said, "I have secured rooms for you and her ladyship." He bowed to Caro. "Miss Nugent is awaiting you, my lady."

A maid standing behind Maufe came forward to escort Caro to her chamber.

Huntley looked at his valet curiously.

"Ah, my lord." Maufe bowed. "My I present Herr Ker-schbaumer. His family has owned the inn since it was built."

Huntley didn't understand why his valet was making a special point of introducing him to the innkeeper, but he inclined his head.

The landlord smiled and nodded several times. "*Ach, gut.* I see the difference. *Grüsse, Herr Graf.*" And went about his business.

What the devil was that about? The landlord acted as if he was a display in some sort of raree-show. Huntley raised a brow. "Would you care to explain what just occurred?"

"Well, my lord, you see it's . . . um . . ." Maufe stumbled over the words.

"He can't even spit it out." Collins snickered from behind Huntley. "Our Maufe here is so grand that the innkeeper thought he had himself a lord. And when he found out Maufe was a servant, it was nothin' for it that the landlord had to see you."

Grinning at Maufe's flushed mien, Huntley chuckled. "I take it they don't get a lot of Quality here?"

"No, my lord." Maufe rushed to reassure him. "But everything is as it should be. I thought you'd want to be as close to the pass as possible and away from the main traffic. I understand the marchese has been taken care of, but just to be safe."

"You made a good choice. Have you by any chance discovered if the chef has a particular chocolate recipe he'd like to serve us?"

His valet's face fell. "No chocolate, my lord. There is a type of cake, made on a spit, which I've ordered. And the chef will serve hot chocolate in the morning."

"Very well." Huntley nodded. "If that is the best we can

do, so be it. Show me to my chamber, and I'll wash. I take it we shall dine within the hour?"

"Yes, my lord. You have time for a short walk, if you'd like."

"I would certainly like it," Caro said from the top of the landing on her way to her chamber.

Huntley glanced up and then bowed. "My lady, your wish is my command. I'll wash after our stroll."

When Caro came back down the stairs, she placed her hand on his arm, and they walked around the outside of the inn and down the street.

"My," she said, staring up, "look how much larger the mountains appear from here, and the air is so fresh."

"Indeed," he replied, but rather than examine the mountains he gazed at her profile. The small lines of concern he'd seen lately in her countenance had disappeared, and her lips curved up.

Now that they were safe, he'd begin his slow seduction of her.

They had at least three weeks before they'd reach Nancy and his aunt. He promised himself by that time Caro would be sharing his bed.

She sighed. "It is all so beautiful."

"Yes. It is."

Caro dropped her gaze from the sight of the Alps and glanced at Huntley. His tone had been so warm.

When they'd started their journey, he had been little more than a stranger to her. Now she could almost sense when his moods changed, not that he was moody like so many gentlemen seemed to be. Indeed, he was amazingly even tempered, but she knew when he was planning something, or when he was on guard because of the marchese.

Despite Huntley's attempts to entertain her in the coach,

he appeared to truly relax only when they were safely ensconced in an out-of-the-way inn. He'd given up so much to
protect her. Giving him an heir would be the one way she
could repay him. Even if he wasn't interested in her physically, she could offer. That way, she wouldn't feel so bad
when he turned her down. But what if he didn't reject her?
He was a man, after all, and they were known to take their
pleasure with any woman.

She felt his gaze on her. "What is it? Do I have a smudge
on my cheek?"

"No, I'm just pleased to see you so at ease, though I don't
know how long your mood will last. I regret to be the one to
inform you, but there will be no chocolate at dinner this
evening."

She almost smiled but could not resist the urge to play
along. Opening her eyes wide in dismay, she asked, "No
chocolate? How could that be? Have you reprimanded the
chef?"

His lips quirked up, and his humorous eyes seemed
greener. "He has promised us a special cake for this dessert,
and hot chocolate in the morning."

Caro formed her lips in a *moue*, and she heaved a sigh.
"Then I must be satisfied. I cannot abide people who will
not be pleased."

"Indeed, my lady, indeed." The sparkle in his eyes belied
his serious tone. "You would not wish to acquire that sort of
reputation."

A small chuckle escaped her. "Especially not in an out-
of-the-way inn on a mountain, which we shall probably
never have cause to visit again."

He smiled. "Just so."

She stumbled. Huntley tightened his grip on her arm as
he stopped her from falling. A small shiver of delight ran

through her from where his hand held her. She glanced quickly at him, but his face held only concern.

"Did you twist your ankle?"

"No, thank you. I'm fine. We should probably return now."

The sun had sunk behind the Alps, and a church clock struck the hour.

"I believe you're right," he agreed. "We don't want to worry the others."

As Huntley guided them back, she thought again about their marriage. Caro had rarely known such fear as when that scoundrel had attacked Huntley. The thought of his being injured or killed made her realize how selfish she was being. He did need an heir and it was her job to provide him with one.

Her mother had taken her to see an old woman after she'd been attacked. Caro tried to remember what the woman had said, and counted the days since she'd last had her courses . . . It hadn't been quite long enough, but perhaps she could let Huntley take her to bed once, and she would become pregnant. Many women had marital relations with husbands they didn't even like very much, and he was being very nice to her.

Caro straightened her shoulders. Giving him an heir was the right thing to do, and the sooner she got the deed over with, the better.

Once they reached the inn, Huntley left her at the door to her chamber. Nugent had already laid out her clothes for the evening. Caro splashed her face and washed her hands before her dresser lifted the pale blue silk evening gown over her head. The color reminded her of blue ice she used to see when she was a child. The bodice was trimmed with lace and two flounces embroidered with flowers decorated the bottom. Twenty minutes later, Caro left her room to find Huntley waiting in the corridor.

He took her hand and placed it on his arm. "You look charmingly."

She found herself smiling. "Thank you. You are very handsome."

A curious look flashed in his eyes but disappeared almost as soon as it had come. He grinned. "Thank you, my lady."

As he started down the stairs to the parlor, she glanced at him. Candlelight brought out the golden streaks in his warm chestnut hair, making him more handsome than before. He was dressed nicely in a Spanish brown colored jacket that fit his frame perfectly. The tight trousers molded to his muscular legs. His cravat, though not extravagant, was tied with propriety. Perhaps it wouldn't be so difficult to allow him to touch her. At least she liked his appearance.

In the parlor, he poured red wine into two glasses and handed her one. "This is from the region. If we don't care for it, I've been assured there is a bottle of Bordeaux to be had."

Caro took a sip. "This is good." She drank half of the wine and held the glass out to him. "I'll have a little more, please."

His brows drew together slightly, but he did as she asked. "It must be good. I don't think I've ever seen you drink wine so quickly."

She put a bright smile on her face. "It's wonderful."

Huntley looked as if he might say something, but the door opened to a waiter carrying a tureen of soup. After she'd been served, she peered at the dark broth. "Do you know what this is?"

"*Gerstensuppe.*" He took a taste. "It's quite tasty."

She tried some of her own. The broth was rich and full of herbs. He also fed her well. That had to count for something, she thought as she took stock of all her husband's good points.

The soup was removed with a pasta that resembled a round ball with melted butter. Caro took a small bite. "This is delicious."

"That is a *Knödel*," he said. "It is sometimes also served in broth."

She swallowed and finished another glass of wine. "How do you know so much?"

"Maufe visited the kitchens."

Taking another mouthful, she sighed. "I shall miss the food. It has all been so wonderful."

As he had all during this trip, Huntley helped her make selections from the dishes set out on a sideboard. Later Caro stared down at the empty plate. "This pork is wonderful, and I never thought I'd like sauerkraut, but I do."

The thought of being with a man caused her stomach to clench in a knot. She poured another glass of wine, sure it would help.

For dessert, the chef brought a small round cake resembling a slice from a tree trunk with a hollow center. It looked delicious, but what caught Caro's attention were several small, irregularly shaped lumps on the plate. "Chocolate drops?"

The chef explained. "We take the droppings from the cake and cover them in chocolate. Normally we don't serve the *Baumkuchenspitzen* to our guests. But *Herr Graf* told me how much his wife loves chocolate."

She glanced at Huntley, trying to figure out what had changed that she now had chocolate. "You told me Maufe spoke with the chef."

With an innocent demeanor, he replied, "Maufe did, but I decided to ask him myself."

She smiled at him before looking at the chef. She had

more than a little trouble focusing on the man but finally managed it. "It is very unusual looking. Please tell me how it is made."

He bowed. "With pleasure, my lady. The cake is made on a spit and the small lumps are what drop from it."

Caro sampled both the cake and the pieces, then said to Huntley, "Excellent. I know French chefs are all the crack, but if it's all the same to you, I think I'd like an Italian one."

Huntley thanked the chef and wondered if Caro realized what she'd said. His wife finished the small pieces of chocolate-covered cake and poured yet another glass of wine. This was the most he'd ever seen her drink, and it was beginning to concern him. What the deuce was she up to?

After the dishes were removed, he stood and walked over to the sideboard for a glass of brandy. When he turned, Caro was in front of him, swaying a little. "Caro, are you all right?"

"Yes, of course. Why wouldn't I be?" She glanced at his glass. "May I have one too?"

Huntley tried to hide his frown. Her eyes were over-bright and her speech a little slurred. She was fuddled. He'd wager that she had never had so much to drink before. "I really don't think it's a good idea, my dear. You've had quite a bit of wine already."

Her brows drew together. "But I want a taste."

Rubbing his fingers on his forehead, he tried to come up with a solution. She was already going to have a headache in the morning. "I'll give you a sip of mine."

Caro nodded drunkenly and tried to take his glass. Instead, he held it to her lips. "Caro, what's all this about? Is something bothering you?"

She shook her head so vigorously that some of her curls fell from the loose knot on her head. "No, nothing's wrong. I have"—she paused and took a breath—"I have decided we should sleep together." Closing one eye, she tilted unsteadily toward him. "Well, not sleep exactly. Why are you moving around so much?"

Sighing, he set his glass on the sideboard and took her hands, drawing her closer. "Caro, my sweet." He touched his lips to her forehead. "When I make you mine, it will be when you want me as much as I want you, and you will *not* be in your altitudes."

Her gaze wide, she stared up at him and wobbled again. To-morrow was going to be a devil of a day for both of them. There were few things worse than being stuck in a coach with a bad head.

Unexpected tears suddenly filled her eyes, and she wailed, "You don't want me."

He stifled a groan. That was it. She was restricted to no more than two or three glasses of wine from now on. He stroked her back and nibbled her ear. "Of course I want you, my dear. God help me"—he wanted her more each day—"but I will not take you when you're disguised."

She poked him in the chest with one finger and, enunciating her words carefully, said, "But you need an heir, and it's the right time."

He decided not to ask why it was a good time. In his experience, those who imbibed overmuch never made much sense. "The heir can wait."

Caro leaned against him, her ample breasts pressing into his chest. Huntley's muscles clenched and an image of her lush mounds in his hands caused his groin to react. Damn, why did she have to be on the go?

"You have nice lips," she said.

He chuckled lightly. "So do you. Very kissable lips."

Caro threw her head back and puckered. "You may kiss them if you wish."

Fate was getting back at him. Here he was with a wife,

his wife, who possessed a thoroughly delectable mouth, and he wanted her like he'd never wanted another woman, but not when she was intoxicated. Huntley sighed. Well, he wouldn't bed her, but no harm could come from kissing her. She probably wouldn't remember it in any event. "Are you sure?"

"Yes." She nodded.

He held her chin between two fingers and bent to kiss the lips she offered. He barely touched his mouth to hers; instead, he feathered kisses along her jaw to the corner of her lips. Caro sighed and started to slide down to the floor. He placed his arm around her waist to stop the descent.

"That was a nice kiss." She giggled. "What else can you do?"

He almost groaned. This was going to be a long night, and he'd have to end his time with Caro soon. "You might like this."

Holding himself tightly in control, he moved one hand over her lush derrière and back up, lightly over the side of her breast. If only she'd asked him to do this when she was sober.

She shivered and sank against him. "Oh, I do." She gave a small hiccup. "Is there anything else?"

Damn. He wanted her so badly, this was killing him. He straightened. That was it, if he stayed any longer he was going to lose what sense he had, and there would be hell to pay in the morning. "I'm taking you to your chamber."

Expecting an argument, he quickly swept her up into his arms before she could protest. "Hold on so you don't fall."

She obediently put her hands on his shoulders, but rather than fight him, Caro started to giggle again. "No one has carried me since I was a child."

She laid her head against his shoulder and her soft breath caressed his jaw. God knew she wasn't a child now, and he needed to get her to her room before he did something stupid. He carried her up the stairs and knocked on her door.

When Nugent saw Caro in his arms, the maid's jaw dropped.

"Hallo, Nugent. Lord Huntley is carrying me," Caro said brightly and with a slight slur.

"What in the name of heaven?" the maid asked.

"Foxed," he said.

"I can't believe it. She's never done that before in her life. Is she able to stand?"

He thought for a moment. "I'm not sure. Her ladyship was none too steady on her feet before." He waited until her dresser closed the door. "Do you need help getting her out of this gown?"

"If she is unable to stand, I will."

"I'll hold her up, and you unlace her."

Nugent nodded. "Yes, that might be best."

When he set Caro down on the floor, she tilted her head back in the same jerky movement of a puppet being inexpertly handled and pursed her lips. He shook his head. "Wait just a moment, my sweet."

Nugent glanced briefly at the ceiling, then worked swiftly, unlacing the gown and stays. "How much did she have to drink?"

Huntley caught his wife as she teetered. "At least five glasses. But she kept refilling hers before it was empty, and the server refilled the jug, so I'm not quite sure. I've never seen her drink more than two before this evening."

"No, that is her limit. Can you help me slip off these sleeves?"

There was going to be the devil to pay come morning. He held Caro up, his fingers grasping his wife's narrow waist over the thin lawn of her chemise as Nugent unbuttoned the long sleeves. Huntley's groin tightened and he tried to stop thinking about what it would be like to skim his hand over her lightly rounded stomach and cup the curls between her legs. This was taking forever. Finally, the bodice of Caro's garment sagged as the maid slid the sleeves off Caro's arms.

"There," Nugent said. "Now, if you'll lift her straight up, I'll get her ladyship's gown off her."

Huntley did as requested and the silk fell to the floor. He finished unlacing her stays, removed them and handed them to Nugent. Caro's soft breasts begged to be touched and every inch of his body was responding to the almost naked woman in his arms.

It seemed as if her maid was taking her damn time about retrieving Caro's nightgown from the bed.

After an eternity, Nugent said, "I'll throw this over her head as soon as you untie her ladyship's chemise."

He glanced sharply at Nugent, but she continued to wait for him. Obviously, the blasted woman had no idea of the torture he was going through. The next time he had Caro like this, he was going to bury himself inside her. He gave the shoulder ribbons a jerk and they fell away. The garment stopped, hanging on the peak of his wife's nipples.

Caro, who'd been docilely allowing him to undress her, tossed her head back again. "Now?"

Bending his head, he kissed her lightly on the lips. "That's enough for now. Nugent, the nightgown, please."

"Yes, my lord."

He'd be damned if the first time he saw his wife naked her maid would be looking on. He raised Caro's arms and the soft linen slid over her as the chemise dropped to the floor. She tipped back against him, her body rubbing against his fully engorged member. *Bloody hell*, he cursed lewdly to himself. His whole body was clamoring for her. She slipped, and Huntley clenched his jaw as he caught her. "She'll have a deuce of a headache in the morning. With any luck at all, she'll be sick to-night and purge some of the wine."

Her dresser nodded and said grimly, "She'll be sick as a cat. What on earth could have got into her, I wonder?"

If Nugent didn't know, he certainly wasn't going to enlighten her. "I'll send Maufe with his remedy."

After putting Caro between the sheets, Huntley couldn't help gazing at her peaceful countenance. With one finger he caressed her cheek and straightened to see Nugent's amused face. He turned toward the door. "Good night, Nugent."

"Good night, my lord."

Satisfied that he'd successfully fought his desires and his now aching shaft, he retired alone to bed. He wondered what Caro's mood would be like in the morning and hoped she wouldn't be too embarrassed.

God in heaven, he was turning into a saint. Getting his wife sober and then into his bed had just become his first priority.

Chapter 11

Caro's head throbbed and her mouth tasted as if someone had stuffed hay in it as well as manure. When she tried to sit up, a wave of nausea hit her, so she lay flat on her back and contemplated trying to open her eyes, which had not yet decided to cooperate. A low moan emanated from somewhere, and a cool, wet cloth was placed on her forehead. Someone hammered on a door. "Oh please, make them be quiet. It hurts my head."

No one answered, but the hammering stopped. Caro finally got her eyes opened, but the room swam, making her stomach rush to her mouth again, and she closed them. She'd been perfectly fine yesterday. Why was she so sick now?

A door opened and closed again. Footsteps stomped across the wooden floor. The pain in her head got worse. Why couldn't they all be quiet? Did they not know how unwell she was?

A brisk hand removed the cloth on her forehead. "Come, my lady, you have to try to sit up. Mr. Maufe's made something that will make you feel better."

Tears sprung to her eyes. "Oh, Nugent, I feel so ill. I think I'm dying."

"Yes, my lady, that was to be expected. Fortunately, you eliminated much of it last night. Can you sit up?"

"No," Caro sobbed, "it doesn't feel good when I sit up."

"My lord, I'll need your help."

Huntley, here? In her chamber? Why? *Oh, he cannot see me like this.* "Oh no, I don't want him to see me so ill."

A strong arm snaked under her and gently lifted her. "Just lean back on me," he said, "and the room won't spin so badly."

She did as he said. "How did you know? Have you had this before?"

His chest was so close she could feel it rumble. "Yes, regretfully, on more than one occasion. Nugent, the glass."

There was a rustling of skirts. Strange how she'd never before noticed how loud they were.

"Here, my love," Huntley said. "Open your lips. I'll hold it for you. The medicine doesn't taste very good, but it will make you feel more the thing."

Caro choked at the bitter taste. "Ugh."

He took the glass away and after a few moments brought it back. "Good girl. Just a little more."

Prying one eye open, she quickly closed it again as a bright light hit it. She turned her head away from the cup. "Do you promise it will make me better?"

"Yes. You'll at least be able to have a piece of toast and a cup of tea before we leave."

She turned her head back to him and opened her mouth to tell him she couldn't go anyplace. Suddenly the vile potion slithered down her throat. Caro sputtered and tried not to sound like a whiny child. "That wasn't fair."

"Come, my lady," Nugent said in a brisk tone. "We don't have all day. I need to get you up, washed, and dressed."

"But I am too sick to travel. You don't understand, neither of you do." She burst into tears.

"You won't die," Nugent said, "though you're bound to feel like you will."

Her husband's solid arm was still holding her, and all she seemed to be able to do was rest her cheek against his warm chest and sob.

Morpheus pulled at her, and she was quite willingly following when the thick, warm coverlet was yanked off her. She tried to grab it back, but her head hurt when she moved. She cracked her lids a bit to glare at him. "No! Give it back. It's cold."

Huntley gazed down at her and shook his head. "We need to leave as soon as it's light."

She closed her eyes again. "But I can't . . ."

"We've no choice. Although I am sure the Austrian envoy has di Venier in hand, I still want to be as far away as possible. You must allow Nugent to wash and dress you."

Lifting her upright, he said, "You can open your eyes. Just don't look at the candles."

Caro really must be ill if she wasn't complaining about his being here, touching her. Turning to Nugent, he raised a brow. "What can I do?"

"Have you broken your fast, my lord?" her dresser asked.

"Yes, I'm at your disposal." He glanced down at his wife. She'd gone limp, and her breathing deepened. Damn, she'd fallen back asleep. At least she could have waited until after they'd dressed her.

Nugent shook her head. "Hold her right there if you will, and I'll bring the wash basin over."

Huntley did as she asked and held Caro while Nugent washed her face and gave her something to rinse her mouth with. He'd make sure she got a bath when they reached their next inn.

Nugent brought over her chemise. "Now, my lord, if you'll unbutton her nightgown, I'll slip this on her."

It seemed he was destined to see his wife partially naked only when she was either foxed or suffering the effects, and in the presence of her maid. Stifling a groan, he allowed the garment to slip down over Caro's breasts. His muscles tightened at the view of the generous, creamy mounds topped by light pink nipples. If only he could taste them, just for a bit.

Nugent went to drop the chemise over Caro's head, which was still resting on his shoulder. She was never going to be allowed to have more than two glasses of wine again. Huntley was starting to wonder if Maufe put a sleeping powder in the concoction.

"Here, my lord, if you'll just hold out her arms." Nugent got Caro's stays on her and laced them loosely. "Now for the gown."

By the time he and Nugent were done dressing Caro, Huntley was sure Maufe was responsible for her inability to waken. He met his valet on the stairs as he carried his wife, wrapped in her cloak, down to the coach. "Maufe, did you put something in your remedy to make her ladyship sleep?"

His forehead wrinkled with concern. "Yes, my lord. I thought it better that she not suffer so much on the trip. Is everything all right?"

"Yes, yes, of course"—then Huntley had a thought—"not laudanum?"

Maufe sprang back in shock. "No, my lord! Not when she's indulged. That would be dangerous."

Huntley let out his breath. "I just needed to make sure. She didn't awaken even when she was being dressed."

Maufe nodded. "Yes, my lord. I can see how that would cause you concern."

One of the inn's servants jumped forward to open the door for him.

Dalle, standing at the coach, glanced at Caro, then at Huntley. "Sick?"

"In a matter of speaking," Huntley replied drily. "Take her ladyship and hand her to me once I'm settled."

He shifted his fair burden to her groom and jumped in the coach. He made sure the jug of tea and package of food was easy to reach before turning back to Dalle. "Hand her in."

Huntley carefully took Caro's recumbent form and settled her on his lap, tucking the fur rug around her. "We're ready when you are."

A few moments later, the coach rolled forward. His small group started off through the pass as the sun began to rise. He gazed at his wife's peaceful countenance. She'd be much better off sleeping than fighting the effects of dipping too deep while she was awake. With one finger, he traced her perfectly arched brow and bent to kiss her forehead. She tried to snuggle in, and a faint line appeared between her brows. He shifted her to a better position, and she settled back into a deep sleep.

He tried not to think of the reason she had drunk so much. Even though he knew it wasn't him specifically she feared, her reasoning still didn't do anything for his pride. Women had always considered him a patient and generous lover, and he gave as much pleasure, sometimes more, than he took.

But he'd never had a woman as broken as his wife, nor had he ever wanted to heal anyone so badly. Until last night, he'd thought they were making progress, but if she'd had to drink that much to overcome her revulsion, they were not as far along as he wished. He'd have to come up with something that didn't include spirits to reassure her.

Huntley awoke hot. A quick glance told him that the sky was gray and there was a scent of snow in the air. The air in the coach was cold, but Caro was burning up. This was not the result of last night.

He banged on the roof. "We need to find an inn. Her ladyship is worse, and it's going to snow soon."

His coach slowed as their other one drew up beside it. A quick discussion took place, and they were moving again. He caressed Caro's flushed face and wished he could do more. She started to toss and turn.

Damn, they'd need a doctor, and soon. Caro continued to be restless. He removed the rug and tried to soothe her. She struck out and almost hit his chin. Huntley remembered the nursery tunes his mother would sing when any of them were sick and tried that. He had a low voice, and after a few moments Caro calmed. He held her closer, rocking her. His chest tightened, and a weight pressed on his heart. She couldn't die. He wouldn't allow it. Holding his lips to her temple, he prayed.

It seemed like an age before the carriage pulled into the yard of an inn. Dalle jerked open the door and held out his arms. Reluctantly, Huntley gave his wife into her groom's keeping until he jumped down and took her again.

Nugent came scurrying up, put a hand on Caro's head and said, Huntley thought rather unnecessarily, "Right, then. We need to get her into her chambers."

He'd been around sick people. He could have told her that.

Nugent strode swiftly into the inn as Maufe came out and said, "My lord, we have rooms."

Huntley bit off the retort he was about to make about stating the obvious. It wasn't their fault a fever had come upon Caro, and he'd not take it out on his servants. "Lead the way."

He followed Nugent up the central staircase and down a corridor to another wing. Caro's maid glanced back over her shoulder. "Mr. Maufe procured the entire floor of this wing."

Shifting Caro, he put his cheek against her forehead. The fever had gotten worse. "Has he sent for a doctor?"

"Yes, my lord." A small smile cracked her grim countenance. "The innkeeper sent out a servant, and Collins went with him. Said if the doctor didn't feel like coming straightaway, he'd help him change his mind."

Caro jerked in his arms, and Huntley almost dropped her. Cuddling her closer, he murmured, "Easy now, we'll make you comfortable soon."

She screwed up her face and began to sob. "I don't feel good."

Ahead of him, Nugent opened a door. "We're in for it now. I'll not lie to you, my lord. She doesn't often fall ill, but when she does . . ."

"You don't have to finish. When she does, she's a handful." He glanced down at his charge. "For some reason, I am not surprised."

He stepped into the chamber, and was pleased to find it not only clean but light and airy as well. A fireplace stood at one end and a large bed with velvet hangings at the other. Doors, flanked by large windows, led to a balcony.

Caro fussed, twisting and throwing out her arms, and he said, "I'll hold her up while you untie her gown. We need to get her comfortable as quickly as possible."

Huntley was concerned to find her shift was soaking wet.

Taking it off, he placed her on the bed and covered his wife with the wrapper Nugent held out to him. "Did you order a bath?"

She glanced at the door. "Yes, it should be here soon." She turned to him. "Do you think we should wait for the doctor?"

He glanced down at Caro and put his hand on her again as if it could tell him any more than he already knew. "No. Put her in a clean chemise. We'll bathe her in that, in case he comes when she's in the tub. The most important thing is to get her fever down."

Nugent went to one of the trunks and brought out a linen shift. "I daresay it won't matter once it's wet, but this is a little thicker than the muslin."

Rather than cooperating, Caro tossed and turned, but only opened her eyes once and gazed glassy eyed at Nugent. "Oh, Nugent, I don't feel at all well."

"That you've made abundantly clear, my lady. We are going to put you in a cool bath and wait for the doctor. Close your eyes."

Huntley strode to the door. "I'll be back as soon as I'm more appropriately dressed to lend you a hand."

He found Maufe hovering outside the door. "Will she be all right, my lord?"

"If it is nothing more than a bad cold, we'll nurse her through this. Though that will be enough to lay her low for several days. My fear is that it's influenza." Huntley started to walk down the corridor and stopped. "Where's my chamber?"

His valet motioned him to the room next to his wife's. "Here, my lord."

The room appeared to connect to Caro's. It had the same view of a garden and a church spire beyond. "Good. Get me out of these clothes and into something I can get wet."

In a very few minutes, he used the connecting door to his wife's room. A copper tub stood before the fire. He tested the water to make sure it was cool. Nugent stood by the bed as if guarding Caro, but stepped aside as he approached.

Huntley scooped Caro up. She was completely limp and unconscious. Wispy curls lay plastered on her forehead. He placed his lips on her temple and put her into the tub. "Come, my lady wife. Let's try to lower your temperature."

Once wet, the linen chemise was almost transparent. He perused her slender form. His eyes traveled over her generous breasts, then to her small waist and gentle swell of her hips. A woman's body. His woman's body and one the doctor was not going to see. "Get something to put over the tub."

His need to protect Caro was growing by leaps and bounds. When had he become so possessive?

He heard Nugent rummaging through the wardrobe, and before long she returned with a sheet that she draped over the sides of the tub.

Huntley nodded approvingly. "That should do it. Please tell Maufe I'll have luncheon here."

"Yes, my lord." Nugent left the room, leaving him holding Caro's hand as he racked his brain, trying to remember everything that one did to help a patient through the influenza.

The door opened, and the swish of skirts, as well as heavy steps, intruded on his thoughts. He glanced up and then had to lower his gaze to the small, slight man carrying a black bag. "Herr Doktor."

The man bowed. "*Ja.* I am Doktor Benner, and you must be Graf von Huntley." He glanced at Caro. "And the *Gräfin.*"

The doctor set about opening his bag in an efficient manner. Huntley felt the weight fall from his shoulders. Unlike many doctors he'd had to deal with, Dr. Benner exuded competence. "Yes."

The doctor took out a long, rather bulky instrument from his case. "First, I shall take her temperature."

Frowning, Huntley said, "Her temperature? I've never heard of that before."

Dr. Benner smiled. "It is not widely used. My father studied at the Medical School of Vienna, as did I, and he was great friends with Doktor Swieten, the founder. They found a correlation between a person's temperature and the illness. In any event, please, if I may?"

Huntley sat on the stool beside the tub and put his hand on Caro's shoulder. Her flushed face concerned him more than a little, and if taking her temperature would help, he'd allow it.

The doctor placed the instrument in her mouth and waited a few minutes before removing it and checking it. Nodding to himself, he touched her neck and throat. "Does she have a rash anyplace?"

"No," Huntley responded.

The doctor nodded again. "With the symptoms she has, it appears to be influenza, but as I don't know where you've come from, that is only my best guess. She is cooling, but be prepared for her temperature to go up and down. It is important that you try to keep her cool when it is up and warm when it is down." He glanced at Huntley. "It must be kept as even as possible."

"Yes, of course. I seem to remember there is a saline draught which can be used to help bring her temperature down."

Nodding, Benner said, "*Ja, ja.* You are correct, and I have brought it with me. I shall leave you a prescription for more. When she wakes, try to have her drink weak tea, or even better, water from the springs. The landlord will know where to procure it. She may also have broth and zwieback . . . what you call toast."

He handed Nugent several vials. "One every few hours. I will return in the morning. If you cannot keep her cool, or if she develops red spots, send for me at once."

"Thank you, I shall." Huntley held out his hand to the doctor.

Benner shook it and said gently, "I can tell she will be well cared for. You obviously love her very much."

"Yes, she will." Huntley turned from the doctor as if to look at his wife but instead blinked back the tears that stung his eyes. Did he love her? At some point he'd have to spend some time trying to discover exactly how he felt about her, but first she had to get well.

After Benner left, Nugent asked, "My lord?"

"Yes, Nugent."

"If you'll just hold her ladyship, I'll tip this down her throat."

He pulled the sheet off the tub and supported Caro's back with his arm while Nugent opened Caro's mouth and poured the contents of the vial into it. His wife choked and sobbed a bit, then settled down.

"She seems a little cooler," he said.

"Well, if we don't get her out soon," her maid said tartly, "she is going to turn into a prune."

Huntley removed Caro's chemise and wrapped her in a towel. Once she was settled back in bed, he sat heavily in a chair and stared at her. The flush had faded, leaving Caro pale but no longer thrashing about in a futile attempt to find a more comfortable position.

Much later, he woke to find the moon making a path through the room. Leaning over her, he put his hand to Caro's head. It was cool but clammy. He pulled up her nightgown and touched her stomach. Cold. *Damn.*

Huntley pulled up the thick feather filled coverlet, called a featherbed, over her, stoked up the fire, then waited. After what he thought was a half hour, the chamber had warmed, and he touched her again. She was still cold. Too cold.

Maufe was still awake when Huntley stomped into his room. "I need a nightshirt."

"But, my lord, you don't have one."

"What do you mean, I don't have a nightshirt?"

Holding his head high and sniffing, Maufe said, "You gave instructions not to purchase them again as you never wore one."

Huntley raked a hand through his hair. "Well, do I have anything I can wear to bed other than pantaloons?"

His valet smiled and nodded. "Yes, my lord. I took the liberty of purchasing something that you may find of use."

Maufe dove into a trunk and came up with a pair of something that looked like an undergarment of some sort.

"What is that?"

"They are to wear under your breeches or"—he looked at the garment doubtfully—"no, probably not your pantaloons. They are of wool."

"I'll wear them." Huntley undressed and donned the wool under-breeches and his dressing gown before returning to Caro's room. He put his hand on her—she was just as cold as before—he climbed under the covers with her. Drawing her to him, he tucked the featherbed tightly around them, trying to infuse her with his body heat. After a short while, the wool breeches began to itch. Easing out of the bed, he removed them and slipped back next to Caro, holding her close.

When he woke, she was warm and dry, but not hot. He kissed her softly, and she snuggled in next to him. "That's right, my love, rest while you may. This isn't over yet."

The moon was still up when he turned to look at the night

table. A vial of the saline draught was there along with two glasses of water. Nugent must have come in to give Caro her medicine. He was a little surprised that the maid hadn't awakened him. It seemed Nugent, at least, had quickly gotten used to the fact that he intended to nurse his wife. He tilted Caro's head and gave her the medicine.

Sometime later, light from the windows and his wife burning up again woke him. He reached to the night table and found another vial, but when he shifted Caro so that he could tip it down her throat, she flung herself around, almost making him drop the medicine. That he had not reckoned on. He could not hold her hands and give her the draught at the same time.

"Here, my lord," Nugent said. "You hold her and give me the vial."

He hadn't even heard her enter. A slow flush rose in his neck and face, but Nugent didn't act as if anything was unusual about his being nude and in bed with Caro. Nugent stretched her hand out and wiggled her fingers impatiently. He handed her the vial and then held Caro still.

Nugent tipped the liquid down his wife's throat and put the empty bottle on the table. "I'll order another bath for her and tell Mr. Maufe you're ready to dress."

Surprised, he stared after her until she'd left the room. One would have thought that seeing his naked chest would have given Nugent hysterics, but the woman seemed to have no nerves at all. Huntley pushed back the cover and turned Caro's pillows for her before swinging his legs to the floor and donning his dressing gown.

Maufe came through the connecting door. "Miss Nugent says she'll come in when you've left."

Taking one last look at Caro, Huntley left the room. "Come, Maufe, I don't want to leave her ladyship for long."

"But, my lord, I am sure her dresser . . ."

Huntley wasn't that tired. No one was going to take him away from her. He couldn't keep the irritation from his tone. "She's my wife, Maufe, and I'll care for her. I will thank you to tell that to anyone else who plans to usurp my position as well."

The next four days consisted of endless baths, changes of nightgowns, and sheets soiled not only by the sweating caused by the fever but also by Huntley's attempts to get nourishment in her. Who would have thought that a slight, mostly unconscious woman could be so hard for two people to manage? The only decent sleep he'd got was when Caro wasn't tossing and turning.

The doctor came every afternoon and proclaimed each time that she would get better. But the second day into Caro's illness, she'd frightened Huntley to death when her fever spiked and they'd had to put snow in the bath water to bring down her temperature.

On the fifth day, he woke to find her slumbering peacefully in his arms. The fever had finally broken. Thank God. They were through the worst of it.

As it had on other mornings, his hand possessively cupped one of her breasts.

Her breathing changed. She'd awakened.

Chapter 12

Caro had strange dreams. She was hot, too hot, then a cooling wave washed over her and a low, soft voice comforted her. Then she was cold and shivering, but something wrapped around her, giving her warmth. When every muscle in her body hurt, a firm, hard hand soothed the aches. The presence was always with her, gently lifting her, giving her drink. Some she hadn't liked, but the presence never got upset or yelled.

Nugent spoke to Caro, telling her, as her dresser had for most of her life, to do as she was told, and the deep voice told her she'd feel better. She did feel more the thing, and the speaker with the deep voice helped her.

She awoke tucked tightly against a hard, warm body. A hard *male body*, and his hand was on her breast. Fear shot through her, and she fought to get free.

"Shh. Caro, you're fine. You're better now."

It was the same voice, Huntley's voice. Except this time

it didn't help. Panic flooded her and she screamed, "What are you doing here? How could you? How could you take advantage of me when I was so ill?"

He jumped out of bed and assumed his dressing gown. *He was naked!* She closed her eyes.

His retort came out in an angry growl. "Take advantage of you, my lady? You honestly think I'd force myself on a sick woman?"

He attacked his hair, raking his fingers through it and faced her. Dark smudges lay beneath his eyes, and lines, deeper than before, bracketed his mouth. Huntley opened the door and called out, "Nugent, come take care of your mistress."

When he strode out and the door to their chamber slammed shut, Caro was suddenly sure she'd never been so alone. So miserable. She burst into tears.

Nugent was at her bed in an instant, her tone as irritated as Caro had ever heard it. "What was that about?"

"Hun—Huntley was in my bed," Caro wailed.

Nugent's hands went to her hips. "Let me tell you something, my lady. His lordship's been taking care of you for the past five days *and* nights. Precious little sleep he's got, with you thrashing about and crying. I've been in and out of this room at all hours, making sure he had the medicine and broth to give you, and a perfect gentleman he's been."

Caro's tears had stopped, and she gave a small sob. "But his hand was on—on my breast."

Making Caro sit up, Nugent shook the pillows. "Well, I don't see how a body can be expected to mind where their hands are while asleep. Which is what he was till you started to carry on as if someone was killing you."

Another door slammed and heavy footsteps sounded in the corridor. "My lord," Maufe called, "when will you be back?"

"I don't know."

Nugent ordered a bath be set in the other room and set about combing Caro's hair. "My lady, you need to get control of yourself. For days, his lordship was the only one who could calm you, and now you act like this."

Really, enough was enough. Caro hadn't been talked to this way since she was a child. In a bid to defend herself, she retorted, "But how was I to know that? I awoke and there he was."

"A little calm reflection would have helped, but you always were one to run off without a thought."

Nugent helped Caro to a small room next to her chamber and into the warm tub. A faint memory of being carried to the same vessel came to her. "Has he been bathing me?"

"He has, *and* making sure the water was the right temperature." Nugent continued her litany. "And helping change you, and feeding you. I'm sure I wouldn't have known what to do without him taking charge as he did."

Nugent poured water over Caro's head and began to wash her hair. "Had the doctor over every day to check on you." A cloth and soap landed in the water near Caro's hand. "You wash while I rinse your hair. He made sure your bed was changed daily and had everything else cleaned."

Caro stood and took the towel Nugent handed her.

Then the final sally came. "When he returns, I expect you to apologize for your behavior."

"*Me* apologize?" Caro lifted her arms for a fresh nightgown, then sat on a stool near the fire where her maid dried her hair.

Nugent scowled. "That's what I said."

This was so unfair. Caro was the one who'd been ill. "But . . . but he was no better than I." She tried to defend herself. "He stormed off without another word."

"He's a man who hasn't had much sleep or his breakfast,"

her maid retorted. "Of course he's going to act like a surly bear."

Bending over so her hair fell forward and the underside could dry, Caro's rush of energy evaporated, and she was suddenly so very tired. "I just want to go back to bed."

"You'll eat first. I have no doubt Mr. Maufe will bring your breakfast soon."

"Who else has seen me like this?" She motioned to her nightclothes.

Nugent sniffed. "Only his lordship, me, and Mr. Maufe."

Maufe brought her tea, toast, a soft-boiled egg, and broth. "If you please, my lady, you're to eat it all. His lordship's orders."

Caro was about to offer a scathing riposte concerning Huntley's orders but stopped. It would only make her sound more childish and difficult than she already appeared. "Thank you, Maufe. I shall do my best." Then, even though really she didn't want to know, she couldn't stop herself from asking, "Where did his lordship go?"

"Out for a walk, my lady. It is his habit when he's in a tiff."

Taking a large breath, she asked, "Would you please have him come to me when he returns?"

Maufe smiled kindly. "Yes, my lady."

Nugent nodded approvingly.

Caro finished her meal, and her maid helped her back into bed, but she couldn't find a comfortable position. Something was missing, and she was afraid to discover what that something was.

When Huntley returned, Caro was in bed, dozing fitfully.

She glanced up as he entered the chamber. Her lips trembled. "My lord."

Still suffering from being ill-used, he bowed stiffly. "My lady."

Her face fell and tears filled her eyes.

That was all it took. He should have known she was still not well. How brainless he'd been to leave like that. In a moment, he was holding her. "Caro, I'm sorry I stormed off. I should have known my being there would be a shock for you."

"No, no," she sobbed. "I'm the one who should have thought." She raised her wonderful turquoise gaze to his, eyes bright with the shimmer of tears. "Can you forgive me?"

"Yes, if you forgive me." He dropped a kiss on her forehead and mopped her cheeks with his handkerchief. She was so beautiful and vulnerable. Although he'd felt reduced to the status of a six-year-old at the time, he was glad now that Nugent had spoken to him, making him realize that Caro was still ill.

"Will you come lie down with me and try to sleep?" She blushed a deep rose. "I—I've discovered there is something missing when I'm alone."

When she'd been unconscious, he'd not been embarrassed about sleeping naked with her. But now . . . "I don't own a nightshirt."

"Oh, so that's the reason you were in"—she lowered her eyes—"in a state of nature this morning."

Strangely, warmth flooded his face. "Yes. Since you're now awake, I shall wear my dressing gown."

"No, if I did not mind before, I should not care now, and I'm so very tired."

"I'll be right back." He left the room and as soon as he could, returned dressed in his banyan. Caro was asleep but tossing. Huntley climbed in next to her and wrapped her in his arms. "Sleep now, my love."

Yet did he actually love her? Did it matter if the tenderness he held for her was love? Yes, it would matter to her, and he needed to know as well.

*   *   *

A couple of days later, Caro stared up at Huntley as he stood next to the bed and gazed down at her. He'd continued to sleep with her. In fact, he was almost never away from her side, yet he never tried to take what was his right as her husband. She should be glad about that. She'd never wanted a man to touch her again, but she didn't want Huntley to leave, and if he did not find himself physically drawn to her, he would.

He put his hand on her forehead and cheeks. "What is it? Aren't you feeling well?"

She shook her head. "I am fine, just a little weak." She had to know the truth. "I have a question I must ask."

He sat on the bed next to her. "What is it?"

Suddenly, this was not so easy. She twisted the sheet in her hands. "Oh, I feel so foolish, but I need to know. Are you not interested in me in an amorous way?"

A deep chuckle rumbled through his chest. "On the contrary, my wife, I'm very interested in you." He brushed his thumb across her cheek. "You may not remember when I said this before, but when we make love, it will be when you are ready. Not when you're ill or have to get foxed to do it."

Foxed? Other than her determination to give him an heir, Caro didn't have much memory of that night, though she did remember thinking wine would help. "Was I very drunk?"

He widened his eyes but smiled. "Extremely. Maufe made you his special remedy and put a sleeping powder in it. I didn't realize you were ill until you were burning up."

He stood and removed his jacket and boots before lying down with her and taking her in his arms.

She wondered briefly how she'd gone from detesting a man's touch to needing just this, him holding her. "I wanted to give you an heir."

Huntley didn't laugh, but his eyes were alight with humor. "Yes, well, it usually takes more than once. Unless one doesn't wish it to happen, then it takes no time at all."

She closed her eyes and concentrated on his warmth. "Did you hold me like this when I was ill?"

"All the time."

"Huntley, you may remove your clothing, if you like."

"I will, when you're asleep."

"No, you can do it now." Part of her screamed in protest, but another part wanted to feel his body next to hers.

The bed moved as his weight lifted from it. Caro turned and peeped through her lashes. Her husband's back was to her. His shirt was off and muscles flexed in his back and arms as he removed his pantaloons and stockings. She opened her eyes wider and was gazing at him when he turned. Chestnut brown curls, the same color as his hair, covered his broad chest. Now she understood why he always seemed so strong.

She'd never seen such muscles. He was beautiful. She allowed her gaze to wander down. His body made a *V* from his chest down to a narrow waist and flat stomach. He didn't look much different from the statues. He held the pantaloons in front of him before dropping them and quickly climbing into bed.

"Am I the first man you've seen naked?"

"The first live one. I've seen a great many marbles."

Tucking her in next to him, with his arm around her, he glanced down. "You'll get used to it."

"Yes." She was amazed at her response to him. She'd get used to it much more easily than she'd previously thought. "I have some questions."

His head nuzzled hers. "Sleep first. You need to finish recovering."

"For what?"

"For traveling," he said. "We're not even in Innsbruck yet."

Hours later, clinking china woke her. She was surprised to find her head and one hand on Huntley's chest. Her first thought was how improper being with him was. Then she remembered she was married, and, for reasons she did not yet understand, she'd asked him to join her in bed. It was like having two people in her head: one who wanted the warmth and comfort of Huntley's body, and the other who wanted to run as far as possible away from him. Right now, comfort was winning the battle.

One of his hands held her buttocks, anchoring her securely against him. His slow, steady breathing whistled in a soft snore. The hand felt—well—how did she feel about the hand? It was warm and oddly comforting. But why was it there? Was it convenient because her bottom stuck out and thus made a good handhold? Or was it because he had long arms, and it was more comfortable than resting his hand on her waist? He stirred and the hand tightened a little and drew her closer. Ah, definitely a handhold.

She glanced back at Huntley's face.

His eyes were open and staring at her. "How are you?"

"I'm much better, thank you." While she'd been trying to watch his hand on her bottom, she'd twisted the rest of her body around so that she was half lying on top of him. "This cannot be comfortable for you. I can move."

"No, stay," he replied. "I like having you here."

Huntley's reply only added to her confusion. What did she want? "If you are sure."

His eyes twinkled gently. "I'm very sure." He found the opening in the bed hangings, which had been closed, and peered through. "Someone's setting up whatever meal it is."

Grabbing his dressing gown, he removed his hand from her posterior without apparently even noting it had been there.

"Who is it?"

"It's probably Maufe, but on the off chance it's not, slip out that side." He motioned to the other side of the bed. "Go into the dressing room. I'll call for Nugent." He sat up and shoved his arms into the banyan. "Go, before you see me nude."

"You remember," she said, "I have seen you as you were born."

Raising a brow, he forbore answering. Though Caro had seen him naked, she'd never seen him naked with a stiff shaft. He was finally starting to make a little progress; it wouldn't do to scare her.

She had such a nice bottom, it was all he'd been able to do to keep from stroking it, but thinking of that wouldn't help his current problem. "Er, yes, but it's a little different now."

Caro's eyes widened in confusion. "How so?"

He wasn't ready to have this discussion. Fortunately, the door opened, and it was Maufe.

"My lord. Dinner will be served soon."

Slipping out of the bed with his back to her, Huntley quickly pulled his banyan together and lost no time striding to his dressing room. "Maufe, please call Nugent. Her ladyship needs to prepare for dinner." Though what Caro would wear other than another nightgown, Huntley didn't know. "I'll be back soon."

He washed quickly and was already in a pair of pantaloons when his valet arrived. His budding desire for his wife, previously dampened by her illness, had surged back with a force that shook him. It hadn't been that long since he'd had a woman. Venice had been populated with willing widows and neglected wives. *Damn*. Fate was determined to have her way with him. Right now, all he wanted to do was make love with his own wife and he couldn't.

His valet handed him a shirt and Huntley drew it over his

head. Somehow, he must convince Caro to allow him to continue sleeping with her. "Maufe, see if her ladyship's ready. I'm starving."

Maufe bowed. "Yes, my lord. I am sure Miss Nugent has everything in hand."

Huntley grimaced. He'd be taking himself in hand soon.

A few minutes later, he entered Caro's chamber and stopped. His stomach clenched as if he'd been punched. Letting out a breath, he remembered to take one again. He'd not had this reaction to her since he first saw her.

Caro was dressed in a pale pink dressing gown of silk and lace. Her long curls were tied demurely back with a darker pink ribbon. Though still pale from her illness, she seemed to be improving, and she'd never appeared more beautiful. His desire surged.

Strolling slowly forward, he took her hand and bent over it. "My lady. You look particularly fetching."

A blush rose slowly into her cheeks. "Thank you. Nugent said this was the only thing I had to wear as all the others were being laundered."

His appreciation for Nugent was increasing by the day, and he wondered what was beneath the dressing gown. "I'm not surprised, as many as you went through."

He kissed her fingers, then helped her to a chair at the table before taking his own seat. Maufe had been pressed to serve the soup. "You may leave after this, Maufe. I shall serve her ladyship."

"Yes, my lord." He bowed and left the room.

Caro took a sip. "What is this, do you know?"

The soup was a broth with tiny balls floating in it. "Yes. The broth is either beef or oxen and the balls are from the marrow. The doctor suggested it."

"Well, it's very good." She took another swallow. "Do you know what else I'll be allowed to eat?"

"Something more substantial than just soup, I hope. I'll take a look when you're finished."

Until her stomach got used to solid food again, Caro wouldn't be able to eat much. He watched as she slowly finished the bowl. "Are you still hungry?"

She smiled. "Yes, and I know that's a good sign."

"A very good sign." Rising, he took the lids off the other dishes on a side table. "We have a chicken dish with small noodles, and a puréed vegetable."

Her face fell. She reminded him of a small child. "No chocolate?"

Huntley gave a bark of laughter. "Maybe to-morrow. Let's see how you handle this first. You don't need to have a relapse."

She raised sorrowful eyes to him. "Nugent always said I was a bad patient." Caro sighed. "I'll do as you say, my lord."

Handing her a plate, he grinned. "Eat what you can. Afterwards, if you like, I'll read to you while you rest."

Huntley took note of how much she ate, then cajoled her to eat a little more. Caro had lost a fair amount of weight, and she needed to put some back on. When she'd finished, he picked her up in his arms.

"Oh," she gasped. "What are you doing?"

"Taking you to bed."

"Huntley, I *can* walk."

Not if he could carry her, she wouldn't. "Of course you can, but why exhaust yourself?"

There would be no backsliding on his progress with her. He was well aware that if she hadn't been so ill, he would never have gotten this far already. He shrugged. "I'm used to doing it. You can walk later. Right now, you should conserve your strength."

He turned sideways, maneuvering her through the door to her chamber.

Caro leaned her head against his shoulder. "I suppose you're right. I shouldn't overtire myself."

"Exactly." He set her down on the bed. "Give me your wrapper. I'll put it over the chair."

He held his breath. She did as he asked. Underneath was a nightgown of the same silk, with just a little band of lace around the neck. No English modiste had made that confection, and it damn well wasn't designed to sleep in. His blood coursed through his veins, and his groin twitched, reminding him it was still interested. Half his brain was concentrating solely on his nether parts. Huntley ruthlessly tamped down his desire. "In you go. I'll get the book you were reading."

Caro slipped under the covers. "Do you know which one it is?"

He reached out for the marble-covered tome. "Yes, I've been reading it to you, and I'm almost finished, but I'll start where you left off before you became ill."

She colored prettily again. "It's a romance."

"So I discovered." Toeing off his slippers, he got in beside her.

"Do you like it?"

He picked up the book and opened it to the page mark. "I don't *dislike* it."

Though with an evil count and an innocent maiden, it bore too much resemblance to his life right now. Yet, in the novel, the hero did not have to beg for his lady's affection. A few pages into the story, Caro was asleep, breathing softly, and he closed the book. Huntley stripped off his clothes and stretched out next to her. Her long, pale, wheat-colored curls were still confined by a pink ribbon.

"You don't need this." Huntley untied the strip of material, tossing it over his shoulder. He pressed his lips to her silken locks before running his fingers through them and spreading her hair out over the pillows. His gaze traced her smooth forehead, straight nose, and her rosy lips. Perfect. Drawing Caro next to him, he tucked her into his side. If he had anything to say about it, and he'd make damn sure he did, this was where she'd sleep for the rest of her life.

Chapter 13

Huntley awoke. The moon made a path across the floor. He figured it to be not long after midnight. During the time he'd spent nursing Caro, he'd left orders for the bed hangings and window drapes to be left open at night so there'd be some light if he needed to get up. Somehow, Caro had moved too far from him.

"Come here." He wiggled his arm under her and brought her closer. The soft silk of her nightdress rubbed against him. His body flamed with need, and he groaned. God, he wanted her, but first she'd have to become used to his touch. Like breaking a skittish horse to saddle but, with her fears, much more difficult. His precious, broken wife. It would take all his considerable expertise to get her to the point where she desired him as much as he did her.

He ran a hand down her graceful form, vowing he'd buy her more of these silk things. He possessively cupped one of her breasts and slipped back into sleep.

When he woke, Caro stirred in his arms and muttered indignantly, "Oh."

They were both on their sides. One of his hands was still on her breast and the other was anchoring her hips to him. He kept his breathing steady and pretended to be asleep, waiting to see what she'd do.

"Well," she said, "his hands really do go everywhere when he's asleep."

He smiled. Breathing deeply, he forced himself not to laugh, and let out a light whistle as if he was still not awake.

She plucked at the hand holding her breast, and he took the opportunity to tighten his grip on her. When he rubbed his thumb lightly over her nipple, it pebbled nicely at the attention.

A small shiver ran through her, and her breast became fuller. She sighed. "Ah. That feels good. How does he do that in his sleep?"

Her small response mattered more to him than he would have thought possible just a week ago. The small kernel of hope he harbored grew as she remained in bed, allowing him to fondle her. He wanted her to experience pleasure and desire. Perhaps he wasn't destined to spend the rest of his life celibate after all. Well, that wasn't quite fair. She *had* offered him an heir. Though he was quite sure if she could manage to get with child without him touching her, she'd have leapt at the chance.

No. She was his wife, and he'd be damned if he'd have sexual congress with her on sufferance. Before he was done, she'd want him every bit as much as he longed for her. His groin twitched. A craving that was growing daily.

"Nugent was right," she said. "It is not his fault."

He didn't know how much Caro was paying her maid, but he'd double it.

"Oh dear, I have to get up. There must be a way to do it without waking him."

He threw the arm that was around her hip over his head, as though to reposition himself while asleep. Released, she scurried out of bed and behind the screen. He cracked an eye and waited for her to return. When she finally climbed back onto the mattress, he let out the breath he'd held, and his body relaxed. She may still be weak, but she was no longer ill, and she'd come to him. Progress. Before too much longer, she would be his, completely.

As Caro got into bed, she slid down the slight indentation and landed sprawled half on top of Huntley. Her night-clothes hitched up above her knees. "Oh my."

He lifted her as if she were a doll rather than a grown woman. When his hand slid along her hip, tucking her back against his side, she braced for the shudder of revulsion but instead experienced a pleasant tingle as she sank against him, taking solace from his warmth.

What did it mean? When did she begin to like being next to him? If she were to leave him, this wasn't good. "Huntley," she whispered. "Are you awake?"

Some part of his head nuzzled against hers. "Everything will be fine. Go back to sleep, my love."

Why did he call her *my love* when he was not in love with her?

The soft whistle of his breath tickled her ear, and she mumbled to herself, "I really must discuss this with him. We cannot continue to sleep together." Yawning, she sank into him more fully. "In the morning."

When she awoke, Huntley was gone. It wasn't the fleeting thought that there was something she wanted to tell him that disturbed her, but her peevishness at waking alone. She missed him holding her. Caro stopped herself from pouting but couldn't keep the tears from stinging her eyes. This must be a sign she was still not quite recovered from her illness. Why else would she want him near her so?

Before she could delve further into her unwanted reaction, Nugent was by the bed. "Are you in pain, my lady?"

Caro shook her head. She would not tell Nugent the cause of her distress. Where was he? "No. I'm just not feeling quite the thing."

With her normal stoic countenance, Nugent said, "That's no surprise. Come, my lady, your bath is ready."

She crawled to the edge of the bed and swung her legs out. "Where is his lordship?"

"Bathing. He said he'd do himself the pleasure of breaking his fast with you." Nugent searched the bed. "What did you do with your ribbon?"

"Nothing. I didn't touch it."

Her dresser bent to pick something up from the floor. "Here it is. You could have just put it on the table."

"But I didn't . . ."

Her maid gathered her hair and pinned it up before helping her from the bed. "Can you walk by yourself?"

"I think so." Caro took one tentative step and then another. Well, that was something, at least. "Yes, I'll be fine."

As she sank into the warm water, a memory teased her. She frowned and reached for a piece of linen and the soap Nugent had placed on a nearby stool. "I remember being in a tub with cool water."

"Yes, my lady. You had a cold bath . . . sometimes several times a day."

"I'm sorry to have been so much trouble."

Nugent was busying herself with something in the wardrobe and didn't turn around. "It wasn't me, my lady."

Caro started to wash and stopped. If Nugent didn't bathe her . . . "Oh no! Who did?"

"I've already told you—his lordship."

"*His lordship?*"

Nugent turned and gave her the same stern look she'd given Caro since she was three. "That's what I said."

Heat rose in her face and chest, and her heart thudded uncomfortably. "How could you have allowed him to—to bathe me?"

Nugent shook out something in a shimmering pale blue and laid it across a chair. "Maybe you'd like to tell me how I was to stop him. *I* couldn't lift you, and we had to get your fever down." She paused for a moment before continuing. "He also helped me undress you after you decided to drink too much."

Caro wanted to submerge herself under the water and never come up. She wished she could forget he'd seen her inebriated. Tenting her fingers over her forehead, she sank further down into the tub. Nugent was right. She couldn't have done it herself. But why would he . . . "I think you'd better tell me everything."

"I've already told you, my lady. His lordship nursed you the whole time you were ill. He would only allow me to help him." Nugent's voice softened. "He never left your side. I'm amazed he didn't take ill himself."

Caro had helped tend her younger brothers and sisters when they were sick, and the enormity of what Huntley had done amazed her. "But I do not understand why he would take on such a burden."

"That," Nugent said with her usual briskness, "is something you'll have to ask his lordship, and before you do, try to remember he *is* your husband. Now finish washing. It's not good to keep a man from his food."

Caro took the towel from the stool and held it to her as she stepped out of the tub. Once dried, she held her hand out for her nightclothes and received another silk gown. She flushed with embarrassment. "Where are my other ones?"

"Drying. Takes a while when it's so cold."

Slipping it on over her head and reaching for the wrapper, she frowned. "I don't remember buying this."

"You didn't. Lady Horatia bought them for you."

Caro was tired of asking why, and she was even more tired of not having any answers that made sense. Huntley did not want their marriage any more than she did. What would make him care for her? Oh, he said it was because she was his wife, yet was that really the reason? And just because she liked having Huntley around and being held by him, didn't mean she'd allow him to have marital relations with her more than once.

Caro pressed her hands to her eyes. He'd said it may take more than once. She shook her head. *I can't. I just cannot.* Caro shoved the thought away. When—*if*—the time came, she'd deal with it then. For now, she should concentrate on getting well.

Huntley ambled into *their* bedchamber, as he now thought of it, wearing a brightly embroidered banyan. Caro continued to rest, and he had every intention of remaining with her.

Breakfast had already been brought, and she was seated at the table. Her eyes lit with laughter when she saw him. "You're very colorful."

Taking her hand, he kissed it and smiled. "It's all the crack. Do you like it?"

Returning his smile, she replied, "I do indeed." She started to giggle. "You remind me of a peacock."

He enjoyed seeing her so happy. "I don't recall ever seeing a red peacock." On the other hand, perhaps she was only amused by his dressing gown. "Breakfast here consists of meats, cheeses, bread, and soft-boiled eggs, as well as yogurt. Would you like to sample a little of everything?"

"Oh yes, please. I'm much hungrier this morning. What is yogurt?"

"It is milk that's been cooked for several hours. The one here is flavored with honey. It's quite good and, from what I've been told, a remedy for stomach problems." He'd never known a woman who had the same interest in food as he did and was adventurous as well. He spooned some in a bowl for her and watched as she tasted it. "Do you like it?"

Caro smiled. "Yes, I do."

His stomach growled, and he ate quickly while keeping an eye on how much his wife consumed. The sooner she regained her strength, the faster they could leave. He wanted to remove to Innsbruck as soon as possible and plan for their onward journey.

Caro smiled. "I think I'm well enough to dress and walk around."

She was still too weak. He stifled his impulse to disagree—that would only put up her back—and attempted to phrase his answer more diplomatically. "I agree. You seem much stronger, but we are under doctor's orders. I'm afraid you must rest until he arrives and gives you permission to try a short walk around the hotel."

Caro's face fell for a moment, then brightened. "You said he'd be here this afternoon?"

He nodded. "If you rest this morning, you are sure to convince him you are recovered enough to take some exercise."

"Very well," she agreed. "I'll rest now."

"Allow me to escort you to the bed." He went to Caro and

helped her up from the chair before offering his arm. "Come, my lady."

She placed her hand on it but leaned on him rather more heavily than he liked. She was not yet as strong as she needed to be to continue their journey. Huntley helped her remove her wrapper and, once she was under the cover, climbed in after her, tucking her into his side. "Comfortable?"

"Yes, thank you." She paused for a moment, her face turned a light pink, and she played with the sheet, twisting it in her fingers. "Huntley?"

"Um?" He lightly kissed her temple.

"Nugent said you—you bathed me when I was ill."

He had told her, but she'd probably still been too sick to remember. "I took care of all your needs. Let me tell you, my lady, you are not the easiest person to feed when you're in a temper."

Caro chuckled. "Was I that bad? Nugent says I'm a horrible patient."

He grinned. "You were, but not as bad as my youngest sister was last winter."

Turning a bit, she gazed up at him. "Will you tell me about your sister?"

He kissed her brow and settled her back against his arm. "After Christmas, the whole house seemed to come down with influenza. Even my father was pressed to help, and he doesn't have the temperament for it. He tried to bully my sister, Alison, into taking her medicine, and she threw it back at him. Of course, his idea was to give her the vial."

Caro chuckled a little. "Did you rescue him?"

"In a manner of speaking." He used a dry tone. "I relieved him of his duties."

Caro turned and seemed to study him. "Thank you for taking care of me."

Her eyes were so blue, deeper than usual. His heart seemed

to be clogging his throat. There was no way he would not have nursed her. He kept his voice as soft as a caress. "Caro, may I kiss you?"

She stared at him for a few moments, but it seemed like an eternity. "Yes."

Huntley had never seduced an innocent before. Her rape didn't count as experience. Opening his senses to her, he took in her faint lavender and lemon scent. He shifted her closer to him and barely touched his lips to the corner of her mouth before lightly brushing them against hers. Hesitantly, she moved her lips on his. He fluttered kisses on her mouth and jaw. Caro sighed. Firming his lips, he moved back to her mouth and ended the kiss. "Thank you."

Caro's cheeks were flushed. "I've never had a kiss like that. It was as if you really meant it."

"Perhaps because I did mean it." He glanced down at her. Was there more to his wife's resistance than the rape? He tried to keep his tone light. "Have you had many kisses?"

She sighed again. "No, and none that I really liked, except that one."

"Ah. If you don't object, I plan to kiss you some more." She turned to him. Her brows were drawn together and raised, as if she didn't understand what he was saying. "Not now, but over the course of the next week."

Her eyes closed and she cuddled next to him. "I don't understand," she said groggily, and her breathing deepened as she succumbed to sleep.

Suddenly she seemed to rouse. "But kissing doesn't fit my plan."

He raised his brows. *Plan?* Huntley pressed his lips lightly against her temple again, and she stirred sluggishly. Was she even awake? "What plan, my love?"

"To make you leave me."

"But you promised me an heir."

She turned and gazed sleepily into his eyes. "Yes, but I thought I'd just . . . um . . . endure it."

He didn't know whether to laugh or scowl. "Indeed? I must tell you, my dear, your idea does not appeal to me at all. *My plan* is to have you enjoy it as much as I do."

Caro snuggled back down against him. "I don't think it will work."

Running his hand over his face, he shook his head. This had to be the strangest conversation he'd ever had with a woman, and he'd had his share. What was she up to? Or had she just told him? One never knew. The female sex had a very different way of viewing things. One thing was certain—he had to find out and stop whatever it was she intended.

"My lord?" Nugent stood at the side of the bed.

Huntley's eyes popped open. The presence of his wife's maid was no longer a surprise. What did astonish him was that he was sleeping almost as much as Caro. "Yes, Nugent?"

"It's time to rouse her for luncheon. The doctor said he'd be round shortly afterwards."

He glanced at Caro curled up next to him, sleeping peacefully, and a tenderness he'd never experienced before washed over him. "Find a warm, thick dressing gown for her to wear. If her ladyship doesn't have one, ask Maufe."

Nugent's lips twitched. "Yes, my lord."

"And, Nugent, I have questions I need you to answer."

The humor left her countenance and she pressed her lips into a straight line. "If I am able, my lord."

Huntley fixed his gaze on her. Demanding her coopera-
tion was not the way to get it. "Fair enough. I hope you
know I only want to help her ladyship. I can't do it blind."

The tension left Nugent's face. "I do know, my lord. Very
well, whenever you are ready."

After the maid left, he lightly kissed his wife on her jaw
and neck. "Caro, my sweet, it's time for luncheon."

When he nibbled her throat, she turned into him and
opened her sleep-fogged eyes. He moved back to her lips,
caressing them lightly with his own. Finally she responded
by pursing hers. There was still a long way to go, but thank
the Lord for small favors and kissing.

Huntley's lips were so warm and firm, yet soft. Nothing
like the quick kisses Caro had shared with Andrew or the
wet, unwelcome ones from . . . no, she wouldn't mention his
name. Holding her to him, Huntley's hands rubbed her back,
soothing the small knots. The heat from his hand spread
through her. Delightful shivers accompanied his every
touch. How good it was to be held like this. She responded
to his kiss, copying what he did. Her lips pulsed, and she
pressed them harder against his.

His arms tightened. "Caro, my darling."

She should stop. It couldn't last. Once they met her godmother in Nancy, he'd leave her, and all this would end. No
man had ever truly wanted her for herself. Why should he be
any different?

When he broke their kiss, she rested her chin on his
shoulder and gazed at him. His eyes were green flecked with
gold. "Your eyes always change, but I don't know what the
different colors mean."

He stroked her back. "You'll have to perform experi-
ments and record your findings, like a scientist."

Caro's throat tightened, causing her voice to hitch. "That would take a long time."

He ran his fingers through her hair, untangling the strands. "We have time. Caro, I'm not going anyplace."

That's what Andrew said, and he left her, even after he said he loved her. She tried to blink back the tears and failed. Huntley held her as she sobbed. "I'm sorry."

He ran the pad of his thumb under her eyes and kissed them. "You're still not well, my love. Don't tease yourself. We'll work it out."

Once she'd stopped weeping, he laid her gently down and rose from the bed. "I'll return shortly."

Several minutes later, Nugent entered carrying a garment that Caro had never seen before and not a particularly pretty one at that. "*What* is that?"

"It's his lordship's. He wants you to wear it when the doctor visits."

She did not understand. "But, Nugent, why must I wear a dressing gown of Lord Huntley's?"

Nugent held it out as if she expected Caro to put it on. "It was the only one we could find that was modest enough for his lordship's sense of propriety."

Caro looked down at the green woolen dressing gown that had bone buttons and was belted at the waist. "Propriety?"

Nugent sniffed. "Yes, my lady. Much in the same way he insisted we cover the tub with a sheet the first time the doctor came."

Caro's brows drew together. "He did?"

"Yes, my lady," her maid said. "He's very protective of you. Mr. Maufe has been the only one other than me allowed in the chamber."

Caro shook her head. He was acting as if they were truly husband and wife. Except for getting her to and from the tub, he could have left her nursing to Nugent. God knows she'd done it often enough. "What I don't understand is why."

Nugent's brows drew together. "It may be because he cares for you. Have you thought of telling him what happened, my lady?"

Caro could feel her face drain of color, and a hole seemed to open up in the floor beneath her. She grabbed onto a chair as the room whirled. "I can't."

Nugent caught Caro before she fell. "Come and sit. There's no hurry, after all."

She couldn't do what Nugent wanted her to. "There is no reason to tell him anything," Caro pleaded. "When we reach Nancy, I'll release him. He'll never have to know."

"You can try," Nugent responded gently. "But he's a stubborn man. What happens if he doesn't want to leave?"

Caro rubbed her forehead. She wasn't making any sense. Her thoughts must still be garbled from her illness. He couldn't leave her in Nancy. He wouldn't go until she'd— given birth. Would she be able to leave the child? And what if it took more than once for her to get with child? A small sob escaped.

Nugent's arm left Caro. "I'll get his lordship."

Caro stared up at her. "For what reason, pray?"

Nugent shook her head. "Because for all your talk about leaving him, lately he's the only one who's been able to settle you when you get fussed."

Caro took a shaky breath and tried to calm herself. "I'm fine. There's no need for you to call him."

"Call whom?" a deep voice asked.

He was dressed in buff pantaloons that showed off his muscular legs. His white shirt was open at the neck, and he wore his banyan. Why did he have to be so handsome? "I'm perfectly fine."

Concern showed in his face. In two strides, he reached her. He touched his hand to her forehead and breathed a sigh of relief.

A tear ran down her cheek; he wiped it away. "What's this then?"

Caro wanted him to hold her. She wanted to trust him, and she wanted to love him. Yet it would kill her if she did.

Chapter 14

After over a week of travel crushed into five days, Horatia and her household had successfully evaded the marchese. She now stood at the rail of the ship as it bobbed at anchor off the old port, waiting for the tide to change.

The ship's captain stood next to her. She shifted slightly to put more space between them and asked, "What is that huge building at the end of the quay?"

Without even squinting, he replied, "That, my lady, is the Grande Hotel Beauvau. It was completed this year. It is the largest, most modern hotel in the Vieux-Port."

"It looks large indeed. The views of the harbor must be wonderful from there." She smiled to herself. La Valle had reserved their rooms at the hotel. She was very pleased about the choice, but had no intention of sharing the information with the overly solicitous captain. The second the man had discovered she was a widow, he'd attached himself to her side like a leech and was becoming harder and harder to lose.

"Alas, I wouldn't know," he replied. "I have my own rooms here." He glanced at her, an invitation in his dark eyes.

Horatia pretended she did not take his meaning. "Very convenient for you, I'm sure. How long did you say it would be before we dock?"

"You have no need to hurry, my lady. It will not be for another hour."

Horatia opened her eyes wide. "That soon? Oh, dear me. I really must get my servants together. Please excuse me, Captain. Thank you for keeping me company."

She walked quickly to her cabin, collapsed on the bed, and scowled. "Risher, please have La Valle attend me."

Her maid frowned. "My lady, what happened?"

"If I have to suffer another lecherous leer from that captain," Horatia said, "I'll not be responsible for my actions."

Shaking her head, Risher replied, "I think La Valle is getting the others ready. Do you want me to take him away from that?"

Horatia considered it for a moment, but pulling him away would only delay disembarking. "No, just tell him that neither you nor he are to leave my side until we're off this vessel. Tell La Valle we will make our journey to Nancy in easy stages. It will take Caro and Huntley much longer to arrive."

"Very good, my lady," her maid responded. "Shall I lock the door and take the key?"

"Please do." Horatia sighed, relieved to be alone for a while.

After Risher left, Horatia rubbed her temples. Why did every man think that because she was a widow, she would be receptive to their advances? After her period of mourning for her husband, she'd been swamped with offers, though not of marriage. No one wanted to wed a barren woman. Eventually all the gentlemen had given up.

Her marriage had not been a love match, but even though her husband was much older than she, he'd still been very well-looking and active. It had been a good marriage. He'd promised her adventure and affection, and, for the years they'd been married, he'd given her both. George had been very sweet about her inability to conceive, first telling her she was too young, then that it didn't matter if she gave him an heir or not. Horatia doubted she'd ever find a man his equal.

The clang of the anchor being lifted and the surge of the ship caused her to glance out. Good, they would soon be at the pier.

Risher returned to the cabin and stayed with Horatia until the ship docked and La Valle came for them. They made their way up to the deck. Fortunately, the captain was busy speaking with someone when she descended the gangway to the wharf.

"My lady," La Valle asked, "would you like me to find a coach for you?"

She glanced to the end of the harbor. "No, thank you. The hotel is not far. If you will ensure everyone else gets there safely with all the baggage, Risher and I shall walk. I'll take one of the footmen as well." Horatia glanced around. One of the stronger, brawnier footmen stood nearby. "Perhaps Alberto can accompany us."

La Valle bowed and beckoned to the footman. "As you wish, my lady."

She was watching the trunks and other baggage being carried down from the ship and stepped aside, only to catch her heel on something. She started to fall, and the next thing she knew she was gazing up into the most unusual pair of sea-green eyes she'd ever seen. They searched her face as if looking for something, though she knew she had never met this man before. She couldn't have forgotten his eyes, the color of the ocean as it surged against the rocks. His grip tightened, and her body sank into his. It had been such a long time since a man had held her.

Good Lord! What the devil was she doing?

She reminded herself to breathe, but was unable to look away. His gaze was mesmerizing, like the snake charmers in India. "Oh, I am terribly sorry. I should have looked before I moved."

The man didn't answer but remained where he was, embracing her. He clutched her so tightly she had to strain her neck to continue looking at him. "Thank you for catching me."

Small lines creased the corners of his eyes as they smiled down at her. His tone was deep, and soft. "My pleasure. I count myself fortunate that I was here to stop you from falling. A dock can be a dangerous place." He glanced around and frowned disapprovingly. "Especially when the lines aren't properly stowed."

His strong arms caused sparks to shoot through her all the way to her core, and her body responded to a need she'd thought long dead. Oh my! That kind of reaction would not do at all. Although the air was chilly, Horatia wished she had a fan. She really must get away from this man and the desire he was stirring. "I take it you sail?"

"You could say that." He flashed a crooked smile.

Horatia tried to keep her eyes from widening, and smiling back. His face was browned from the sun. His jaw was square. He had an aquiline nose that appeared to have been broken at some point. Yet what held her interest were his well-molded lips and straight white teeth. Then a dimple popped out, looking so incongruous in his strong face. From his voice, one could tell he was definitely gently bred and English.

Good Lord. She was acting like a peagoose. Straightening, she tried to put a little distance between her and the man. "Well, thank you, we really must be going." Horatia glanced around to find Risher standing a little way away talking to Alberto, apparently oblivious to Horatia's problem. "Risher."

The maid hurried over. "Yes, my lady? Are you all right?"

"I tripped, but I'm fine. We must leave." Horatia turned to the gentleman. "We must be going."

Why was she repeating herself?

She started to walk but was still held firm by his strong hands. What would they feel like on her bare . . . This was not going at all as planned.

He took one of her arms and twined it in his. "I'll escort you, my lady. The docks are not safe for a female like you."

Horatia hadn't wanted to do anything reckless in years, yet the urge surged forward. She had to get away from him. "I have a footman. Alberto, make your bow to . . . to . . ." She raised a brow.

"Allow me to introduce myself, my lady. Captain, the Honorable John Whitton."

"To Captain Whitton."

He inclined his head, acknowledging her young footman, but didn't seem at all impressed.

What was she doing? Normally, while traveling, she abandoned English proprieties. Really, how could one expect to always be in the company of someone who could perform an introduction? But at the moment, she did wish they had been properly introduced.

Men with strong jaws ought not to be allowed to have

dimples. It was far too distracting. *Oh drat*. "I beg your pardon." She tried to curtsey but he held her up. "Lady Horatia Laughton, widow of Mr. George Laughton."

Captain Whitton's mien became serious. "Of course you are," he said as if he'd already known her name. "I was sorry to hear of George's death."

Horatia nodded. "Yes, though it's been quite fifteen years now. How did you know my husband?"

"He was a mentor of sorts," Captain Whitton replied. "When I first arrived in the West Indies, George took me under his wing." The captain turned her and they walked toward the hotel. "I assume you're staying at the Beauvau?"

Her heart, which had started to thump painfully, was interfering with her throat. "How—how did you know?"

"You're walking." He grinned. "It's the only hotel in the area to which you'd be likely to give your custom."

"Yes, of course." Her voice sounded breathless, but that wasn't surprising, the way her body was set on betraying her. God Almighty, she was acting like a girl again, and she'd *never* been a well-behaved young lady.

"Allow me to escort you. Marseille is a busy port town," he continued. "As such, it has its share of crime, especially around the docks. Do you plan on making a long visit?"

"No," Horatia replied, grateful she would not be in his company long. She'd never met a man who so captivated her on a purely physical level. She was much too attracted to him. Resisting the urge to twist the fringe of her scarf, she replied, "We shall rest for a few days, then travel north."

They entered the hotel, where La Valle waited for her. "Thank you for your arm, Captain. I wish you a good day."

He bowed, but when he rose a flash of humor entered his eyes, as if he knew some secret joke. "It was my pleasure."

"My lady?"

"Yes, La Valle, do you have our rooms arranged?" She

resisted the urge to watch the captain leave. He'd probably return to his ship, and that was the best place for him. Away. Far away from her, and her overeager senses.

"Of course, my lady. If you will follow me."

Horatia had a large chamber with a balcony overlooking the harbor. Though she searched, and could see the ship they'd been on, she could not find Captain Whitton. "Risher, come look how interesting it all is."

"Yes, my lady. Much like your view of the Grand Canal."

"I suppose you are right," Horatia replied. "I do love being around the water."

"Why don't you go down to the parlor, my lady, and drink tea, while I put your clothes away?"

"I think I shall."

She changed into a day gown and picked up her book. "I'll be back later."

Horatia opened the door and walked into a wall of male muscle. His arm shot out to stop her from bouncing off him.

"Oh!" She glanced up. Captain Whitton. Her breath caught. "Good day, Captain." His hand seemed to burn through the thin cashmere of her gown and three petticoats. This was not good. She didn't need a man to offer her carte blanche again. Even if he was sinfully handsome and her body responded to him as it never had to anyone. His heat soaked into her. No, she could not do this. Whatever *this* was. "I was just going . . ."

Horatia's voice faded. He stared down at her. His eyes twinkled with humor. Her gaze dropped to his lips, tilted once more into his crooked smile. The dimple made an appearance, and her lips tingled in response.

His arm tightened, causing her breasts to brush against his coat. A shiver shot straight to the apex of her thighs, and she stopped breathing. Horatia closed her eyes, resisting the urge to rub against him like some wanton cat.

She inhaled and opened her lips to tell him they were standing much too close together and he really shouldn't have his arm around her. Oh Lord, he looked as if he'd like to devour her. Slowly, he bent his head, kissing and nibbling his way from the edge of her lips to the center. By the time he got there, her mouth opened, wanting him, begging him to continue. His tongue ran across her teeth, teasing. When she could stand it no more, she put her hands on his face and caressed his tongue with hers. He tasted like tea and the ocean. He lifted her as he tilted his head, and she pressed into him, moaning. After several moments, her brain finally caught up with her long-starved senses. What was she doing, kissing him like this? She tried to jerk away. "*Captain Whitton.*"

The indignation she'd tried to infuse into the words didn't come out quite as she'd planned. Her voice was much too soft and breathy, as if she meant to encourage him rather than the opposite. She put her hand on his chest and pushed. He loosened his hold but didn't move away. She could not allow this to happen, not now. She had too many duties to focus on.

Horatia tried again. "Captain Whitton, I may be a widow, but I am a chaste widow. I do not engage in love making outside of the marital bonds."

"Very well."

As his head bent to kiss her again, she hauled back one arm and slapped him.

Whitton's head jerked up with a frown. "What the deuce was that for?"

"I told you . . ."

"Yes, you told me you had to be married to make love with me, and I agreed."

Something was terribly wrong with this conversation. She narrowed her eyes. "Agreed to what?"

"Marry you, of course."

All the air rushed out of her as if her lungs were a bellows. "*Marry me?* Have you lost your mind? Or do you go around suggesting marriage to every lady?"

"Of course not. If I made a habit of that, I would have been married a long time ago."

"This—you—are outrageous!"

"I'm merely taking the initiative." John grinned. Her lovely countenance was full of virtuous outrage, yet her body was still flush against his. God, she was a beautiful woman, and she looked even better with her face rosy and her green eyes flashing.

One nicely arched brow lifted, and her stubborn chin tilted up. That was even better. He liked a woman with spirit, and Lady Horatia had plenty of that.

"You are very sure of yourself, sir."

Resisting the urge to smile, a gesture sure to anger her even more, he said, "I am thought to be a rather good catch."

"Well—well good for you." She backed up a little. "Go find someone who wants to catch you. I am perfectly happy and have no wish to change my life."

He rubbed his chin and studied her for a few moments, taking in her rapid breathing and dilated eyes. She'd responded to him as if starved for his touch. "I don't believe you."

This time she rose to her full height, which, although much shorter than he, was not inconsiderable for a woman. "Are you calling me a liar, sir?"

"Not at all." Lady Horatia reminded him of a hen whose feathers had been ruffled. "I just think you're mistaken. Have you been kissing men on a regular basis?"

"I just told you . . ."

He stifled a laugh. "Yes. Yes, so you did. Which, I must say, is a relief. I really couldn't marry a woman who went around kissing other men."

Passing her palm over her brow, she gazed at him. "I think you must be mad. At least, this conversation is."

Whitton caught her hand and drew her in, placing his arm back around her waist. "I'll tell you in a minute."

He bent his head and kissed her again. She melted into him, then seemed to realize what she was doing. Her body tensed. "No," he said, "I was right." Lady Horatia raised her hand to hit him again, and he caught it. "Enough of that, my lady. I've no intention of allowing you to make a habit of pummeling me. Particularly when you enjoyed our kiss as much as I."

She blushed charmingly. "I did not."

Lady Horatia didn't seem to have changed very much since she was young. She was every bit as delightful as he knew she would be. "You're a very poor fraud, and it's clear you need to be kissed more often. Though you really shouldn't go around doing it in the corridor—unless you're betrothed, that is."

Her lips tightened in frustration, and he thought for a minute that she'd stamp her foot.

"But I do not. I did not, and—and it's not proper in any event, even if one is betrothed," she said, flustered. "Besides, *you* kissed *me*."

John pressed his lips firmly together, trying not to laugh out loud. He hadn't had this much fun in years, perhaps his entire life. He made himself nod thoughtfully. "So I did, but you kissed me in return."

"Humor him," she muttered more to herself than to him. "Captain Whitton. You cannot possibly wish to marry me. For all you know, I could have many bad characteristics."

"Such as?"

Her brow wrinkled for a moment, and then, with an air of satisfaction, she said, "I—I could be a shrew."

"You could be," he acknowledged. "But you're not. Laughton would never have married a bad-tempered woman."

George had been right about his wife. Any other lady of John's acquaintance would simply have walked back into her chamber and closed the door. Not Lady Horatia. Once engaged, she was unable to back down and would give as good as she got. Holy Jesus, he loved her. Everything about her. In his heart, he'd known she was for him, and this was the proof.

"You still don't know me."

Her pretty lips formed a *moue*, and he wanted to kiss her again, but first she'd have to talk herself out.

"I could still have any number of bad habits."

John was pretty sure he had heard about all of her foibles. He raised a skeptical brow.

She nodded, warming to her topic. "Truly I do. I'm impatient, I have a dreadful temper, sometimes I drink too much, and, oh, I am very fond of arranging things to my way of liking."

She glanced up at him and searched his face.

He grinned at her. So far, this was nothing new.

She scowled. "Are you listening to me at all?"

"Yes," he assured her. "I've heard every word you've said. What other arguments do you have?"

"Well." She gave him a calculating look before addressing herself to his top coat button. "I am past the age of wanting children, even if I could have them, and I have no intention of giving up even a farthing of my property. Any way, I am too old to be thinking of marriage."

She seemed to think her last arguments had clinched it and glanced up hopefully. Lady Horatia's hair was still a rich mahogany brown shot through with gold. Her clear complexion made her appear much younger than seven and thirty. She was exactly what he'd been waiting his whole life for. The only thing that bothered him was the lie George obviously fed her about not being able to have children.

"I have no need for offspring." It wasn't exactly a falsehood. His brothers would be more than happy to have their sons inherit. "I have plenty of nieces and nephews. I've enough wealth of my own. I don't want yours. We may have to work through who is going to order what, though. I, too, am pretty used to having my way. However, I'm sure we can come to an accord."

"Well then, you see, I am not the wife you . . ." She narrowed her eyes again. "What did you say?"

Captain Whitton heaved a sigh, but his eyes twinkled with humor. Horatia had the distinct sense she was losing the battle. She'd never been so confused. Her life was well-ordered, and she planned to keep it that way. She had enough responsibilities managing her servants, not to mention Huntley and Caro. She tried and failed to keep her gaze from his lips. The dratted man had so easily awakened feelings she'd thought long buried. Why did this have to happen now instead of years ago?

"Now who's not listening?" he retorted. "I just told you I don't need either children or your money."

"We cannot continue to discuss this in the corridor." She turned to go. His hand stroked her from neck to waist. The shiver of desire that coursed through her almost made her knees buckle. Oh no. Even with George, that had never happened. Swallowing, she fought to bring her errant body back under control, when all she wanted to do was lean into the rogue. "I shall leave you now."

Captain Whitton took her arm. "I'll escort you."

Glancing up at him, her mind warred with her senses. What was going on? "Why?"

His eyes seemed to grow warmer. "I'll explain over tea. Shall we go to my parlor or yours?"

She knew exactly what would happen if they were alone. He'd have her skirts up in a matter of seconds, and she'd probably help him. She'd never wanted a man before like she did Captain Whitton. "I am not going to any private parlor with you."

"Come with me, then," he said. "I know a place where you'll feel safe."

Captain Whitton led her down the stairs and out to a large terrace where several tables were situated in a garden-like atmosphere. After selecting a small table near the wall in the far corner, he pulled out a chair for her and motioned for the attendant. "Tea for two."

The waiter bowed and hurried off.

Horatia reminded herself to breathe and finally succeeded in calming herself. As long as she didn't look at his lips, she'd be fine. Or his dimple. Or his . . . that was quite enough. She pinched herself hard on her leg. "Now, Captain Whitton, I consider myself to be a reasonable woman, but none of this makes any sense."

He rubbed his chin for a few moments and studied her. "I suppose I could blame it on the *Sucooua*."

She shook her head, thinking that she'd not heard aright. "The what?"

"The witch on Dominica."

Chapter 15

Horatia couldn't believe what he'd said. "What do you mean, a witch?"

The dimple popped out—God help her—and he grinned. "It's common to visit the *Sucooua*. They give advice and readings. She told me I kept the woman who would be my wife close to my heart."

It must have been all the sun he had been exposed to or too many days at sea. The man was definitely mad. "I fail to understand how you could have kept me close to your heart when I've been in Venice for the past sixteen years."

He pulled out an ornate gold pocket watch, opened it, then handed it to her. All the air in her body left in a whoosh. It was a miniature taken of her when she was sixteen. When the match with George had been proposed, her father sent it to him. Her hand trembled. "How—how did you get this?"

Closing one eye, he studied her as if to decide how he'd answer.

"It was George's. We shared quarters in Kingstown. One of the maids found it after he'd left." He kept his gaze on hers. "I wrote him, asking where I could send it. He told me to keep the watch and give it to him when he saw me again." The captain pointed to the portrait. "That doesn't do you justice."

She stared at the miniature. "After we married, George ordered another. Still, I fail to see how you could know me from a picture."

Captain Whitton had actually carried her portrait all these years. Her chest ached. Things like this weren't supposed to happen to women of her age. She picked up the cup of tea that had arrived and tried to force a sip down her suddenly tight throat. What was she to do? She could not allow his actions to affect her plans. There had to be something she could say to convince him that she wasn't the right woman for him. She had Caro to care for. At the moment, Horatia's life was complicated enough without adding a lover to it.

"It was more than the miniature," he said. "George wrote to me until he died. Most of his letters included something about you." Captain Whitton leaned over the table toward her. "Lady Horatia, I fell in love with you a long time ago."

"I was much younger then. I'm older now." Though apparently not any wiser. She passed a hand over her forehead. This wasn't happening. He belonged in Bedlam. She belonged there as well for just listening to him.

His lips tilted up crookedly. "I expect you are. So am I."

"Be that as it may," she said, trying to regain control of their conversation, if she'd ever actually had it. "Even if you are correct, and you do know me, the fact remains that I, sir, do not know you. And I will not . . ."A slow blush rose in her cheeks as, belatedly, she thought about her husband's letters and what they could have revealed. With those George considered to be close friends, he had not been the most circumspect of fellows.

"You could get to know me." The captain's green eyes held a hopeful look. Almost like a puppy's. Except puppies did not gaze at one as if they'd like to devour one whole.

Her lips were suddenly dry. She licked them. This was not going well at all. Though why she could not bring herself to just stand and walk away, she didn't know. "I am leaving in a few days. I am afraid there will not be sufficient time."

"I have no immediate plans. I could travel with you," he suggested.

Oh Lord. Closed carriage, his lips, his hands . . . An ache of desire made sitting uncomfortable. "I cannot possibly countenance traveling in a coach with you."

Leaning back in his chair, he took a sip of tea. "No, that wouldn't do at all. I can't abide being cooped up."

This was clearly a trap. Captain Whitton had more moves than the old Romany who fooled people with the shell game. "What are you proposing?"

"I shall ride on horseback, and you will agree to take walks and dine with me."

Perhaps he was not *totally* unreasonable. Strolling, dining, his hard body. She wasn't going to be able to sit here much longer. "Just until Nancy?"

"Yes," he replied. "If you cannot bring yourself to marry me by the time we reach Nancy, I'll agree to go my own way."

No, no, no. How was she going to stand being in such close proximity to him every day for more than two weeks? "Very well."

She rose and held her hand out to shake on their deal, but instead he took it and brushed his lips softly across her knuckles, his warm breath a whisper against her fingers. Her hand trembled, and when she tried to snatch it back, he held it.

His gaze captured hers. "We must agree on complete honesty."

Straightening her back, Horatia gave him her most offended look. "Of course I shall be honest with you."

Drat the man. She needed to get out of this somehow. Away from him before her knees gave way with a lust she hadn't known in years, perhaps not even then.

"Good," he said. "Then we have a deal."

When he released her, all the heat in her body left with him.

"Indeed," Horatia said. "Be ready in three days' time at eight o'clock in the morning, sharp. I shall not wait."

"A punctual woman. I will be ready." His countenance was serious, but he had a twinkle in his eyes.

"Very well." At least she had some time to attempt to recover her senses, both physical and mental. She glanced at the captain as she rose, and got the impression he found her amusing.

"But you'll see me before then . . . at dinner this evening."

This evening? Panicked, she cast her mind back over their deal. She'd set no time to begin the getting-to-know-him phase. Hoisted with her own petard, as George would say. "Very well, we will dine together this evening."

In two steps, Captain Whitton was beside her and had possessed himself of her hand, which he placed on his arm. "I shall make the reservations in the dining room. It wouldn't do for you to be alone with me in a parlor."

Horatia's jaw almost dropped. After practically ravishing her in the corridor, *now* he was concerned about propriety? Perhaps it was because she'd refused to be alone with him earlier. The scent of him, fresh like the ocean, wrapped around her. She had never before wanted a man this badly. "It's all right, I don't mind. We may dine alone."

As if he could read her wanton thoughts, his disapproving green gaze speared her. "No. That would not be advisable."

Drat.

By the time they got to her chamber door, and he lifted her hand from his arm, she thought her body would crumple to the floor from yearning. When he reached around her, she raised her face, ready for the kiss that was coming. But it didn't. He knocked on the door.

If she could just have him once, she'd be over this madness. She was a widow, after all. She was allowed to have an affair. One could even say it was expected.

He bowed and lifted her trembling fingers to his lips. "I shall do myself the honor of fetching you at seven of the clock."

"Thank you. I shall be waiting." He squeezed her hand and another jolt of lust shot through her. God, she was going to kill him.

Once inside, Horatia collapsed on a chair. Every nerve in her body had been set for the feel of his hard, warm mouth, and he'd left her frustrated. Yet she had too much to do to add a man to her life right now. "Oh, Risher, what a scrape I've got myself into, and I cannot see my way out of it."

Risher shook her head. "Well, my lady, it's like the old master used to say. You run headlong into things without a thought. What have you done now?"

When John had escorted Lady Horatia back to her chambers, he caught her casting him sidelong glances. Her gaze simmered with barely suppressed desire. He resisted the urge to smile. George had written that she would be just the woman for John, but George was going to marry her any way. At the time, John was a second son, trying to make his fortune, and in no way an eligible marriage prospect. Well, he wasn't young anymore, nor was he ineligible. Horatia was going to be his.

He'd seen the moment she realized she had trapped herself. Beautiful, bright, and reckless. He'd kissed her trembling hand and resisted the urge to take her lips again. He'd never had such a reaction to a woman, nor had a lady ever responded to him the way Lady Horatia did. Her whole body seemed to simmer with desire. The portrait hadn't prepared him for the person she was. She was so much more, so alive and passionate. As much as he wanted her, to taste her, to have her beneath him, an affair was not the answer. She'd promise to marry him before he bedded her.

As John entered his chamber, his valet, Smyth, glanced up. He'd been with John since he'd left Oxford and made his way to the West Indies. The valet had been an incongruous figure aboard ship, never quite fitting in with the rough crew, but respected nonetheless.

"Smyth," John said, "I require a table for two in the dining room this evening. Lady Horatia Laughton will be joining me."

Smyth bowed. "If you will trust me with the menu, my lord, I shall make all the arrangements." When John nodded, his valet turned to go and then stopped. "If I may add, my lord, I'm very happy for you."

John raised a sardonic brow. "Don't be happy yet. We've a long trip to Nancy to get through before I know if she'll agree to be my wife. And no 'my lording' me. I don't want her to know yet."

"Yes, sir. Fortunate thing we did not journey all the way to Venice and have to retrace our steps."

"You have a point. One could call my meeting with her fortuitous." John walked over to the small sideboard and poured two fingers of brandy.

It bothered him that Laughton, the randy old goat, had apparently allowed Horatia to believe she was the reason there were no children of their union. John knew better. During all the years Laughton lived in the West Indies, there'd never been even a hint that he'd actually sired a child, though he'd supported a few just to keep up appearances. John tossed back his brandy, welcoming the familiar burn as it ran down his throat. Convincing Lady Horatia to marry him was going to be a challenge. One he looked forward to.

"Caro, why are you crying?" Huntley held her gently and stroked her hair, which Nugent had tied back with another pink ribbon.

"I don't know. I don't understand any of this." Caro sobbed against his shirt.

He sat on a chair and lifted her onto his lap and murmured to her, "Tell me what it is you don't understand."

"Why I still don't feel well, and I cry all the time."

He wished he could will her to get healthy faster, so she wouldn't be so miserable. First the marchese, then the influenza, and now her slow recovery, and he was helpless to do more than what he was already doing. "You don't cry all the time." He smiled. "I rarely see you weeping. You're just not as fit as you'd like to be."

"I suppose you are right."

"If the doctor allows it, and you agree," Huntley said, "I'd like to remove to Innsbruck to-morrow. It's flat there, and the air is not quite so thin. Perhaps then you can take some gentle walks to increase your strength."

Caro leaned her head on his shoulder. "Yes, I'd like to go for a walk. Even a short one."

A knock came on the door and Nugent showed the doctor in. He bowed. "Good afternoon, *Herr Graf*. How is her ladyship today?"

Huntley tucked in a bit of Caro's woolen dressing gown that had gaped open. "I think the fever is gone for good, but her ladyship is still very weak."

Dr. Benner nodded and examined Caro while Huntley continued to hold her on his lap. "My lady, you are improving, though not as quickly as I'd like. My lord, what are your plans?"

"I'd like to travel to Innsbruck as soon as possible," Huntley said.

"*Ja*. That might be a good idea. It is not so cold, and I can refer you to a colleague of mine."

"Would it be possible for me to go for short walks?" she asked.

"Once in the city, yes." Dr. Benner grinned and wagged his finger at her. "But you are not to overdo it." He glanced at Huntley. "Do you have a hotel in mind?"

"The Goldener Adler."

"*Ja, ja*, it is a very good hotel. I shall write you a note for Herr Doktor Hans Grunner." Benner bowed. "It has been a pleasure, my lord, my lady."

"If you'll give me a moment, I'll come with you." Huntley picked Caro up and deposited her gently on the bed. "I'll be back in a few minutes, my dear. I want to give the orders for our move."

"You won't be long?"

He tucked the featherbed around her, trying to make her as warm and comfortable as he was able, before placing a kiss on her lips. "No, I'll be back as soon as possible."

When he reached the door, Huntley looked back at Caro. Her forlorn expression almost made him return. It was clear she needed him now, but what would happen when she regained her strength, both physical and mental? He could not allow her to pull away from him. Even if he wasn't sure if he loved her, she was his, and would always be his. Closing the door behind him, he entered the adjoining parlor where Benner sat at the desk, writing. Maufe hovered nearby.

"Maufe," Huntley said, "please advise the hotel and the rest of the staff we leave in the morning for Innsbruck. Also, make arrangements to pay the doctor."

Bowing, his valet responded, "Right away, my lord. I take it this means her ladyship is better?"

"She will be." Huntley lowered his voice. "Maufe, there is no reason for her ladyship and I to have separate chambers while she is so ill."

If his valet had any thoughts on the matter, they did not show. "As you say, my lord."

After receiving the letter from the doctor and thanking him for his care of Caro, Huntley turned and re-entered the bedroom. Caro glanced up at him and smiled. He quickly undressed and slid in next to her. "Time to rest, my love."

She curled in against him and gave a small, satisfied sigh. "The bed is so cold when you're not here."

"Caro . . ." No, she was his wife, and had enjoyed the last time he'd kissed her. He would not ask permission to kiss her. As gently as he could, he pressed his lips against hers. When she responded, he ran the tip of his tongue along her lips until she opened them, allowing him to take possession of her mouth.

She gasped in surprise but then returned the strokes of his tongue with hers. His blood thickened with desire for her and only her as he reveled in her hot, moist cavern. Running his tongue over her teeth and tangling with her tongue, he tasted the honey she'd had with her tea.

One of her small hands clutched his neck. A breathy moan escaped her and drove him on. If he didn't stop soon, he'd regret it. Slowly, he eased out of the kiss and gazed down at her. "Are you all right?"

Desire-glazed turquoise eyes returned his look. "I think so. What was that?"

"The kiss?"

Her brow wrinkled. "That time it seemed so much more than a kiss."

Cautioning himself to probe slowly, he said, "It was our kiss. One that belongs only to us. Did you like it?"

"Yes. It was just so different. I wasn't prepared for it." Her brow smoothed and a small smile tugged at her beautiful lips. "I did like it."

He nuzzled her neck. "Then we shall add that to our répertoire of kisses you enjoy."

"Yes," Caro said more to herself as he tucked her close to Huntley. *I do like kissing him.* She breathed in his musky scent. The surge of energy that had accompanied his kiss receded, and she struggled to stay awake. "Did you like it as well?"

"More than you know," he murmured.

Nugent was right. With his arms around her and the way he gently stroked her, she began to settle. A man's touch had never had that effect before. Mostly it brought terror. When she was better and didn't need him all the time, she'd have to figure out how it was he was able to comfort her so. Tired and warm in his arms, she refused to allow herself to think about the future.

Hands grabbed at her and wet lips tried to capture hers. Caro tried to get away.

"Caro, Caro. My love. Wake up. I'm here. I won't allow him to hurt you."

Her eyes flew open to see Huntley's worried gaze. Thank God. She was safe. For the first time in five years, she hadn't had to live through the attack again. Lying half on him already, Caro threw her arms around him and buried her face in his neck.

He held her tightly against him until her trembling slowly faded. "Do you want to tell me about it?"

"No." She didn't want to talk about it or think about it. What she wanted was his firm, hard lips on hers to erase the memory of the others. "I want you to kiss me like you did the last time. I want our kiss."

Thank the Lord he didn't ask why but just did as she wished. Relief flooded through her as his tongue probed her mouth, and she returned the caress. A strange stirring started to spread through her. Little tingles and more. A deeper need to feel more of him grew.

Caro rubbed her hands over his back, pressing her fingers into his hard muscles. She couldn't imagine how she'd ever thought he wasn't a strong man. His back tightened as she pushed into him and tried to possess his mouth as he possessed hers. Her skin was so sensitive, it seemed to be alive. Every movement abraded her senses, heating her and making her heart flutter. When he stroked her hair and back and then down over her bottom, she shivered with delight. Yet, as before, he slowly drew back from the kiss.

When Huntley's lips left hers she was bereft. "Why did you stop?"

His eyes sparkled blue with gold flecks. "If we continue, more will happen than you're ready for."

Warmth of another kind rose from her neck to her cheeks as she blushed. "I—I didn't think."

He kissed her lightly as the pad of his thumb stroked her cheek. "You just don't know. Despite what happened to you, you are still an innocent and have no idea how quickly this could spin out of control."

His eyes smiled, but his body was hard and tense. Huntley really did want her.

"Why?" she asked.

"Why what?" His brows rose.

She shifted in his arms. "Why do you want me and why are you afraid to—to . . ."

Dipping his head, he placed light kisses on her jaw. "I don't quite know the answer to your first question. As for the second, you are still not well."

Her head dropped to one side, giving him better access to her neck. Something had awakened within her. Something that wanted to encourage him to kiss and touch her.

When he reached her lips, he asked, "Will you allow me to set the pace?"

Right now, she'd allow him to do almost anything, if he'd just kiss her again. "Yes."

Caro got her wish and his lips and tongue teased her mouth open. As they explored each other, frissons of pleasure shot through her and her nipples started to ache. All too soon, the kiss ended, and he moved her around so that she was next to him again.

"My love," he whispered, "you need to rest."

A few minutes later, she listened to Huntley's soft snore and sank into his warmth. She wanted so much to be a normal woman again.

Huntley watched as Caro's breathing deepened and a smile played on her lips. He'd been terrified she'd reject him after her dream. Instead, inexplicably, his kiss had helped her. Not for the first time, he wondered exactly what the blackguard had done and who he was. Was it possible that Huntley making love to her would heal her completely and enable Caro to exorcise her memories?

His engorged shaft throbbed as he held his sleeping wife to him. She'd responded with more fervor than he imagined she would, and his hunger to make her his became his most important quest. Yet her first question brought him up short. Why did he want her? She was a beautiful and desirable woman, and she was his wife. For most men, that would be enough. Yet he was sufficiently wise when it came to women to know that if he wanted a chance at a good marriage, he'd better have a completely different response to offer her. One that was not limited to her appearance and his physical needs.

Caro's soft breathing distracted him, and the protectiveness that'd been growing in him increased. Fate had thrown them together, and she was his; yet, unless he could give her what she needed, she would never be his wife in truth.

He slipped out of the bed, tucking pillows around her to keep her warm, and went in search of Nugent. He found her and Maufe down the corridor in a small parlor, having a comfortable coze. She was seated on a small sofa, mending, and Maufe was at the table, blacking boots.

"Nugent, it's time we talked. Her ladyship had another nightmare."

Nugent rose but Huntley stayed her. "Her ladyship is fine and sleeping peacefully. I need to know what happened."

Caro's maid lowered herself back to the chair. "I agree, my lord. This should not be kept from you any longer." She stared at him. "I promised her I would keep it to myself, but I can't stand by and see her ladyship continue to suffer. She needs help to move on with her life."

"I'll do anything I can to make her whole again."

Nugent nodded.

Maufe stood and picked up the boots.

"You may stay, Mr. Maufe," Nugent said.

Huntley took a seat at the table, drumming his fingers impatiently while Nugent gathered her thoughts.

"My lady fell in love with the son of a neighboring peer, whom she'd known most of her life," Nugent began. "Her ladyship was not but sixteen, but passions at that age run high. He was a few years older, and I do think he returned her ladyship's affections. Yet he needed to marry money. Not just the respectable portion her ladyship had, but a large fortune. After he went on the Town, he found a lady who was the only daughter of a banker and wed her before a month was out."

Huntley stopped breathing for a moment before asking, "Did anything occur between her ladyship and the gentleman?"

Nugent slowly shook her head before glancing at him. "A few stolen kisses in the garden, if that. Her ladyship's mother, Lady Broadhurst, knew about the attachment and made certain they were properly chaperoned. He was an honorable young man. If he could have married her, I believe he would have done so, but his father made it impossible."

The young man would not be the first to have been put in that position by intemperate relations. Nodding, Huntley motioned Nugent to continue.

"Her ladyship's father wanted an advantageous marriage for her. After the young gentleman married, her father arranged a marriage to another man. My lady's heart was broken, and at the time, she didn't care who she married. Still, Lady Broadhurst insisted my lady have a full Season. A few months later, my lady discovered she couldn't abide marrying her betrothed. I didn't find out what made her change her mind until after we left England."

"Which was?" Huntley asked.

"A friend of my lady's told her the man had taken advantage of a young serving girl." Nugent picked up the tea-cup and took a sip. "We were still in London. My lady decided to speak to her betrothed alone and tell him she didn't want the marriage. I tried to go with her, but she smiled and said there was no reason to make such a to do. I never should have let her go by herself, and I'll never forgive myself for allowing it." Nugent stopped, her hands shook. Maufe poured her a glass of water and handed it to her. Taking a drink, she calmed herself. "Lady Caro was gone too long for my liking. I went to look for her and heard her scream. When I opened the door to the front parlor, the man pushed past me, and I found my lady on the floor, sobbing. Her bodice was torn and a bruise was starting on her face." Nugent stopped again. "My lady's skirt was hitched up around her hips and there was blood."

Rage coursed through Huntley as every muscle in his body clenched. "Go on."

"I told the butler to clear the hall and corridors, and I got her up to her room, then called for Lady Broadhurst. Lord Broadhurst was in the country taking care of some business, so Lady Broadhurst, my lady, and I traveled that evening to a small estate in Suffolk near the coast. Lady Broadhurst made arrangements for us—my lady, Dalle, and me—to leave. We ended up traveling through the Netherlands because when we tried to board the merchant ship, my lady panicked at all the men on board."

Nugent took another sip of water and a grim smile appeared on her face. "I guess the gentleman who raped my lady didn't count on his lordship being out of Town. The man thought he'd be able to force the marriage. By the time his lordship returned, we were already on the Continent, and Lady Broadhurst had told Lord Broadhurst what happened. He agreed with her ladyship that my lady should remain in Italy until she wanted to return."

Silent tears slid down Nugent's cheeks. Maufe pressed his handkerchief into her hand.

Huntley's throat closed. "Who—who was it?"

Shaking her head, she said, "That's not my place to say."

He'd find out and kill him, if someone else hadn't already. "The bad dreams, how often does her ladyship have them?"

"For the first year or two, she had them a few times a week. Until recently, she hadn't had one for several months." Nugent raised her gaze to his. "She relives the attack."

Huntley's heart constricted, and he swore under his breath. That filthy bugger, whoever he was, would pay for hurting Caro. For each year she suffered and for every bad dream. When Huntley found the scoundrel, he'd tear him apart. No wonder she didn't want to be touched. He'd keep her safe now. No one would ever hurt her again. Somehow, he'd find a way to heal her, make her whole again.

He glanced at Maufe, who was holding Nugent's hand, before rising. "I'm going back to her ladyship now."

Shunning his parlor and the bottle of brandy in it, he went straight to Caro. After shedding his clothes, he removed the pillows he'd propped up around her and climbed in the bed. Wrapping his arms around her, he gave in to his need to hold her close to him. The fluttering of her dark brown eyelashes was the only sign she knew he was with her again. After what she'd been through, it was a miracle she'd wanted him to kiss her. Would she ever tell him, or was it too horrific a memory? His mind wandered back to the maid who'd been raped. At least Caro was alive and with him. He'd just have to keep her there.

The next morning, Huntley gathered his wife and their servants and traveled down the mountain into Innsbruck. Caro had dozed off and on while he divided his time between looking at her and admiring the changing landscape. Towering mountains still surrounded them as they made their way to the Inn River valley. The forest gave way to fields showing signs of a recent harvest.

Innsbruck was an elegant town with tall painted houses. Their hotel was a few blocks from the river and right in the middle of the main shopping area. They were shown the most luxurious quarters they'd had thus far on their journey. Tall ceilings were decorated with carved, brightly painted beams. A large bed with royal blue and gold hangings stood against one wall. From the windows, he glimpsed the Inn River and the snow-covered mountains beyond.

They'd arrived in time for luncheon, which Huntley had ordered served in the parlor adjoining their bedchamber.

"What do you think?" he asked as he set down his serviette.

Caro wiped her lips and smiled. "I like all of it. Shall we try for a short walk?"

She did look better. Her cheeks had a little more color, and she'd rested most of the journey.

"Why not?" He rose and tugged the bell-pull. Maufe and Nugent both answered. "Maufe, I commend your choice of hotel. Her ladyship and I are going to take a short stroll."

"Thank you, my lord. I shall get your coat."

Once Caro had donned a pelisse and cloak, and he his greatcoat, they walked down Maria Theresien Strasse, the main street. With her hand tucked in his arm, she glanced into the shops. "I'm going to need some warmer clothes."

"Both you and Nugent, I suppose. We can inquire into a good modiste when we return to the hotel."

She glanced shyly at him. "I don't know how much money I have with me."

He raised a brow. Her money was hers. He'd clothe her. "You do remember we're married. It is perfectly proper for me to provide for you."

A slow blush rose in her cheeks. "I haven't forgotten. I just didn't think of it in terms of gowns."

He brought her closer. "If it makes you uncomfortable, then don't think of it. We have time to figure it all out." When she didn't reply, he asked, "Would you like to continue on our outing or return?"

"I can go a little farther."

Keeping a frown from his face, he wondered what was going on in her head. "Look at this shop. They seem to have a good assortment of woolens."

She nodded. "So they do."

After a few minutes of looking at the capes, coats, and other items, they turned back to the hotel, ambling down the other side of the street. Huntley noticed a bake shop and decided to visit it the next day. Surely he'd be able to find something containing chocolate for his wife.

By the time they arrived back in their chambers, Caro appeared tired and willingly accepted his help undressing and donning her nightgown. When he settled in next to her, rather than allowing him to gather her to him, she wrapped her arms around him and moved her lips against his.

Huntley grinned. "I thought you were worn-out."

"I am, but this helps me sleep."

It had the exact opposite effect on him. "I wouldn't want to deny you a medicinal kiss."

When she ran her tongue along his lips, he opened his, encouraging her to probe. She was getting very good at this.

Knowing she needed rest, he tried to keep the heat low, but when her hands slipped behind his back and she pressed against him, flames licked at his skin, and he groaned.

He'd felt desire before but never a craving so deep it came from his soul. A need to possess her as he never had another woman. To make her completely his. He cupped her now swollen breast, then brushed and toyed with her nipples. Caro gave him a low moan and shivered. His shaft, which had stirred at the first touch of her lips on his, was ready to play. But not yet. How much longer he didn't know.

His muscles tightened as he allowed her to lead. If he wanted to make love to her, she must understand she had a say as well. He ran his hands down her back and up again to her full, heavy breasts. He pulled the silk and rubbed it against her skin, all the time wondering how long he could last.

By the time Caro broke the kiss, her skin was flushed, and breaths came in gasps. Her eyes were warm as she gazed into his. "That was even better than before."

He started to absently agree with her, but it struck him that he'd never kissed another woman as deeply or enjoyed it so much. His lips quirked up. "Yes. It was. Try to sleep. I'll wake you for dinner."

"Someday," she said ruefully, "I'd like to be able to stay up long enough to have tea."

"Maybe in a few days." He'd consult with the hotel's chef after he went to the bake shop.

They'd remain in Innsbruck until Caro's health was restored, and by the time they left, she would be his wife in truth.

Chapter 16

The following morning, Huntley rose early and went in search of a chocolate confection for Caro. Though barely dawn, the streets of the old city were bustling with vendors and farmers in town for the market. After trying two bake shops, where he discovered only bread, he was directed to Café Munding at Kiebachgasse 16, a short walk from the hotel and close to Maria Theresien Strasse. There, he found a chocolate torte.

Yesterday afternoon, once Caro had rested, she'd been able to take dinner in the parlor. Just moving to Innsbruck seemed to make a difference. To-day they'd start shopping for sufficient clothing to make the rest of the trip. He'd take her to the café when they finished their errands.

Nugent was arranging Caro's hair when he strode into their chamber. The dresser narrowed her eyes at him. "I'd appreciate it if you could leave it up for a while this time, my lord."

His wife blushed, and he gave Nugent his most innocent look. "I will, at least until after luncheon. However, if her ladyship needs to rest, I don't see how she can with all those pins sticking in her scalp."

Caro choked and met his eyes in the mirror. Hers were twinkling with mirth. Nugent shook her head and left.

The day before, he'd incurred Nugent's ire when he'd taken all the pins out of Caro's hair so that she could rest more comfortably. Well, that's what he told her maid. What he'd really wanted was to run his hands through her silken curls.

"If I'd said that to her," Caro said, "she would have made me feel six again."

He crossed the room and picked her up and headed for the bed. "Fortunately, only Collins has been with me long enough to do that, and he rarely does." Huntley studied her face. "You look well. How are you feeling, and what are you doing up so early?"

She met his gaze a little shyly. "I awakened cold and could not go back to sleep. As a result I decided I may as well be up to greet you. Have you broken your fast yet?"

"No, I wanted to breakfast with you." He set her down, drawing her close.

When she tilted her head up, he kissed her. That part was going well. Caro hadn't objected to his continued sharing of the bed or their increasing physical closeness.

He glanced at her hair, and she chuckled. It was such a light, carefree sound, one he'd never heard from her before. His heart swelled. Feelings he'd never experienced, and couldn't name, flooded him. He wanted to hear her laugh like that often.

She put her arms around his neck. "Nugent will forget herself if you take it down now."

"Um, I suppose you're right."

"We have a lot to accomplish after breakfast."

"I expect not all of our errands will be completed this morning. We'll do as much as we are able, and no more, so that you can regain your strength."

He considered his wife's soft, shining hair, and sighed. He would rather have it down.

"I'm feeling better already," she said. "Come, the city is already awake. Let's eat."

A half hour later, Caro's hand was tucked in his arm as they made their way to the modiste. She'd glanced at him questioningly a few times as she considered her purchases, and he'd done his best to let her know he approved of them all. Still, he wished he knew what she was thinking. His wife was too good at keeping her own counsel.

Strolling through the vegetable market, they discussed what types of provisions they should carry with them and the best route to Nancy.

"It is getting colder," Caro said. "We can take almost anything we want as long as we store it on the outside of the coach."

"There are storage areas under the seats we can use as well."

She looked at him. "Is that where you put the tiramisu?"

"Indeed." Huntley looked around and found the street sign. "I think the quickest way is through the Fernpass."

"Isn't there also a route around the Bodensee on the Swiss side?" she asked.

He turned her down a side street. "I saw a book shop this morning. I think it's down here." He made another turn and was pleased to see he was right. "Now, let's hope they have maps."

A bell jingled as they entered the shop.

A middle-aged man greeted them in German. "Good morning. How may I help you?"

Huntley answered in the same language. "Good morning. We will be traveling to Nancy and need some maps to decide the best route to take."

The shopkeeper brought the maps and told them snow had already fallen near the Swiss border. Though Huntley knew Caro would have liked to travel that way, she agreed the Fernpass was a better option.

"Thank you." Huntley paid for the maps and gave the man his card. "Can you have them delivered to the Hotel Goldener Adler?"

"It would be my pleasure." The shopkeeper bowed, and they took their leave.

When they had regained the street, Huntley glanced at Caro. She seemed to have more energy than the previous day. "How are you feeling? We can go back to the hotel if you wish."

She took his arm. "I'm not tired."

He grinned. "In that case, I have a surprise for you."

She smiled as if she didn't have a care in the world. "Will you tell me?"

"You'll see when we get there." He led her back to the market and down another small street to a square. "Here we are."

Holding the door to the café open, Huntley followed her into a warm room trimmed in light wood. Paintings of nature scenes hung on white walls, giving the café a cozy feel. As a server came forward to greet Caro, she spied a large wooden cart with a curved glass cover. Centered on the top shelf was a round chocolate torte. This was what he'd been doing this morning. She was so glad she hadn't taken him to task as she'd wanted to when she woke up alone. Her heart surged with joy. No one had ever treated her so well. As if her desires were foremost in his mind.

Tears pricked her eyes, and she turned to him, lifting her hand to his cheek. "Oh, Huntley. Thank you."

He kissed her fingers and murmured, "Don't cry. What'll people think?"

She glanced around. The café was full of women. "They'll understand."

Huntley nodded to someone, and a woman in a plain gray gown with a white apron smiled and motioned for them to follow.

When they reached the small table in the corner, he helped her with her pelisse, and she started to try to untie her gloves. Whatever had possessed her to buy them? They were of soft black calf's leather, lined with cashmere and very comfortable, but had ties that she could never manage to unfasten.

He took her arm and slowly released the six small bows, caressing her inner wrist as he drew them off. She shivered slightly. His lips quirked up as she caught her breath. Oh, he was a devil. The problem was she liked it a great deal too much and didn't know how to pull back.

This morning, when he wasn't beside her when she'd awakened, she had casually asked Nugent about his bedchamber and was told that he had no separate room. Before Caro had fallen ill, she would have insisted he find his own room. Yet now, she didn't want him to leave her. She didn't understand what was happening to her.

"Caro?"

She glanced up. Concern etched a line in his brow.

"Are you all right? I thought this would make you happy."

Summoning a smile, she pushed her apprehensions aside. She would not ruin their outing by worrying. What was it Nugent always said? Don't borrow trouble. "I am happy. Happier than I've been in a long time."

The fine line went away, and he returned her smile. "Ah, here's your cake."

Picking up the fork, she cut off a small piece and tasted. It was so good she closed her eyes to savor it before taking another bite. "Mmm. Huntley, you must try it. It is heaven." Opening her eyes, she was shocked to see he didn't have a slice, but something else covered in a cream-colored sauce. "What is that?"

He gave her a wry smile. "I hope I haven't disappointed you, but I have a weakness for apple strudel with vanilla sauce."

"Oh." She feigned sadness. "I suppose not everyone can like chocolate."

"Minx." He gazed at her, causing her cheeks to heat. "I eat considerably more than you, and you wouldn't want me eating all of the torte."

Somehow she had the feeling he wasn't talking about the torte. She swallowed another bite, her fork still suspended over the cake. "You may have a point I'd not considered. Please, enjoy your strudel."

After they'd finished and were once again on the pavement, she leaned on him, just a little, as they strolled and took in the scenes painted on the buildings and the colorfully trimmed wooden porches. "This is a very lovely town. All the buildings are decorated so beautifully."

"It is." He glanced down at her. "I'd like to spend more time here."

"But you are worried about the snow?"

"Indeed," he said. "If it wasn't for our commitment, I'd winter here."

"I would have liked that." This town could have become their special world. Where no one knew Caro, and Huntley would not allow anyone to threaten her.

"If you're feeling up to it," he said, "we'll plan to see the sights after we've accomplished all our tasks."

"I'd like that. I would hate to leave after seeing only the market."

She was feeling much stronger. The air here was not thin as it had been in the mountains. Even though it was only their second day in Innsbruck, the walks were already helping her regain her strength. When they returned to their chambers, Huntley ordered a hearty soup for luncheon, which consisted of tomatoes, beef, and peppers. Caro was surprised she ate it all.

She felt him studying her closely and glanced up. "What is it?"

He placed his serviette on the table and rose. "You seem a little tired."

She hid her smile. "I am just a bit."

"If you rest now, we can dine together."

Rising, she gave him a sidelong glance. "Yes, of course, and Nugent would have to re-dress my hair before dinner in any event."

He came around the table and swooped her up into his arms. "I wouldn't want you to overtax yourself by walking to the bed."

She was content, more so than she'd ever been in her life. He deposited her on the upholstered stool in front of the dressing table, and she watched as he slowly took out one pin at a time, letting them drop to the floor. As the tendrils fell, he teased them out or twisted them around his fingers. Each one received special attention until her hair flowed over her shoulders and down her back.

Huntley leaned over, placing kisses on her neck. Her gown and stays loosened, and fell away. After she rose, he drew her garments off her arms and slowly pushed the gown over her hips. When she was clad in nothing but her chemise, he took her in his arms and carried her to the bed, holding her against him as he climbed in.

But when he rose over her, Caro's throat constricted, and her heart raced as panic gripped her.

Huntley backed away and leaned against the pillows. His fingers caressed her jaw as he studied her. "Tell me how he hurt you."

Fear threatened to strangle her as it had before. "I—I don't like to think about it. When I do, I have bad dreams."

He slid one arm beneath her. "If we want to have any kind of marriage, we need to be rid of him." He whispered against her ear, "Tell me what he did, and I'll replace those memories with new ones."

When he'd kissed her the last time she'd had a bad dream, it had helped. Could he help with the rest of it? Her chest tightened in fear as she gazed up at him. His face was calm, his eyes reflected his concern. Most importantly, Caro knew that if she said no, he would stop. "I'll try."

He touched his lips to her hair. "When you're ready."

Closing her eyes, she swallowed. "My father made the match, but I couldn't go through with it. When I told him I didn't want to marry him, he tried to kiss me. It was horrible. His lips were wet and slimy."

Huntley fluttered kisses on her lips before he tilted his

head and lightly ran the tip of his tongue across the seam. She opened her mouth and touched her tongue with his. The caress heated her and sent tiny flames flickering through her body.

Raising his head, he asked, "Like that?"

The knot in her stomach started to uncoil. "No. Not at all like that."

"Look at me," he said.

She met his eyes. They were gentle, but there was something else as well. A determination she didn't understand.

"Then what did he do?"

"He—" She shuddered. Huntley stroked her back until she was ready to go on. Caro sobbed and tried to blink back the tears. "He grabbed my breast and twisted it."

Huntley's hand closed over her breast and kneaded lightly. His thumb caressed her nipple and it formed a tight bud. A warm need filled her where the fear had been.

"Like this?" he asked again.

She shook her head. "No."

"What did you do?"

Keeping her eyes on his, she replied, "I tried to scream, but nothing came out."

Without moving his gaze from hers, his hands roamed down her body, touching her softly and intimately, leaving a trail of flames. "Do you want to scream now?"

Moaning, she tried to move closer to him. "No."

"The next time you scream," he whispered, "I promise you, it will be with pleasure."

The golden flecks in his eyes burned brighter. She caught her breath. "And then he hit me, and held me down, and hurt me."

His voice turned grave. "Where did he hit you?"

She touched the side of her mouth, and he lightly caressed the spot before kissing it.

He ran the tip of his tongue down her neck and back up to her jaw. "Caro, let me make love to you."

His gaze was warm and kind. It was time for her to try to put her demons away. "Yes."

His fingers caressed her mons and a breathy sigh escaped as he slipped one finger in her and caressed. With each stroke, the tension in her core rose. She didn't understand what she was feeling, but her legs opened to encourage him, and a primitive need clamored to have him inside her.

His firm, well-molded lips captured hers, and she was kissing him with a desire she didn't know she was capable of. Flames burned under her skin. Her palms caressed his strong chest. Her fear slithered away. There was only him as he placed open-mouthed kisses on her neck and throat before moving over her bosom.

One thumb ran lightly over her nipple, and she arched up. More, she wanted more. He chuckled. His mouth closed on the other nipple and lightly sucked. This must be the most exquisite sensation she had ever experienced. Another high-pitched sigh came from somewhere, and longing coursed through her veins, pooling between her legs.

Oh, please do that to the other one as well.

As if he'd heard her, Huntley switched breasts. This time, Caro knew the sounds came from her. Her voice was low and breathy. "Oh, that feels good."

His lips left her bosom, and he covered it with his hand, rasping the wet muslin against her nipples. "I'm glad you like it."

As he blew on one nipple, it furled into a tight bud before he took it and her chemise into his mouth again. The fire coursing through her threatened to ignite. How much more could she take before she exploded?

Her fingers gripped his neck. More, she wanted more of him. One of his hands kneaded her bottom and the other held her head. "More."

Had she really said that out loud?

He groaned, and the ribbons of her chemise gave way and slipped down. Huntley's teeth grazed a breast, and Caro found herself holding his head to her bosom as he sucked. He rubbed and twirled her other nipple between his fingers. Now she knew what he'd meant when he told her she'd scream with pleasure. That she would desire him.

Caro wanted to give him everything he wanted, all of herself. What was more amazing was she wanted him and all he could give her. She hadn't known it could be like this. He was torturing her. Her body sang with desire as he kissed his way down her stomach. All the spots of tension seemed to coalesce in her mons.

Her hands clenched the pillows and she brought her knees up and squeezed his shoulders. When she tried to cry out, her breath was gone and the spiraling tension threatened to overwhelm her. In the next instant, the most wonderful feeling came over her and she shook from the inside and shattered.

Still she knew there was more. Huntley had been caressing her, pleasuring her, for days and taken nothing for himself. She'd seen his tension as he held back. "Please make love to me."

He slowly kissed his way back up her body and gazed into her eyes. "Only if you're sure."

His gaze burned like the blue flames of a fire flecked with gold. If she was ever going to put the past behind her, this was her chance. She could dream of him instead of the other. "I'm ready."

Taking her lips in a deep caress, she barely noticed his fingers enter her. They slid in and out, causing the fire to light again. When he moved over her, she tensed for the pain, but there was only a stretching and wave upon wave of delight as she reached for the explosion to take her again. She grasped him with her sheath and cried out.

Her heart swelled with happiness. For the first time since the attack, she was whole again.

Caro's skin flushed with desire and her breath came in short pants. Huntley needed to erase all her fears and doubt. Teach her how much pleasure he could give her. Capturing her mouth, he languidly stroked her tongue as he ran his hands under her breasts and down her body, pushing her chemise lower with each caress.

Moving over her, he'd kissed her long neck and her creamy mounds. When he got to her still too flat stomach, he paused and glanced up. Caro's head was thrown back, the tip of her tongue licked her lips. Moving slowly over her nether-curls, he caressed her with his mouth and almost shouted with joy when she pushed her hips up to him. Circling the small pearl nestled in her curls, he inserted a finger into her wet silk. She tossed and writhed as he drew out her tension before he entered her hot sheath. One last flick of his tongue, and she convulsed around him.

She'd tensed when he rose over her. Knowing she'd expect the same pain as before, he entered her slowly, keeping himself attuned to any discomfort she might have. Then she relaxed and accepted him. He used a slow, even pace until she quavered around him and brought him to completion.

Finally, she was his.

He kissed her lips and cheeks. Wet? Why was she crying? "Caro, what's wrong?"

"Nothing, nothing. It's all wonderful."

He held her face gently between his hands. "I hadn't planned . . ."

She smiled and put her fingers over his lips. "It was perfect. I could not have asked for more. No matter what happens now. Well, what I mean is, whatever we decide to do. It will be fine."

What in damnation did she mean, whatever we decided to do? *Women!* Why did they have to be so damn difficult?

Chapter 17

A shard of weak winter light stole into the chamber. Caro relished the feel of her husband's strong arms around her. *Her husband.* It was the first time she had truly felt that he was. What the future would bring, she didn't know. Yet, for the first time in years, she had hope for a normal life. One with love and children.

Huntley stirred. His hand caressed her breasts and wandered down over her stomach. His breath feathered her jaw. Sighing softly, she gave her neck over to his lips. She never would have believed that she'd welcome a man's touch. The curling hairs of his chest tickled her back, and she resisted the urge to turn and run her palms over his muscles.

Then his fingers reached between her legs and stroked, focusing all her attention on his caress. She sighed. "Oh, Huntley."

"Gervais." His voice was a low rumble, as if he hadn't awakened yet. "I want you to call me Gervais."

"Gervais." She tested the name on her tongue. It felt right. "Who else calls you that?"

"Only you."

She wanted to think about what he'd said, but his fingers slipped into her already wet sheath and she moaned. Every nerve in her body was focused on the apex of her thighs. His hard erection slid between her legs, rubbing her sensitive place, adding to the sensations. She encouraged his fingers deeper.

Huntley-Gervais's voice was low and rough. "I want you."

The tip of his shaft hovered at her entrance, waiting for her answer. "Yes."

Unlike earlier when he'd slowly filled her, this time was a sharp thrust that sent spikes of pleasure soaring through her body. He held her even tighter, and his hand never left her mons as he possessed her.

Tension spiraled up until each breath she took ended on a cry. His breathing rasped in her ear, and his body tightened. One hand gently squeezed her breast, while the other pressed in her curls. He seemed to know just what to do to bring her bliss. Her breath caught as he thrust deep within her. She wanted him more than she'd ever thought possible. Hot streaks flew through her, and she came apart. Unable to pull a coherent thought together, she slumped against him, reveling in his strength. If only she could live like this forever.

When Huntley next awoke, Caro lay limp and sated in his arms. Keeping one arm around her, he gently pushed her damp hair from her face. He kissed her neck and the curve of her jaw. His chest ached. He'd never wanted a woman as much as he wanted her. No, needed her. Whatever happened, he would never let her go. He'd show her how much she meant to him, that he needed her in his life, forever. Listening to her soft breathing filled him with a sense of peace.

"Hun—Gervais?"

"Yes, my love?"

"Is it always like this? So intense?"

"Between us, it will always be that way." He reached back and pulled the bed hangings closed, enveloping them in semi-darkness and shutting out the rest of the world. "How are you feeling?"

Caro rolled to face him. "I feel well. Much stronger."

Even in the dim light, her face glowed with contentment. He kissed her lips and forehead. "Caro, I . . ."

"Hmm?"

"I think if you rest now you'll be well enough to dress for dinner."

She smiled and turned around so that her back was once more to his chest. "I hope so. I am so tired of not being able to do things."

He drew her closer. Sometime over the past week, he'd fallen deeply in love with her. Perhaps he was a coward for not telling Caro he loved her, but she hadn't told him how she felt. He couldn't bear for anything to set them back. One never knew how a woman would react. Particularly after what she'd said earlier about whatever they decided to do. His love for her, his feelings, were too new and fragile to risk. He'd wait until the time was right, after he was sure of her affections toward him.

How his married friends would laugh if they could see him now. Still, he wished for their counsel, Marcus's and Worthington's especially.

Caro's steady breathing drew his attention. Her lips, still swollen from his kisses, tilted up in a smile. She was so beautiful his heart ached, and she was his, forever his. He held her tighter, as if that could stop any thoughts she may have about leaving him.

After a while, he mentally reviewed the route they'd take from Innsbruck to Ulm in Germany. He trusted Maufe would remember some of the inns at which they'd stayed on their journey to Italy.

The Fernpass was an old, frequently traveled, and well-guarded passage through the northern part of the Alps. There were many posting houses and the like that had been there for centuries. As long as they didn't experience a heavy snowfall, it would take about a week to reach Ulm.

The door opened and someone snorted.

"This is the first time I've seen the hangings closed," Nugent remarked.

Maufe coughed. "Um, yes. Well, I should probably order a tub to be set up. They will want to wash."

"Indeed?" Nugent commented in a satisfied tone. "Well, it's about time." She paused. "How do you know?"

Maufe's voice was so low, Huntley couldn't hear what his valet said, but he knew. Huntley always closed the hangings when he had a woman. It occurred to him Caro never needed to know about that particular signal.

She stirred. "Was that Nugent?"

"Yes, she's having a tub brought up."

"Where is . . . ?" When Caro sat up, the coverlet fell off her and exposed creamy breasts topped by light pink nipples.

Not able to resist, he reached out and cupped the one nearest to him. His groin twitched "What are you looking for?"

Long, light flaxen curls cascaded down her back and over her shoulders. "My chemise. It must be here somewhere."

"You don't need it." He lifted Caro and sat her on top of

him. "You are the most exquisite creature in the world, just as you are."

A faint blush rose from her chest up her neck. "Flattery?"

Reaching up, he drew her to him. "No, truth."

He kissed her and raised her hips up to meet his fully erect shaft. The door opened. *Damn.* "They are going to have to start knocking."

Her face turned a fiery red, and she reached for the cover. "Do you think they've guessed?" she whispered.

Raising a brow, he tried not to laugh. "We *are* married."

"Yes, but . . ." She hid her head in his neck. "Oh dear."

Even through the sounds of the tub being brought in and water being poured, the position of her mons with respect to his groin kept him hard. If he didn't get her off of him, he'd take her and complete her embarrassment.

Whispering in her ear, he said, "Caro, I need to move you."

"No, not yet," she replied in a soft voice. "Wait until they leave." The tip of his shaft brushed her nether curls, and her head shot up. "Oh, oh, I see."

She helped him slide her off, and he tucked her next to him. "It is remarkably single-minded."

Though the light was dim, he could see the worry in her eyes.

"Can you not manage it?" she asked.

"Not easily." *And not around you.* "Give it a few moments."

Wrinkles formed in her forehead. "But if you cannot—"

"I can control whether or not to use it." He studied her frowning countenance. "Caro, what was done to you before was not out of affection. All men can decide whether to take a woman or not. Too many decide wrongly. Forcing a woman is never right."

Maybe someday he'd explain that some men derived pleasure from hurting women, but that discussion would not happen any time soon. He ran his fingers along her spine and down to her buttocks. Her tension eased. "Do you understand?"

She nodded. "Yes. You would never force me."

"No, never." He drew her down for a kiss. "I take no joy in your distress. I want you to be happy."

He wanted her to love him.

"My lord, my lady, your bath is ready," Nugent said. "I'll be in the other room with Mr. Maufe when you're ready to dress."

The door closed. "Well, my lady," Huntley said, "are you ready to bathe?"

Caro threw back the cover and opened the hanging bedcurtain on her side of the bed. "I need to put up my hair."

Of course she did. "I'll find your hairpins. I know they're here somewhere."

He'd just picked one up from the floor when Caro pulled her hair to one side and started to braid it. The slender line of her back distracted him. *Hell.* All of her distracted him.

"Have you found them yet?"

"Just a moment." Turning back to his task, he hunted around the floor and found enough of the pins to keep the braid up. Clearly, he'd need to be more careful with what he did with them the next time.

Steam rose from the wide copper basin as he handed her in and followed, sinking down into the warm water. Grabbing the small piece of linen, he applied soap and turned to Caro. "Now, my lady wife. You will see just how proficient I am at washing you."

Her eyes grew wide and her color deepened.

"I did it before, when you were ill."

"So Nugent told me, but I don't remember."

Though he tried to attend to her in an efficient manner, he was clearly no good at it. He drew the linen down over her breasts, and her nipples peaked. Then he kissed her and water splashed as she came to him. There'd be a mess to clean up after this.

Hotel Vieux-Port, Marseille, France

Horatia's plan to leave quickly was thwarted by work required on two of the carriages. She and her household spent almost a week in Marseille before the carriages were ready for travel. Captain Whitton lost no time gaining a foothold into her life. Though she must give the devil his due, he was the one who found the damage to the carriages, and he'd gone with her and La Valle when she needed to select horses that could make the trip in the easy stages she'd planned. The captain not only made very good recommendations but successfully bartered the price down. Based on his interactions with the horse dealer she suspected he was not a particularly easy man to deal with. Yet he'd not interfered in any of her decisions for the journey.

Horatia wanted to kick herself as she joined him for breakfast. Apparently his demand that she dine with him extended to all meals. Why hadn't she paid more attention? It must have been the dimple.

She held up a list of preparations. "Have you nothing you wish to add?"

He rubbed his chin and glanced at the sheets of foolscap on the table. "No. It appears as if you've thought of everything."

Narrowing her eyes in disbelief, she said, "If you're sure."

His eyes deepened to the color of green water near the

rocks. "It has always been my desire to marry a woman who is capable of planning."

"Humph." She rose, as did he. "Very well then, I have matters to attend to."

"I shall walk with you."

As always he was beside her, prowling like a large lion stalking its prey. His hand at the small of her back guided her to the stairs. Whitton had not kissed her again, but his numerous small caresses caused her senses to flare. The touch of his hand on hers, even through her gloves, made her fingers tremble. His lips on her knuckles, fingers playing with the wispy curls against her neck, all served to encourage her errant, long-denied body to respond and yearn for what it had not had for years.

She wondered how his hard, lightly calloused fingers would feel on her breasts. Shivering, she tried to stop her thoughts. They were becoming as difficult to control as her body.

"Is anything wrong?"

When she glanced up at him, his eyes twinkled. The wicked man knew just what effect he was having on her. "Nothing, I'm just a little cold."

A slow smile spread across his face and the dimple made an appearance. His voice was low. "I'll remind you to bring a shawl the next time."

Just the thought of him placing it around her shoulders made her heart race. "I must tell Risher it is becoming cooler."

The combination of him and the heat emanating from the stone walls of the enclosed terrace made her want to fan herself. Perhaps he wouldn't notice how warm it actually was.

Whitton leaned close to her, his warm breath fluttering against her ear. "What happened to honesty, my lady?"

He stopped strolling, and she glanced around, surprised to find herself at her chambers. *Damn. Damn the man*. Now he had her cursing. Swallowing, she glanced up at him. "What did you want me to say?"

"The truth. That every time I touch you, each caress I make, affects you."

Her eyes widened as she gazed at him. An affair would be just the thing. Get him out of her system and go on with her life. "Perhaps . . ."

"No." Whitton's thumb lightly stroked her jaw. "We are not going to have an affair."

"How did you . . . ? I was not considering that at all."

His eyes smiled. "*You* are a very poor liar. Everything you think runs through your eyes and your face."

Her gaze dropped to his lips. He bent his head, kissing her lightly. "There's someone coming, and we must have a care for your reputation."

Taking her hand, he kissed it while reaching behind and pushing the door handle. "I must be out the remainder of the morning. If you need me, call my valet, Smyth, and he'll send word. I'll see you at luncheon."

When he turned to leave, Horatia pressed her fingers to her lips. Oh, she was in so much trouble.

Risher pulled her into the room. "My lady, you cannot stand in the corridor moonstruck over the man."

"I am not *moonstruck*."

"So you say. Have you decided if you'll marry him or not?"

Horatia threw herself down on a chair. "No. Why should I?"

"You always said if a gentleman came along who tempted you, you'd wed him." Risher shook out a gown before folding it carefully and placing it in a trunk. "Seems to me, you're more interested in him than you want to let on."

"Giving up my freedom is a large price to pay for . . .

companionship. He'd have complete control over me, whether I wanted him to or not." And she was starting to like him much too much. If she could only get what she wanted without marriage, her life would be perfect again. There must be something about him that made him ineligible. "Risher, you've met his valet, have you not?"

Her maid glanced at Horatia sharply. "I have."

"Could you discover more about Captain Whitton?"

Risher's lips pressed in a thin line. "I could, but I'm not going to."

Horatia used the voice she always did when she wanted her maid to do something and Risher was resisting. Though it *had* been a very long time since Horatia had asked Risher to do anything out of the ordinary. "Please, Risher," Horatia wheedled. "It will help me make my decision."

Risher's lips twisted wryly. "Very well. But mark my words, my lady, Captain Whitton is not a man to be trifled with. He'll catch you out."

Horatia took her maid's hand in hers. "Not if you are *very* careful."

"Smyth." John strode into the parlor adjoining his bedchamber. "I'm going to make the banking arrangements and check on the sale of the ship. I don't expect it to happen, but if Lady Horatia should ask for me, send word immediately."

"Of course, sir," his valet responded. "I posted the letter you wrote the London solicitor, by messenger."

"Thank you."

"May I ask how the courtship is proceeding?"

"Slowly, very slowly." If only he could read her devious little mind, he'd know more. He'd never exercised so much control over himself in his life. After so many years as a widow, Horatia was justifiably wary of giving up control of her life to a man. If only he could have come to her a year after George died, before she'd grown so independent. If it hadn't been for John's obligations to the Crown, he would have. All he could do was stay on his course and convince her he was necessary to her future happiness.

As he walked out of the hotel and down the street to the banking area, he thought about the work waiting for him in England. His brother had left the estates in shambles. Although John had hired a well-recommended steward to start putting things to rights, he needed to return home soon. For the present, fixing his interest with Horatia took precedence. He'd no intention of not having her in tow as his wife when he arrived as the new earl. Yet, God knew, she wasn't making it easy.

It had taken him a while to discover why the eldest daughter of a marquis was wasted on a mere mister, even if the gentleman was the grandson of a duke. He'd found that George Laughton had been a childhood friend of Lady Horatia's father, and after her last hoydenish trick—taking one of her father's carriages without permission and driving it down St. James's Street—her father'd been more than happy to marry her off as soon as possible.

Laughton promised to take Horatia overseas and look after her, which he did, successfully staying out of the hands of any French troops. After George's death, her father couldn't get her to return to England. No doubt the Marquis of Huntingdon had planned another marriage for her, and she was having none of it. John chuckled to himself. The vixen. It was her spark of mischief that had so captivated him.

The back of his neck prickled, and he whirled around but saw no one other than ordinary people going about their business. That was the second time since landing in Marseille he'd sensed danger. He turned down another street, hid in an alley, and watched. A few moments later, a man with a familiar limp hurried by. *Scarper*. What the devil was he still doing in Marseille?

The rest of the crew had quit the city over a week ago. Whitton debated going after his former crew member, but after a moment decided against it. Nothing was going to stop him from leaving on the marrow with Horatia. She was everything he wanted, and he was everything she needed. A firm but light hand on her rudder.

If Scarper was looking for John, he would take the precaution of leaving before his future wife so, if he was still being followed, she wouldn't be in danger. He waited a little while longer before doubling back to the main street and the bank. By the time he'd arrived at the shipyard to meet with the broker, it was already half past twelve. Horatia ate luncheon at one.

"I've good news for you, Captain Whitton." Monsieur Dufore, a dapper, middle-aged merchant, ushered John into an elegantly appointed office. The polished wood and leather chairs were a distinct contradiction to the almost shabby exterior of the building.

Once he was seated with a glass of wine, Monsieur Dufore continued. "We've received a very respectable offer for your ship. Considering the condition it's in, the offer far exceeded my expectations."

"That's good news indeed," John replied, "and it comes just in time. I am leaving for England soon. I'd been prepared to authorize you to sell it for scrap."

Dufore's eyes widened. "Its state is not that bad."

"I need to move ahead with my plans, and the ship no longer enters into them." The schooner had hit heavy weather crossing the Atlantic, but she was still a damn fine ship.

"Ah, *oui*. I understand. Life moves on." Dufore busied himself with the papers on his desk. "I have all the documents in order, in anticipation you would agree to the price."

John took the file the agent handed him, then, after carefully reading them, approved the terms. "Send the letter of credit to Rothschild's. They have my instructions."

When John rose, Dufore did as well. "Thank you, Captain. I will send a messenger immediately. It has been a pleasure doing business with you."

"On my part as well," John replied. "Thank you for effecting the quick sale."

He had less than fifteen minutes to make it to the hotel. Once he'd attained the street, he lengthened his stride and immediately turned. Scarper again. "You've been following me all day. What the hell do you want?"

"Aye, Capt'n. It's good ta see ye."

John had no time for the man. He'd been a liability on board, and John was not going to allow Scarper to scuttle his current plans. "Cut line. Why have you been watching me?"

The seaman's gaze shifted from one side to the other but couldn't seem to make contact with John's.

"Out with it. I have an appointment." From the corner of his eye, he saw a lad dressed as a courier exit Dufore's and take off down the street toward the commercial area. Scarper still had not answered. Whitton moved so his back was to a building and shifted his leg to feel the dagger in his boot. "Never known you to be so slow to voice your complaints."

"Weal, ye see, I jus' wanted ta see the old girl again."

"Is that all?" John asked with exasperation. "Then be my guest. She's in the yard at the end of the docks."

Scarper stared at him in surprise. "Ye don't mind then?"

John narrowed his eyes. What the devil was the man up to? "No, why should I? Is there something I should know?"

"No, no, Capt'n," Scarper said. "Naught at all. Then I'll see ye around." He turned to leave and stopped as if he'd forgotten something. "Will ye be heading back ta England then?"

Something was definitely going on. John reminded himself it was no longer his concern. "After I've finished my business here," he said. "It will be a change to be a passenger."

"Aye, it would at that," the sailor responded. "I'll be seein' ye around."

"Most likely." Not if John had anything to say about it. He stared at Scarper as the man made his way down the docks, and wondered what rumor had started about the ship. It was going to make John late to luncheon, but he needed to lay a false trail. If anyone wanted to find him, he'd make damn sure they'd have to work at it.

Turning the next corner, he entered the booking office and was surprised to find it completely empty of customers. After paying for passages for two on a ship leaving next week, he strode as quickly as possible to the hotel.

Horatia was just preparing to take a seat at a table in the courtyard when he arrived.

She glanced up. "I was beginning to think you had abandoned me."

He dismissed the waiter and held her chair. "Thinking or hoping?"

She waited until John poured their wine. "If you know you are upsetting me, why do you persist?"

Taking a sip of wine, he studied her over the rim of his glass. Horatia's color was a little high and her breathing shallow. "You're not such a poor creature as that. I'm only disconcerting you because you want me and I insist on marriage."

She set her glass down with a snap. "Oh, how dare you?"

He grinned at her. "Truth?"

"You are completely odious." Picking up her glass again, she took a sip yet made no move to leave.

He glanced around to make sure no one was within hearing. "I'll make you a wager, my lady."

She lifted her chin and replied haughtily, "I do not wager for money."

"Not money. In fact, it is actually more of a dare." The last time she'd gambled for money, she'd lost a fine pair of pearl earbobs one evening in Baden-Baden. Laughton had boxed her ears. John still had the letter telling him of it.

Part of his plan to convince her to marry him was to keep her off balance by changing the rules of the game each time she became comfortable with them.

Her eyes took on a curious sparkle, and she had another taste of wine. "Yes?"

Ah, this was the girl who drove down St. James's Street. "I shall wager you'll be betrothed before you bed me. If you are not, and I succumb to your not inconsiderable charms, I shall free you from your commitment to allow me to accompany you to Nancy."

The tip of her tongue lightly licked her full bottom lip, as if she was already savoring victory. "You, Captain Whitton, have a deal."

"Perfect." He fought to keep a satisfied look off his face. "In the interest of honesty, I should tell you that I sold my ship today. Mr. Whitton would be more appropriate, or John."

Horatia considered him. It was always appropriate to address a former captain by that title. But since he suggested it, calling him John might work in her favor. "John it is. You may call me Horatia."

"Horatia." He took the hand she held out, but instead of

kissing her knuckles, turned it and lightly grazed his teeth across her inner wrist.

She sucked in a breath. It appeared the dratted man was going to make her seduction of him extremely easy. She felt a bit cast down, but reminded herself this was what she wanted, only a short affair. He'd probably changed the rules because he realized he did not wish to marry her after all. A small stab of disappointment sliced through her. Well, good. She could bed him and be rid of him before she reached Nancy.

"I must leave early in the morning," he said, "to attend to some business. Your major domo told me you'd be staying at the Hôtel du Jardin in Salon-de-Provence. I'll meet you there."

She knew it. He was leaving her. She raised a brow. "Running away?"

The look of pure lust he shot her sent a streak of desire straight through her.

He was still holding her hand, and he stroked her wrist. Lowering his voice and making it seem like a caress, he responded, "No. I intend to rid myself of any distractions so that I may devote all my time to you on our way to Nancy."

She quickly brought herself back under control, raised her gaze to his, and smiled slowly. "If you make it to Nancy."

"Indeed. At this point, the only known outcome is that one of us will win."

Her head was in a whirl as he escorted her back to her chamber. She'd been so sure he was going to leave. This time, rather than rush back into her room like a breathless girl, she slid her arms around his neck and kissed him. "Until dinner."

His lips quirked up. "Until then, Horatia. Oh, and by bed, I meant full copulation."

Oh, he was wicked. She'd be purring in a moment. She caught her breath, responding evenly, "Of course. What else?"

She backed into her chamber and watched as he ambled down the corridor. "Yes, that is definitely what I meant as well."

Her heart pounded so hard she had trouble catching her breath. She'd had a full marital life. He was right. She did want him. To be held in a man's strong arms again and made love to. Men were easy to get into bed, at least that's what George always told her. Soon she would have the experience she wanted and be on her way. She wondered if John tasted as good as he smelled.

An hour later, Horatia set down her book and gazed out over the harbor. If she wanted only an affair with John, why then did she feel as if she was in danger of losing something? She shook herself. This was ridiculous. Her life was complete as it was. There was no reason to marry again. Not that she had anything against marriage, but it was such a gamble. It had been a week since he kissed her fully. What would it feel like to do it again? Perhaps she'd find out this evening. Of their own volition, her fingers touched her lips.

This was silly and not at all helpful. *Think about something else.* Huntley and Caro. She should be worrying about them instead of lusting for John Whitton. Unable to settle herself, Horatia paced the room. There must be something she could do until it was time to dress for dinner.

Strident voices rose from outside in front of the hotel. Stepping out onto the small balcony, she gazed down. A ship must have docked, and by the looks of it, all the passengers were English and planning to stay *here.* Just what she did not need. Thank heavens she was leaving in the morning.

Risher called to her, "My lady, Mr. Whitton sends a message that the English have invaded, and you might want to dine alone in your parlor this evening."

A burble of laughter rose in Horatia. Of course he'd say that. He'd been away from England as long as she had, or longer. "I agree. Meeting or being stared at by a lot of my fellow countrymen is not what I wish for. Not to mention that I'm traveling without a companion. It's just my luck I'd see someone I know. Please send a message to him that I will meet him in Salon-de-Provence."

Risher bobbed a curtsey. "Yes, my lady."

"And, Risher, let us plan to leave even earlier than planned. I shall take my breakfast up here as well."

"As you wish, my lady."

Horatia dined alone and tried once more to read, yet after staring at the same page for an hour, she finally had to admit that she missed dining with John and exchanging interesting barbs with him. She wished she'd found out more about his life. Well, that was not to be, and she may as well get used to being without his company. He would not be around much longer. Tears pricked her eyes, and she blinked them back. What was happening to her?

Chapter 18

Innsbruck, Austria

Gervais had finally decided Caro was well enough to take dinner in a regular parlor rather than in the small one next to their chamber. Though it was only a few doors down, at least it was a change. She glanced up from her soup to study her husband from under her lashes. Bathing with Gervais, kissing him, and touching him had been so easy and natural. He made it so. A smile tugged at her lips. She could not believe they'd made love in the tub.

When Nugent dressed her hair, she'd tsk-tsked over the tangles. But Caro could tell her dresser was happy for her. It had been just over three weeks since their small group had set out from Venice. She hadn't wanted to go and, most particularly, had not wanted to be with Gervais. Yet he'd protected her, cajoled her out of her sullen moods, and taken care of her when she'd been so ill. The result being she was happy and rapidly falling in love. Not at all the same woman who'd left Venice, but who was she now? For so long she'd shut herself away and allowed hurt and fear to keep her captive. Thinking she'd never have any children of her own, her only outlet had been visiting the orphanage. Even now she could be carrying Gervais's child. How would she know? Her mother had never explained anything, and, since Caro was still single, she'd heard no gossip of the type married women are privy to. She supposed she could ask Gervais, but he was a man. He probably wouldn't know either.

"Caro?"

She focused her attention on him. "I'm sorry, I must have been woolgathering. Did you say something?"

A slight frown marred his countenance. "I asked if you'd like to leave in four days. That will have given everyone a solid week to rest, and we can take in some of the sights."

She smiled. "Yes, that would be perfect. It will be nice just to be able to walk around without having to do anything."

His face relaxed. "I agree. We'll visit the café every day."

The place he had found just for her. "May we take a whole chocolate torte with us when we go?"

Huntley leaned back in his chair and laughed. "If you wish, we'll take two and hope we find more along the way."

Her heart soared. This was exactly as it should be. Joking and laughing, each learning about the other. She felt absurdly young and hopeful. "And you can have your strudel."

"Indeed." He nodded toward her soup. "Do you not like it?"

The soup was a rich broth containing small round bits of something. "I do. What are these things floating in it?"

"Marrow, rolled and fried."

She knew he wanted her to eat, and she was very hungry. The next course was roasted pork with sauerkraut and savory dumplings, accompanied by several removes. By the time they brought the cheese, she hardly had any room left. "I don't know how I can eat another bite. Though I am determined to taste all the cheeses. I understand they are local."

"Here, try this." He handed her a piece of smooth, hard cheese with holes in it. "It has a nutty taste."

She'd started watching what he ate, taking note of his likes and dislikes. It was time for her to begin acting like a wife and start taking care of their household, such as it was. Perhaps she could find a recipe for the apple strudel. By the end of dinner, she was replete and very tired. All she wanted to do was to climb into bed and sleep.

He stood and came round to her. "Come. You look exhausted."

When she rose, he picked her up and she giggled. "Gervais, do you intend to carry me everywhere?"

"At least until you've regained your strength."

He gazed down at her, and his eyes seemed to change from green to blue.

"Besides, I like having you in my arms."

She held on tighter. "I enjoy it as well. Will you ring for Nugent?"

"No, I'll attend you." His deep voice caressed her. "Unless you have an objection?"

Caro's heart fluttered. "No, you may do it. Though I think, this time, we should keep track of my hairpins."

"I'll have to buy you more," her husband said, chagrined.

Caro tried to hide it, but in the short distance from their parlor to the bedchamber, she'd yawned twice, and fought to keep her eyes open.

His chest rumbled as he quietly chuckled. "You, my lady, need to sleep."

Her brows drew together. That meant no more love making. "No, I'll be fine. I can sleep later."

Setting her down on a stool, he propped her up against his legs and started to untie her laces. "Later?"

"Yes." She swayed, and he caught her. "After we—we . . ."

Placing his lips close to her ear, he murmured, "Make love?"

Caro fought sleep as her breathing deepened. "Yes, after that."

"What if I promise to wake you up for it?" he asked.

Her gown and stays loosened. Gervais stood her up before pushing those garments, along with her chemise, down over her hips. "Very well. You won't make me wait too long, will you?"

He lifted her out of her clothes and threw the bed-cover back. "It will seem like a very short time," Gervais said as he laid her on the bed. "Sleep now, my darling."

Caro let the words of endearment wrap around her. She truly was falling in love with him, but did he feel the same way? She couldn't bear it if he didn't return her affections.

Huntley gazed down at his wife's slumbering form. He wished he knew how long it would take for her to come to love him. He stripped and climbed in next to her. She made soft noises of satisfaction as he drew her near. Holding her close, he cupped one bare breast and buried his face in her hair. *Oh, damn!* He'd forgotten to take down her hair. Careful not to wake her, he drew out all the pins and set them on the table next to the bed. Combing out the long tendrils with his fingers, he wished she would always leave it down.

The style she wore was flattering and very fashionable, but the idea of touching her curls whenever he wanted to appealed to him. He stopped. It would probably tempt other men as well. He wrapped a tendril around his fist. No, better she should have it up when they were out. He cupped her breast again. Perhaps he would buy her a fichu to cover more of her very fine bosom. In fact, he really needed to pay more attention to her gowns. Why had he never thought of all this before? Strange dreams of him whisking Caro away from lecherous men staring at her breasts and hair troubled him before he fell into a deep sleep.

Huntley awoke as he was protecting her, yet again, from some loose fish. After reassuring himself Caro was next to him, sleeping peacefully, he rubbed a hand over his face. His friend, Robert Beaumont, was right. Being in love was a damned uncomfortable feeling. How did his friends manage it? Well, maybe it was different for them. Except for Anna Rutherford, all his friends' wives were older or had more experience than Caro—and Anna was well able to take care of herself.

But his Caro was fragile, and he needed to protect her. The curve of her jaw drew his lips to her slender neck, and his groin stirred as he kissed and nibbled his way to her breasts.

She turned into him and sighed. That was all the encouragement his shaft needed. Moving over her, he sucked her breasts. Caro's sighs turned to moans as his fingers dipped into her hot, wet sheath. "Gervais."

"Yes, my love."

"I want you."

As slowly as he could, he filled her and withdrew, wanting to show her how much she meant to him. She wrapped her legs around him and arched up, trying to hurry him. He entered her again and used long, slow strokes to increase her tension. Soon she was writhing beneath him and cried out. Not until then did he find his own release. Collapsing to her side, he held her tightly to him. If only he could tell her he loved her, all would be well.

Later, Caro awoke to find her breasts already swollen and her nipples hard. An ache that started between her legs swirled up and tightened. His lips were everywhere, pleasuring her, and the slow thrusting made her cry out. Holding on to him with her arms and legs, she tried to make him go faster.

Fire lanced through her and the flames engulfed her body. She shook and convulsed around him, and he was deeper than he'd been before. Gervais held her close as he thrust one last time and emptied himself into her.

She didn't know who clung to whom; the beats of their hearts thumped together. Her head was buried in his neck as his was in hers. Caro thought she heard him tell her he loved her, but it was so faint, it must have been her imagination. If he would just love her, life would be perfect.

When she awoke again, the room was light. Gervais snored softly next to her. Reaching out, she touched his chest and ran her fingers through the soft brown hair. The flat disks of his nipples hardened under her touch. What would he do if she touched them with her tongue as he did to her? Choosing the one closest to her, she gave it a small lick. He tasted pleasantly of musk and salt.

When she touched it again, he groaned, and his hand covered her bottom, sending sparks through her. Applying herself more fully to the one nipple, she lightly pinched the other. This time, he lifted her so that she was on top of him.

Caro's legs fell onto either side of his body as she straddled him and gazed into his eyes. "Didn't you like it?"

"I liked it very much. This way you have access to both, if you choose."

His eyes were greener this morning and, for the first time, she noticed stubble on his face.

"In fact"—he grinned—"I'm yours to explore."

Lowering her lashes, she smiled. "Hmm, that sounds like a fascinating invitation."

She pushed herself down toward his legs until something soft rode up against her derrière.

Reaching behind, she touched it, surprised that anything on Huntley could be so soft.

His voice was a low rumble. "If you keep playing with that, your explorations will be much shorter."

While she was trying to decide which of her options to choose, Maufe called through the door.

"My lord, there is a matter with one of the carriages that needs to be settled if we are to leave soon."

Gervais flopped his head back onto the pillows. "Devil take them."

Disappointed but determined not to show it, she said, "We have this afternoon and this evening."

A wicked gleam came into his eyes. "If you don't mind taking me hard and fast, we also have this morning."

Suddenly she was on her back, and he loomed over her.

Her voice squeaked. "If I do mind?"

"Then we have this afternoon and this evening."

He lowered himself so that his chest barely touched her breasts. The now welcome ache started between her legs. His hard shaft rode near the apex of her thighs. His muscles stood out, tensed. For a moment she'd been afraid, but he waited, and her dread subsided. It was her decision to make. "Show me hard and fast."

"My lord," Collins asked, "are you listening to me?"

Huntley jerked his head up and brought his mind back from the vision of Caro's sultry smile as she'd welcomed him into her earlier.

He brought his attention back to the coach. "Yes, the wheel. It has a slight crack and needs to be replaced."

"As I was saying," his groom continued, "we must get it taken care of before we leave, and they're going to charge us extra to get it done in time."

"Then do it," Huntley said. "Just don't let them rob us."

"No, my lord." Collins raised his brows. "But if we need to find you to-day?"

"I'm taking her ladyship to see the sights," Huntley replied. "We'll be back by dinner. Pay what you must. I'm not going to make a mad dash to Ulm, and we need to be on our way."

His groom nodded. "Yes, my lord."

Huntley had bought larger, heavier horses for the trip through the Alps. "You're happy with the horses?"

"I am," Collins said. "They're what we need right now."

"Good. Is there anything else?"

"No, my lord."

His groom had his hands stuck in his pockets and was looking down at the ground.

Now what was going on? "Out with it."

"Well, my lord, it's just that I've met a woman, and I'd like to marry her and have her come with us."

"You decided this all in a week?" he asked, amazed.

A flush infused his groom's face, and Collins scratched his head. "Not exactly. You remember we came through here on our way to Italy?"

Aha, this was making more sense. "I take it you met her then?"

"Yes, my lord, I did."

"I'm the last person to stand in the way of your joy. How soon can you be married?" He could not very well object to any of his servants wanting the same happiness he hoped to find with Caro.

His groom's weathered face cracked a smile. "We can slip the noose this afternoon. If it wouldn't be too much trouble, we'd like you to be there."

"Very well, I still need to bathe and change. Send word where and when, and her ladyship and I will be there. Order a parlor for a celebration." Collins had been with Huntley since he'd sat his first pony. They would celebrate his groom's wedding properly.

"No need to do that, my lord. Her family has a tavern with a back room."

A tavern wench? Huntley raised a brow, and Collins hurried to reassure him. "It's respectable, what they call a *Gasthaus*. As is her family. I wouldn't marry no light skirt. My mam wouldn't be happy if I did."

"Very well."

Huntley turned to go, but his groom said, "She was in service when she was younger."

He stopped and took a moment to curb his impatience to be off. This was his last day in Innsbruck with Caro. "I'm sure we'll find a position for her." He softened his tone. "She'll be made welcome. You know she will."

Collins's lips tilted up, and he looked relieved. "Thank you, my lord. That's what I told her."

"I shall speak to her ladyship before we go out." Huntley strode out of the carriage yard and through the back of the hotel, taking the stairs two at a time. They should have done their sightseeing yesterday or the day before, but he'd been afraid she was still too weak. He only hoped she could make the trip without suffering. He'd remain in Innsbruck longer, but it was almost the middle of November and the snow wouldn't hold off forever.

Caro was having her hair arranged when he entered the room. Her dresser made the finishing touches, bobbed a curtsey, and left.

"We have a wedding to attend sometime to-day and a new member of the staff."

She caught his gaze in the mirror and grinned. "Yes, I'm very happy for Collins. Nugent and Maufe agree we need a maid of all work. Her name is Elsa, though it has been decided she will be addressed as Mrs. Collins. She was in service with an aristocratic family here in Innsbruck. The wedding is at two o'clock at the Kapuzinerkirche. We'll travel by carriage."

She stunned him. This was the first time she'd had a household issue to deal with, and she'd mastered it. Though why that should surprise him, he didn't know. She was, after all, the daughter of a marquis and practically ran his aunt's household. "Very well. As you have it in hand, I shall wash and change. We have a busy day ahead of us."

Maufe was waiting for him with a basin of warm water and his kit for the day laid out. "I take it you've been told about the wedding, my lord?"

He cut a glance at his valet. "Yes. I wish I'd had some warning."

"I did offer to tell you, but Collins was insistent that he be the one."

Huntley rubbed his hand along his jaw. "Maufe, I do not like being the last person to know what is going on in my household. If anything like this happens again, I expect to be forewarned."

Maufe flushed. "Yes, my lord. I should have given you a hint."

"Knowing what you did, you should also have had my bath ready and seen me dressed before I saw Collins." Huntley washed and held out his hand for the razor. "I wanted to have an easy day for her ladyship, and now we shall be rushed."

His valet remained silent.

"Don't let it happen again."

"No, my lord."

When he finished shaving, he tied his cravat and Maufe helped him with his jacket. "What time do we have to return in order to be at the wedding on time?"

"One o'clock. My lord, her ladyship has a list of the sights she would like to see, and I've made arrangements for two of the chocolate tortes to be delivered."

Huntley heaved a sigh. "Good work. Thank you."

His valet still looked aggrieved.

"What is it, Maufe?"

"It is only eight o'clock, my lord."

Taking out his watch, Huntley checked it. He hadn't been paying any attention to the time. "By God, you're right. I had it as at least past nine. I must have been up earlier than I knew. We won't be as rushed as I thought."

Maufe sniffed. "No, my lord."

Huntley glanced at the ceiling. "I should not have snapped at you, but I want this day to be a good one for her ladyship. She is finally on the mend, though I am concerned the travel may be too much."

"Yes, my lord," his valet said, "I understand. I should have given you some warning about the wedding, and we will all help her ladyship."

Huntley joined his wife at the breakfast table. Caro was such a wealth of information concerning their new staff member that he finally said, "It's almost as if you've met her."

She swallowed her yogurt. "I have. While you were with Collins, I was with Elsa. Though my German is passable, her English is excellent. Her father is not happy about the match, but her mother is thrilled." Caro took a piece of a roll and popped it in her mouth. Once she'd swallowed, she continued. "And she's thirty. Her mother despaired of her finding a husband."

He took the cup of coffee she handed him. "Why did she leave her position?"

Caro tensed. "A gentleman guest attempted to take advantage of her. When she told her mistress and the woman did nothing, Elsa resigned. She received an excellent reference and returned home."

"Good for her," he said approvingly. "I take it that you believe she'll be an asset to our household?"

Smiling, his wife replied, "Yes. I have several ideas I'm mulling around."

"If you wish to discuss them with me," he said, "I'll be happy to listen, but I have no intention of interfering. The household is yours to run."

Caro chuckled. "Such a large one as we have."

He wouldn't mention returning to England yet. "We will eventually stop traveling."

Her countenance became serious. "We have decisions to make, don't we?"

Standing, he came around the table and took her in his arms. "Yes, and we'll make them together."

She tilted her head up and suddenly looked much younger than her two and twenty years. Her voice wobbled a little. "Will we?"

"Yes, we will." If there was one lesson he'd learned from his friends' marriages, it was to form a partnership with one's wife. He was used to ordering things as he wished, but it was more important to do what he needed to keep Caro happy and in his life.

Caro's list of places to see was shorter than he'd thought it would be. The Golden Roof was the first sight she wanted to visit, followed by an arch, the city tower, and the cathedral. She sighed for what she thought was the last time over the chocolate torte at Café Munding. He didn't tell her two of them were coming with them. That would be a surprise. They returned to the hotel for luncheon, and afterwards, an open carriage ride took them along the river.

She held his hand and snuggled into her new fur cloak. "Elsa's brother is a priest at the church. He is happy she's marrying, as well."

Grinning, Huntley replied, "It seems to me that they are all extraordinarily happy to send her away."

"Well," she explained, "Elsa and Collins have been corresponding since you came through this past summer."

He glanced down at her. "Have they? It's amazing the things I don't know about my own servants. Is there anything else I should be made aware of?"

Her eyes twinkled with mirth. "It's early days yet, but I think Nugent and Maufe may be becoming close. They went out together and shopped for our wedding present to Collins and Elsa."

Huntley put his arm around her. "Do I dare ask what it is?"

"A mantel clock for their new home, when they have one," Caro said shyly. "And I do think you should give Collins a raise."

"As you say, my lady," Huntley agreed. "I'm happy to see that I've married an astute woman."

She cuddled next to him until the carriage turned back into town.

Perhaps Collins's marriage was fortuitous, Huntley thought. It seemed to spur Caro's desire to take charge of the household duties. Maybe now they could begin forming the partnership he wanted with her.

They arrived at the church, which was a small, half-timbered building with the door opening straight onto the pavement. The nuptial ceremony was shorter than the full mass he'd expected. Due to their early departure the following morning, the festivities lasted only a few hours.

The new Mrs. Collins was very pretty and plump with a cheerful countenance. What most gentlemen would call an armful. As was his experience with most plump, cheerful women, Huntley could tell she was a force to be reckoned with. While she directed everyone around her, the normally taciturn Collins towered over her with a smile that seemed permanently affixed to his face.

Huntley and Caro exchanged glances.

He placed his lips close to her ear. "I can tell who will rule the roost in their house."

A smile tugged the corner of her lips. "I think they'll be very happy. See how Collins looks at Elsa."

After taking their leave of the newly married couple and the bride's parents, Huntley and Caro made their way slowly back to the hotel. He wondered how much she missed having a real wedding of her own. "It was a nice ceremony and party."

She glanced at him. "Yes, it was."

He drew her closer. "Caro, do you wish you'd had a proper wedding?"

Opening her eyes wide, she replied, "I did have a proper wedding."

"You know what I mean," he said. "In a church, with a breakfast afterwards, and our families in attendance."

"It wouldn't have happened," she said firmly. "I am happy now. That is the only thing that matters."

"Is that the truth?" Perhaps she was right; neither of them had wanted to marry. Who knows what would have happened if fate hadn't contrived to throw them together. They were within view of the steps to their hotel when he stopped.

Caro gazed up at him. "Yes, I've never been happier."

Pulling her to him, he kissed her. His throat ached with a depth of emotion he'd never thought he'd feel. None of the other women he'd had ever affected him like this. His life would not be complete until he found a way to make Caro love him.

Chapter 19

Horatia glanced out the coach window as she and her entourage arrived at the Hôtel du Jardin in Salon-de-Provence in mid-afternoon, John was already there. His lips quirked crookedly as he saluted her with a glass of wine. She sighed as he came toward her. As much as she disliked admitting it, she'd missed him yesterday evening and this morning. Without his teasing banter, dinner and breakfast had been boring and the trip almost unbearable. If he'd accompanied them, Horatia imagined the journey would have been punctuated with him trying to converse from horseback or suggesting they stop at one place or another. The wicked man was worming his way into her thoughts and life, and she didn't know how to stop him.

The waiter brought John a bottle of wine and another glass. As the coach rolled to a stop, he stood and strode swiftly toward her. Her breathing quickened as he opened the door and waited. She tried not to smile and failed. "Have you been waiting long?"

He took her hand and helped her from the carriage. "No longer than I expected. I walked around the town and got directions for the major places of interest you might want to visit." He led her to the table and poured a glass of wine. "We have plenty of time before dinner. Our table is reserved and the meal ordered."

Keeping her gaze down, she removed her gloves. "You didn't have to go to so much trouble."

"It was no trouble at all," he replied cavalierly. "Smyth made the arrangements."

She jerked her head up. "Well!"

John grinned.

"Oh! You odious, odious man."

Shrugging, he replied, "I had to say something to get your attention."

Taking her bare hands, he kissed first one then the other, making them tingle and other parts of her yearn to be touched. He lowered his voice. "Horatia, I've missed you. Come, drink wine with me."

"I really should go to my chambers." She shivered slightly and found herself leaning toward him, then sat quickly in the chair he held for her, hoping to hide her reaction.

"Why? Your servants have no need of your supervision. Are you trying to avoid me?"

Opening her mouth, she closed it again. "I'm not sure."

He was embarrassingly astute and direct. What was the matter with her? She'd pined for him all day and now—now his presence made her feel more than she wanted to. Thousands of tiny jolts ran through her. She wanted his arms around her again and his lips on hers.

He smiled broadly. "*That* is the truth." Lifting his glass of wine, he toasted. "*À Santé.*"

She raised her glass to him. "*Et bonne chance.*"

The afternoon sun warmed her back and the cool rosé wine was dry and fruity as it slid over her tongue and down her throat. "This is wonderful. Is it local?"

"Yes." He brought his chair closer to hers so that he was now next to her. "If you look across the road and up the hill, you'll see the vineyard."

Horatia turned in the direction he indicated. "Oh yes. I see it."

He lightly touched the back of her neck. Suppressing a shiver, she turned. Their mouths were so close she almost touched her lips to his. His warm, light peridot eyes captured hers. She drank half her glass of wine in one gulp.

John emptied his, stood, and held out his hand. "Come walk with me. The wine will be here when we return."

When she rose, he tucked her hand in his arm and they strolled around the side of the stucco building, keeping to the flagstone path. Some hardy roses, still in bloom, climbed trellises. High boxwood bushes formed a background for a few late summer annuals, now giving way to chrysanthemums and asters.

He led her down a passage that ended in an arbor next to a tall, weathered stone wall. What was he thinking? "Where are you taking me?"

He grinned but didn't stop. "You'll see in a minute."

She tugged to disengage her arm. He held it tight. "Just a little farther."

When they reached the arbor, he stood in front of her and slid his hands slowly down her arms and back up them again, lighting fires under her skin. Her mouth was suddenly dry. "Where are we? I cannot see anything."

"In the far back corner of the garden. Where we won't be disturbed."

"What do you—"

He covered her lips with his. Oh, she'd missed this. Her mouth opened. His tongue languidly stroked hers as his hands ran freely over her body. When he cupped her aching breasts, she moaned and pressed into his palms.

She'd never been kissed like this. As if he'd devour her. She stepped closer, and John stroked her from the back of her neck down over her derrière, setting her on fire. Horatia tried not to sink into his warmth, but his hard chest beckoned. She gripped his neck and played with his sandy curls. His arousal rode between them. She deliberately rubbed against it. What would it be like to touch him?

He groaned. Finally. Some indication he was as affected as she. She moved one hand down over his buttock, then around to the front of his hard, muscular thigh, inching it higher. Wetness pooled between her legs. She'd never wanted a man so much. Perhaps it was only because it had been so long, so very long.

Three petticoats and a silk twill gown—she may as well have been naked when his palms cupped her bottom. Then his fingers touched the spot already on fire between her legs and stroked. She hung on to him with both arms. Hot streaks coursed through her as she rubbed against his hand, wanting more.

She tried to draw her mind back to think, but as if he knew what she was doing, he deepened the kiss, overwhelming her mouth as his fingers played. A keening sigh escaped her as flames licked her mons and ran up her body. Did he even know what he was doing to her? If he didn't, he'd find out soon enough.

Suddenly, it happened. The shuddering relief she'd not

experienced in so many years coursed through her, causing her to explode. Horatia's arms loosened, and he caught her. She wanted more. If only he'd ruck her skirts up, she would happily sink down onto him and let him fill her. He was as hard as rock. What was the devil waiting for? *Drat. The wager.* He'd lose the wager.

Then she remembered where they were and her face flamed, mortified. He hadn't even been skin to skin with her. She never should have allowed it. She'd known how it would be if he touched her. George always said she was a wanton, and he'd been right.

The next thing she knew, John sat on the arbor bench with her on his lap. "Horatia, my love."

She couldn't face him. Not now.

"Horatia. Look at me." He placed one finger under her chin and tilted her head up. "What's wrong?"

What did it matter what she said to him now? He knew it any way. "I am shameless."

When she tried to hang her head, his finger kept it up. "What put that thought into your head?"

"George said it." She raised her gaze to John's eyes. Desire and humor mixed in their green depths. How humiliating.

"I'll wager he didn't mean it in a bad way."

Tears started in her eyes. "No, probably not, but that doesn't make it any less true."

"You are a passionate woman." John lowered his voice to a soft murmur. "Who has kept it all hidden for years." He kissed her gently. "You're like dry tinder ready to burn."

He shifted her into a more comfortable position but did not release her gaze. "Ask yourself why now and why with me? Why did you never remarry?"

She wished she knew the reason she was so attracted to

John. It might help her resist him. "No gentleman is interested in a woman who is barren. At least not for marriage, and I will be no man's mistress."

John caressed her cheek with the pad of his thumb. "I want to marry you."

If only it was true, but he didn't know her. "You only think you do. You're in love with an image."

He blew out a frustrated breath. "Though I've had to rely on letters from George and from friends who came across you after he died, I've known for years how much more than that portrait you are. You're an intelligent, vibrant woman. I wanted to come to you years sooner, but was unable to leave. Instead, I had to rely on news from friends. I was on my way to find you when we met in Marseille."

Her heart drummed hard and fast, as if it would burst from her chest. Whatever she'd expected him to say, it was not that. "You are serious?"

He grinned a little. "I did tell you."

She rubbed her brow, trying to make sense of it all. When she was young, she believed everyone had one person they were supposed to love. She'd married a man who was kind, and whom she loved but was not in love with. For years she thought that was how it was supposed to be. Yet her feelings for John were different. Was she falling in love? "I don't know what to do. Everything, the flight from Venice, meeting you, it's all happened so quickly."

Beneath her, his muscles clenched, turning him from a fairly comfortable chair into hard wood. "Flight from Venice?"

"Yes, of course." She searched his face. "Did I not tell you? No, I suppose I haven't. My goddaughter was being persecuted by a Venetian marchese . . ."

Sitting up straighter, he fixed her with a curious look. "So that's the reason you have so many servants with you. You're not returning."

She frowned. What did he think? That she traveled with almost twenty servants all the time? How absurd. "Yes. Most of them have been with me since I moved to Venice, some, like De Valle, have been with me since I married, and my dresser since I came out."

John leaned back against the bench, resettling Horatia on his lap. "With all that on your mind, I'm surprised you didn't send me to the right about."

His arms held her nestled against him. Well, that was an unfair remark. "If you will recall," she retorted tartly, "I did try." She glanced up from under her lashes. "You just wouldn't go." She tried to sit up straight, but he held her where she was. "So you see now, I have a great many responsibilities I cannot ignore."

John was quiet for a few moments as he stroked her back. Probably trying to figure out a graceful way to leave her, all her dependents, and her problems. What was she doing sitting on his lap?

She struggled again to get up but was defeated by his arm clamping around her waist.

"Give me a moment."

A moment for what, pray? "If you wish to leave," she said with as much dignity as she could muster under the circumstances, "I'll understand."

"No." He glowered, radiating anger.

Well, what had he to be upset about? She was the one who'd made a fool of herself.

"I do not wish to leave." He nuzzled her neck. "I'm trying to think how we can make it all work."

A minute or so later, he said, "I have a proposal."

Horatia raised a brow. "You've had several already."

"A new one, which will nullify the others."

Well, that was probably a good idea. She knew now she'd have lost the bedding-betrothal wager. As she waited for him to continue, the scent of the roses floated through her senses. What a beautiful place. Flowers and vines everywhere. It did not even seem as late in the season as it was. A tall box-wood hedge helped to screen the rest of the garden from this little alcove.

"I have it."

He sat up so suddenly Horatia tightened her grip on his neck to avoid being tossed off his lap. Where she should not be in the first place. His arm kept her in place.

"Allow me to court you, as we'd agreed in the beginning, but this time I will not demand we spend time together. It will be your choice."

Drat the man. He'd truly trapped her. Now she'd have to admit she wanted to spend time with him. And she'd been having so much fun testing her wits against his. "To what purpose?"

"To put less strain on you." His fingers made patterns on her back. "Our little game has been fun, but it's not fair for me to add to your burdens when I wish to ease them."

She shouldn't have said anything to him about her troubles. "Yes, well, I suppose we can go on in a companionable fashion."

He shot a concerned glance at her. "You don't sound happy."

Horatia gave a light shrug. "I enjoyed our conversations."

John settled back against the bench again. "We'll still have them, and perhaps more moments like this as well. Will you dine with me this evening, my lady?"

On the other hand, being here was very nice. "Yes, if you'll have a glass of wine with me now."

"My pleasure." He kissed the tender place beneath her ear.

A shiver of desire coursed through her. Perhaps a more regular courtship wouldn't be so boring after all, especially if he would allow her in his bed.

After easing her off him, he placed her hand on his arm and led her out of the arbor.

John sensed the small quiver running down her neck as he kissed it. He should've found her sooner. But from all he'd heard, she had been living a safe, quiet life in Venice. Sooner rather than later, he'd have to tell her about both his title and the possibility that she might be able to become pregnant. If he waited too long, she'd think he'd deceived her. Or perhaps he could simply tell her about the earldom and leave the other to chance. After all, he wasn't positive she could bear a child, only that George couldn't get one on a woman.

John and Horatia ambled around the garden on their way back to the table.

After they finished the wine, there was still time to stroll around the small town and view the sections of the city wall that still remained.

Later that afternoon, they stood on the ramparts of the city wall looking over the rolling hills of the countryside. Some of the fields were still green, others yellow or purple. She told him about the route she planned to Nancy.

He took her hand and kissed it. "How long would you like to stop in Avignon?"

"Three days or so. Time to rest and enjoy what the city has to offer. I've never traveled in France, you know."

He turned to face her. The green of her eyes made the fields look sallow. "Yes, it would have been too dangerous in '96."

Horatia nodded. "All of Northern Italy was unsafe then.

We sailed to Greece, and eventually made our way up from Naples."

Leaning against the rough stone of the parapet, he ran a finger along her jaw. Horatia sucked in a breath.

"Do you ever think," he asked, "about going back to England?"

She raised her gaze to his briefly, then stared out over the landscape. "I might have gone back after George died, but my father already had another match in mind. Even though I was independent, he would have made life difficult."

"I can see how the idea would not have been welcome." Just the idea of her with another man made John's muscles tense. The primitive beast lurking just below the surface pushed John to make Horatia his as soon as possible. He'd make sure no other man would ever possess her.

She gave a small smile. "I was very lucky in my marriage. Now I've been away from England for so long, returning would seem very strange. Then again, I do not know if I shall ever return to Venice. I may need to find a new home."

He held his breath and said a short prayer. "If you had a reason, would you live in England?"

She lightly shrugged one shoulder. "If there was a need. Though first, I must ensure my nephew and goddaughter are well and happy." Horatia glanced at John. "And wherever I make my home, my dependents must have a place as well."

His arm circled her waist. "I do understand how important that is. I did my best to place my crew with other captains."

She nodded and glanced around. "We should go back before it becomes too dark."

The sun hung low in the sky, a bright ball before it sank. Pink and lavender clouds stretched out across the horizon.

"Yes."

As they walked to the steps, Horatia asked, "Do you miss being on your ship?"

John steadied her over the rough ground as they descended. "At times I do. I miss the freedom of being able to haul anchor and change my harbor." He placed his hand over hers. "But right now? No. I'm exactly where I want to be."

She tucked her hand in his arm, leaning on him a little. "Later what will you do? Do you wish to go home?"

John glanced down at her, but all he could see was her hat. "I want to make a home."

One with her, whether or not she could bear children. George had been correct. Horatia was the right woman for him, and John would convince her that he was the right man for her.

Horatia stepped into her chamber. John had been so evasive about what his future plans were, it caused a memory to stir in her mind. "Risher, how much time do I have before I must change for dinner?"

"Not long, my lady. Why?"

"After I go down, look for the letters from my sister and Lady Watford. I've a recollection of something nagging at me."

"I think I know where they are," Risher said. "They'll be waiting for you when you get back."

"Thank you. What would I do without you?" Horatia untied her hat and placed it back in the box.

"With the good Lord's help, my lady, you won't have to worry about it for a long time."

Horatia turned to her maid and gave a small smile. "I shall depend on that."

Her dresser motioned for her to turn around. "Have you decided where we're all going to live?"

Risher untied the laces of Horatia's gown, and she stepped out of it. "Not yet. Bear with me for a while."

After donning her wrapper, she splashed her face with water and dried it, then sat at the dressing table. "First there is a mystery I must figure out."

"About the captain?"

"Indeed. He's being very cagey when it comes to answering questions regarding his family. I think he is withholding information."

Risher's hands stilled.

"Nothing so bad, mind you. I feel as if he may not have told me everything about who he is." Horatia met her maid's gaze in the mirror. "Think of it as an adventure. Like the ones we used to have."

Narrowing her eyes, Risher replied dryly, "If I remember correctly, my lady, *you* were the one having the adventures, and I was wringing my hands."

Horatia raised a brow. "Are you going to tell me you did not have fun distracting the head groom when I took my father's carriage?"

Risher's face turned bright red. "That was a long, long time ago, my lady," she said repressively. "And I did not have any joy at all trying to cover for you when you sneaked off to Vauxhall. Thankfully, I've never done anything like it since."

"Yes, well, neither have I, really." Horatia lowered her lashes and grinned. "It's sad how staid we've become in our old age."

"When you have us running off across the Continent?" her dresser asked in shocked tones. "There's nothing abstemious about us at all."

Horatia sobered. "That is an adventure I could have done without. I hate not knowing what is happening with Caro and Huntley. I hope di Venier did not find them and they haven't killed each other."

"Mayhap we'll have a letter when we reach Nancy."

Risher deftly twisted Horatia's hair up into a knot, teasing curls out to dangle on her neck and over one shoulder.

"Do you think I should start wearing a cap?"

"I suppose most people would say you should," her dresser said thoughtfully, then perked up. "But when did you ever care about that?"

"Never." Horatia gave her head an emphatic nod. "And I hope I never shall. Have you been able to get any information from Mr. Smyth?"

"No, my lady. Although I was not given a set down, he made it very clear that he does not gossip about his employer."

When Horatia opened the door, John was waiting in the corridor.

"You should have knocked."

He took her hand and pressed a kiss to the inside of her wrist. "There was no need. You're always punctual."

While they dined in the courtyard terrace, she asked him about his childhood and why he left England.

"We younger sons," he said, "must make our own way in the world. I was fortunate enough to be able to take advantage of the opportunities offered me. In other words"—he grinned ruefully—"I was not penniless."

Horatia raised her glass of wine to the candlelight and twirled. "Neither am I."

He stiffened as if she'd hit him. "Your wealth shall remain your own. I have no need of it."

That was interesting. A sore spot with him. She wondered which heiress he was accused of trying to win.

"Did you make your fortune?" She studied him as he considered her question.

"Yes. I made more than enough to have a home and support a wife in some elegance." He took a sip of wine. "Am I being evaluated, my lady?"

"Yes. Would you expect anything else?" Horatia refused to be embarrassed or cowed. If she was seriously considering him as a husband, she should ask these questions. After all, she had no one to inquire on her behalf.

His lids lowered a little as he regarded her. She kept her gaze on him, waiting for his response.

After a few moments, he smiled and the dimple appeared. "Not only would I expect nothing less, I need a *savvy* woman to accomplish what I want to do."

He helped her rise then blew out the candles, leaving them in relative darkness. "Look at the stars." He waited until she glanced up. "Do you know which ones are which?"

She bit her lip. "No."

He stood behind her, his warmth seeping into her, causing her senses to come alive.

"Someday, I'd like to tell you about them."

Horatia turned into him and tilted her head back. "Maybe someday you shall."

John placed a brief kiss on her lips. "We're not alone."

She blinked. They'd rented the entire hotel, but the restaurant was open and there were other customers. "No." *Unfortunately.*

When they reached her bedchamber door, John drew her close. "Now, my lady." Bending his head, he slowly laid siege to her lips, nibbling and caressing. Heat, need, and desire rose in her again. Her toes even started to curl. Then he lifted his head. She sighed. It was the best kiss he'd given her so far. If he hadn't stopped, well . . . Drat, she wanted him.

His voice was deep and soothing. "Shall I see you at breakfast?"

"It would be my pleasure."

When she entered her chamber, her dresser had the letters on the desk. Horatia untied the ribbon holding her sister's letters and looked through them as Risher took down Horatia's hair. Finally, she found the one she'd remembered from Huntley's mother.

> *The 16th of June in the Year of Our Lord 1815*
> *My Dearest Sister,*
> *Thank heavens the Season is at an end. I am happy to report that your oldest niece has had the good sense to . . .*

Horatia skipped down to another paragraph.

> *In other news, the Earl of Devon finally managed to get himself killed. At his age he should have known better than to engage in a carriage race. But after all, the Whittons, if you remember, are reckless wastrels. I am amazed there is anything left of the estate . . .*

Horatia pulled the bow loose from the second stack of letters and found Adele Watford's letter dated around the same time.

> *My Dearest Friend,*
> *If Watford will not allow me to visit you next year, I plan to run away. I so wish to see your Venice . . . The biggest news of the season, other than Miss E convincing the D of F to marry her, is the death of the Earl of Devon. Carlotta, C of D, is one of my dearest*

friends. And although you have not met, you would love her. Thankfully, she and her daughters are well taken care of, for her husband left only debts. Nothing, of course, can be settled until the younger brother can be found. He left years ago and has not returned to England since. I don't suppose you have run into a John Whitton during your travels? Now I am being silly. One other matter . . .

Hmm, that is what he's hiding. John Whitton is the new Earl of Devon. But why would he not want her to know? Horatia tapped her chin. Was it only his family's reputation he was trying to bury?

Chapter 20

Austria, traveling from Innsbruck to the Fernpass

Caro and Gervais's small household left the comfort of Innsbruck as the sun crept up from the river valley. She agreed with him that they needed to leave early and get as close to the Fernpass as possible, but when he kissed her awake, she'd done her best to keep them in the warm bed.

"Caro, my sweet, we must break our fast and start out."

She cracked an eye and stared at him. One rich brown lock fell over his forehead, making him utterly irresistible. Stirrings of her own arousal snaked up and she breathed in his musky scent as she pressed closer to him. Even to herself, her voice was low and sultry. "Make love to me."

He raised a brow, but his lips tilted up at the corners. "We made love twice last night." One large hand caressed her derrière and the place between her legs throbbed in earnest. He kissed her behind her ear. "You won't have time to bathe."

"I don't care." Keeping her gaze on his, Caro did what she'd never done before and reached down to purposely touch him. How hard and soft it was at the same time. Fascinating. Even the skin over his buttocks wasn't this soft. His shaft grew and twitched. When Gervais sucked in a ragged breath, she smiled. For the first time she understood the power she had over him.

His eyes warmed with desire as he covered her, spreading her willing legs apart. "What has got into you?"

Caro tilted her hips toward him. "You. Will you take what I am offering, my lord?"

His deep voice caressed her. "Always, my lady."

Gervais's large body descended just enough to bring her breasts in contact with his chest. Kissing the spot where her neck and shoulder joined, he filled her so slowly that she pressed down on him with her feet, trying to make him go faster. When he was deep within her, she sighed. He withdrew and repeated his excruciatingly slow invasion.

"Gervais, please, you're torturing me." Faster, she needed him to go faster. Gripping his waist tighter, she tried to gain leverage and thrust her hips up to meet him.

He chuckled wickedly. "Patience. All things come to those who wait."

The tension rose under his unhurried onslaught until her body convulsed hard and deep around him. Not the fire she was used to, but inexorable waves of pleasure washed over her as he thrust up so far, so deep, they were truly one body. Then the swells carried her out, and with one hard thrust, he sent her flying higher than ever before.

Happiness and fear warred within her. Caro could no longer deny she belonged to him like she never had before. Tears pricked her eyes. Somehow, she had to find a way to make him love her. She was positive she loved him, and she needed him to belong to her as well. If only they had the type of marriage that allowed each of them to speak freely.

Collapsing to one side, Huntley rolled Caro on top of his chest. He'd meant only to show her another way to make love, but instead he'd fallen more deeply under her spell than he'd thought possible. It was no bad thing to love one's wife, just as long as she returned his affection. They had one week before they'd arrive in Ulm and then another ten days or so to Nancy. Somehow he needed to find a way to tie her to him permanently. It had been a while since she'd mentioned leaving him. Still, he couldn't be certain she planned to stay.

Caro's soft breathing tickled his ear. He held her just a few moments more. "Sweetheart, unless you wish to winter in Innsbruck, we must go."

Pushing her locks back, she gazed down at him and sighed. "Very well."

He opened the bed hangings. Tightening his grip on her, he rose from the bed, taking her with him. Someone had been in to stoke the fire, and the room was already warm. As he released her, he said, "I'll send Nugent to you and see you at breakfast."

His banyan lay over a chair. After donning it, he went through the door into a dressing room. Maufe had hot water ready.

Other than keeping her in bed, how was Huntley to convince her to love him? He mulled over and rejected ideas for keeping his wife from leaving. His biggest fear was that she'd decide to leave him after she had a child. As he'd done nothing to stop her from getting pregnant, that was a real concern. Why hadn't he insisted she promise to remain before he'd taken her? *Damn*. He was far more adept at keeping a woman's claws out of him than trying to encourage one to hang on. *Ow!* Blood welled from the cut on his face.

Maufe hurried forward with a jar. "Is anything wrong, my lord?"

Too much was wrong. "No, I was just preoccupied." Huntley blotted the blood and applied the basilicum powder his valet handed him. "Thank you."

Perhaps promising to give her what she wanted would be worth a try. Unless, of course, she wanted her freedom. Which was not going to occur. It couldn't. She was his. Every bit of silken skin. Every lock of hair. He was determined to have all of her, body and soul. There must be a way to discover what she desired without asking her. Nugent might be willing to help. No, that wouldn't do. He couldn't suborn Caro's servants for his own needs.

He entered their parlor and caught his breath. Caro was a vision, dressed in a lemon-yellow twill carriage gown. It was made high on her neck and trimmed with lace. Going forward, he took her hand and kissed it. "You are beautiful, my lady."

Her smile of delight was all he could have asked for. "Thank you, my lord. You look very handsome."

He seated her, then joined her at the table. "I'd like to return here someday."

Caro seemed focused on the roll she was buttering and didn't look up. "As would I."

"Perhaps we could . . ." Her gaze flew to his face. Was that fear lurking behind her eyes? *Hell.* He'd spoken too soon. Despite their love making, she wasn't ready to commit to him. Now what was he to say? "We could get the recipe for the rolls. You seem to enjoy them."

Her gaze dropped back down. "Yes. Perhaps." She pulled the pot of jam toward her. "Maybe Elsa will know."

"Yes."

He quickly finished eating and said, "Please excuse me. I'll check on the coaches."

Caro gave him a small, tight smile. "I'll not keep you waiting."

Huntley strode out of the parlor, his hands curled into fists. He wanted to hit the wall or something—better yet, someone. They'd been going along so well together, and he'd made a muddle of it by speaking of their future before she was ready.

He attained the hotel's coach yard and watched, without interest, the preparations for their departure. He'd not approach the subject with her again until she gave him a clear indication that she wished to speak of it. He scowled. She would not leave him. He couldn't allow it.

"Is everything all right, my lord?"

He glanced up to see Collins, brows furrowed, staring at him. "Yes. Are we almost ready to be on our way?"

"Just waiting on her ladyship and Miss Nugent." He turned his head. "Here they are now."

Huntley walked to Caro and held out his arm. "Allow me."

"Thank you."

Drat all this formality. What he wanted to do was lift her in his arms.

Hot bricks were loaded in the boxes under the floor and the blankets he'd purchased placed on the seats in their coach.

"That should do us. Maufe, do you have her ladyship's hot chocolate?"

"Already packed in the hamper, my lord."

Smiling, Huntley helped Caro up the steps and then climbed in himself. He tucked the blankets around her and retreated to the opposite seat as the coach rolled forward. "Are you warm enough?"

She regarded him for several minutes as the coach made its way over the cobblestone streets. "I'd be warmer if you sat next to me."

After her reaction at breakfast, her request surprised him. "If you are sure you won't be too crowded."

Caro patted the empty place next to her. "No, not at all."

After he switched seats, her hand crept into his.

"Caro?"

"We do not have to speak. If you don't mind, I think I'll sleep a little."

"Let me take your bonnet." If the small wool confection with a feather and netting could be called that. She pulled out the pin and handed it to him. Huntley carefully placed the hat on the opposite seat. "There, rest your head on my shoulder."

Nodding, she did as he suggested. She sniffed a couple of times. He hoped she wasn't sickening again. "Are you feeling well?"

"I'm fine."

She glanced out the window, the buildings she loved barely impinging on her consciousness as she blinked back the tears threatening to fall. All her hopes had dissolved, and the fear that Gervais would never love her pushed to the fore. He'd not wanted to discuss their future. Did that mean he didn't want one for them? She needed his strong, steady presence next to her. Without him, nothing was right anymore. Gervais's arm came around her, and he settled her more comfortably against him. Caro swallowed and sniffed to keep the tears at bay.

What a fix she was in. Years ago, she'd promised herself that she'd never fall in love again, and here she was. Nothing had changed. She was not any wiser now than she'd been at sixteen. Yet he was so kind and attentive to her. He always saw to her needs. Perhaps she could live with him even if he didn't love her. If she did not become greedy, her life could be good. No decision had to be made now.

By the time Caro awoke, they were already climbing into the mountains. This was so much different than the road to the Brenner Pass. Here the hills rose up more sharply. Snow-topped crests towered over them. At least this leg of their journey was not so hurried. Since they decided not to change their horses, they'd make longer stops. She straightened. "Where are we?"

He kissed the top of her head. "Not far from Telfs, our first resting place. Did you sleep well?"

"Yes, thank you." She always slept well in his arms. Perhaps if she told him, it would make a difference, but there was always the chance he'd reject her for wanting more than he could give. He'd been quite popular with certain ladies in Venice, but they were all fleeting affairs that he'd ended. Was he not capable of deeper feelings? Or perhaps he showed them by taking care of her.

When she moved to stretch a little, his arm dropped and the warmth seeped out of her. "Would you like to dine in the common room again?" he asked.

In an attempt to encourage Gervais to hold her again, Caro snuggled into him. "I'd love it. The last time was so interesting and it is not something I'll be able to do a lot."

His arm went obediently around her shoulders, and she gave a small sigh. How long had they calculated it would take to reach Nancy? With any luck at all, she'd find a way to make him fall in love with her.

Not more than fifteen minutes later, they turned off the road into the yard of a busy inn. Gervais jumped down and waited while Caro stood in the door, gazing up. The inn was three stories. The ground floor was whitewashed, but the first and second floors were of timber, giving it a cozy feel. Greens and winter heather, *Erica carnea*, filled the window boxes. "Very pretty. I wonder what the inside looks like."

Holding his arm out, he replied, "Shall we see?"

"Yes." She placed her hand on his sleeve and stepped down.

He bent his head to hers and spoke softly. "If you don't like it, tell me and I'll arrange a private parlor."

What she wanted when he spoke in that tone was a private room. "I am sure it will be fine. How long do we pause?"

"About an hour."

Maufe was in the hall when they entered. "My lord, I did not know if you wanted a parlor or if her ladyship would like to visit the common room. It is busy but clean, and the patrons look respectable."

She was able to glance into the room in question. Though the ceiling was not particularly high, the room was bright, with benches placed below the windows lining two walls. "The common room, if you please, Maufe."

"Yes, my lady."

A serving girl came with a large mug for Gervais and a smaller one filled with warm spiced wine for Caro. The other servants sat at a table not far away. Caro inclined her head at Maufe. "Thank you again, Maufe. You may go eat as well."

Although no one stared, the other guests stole surreptitious glances at her and Gervais. After she removed her gloves, he took her hand and kissed it. Deep voices snickered and more than one feminine voice could be heard shushing them.

He grinned. "I think some of the men here will get an earful from their women."

This was the perfect time to start telling him how much she loved him. "And so the women should. You are a perfect example of how a husband should behave."

His head swung from his contemplation of the room to her. A blush rose in her cheeks.

"Is that the way you really feel?"

Lifting her chin, she managed a small grin. "Yes, of course. Else I would not have said it."

He leaned so close she thought he'd kiss her, but he merely tucked a curl behind her ear. Even that small touch caused her heart to flutter. When he didn't draw back, she stilled, waiting, as he searched her face. Then two pans were set on the table and the moment was over. Caro was sure he'd been about to say something to the purpose. Well . . . *drat*.

He picked up a fork and dug into a dish of sliced potatoes with fried eggs. "Shall we eat?"

"What is that?"

"It's called *Gröstel*. I had it the last time. Very flavorful." He pointed to the small skillet in front of her. "That is *Kasnocken*. Small dumplings with cheese and onions. It's quite good. Try it first and then, if you wish, you may have some of the *Gröstel*."

She picked up her fork and took a bite. The tang of fried onions contrasted nicely with the nuttiness of the cheese. The noodles were softer than Italian pasta, and the cheese clung to them, infusing the noodles with flavor. This was so good. After she'd finished more than half of hers, Caro glanced longingly over to his. "May I taste some of that now?"

He speared some of it onto a fork and held it out to her. She closed her lips around it. The smoky flavor of streaky bacon mixed with fried egg and onions filled her senses as she chewed. She sighed. Not as good as the chocolate torte, but delightful all the same. "Wonderful."

A smile pulled at his lips. "If I feed this to you, which I'm of half a mind to do, I'll have every other husband here in trouble."

Her eyes opened wide. "What do you mean?"

"Don't look, but we're the center of attention."

She grinned as wickedly as she felt. "What if you fed me just one more bite?"

"You, my lady, are a hoyden," he responded severely, but his lips tilted up and he held the fork out to her.

"I have never been called that before. I was actually a very dutiful daughter," she said in her primmest voice.

Had she ever been so bold? No, not even when she was younger. While she chewed, she stole a sidelong glance at the room and was not surprised to see wives with their eyes narrowed at their mates, mayhap wanting attention from them that she received from Gervais. Even if he didn't love her, he was still a very good husband.

"It must be Horatia's influence," Gervais said. "From what I've heard, she was anything but dutiful."

"No. Even the milder stories I've heard put me to the blush."

He studied her for only a moment, and Caro wished she could read his thoughts.

He glanced around. "The others are finishing up. We must leave soon."

He wiped his lips with the serviette. Oh, what those lips had done to her as they trailed kisses down her body. But not in the common room. They'd already caused enough trouble. Placing her serviette on the table, she turned to him. "I'm full."

Pulling the *Kasnocken* pan toward him, he ate the rest of it. "Shall we go?"

Several men glared at him as they left the room. Gervais's countenance showed nothing, but a telltale twitch in his jaw made her realize how hard-pressed he was to keep from laughing. Those men would have a difficult time, for a few days at least.

He had to be in love with her, but how to tell for sure when he wouldn't say it?

Six days later, they settled into their hotel in Ulm, once a free city, now part of the Kingdom of Württemberg. The city walls were a shambles from the sieges during the war, and an air of depression hung over the city. From their bedchamber windows, she could see the rubble.

Over the course of the week they'd been traveling, Caro had taken on the responsibilities of Gervais's wife, as much as she could under the circumstances, conferring with Maufe over their lodgings and breakfast. Gervais still insisted on selecting their evening meal, choosing dishes he thought she'd enjoy, and finding chocolate for her. She'd never been so well cared for.

Taking her in his arms, he asked, "How long do you wish to remain here?"

Caro stretched up against him and planted a kiss on his lips. "Two nights, if that is enough time to arrange the new horses. I've never before been in a city so damaged by the war. It's sad."

"I'll inquire about a new team this evening." Holding him tight to her, she breathed in his musky male scent. He used no colognes or other scents. He bent his head and teased her lips open to him. When she pressed herself full length to him, he pulled out the first hairpin. "Gervais?"

"Um?" He placed more hairpins on the table.

Perhaps now was the time to tell him she loved him. "There is something I want to say to you."

Sharp voices raised in anger rent the relative quiet. His head jerked toward the window. "Wait a minute."

He strode over then leaned out. Soon the voices stopped. "What was it?" she asked.

"An altercation," he responded. "It's fine. None of my people were involved." He turned back to her and took her in his arms again. "Now, what is it, my dear?"

After everything they'd gone through, she couldn't believe he still thought in terms of his servants and not theirs. Obviously, this was not the time to open her heart to him. She lowered her lids. "It was nothing. Kiss me."

Antonio held his sobbing son in his arms. An ache spread over his chest as his heart broke in two. "Don't cry, Geno. Your servants, Cappi and Donato, will be with you. If anyone mistreats you, they will bring you back."

Geno shook his head back and forth. "Papa, I don't want to go!"

Holding his son tighter, Antonio kissed his forehead. "The duke will not change his mind. We must accept his decision. You will come for a visit after Christmas and in summer. Now you must go."

His grandfather was right. Geno should take his rightful place, no matter how much it hurt to let his son go. Antonio had wanted to make the trip with his son, but Nonno would not allow it. Other than burying Geno's mother, this was the hardest thing Antonio had ever done. Damn her family for marrying her to the baron when she had Antonio's child in her belly.

He handed his son to Cappi. "Take good care of him."

"Yes, milord."

Turning away as the servant carried Geno off, Antonio tried to stop the tears from coming. He needed something to take his mind off losing his son. "Have you received word of where Lady Caroline is?"

His *maggiordomo* sighed. "No, milord. The man was unable to find her. However, he does know where Lady Horatia is. She is traveling north from Marseille. He thinks Lady Horatia will meet with her goddaughter."

"I agree," Antonio said. "I will leave in two days' time. Tell the man to expect me."

"*Sì*, milord. Everything shall be ready."

If Antonio couldn't have his son, he'd have Lady Caroline. It was too much to expect him to give up both. Once his grandfather saw how much she would love Antonio, Nonno would relent and let Antonio keep her.

Chapter 21

After her discovery last evening that John was the new Earl of Devon, Horatia needed a plan to ferret out what the man was up to. Why would he want a wife who could not bear him children? It did not make sense. Unless—her heart thudded, making her breathless—he truly *was* in love with her. She hadn't believed him before, but now . . . She dropped to the chair. No gentleman had ever been *in love* with her. George certainly hadn't been. Oh, he'd loved her, but he was never *in love* with her. She'd never been in love, not even in her salad days when her friends were falling in love with dancing masters and other unsuitable men. Yet what did it mean that John so fascinated her, she engaged in madcap wagers with him? Even George had not encouraged her wilder side, at least not outside of the bedchamber.

Still, John needed an heir. She could not allow him to make such a sacrifice, even if he did not see it as one.

Horatia tapped one finger against her chin. After what happened between them, John would not believe she had no attraction to him. If she continued to turn him down, he was just the type of man to see it as a challenge. Never a good thing.

When did he plan to tell her about the earldom? Surely he wouldn't wait until after the marriage. She shook her head. After the betrothal. Yes, that was it. After she agreed to marry him, and he told her, she could begin making him understand she was not the right type of wife for him. And since they'd be engaged to be married, she could indulge, just a little. A few kisses, some touches. No. There was no reason at all she couldn't bed the man.

Rising, Horatia rang for Risher. "I am going down to breakfast now and may not return for a while. Take the morning, if you like, and see some of the city."

"Thank you, my lady. Mr. Whitton is waiting in the corridor for you. He said for you to take your time."

John was leaning against the wall, looking impossibly handsome in a coat of dark brown, white shirt, and tight buff pantaloons. Oh, Lord, his legs had never appeared more to the advantage. So strong, so muscular. The bulge of his member appeared to grow larger. Repressing a shiver of delight, she licked her lips. A temporary betrothal would do nicely.

He straightened and smiled, making the dimple appear. Horatia stifled a sigh. "Good morning."

"Good morning, my love." He offered his arm. "Breakfast is on the terrace."

"I'm glad the weather is still so pleasant. I imagine it will grow cooler as we travel farther north."

When they reached a small table set for two, he seated her and took the place opposite, signaling to a waiter, who brought a large tray laden with tea and coffee-pots, breads, jams, meats, and cheeses.

"We'll have to make sure all the hotels we stay at have a good common dining area, so we may continue to take our meals together."

Horatia broke off a piece of the croissant. "Ah yes. The proprieties."

John studied her, and she wondered if she was doing anything to give herself and her idea away. He was extremely astute when it came to countering her.

But he merely asked, "What do you wish to do to-day?"

Horatia swallowed and endeavored to keep her tone even. If he suspected her subterfuge, he'd be very angry. "I would like to tour the city and decide which sights I wish to visit in the morning." Taking a sip of the tea, she gazed at him over the rim of her cup. There was one sight she definitely planned to see this evening.

Once she'd finished eating, she rose. "Shall we go?"

He stood in one elegant, fluid motion. How had she missed that before? Her heart skipped like a stone across water.

"Horatia, is there something you'd like to tell me?"

Opening her eyes wide, she answered, "I wondered if you would like to dine at a restaurant this evening. If we find one during our walk."

"If that's what you wish."

He didn't appear to be entirely convinced.

She'd had years of practice dissembling, yet he seemed to see right through her ruses. She took his arm. "It is."

Strolling through the ancient city, she was saddened and angered at the destruction caused by both the rebellion and the army. "Why do they feel the need to destroy what should be preserved?"

John shook his head. "I wish I could tell you. Anger at the

wealth accumulated by a few, perhaps." He led her to the lone free table at a café. "Have you changed your mind regarding remaining here for a few days? You might find less devastation farther north."

She frowned. "I don't yet know. I so looked forward to seeing the sights George described to me. He was here on his Grand Tour in '83."

A waiter came over and John ordered coffee for them both.

Horatia smiled. "There is one good thing about France. In England, I would still not be allowed in a coffee shop. Here, you may see ladies in all of them."

John gazed at her. "Horatia, have you thought about living in England, but with a home in Paris as well?"

What was he about? She took a sip of the rich, slightly bitter coffee and considered her answer. "Whether I return to England or not, I would buy a house in France. It has become very fashionable. From what I hear, Paris is the most lively and interesting city in Europe."

He exhaled as if he'd been holding his breath. "I'd like you to come back to England with me."

John had asked her to marry him, but this was different and inexplicably much more serious. She gazed into his stormy green eyes. "I'll give you an answer soon."

After he paid for the coffee, they ambled slowly back to the hotel.

"Dinner at the small restaurant down the street?" he asked as they reached the door to her chambers.

"Yes."

He leaned forward, pressing his arm against the wall, holding her in his web. "Kiss me."

The corridor was empty. She reached up and touched his lips lightly with hers. Licking his lower lip, she tasted coffee and salt and desire. If he opened his mouth, she'd let him take her against the wall. It was all she could do not to flatten herself against him. He raised his head, breaking the kiss, yet continued to hold her for a while longer. To-night, he'd get at least a temporary answer, and she'd have him, for a while. Until he came to his senses.

Later that evening, Horatia sat at the dressing table as Risher combed out her thick, dark curls. Horatia dismissed her maid and waited a few minutes before shedding her wrapper and donning a morning gown, in the unlikely event anyone saw her. Quietly unlatching the door, she padded softly down the corridor to John's chambers and listened for any sign his valet was still up. Her heart pounded. Hands shaking, she reached out to try the door. So long. It had been so long and she wanted him so very badly. Surely he'd understand. She pressed the latch down and pushed. The door opened.

He stood tall, bronzed, and naked. Her mouth dried as she took in his broad shoulders and narrow waist and hips. She licked her lips. Dark curls covered his chest. Horatia's hand twitched, wanting to run her fingers through them.

A pistol was in his hand, pointed at her.

"John!"

"Horatia!" His eyes widened. Quickly setting the gun down on a table, he strode forward and grabbed her shoulders, giving them a little shake. "I could have shot you! Why are you here at this time of night? Come to think of it, what are you doing in my room at all?"

"I came to tell you I'll marry you." Glancing up, she bit her lip. Would he forgive her for what she planned to do? Did it matter? She'd lusted for him since he saved her from falling on the docks. Even if he hated her, she'd be safely settled in France, far enough away from him and his wife.

Kicking the door shut, he enveloped her in his arms. He still smelled of fresh air and the sea. When his lips descended

on hers, she shuddered in delight. Running her palms greed-
ily over his back, she reveled in the strong muscles flexing
as he caressed her. George had been strong and lean, but he
never felt like this. John's chest and back were hard, his
stomach taut. She rubbed her cheek against his chest, soft
hair tickling her as she searched for and found his nipples.

With the first lick, he moaned. She grazed the other one
with a nail.

"Horatia, how does this gown come off?"

She murmured against his ear, "Buttons in the front." She
reached down, touched his already hard shaft, and stroked.

His tone roughened. "Get rid of it, now."

Cool air wafted around her legs as he rucked her skirts up
to her waist. A deep shiver shot through her as his fingers
probed and fondled.

His hand held her hip as she leaned back and quickly unfastened the small pearl buttons before he decided to rip her
gown apart. The printed muslin was the only thing standing
between his naked body and hers. Finally the last one came
loose. She shrugged out of the sleeves as he tugged on the
gown. It slid off her hips and in a soft swoosh fell to the
floor. Need and desire overwhelmed her. Horatia pulled his
head down and kissed him with the longing of all the years
of built-up denial.

When he lifted her, she wrapped her legs around him.

"Horatia, my love, it's been a long time for you. Slow
down a bit. I don't want to hurt you."

She knew she was already wet for him, and she wasn't
waiting any longer. "I'm not an innocent. Take me, take me
now."

John had a very good idea how experienced she was and
thanked God he wouldn't have to bother with a virgin for a
wife. Still, it'd been many years for her. Walking to the bed,
he placed her in the middle of it and followed. He tried to

kiss her slowly, but her lips were hungry and demanding. When he thought to ravish her with his tongue, she caught it and sucked. The sensation was so exquisite, he groaned. Lightning coursed through his veins as he struggled to keep up with her, give her the pleasure she gave him. He'd never had such a woman. Reaching down, he stroked her curls and rubbed the small nubbin buried within. She made a sound between a moan and a soft growl. When he inserted his finger into her sheath, it was hot and sodden, like silk to the touch, and tight. "You may need some time. Let me—"

She arched up and gave a sharp noise of frustration. "No, I am ready. I need you inside me now."

"Very well. But we do this my way." John entered her slowly, withdrew, and entered again, giving her sheath time to stretch. Horatia met him thrust for thrust, moaning deeply. What had George called her? His houri. John believed it. And now she was his.

He plunged deeply, possessing her, branding her. Horatia shook and cried out. She convulsed around him so strongly he couldn't withdraw to push again. His heart pounded and a roar filled his ears. With a groan, he spilled his seed and collapsed next to her. For the first time in his forty-two years, he'd been taken by a woman instead of the other way around.

He must have slept, for when he opened his eyes, the sky was softening as it did before dawn. Horatia, a warm bundle of woman, slept soundly next to him. He studied her soft, plump curves. Magnificent breasts that begged him to taste led to the soft indentation of her waist flaring out to beautifully rounded hips. She was what men called an armful. He wondered how much sleep she required and how long they had until the hotel began to awaken. John gave into temptation and took one rosy, pink nipple into his mouth. Honey couldn't have tasted sweeter. Horatia sighed and pushed toward him. As he caressed her other breast, it became heavier in his hand.

By the time he'd finished, Horatia was writhing under him. Her body flushed.

"John."

He hoped she didn't mind that he'd started without her. "Are you all right?"

She reached down and guided his shaft to her entrance. "I will be."

Some sort of primitive need to show her who was in charge surged through him, and he plunged into her. Horatia rose up and gripped his shoulders before biting one as she came, milking him so hard he had to push her down to stay in her. He held her close as she kissed the mark she'd made.

"How bad is it?"

Her lips moved to his neck and nibbled. "There is no blood. It should be fine in a day or so."

He made a useless attempt to smooth her hair and then he had to ask, "Are you always like this?"

She stilled. When she spoke, her tone was tentative. "Why do you want to know?"

What had he done to upset her? He feathered kisses on her neck. "I've never been ravished by a woman before, and I'd like to know if it's something I can grow used to."

Her laugh was low, sultry. "I've always enjoyed love making. With you, it is deeper, more primal. Yet it may also be because it has been so long for me."

He gave her his affronted look. "I hope it's because you can't resist me."

She studied him soberly before meeting his eyes. "Perhaps."

"You should go back to your room soon. At the next hotel, I'd like our chambers to be closer together."

"I think they should connect. I'll have La Valle make the arrangements."

Smiling, she kissed him with an open mouth, slipping her tongue in to caress his. She was a siren. His siren. Yet this surprised him. "Am I understanding you correctly? You intend to tell your major domo we're sleeping together?"

Horatia frowned. "Of course not. I'll tell him we are betrothed. He's French. He'll figure it out on his own. Does that bother you?"

He didn't want anyone thinking badly of her and wondered how soon they could marry. "Not in the least."

Two days later, they made their way north, stopping at Orange to see the ruins of a Roman theater and an old Roman arch. By the time their caravan arrived in Valence five days afterward, he'd abandoned his horse for his sensually abandoned betrothed, who insisted no one would know what they were doing. Of course, the way the coach normally rocked on some of the roads, she may be right. "What sights are we viewing here, my love?"

Horatia took out her notebook. "The Maison des Têtes and the Romanesque Cathedral of Saint-Apollinaire. That shouldn't take long. Two nights, I think. When we arrive in Lyon, we shall plan to stay several days. It's a large city with many interesting things to see, and shops."

He hopped down from the carriage, now halted in the yard of their hotel. "I'd also like to have a few repairs done on a couple of the coaches."

Horatia waited for him to lift her down. "Nothing serious, I trust."

"No. At least, La Valle doesn't think so." He escorted her into the hotel lobby, where her major domo waited to show them their rooms. Most of the time, their group occupied the entire building.

Horatia came to him every night and didn't leave until she was ready to dress in the morning. La Valle began to defer to John, and the rest of her servants treated him as their new master. The more he found himself acting the part of her husband, the more he wanted the role in truth. With all the English supposedly traveling on the Continent, one would think he'd have run across a clergyman.

A little way from the hotel stood a park, bordered on one side by the Rhône river. He and Horatia walked along the outer path to the water. On the way back, they stopped at a café, where they enjoyed coffee with *les Suisses*. The waiter explained that the sweet, orange-flower flavored pastries were made in the shape of the Swiss Guard stationed in the city to protect the remains of the exiled Pope Pius VI.

"Well, I think them very tasty," Horatia said as she finished off hers.

"I agree. We'll tell everyone else about them."

Despite the sun, she shivered. "It is becoming colder. I must have Risher find my cloak. When we reach Lyon, I'll have everyone shop for warmer clothing."

Something was wrong. Though they'd become physically intimate, her mind seemed more distant. As though she was purposely remaining apart from him. What was she up to now?

Chapter 22

Horatia claimed John's mouth as he thrust into her one last time before he groaned. Her skirts were bunched around her waist as she straddled his lap, sated. All too soon, the coach began to slow.

He reached over, pushing the leather curtain aside. "We're entering Dijon. It won't take long to reach the hotel."

She swung her legs around to sit on the seat again, then buttoned her gown and donned her pelisse. She put the last pin back in her hair and covered the mess with her bonnet.

"Try to stand and I'll straighten your gown," John said. "You can't leave the carriage looking like you've been through a storm."

"Well, whose fault is that?" Horatia tried to make her tone severe, but grinned. He was just as disheveled as she. Once he'd tugged her gown in place, she leaned forward. "Your cravat is a mess."

"If anyone says anything, I'll tell them it's a new fashion."

A giggle escaped her. "Ah yes. *L'ébouriffé*. If we see any of our countrymen, they'll be so impressed they'll try to emulate you."

The look he speared her with was so hot, she almost demanded he kiss her, but the coach slowed and went through an old arched entrance way. "I think we have arrived."

She hurriedly smoothed John's neckcloth before the door opened.

A middle-aged man with a large mustache bowed. "Milady, milord, *bienvenus à l'Hostellerie le Sauvage*. We have all in readiness."

Horatia allowed him to assist her from the coach. "Thank you, monsieur." She glanced around and was immediately entranced by the ancient building. The bottom level was of worn gray stone and the upper stories of wattle and daub. Long mullioned windows graced the front façade. "How beautiful!"

La Valle stood at the bottom of the steps into the building. "My lady. A light nuncheon and a bath have been ordered."

As it appeared her major domo wasn't quite finished, she said, "Go on."

"I have discussed our journey with the landlord and he advised us to use the road from here to Paris rather than from Nancy to Paris. It is much shorter and in better repair."

John came to stand next to her. "What do you think, La Valle?"

His attention shifted to John. "I have studied the maps and agree. If we continue to Nancy, we will either have to return here or take a much longer route to the north."

Horatia nodded. "I'll send a note to Caro and Huntley to meet us here."

Later that day, she lay in John's arms, drawing patterns

on his chest with her finger. She did so like a man with chest hair. They'd been betrothed for over two weeks now, and he'd still not broached the subject of his earldom. What was he waiting for, or was he afraid to tell her the estate was practically bankrupt?

No matter, he needed to leave before her nephew and goddaughter arrived; otherwise Horatia's life could become even more complicated. Huntley, she suspected, would take John's side and Caro might, as well.

Well, if John was not going to mention it . . . "My love, when are you going to tell me you are an earl?"

The muscles in his chest tightened and he sucked in a sharp breath. "How did you know?"

His tone was somewhere between tense and resigned.

"I do receive mail, and your brother's death occurred at a particularly slow time for gossip. I had it from two of my correspondents." She turned herself so she could watch his expression. "When?"

He grimaced. "After we married."

Horatia planted both palms on his chest and pushed up. "*After* we were wed? Are you mad? Have you not yet realized you cannot marry me?"

John's sharp gaze pierced her. "*That* is precisely the reason I didn't plan to tell you until afterwards. I knew you'd get some sort of damned stupid idea like that into your pretty head."

Oh, that was it. He could leave to-day. "*Stupid?* If I am so dim-witted, *my lord*, I am amazed you wish to marry me."

"I didn't say you were dim, I said your idea was."

She struggled to rise, but her legs were caught in the sheets and he'd clamped his legs around them. "Unhand me."

He raised his hands as if in surrender, and even though he still glared at her, a twinkle appeared in his eyes.

"You know what I mean." She wiggled her legs, trying to get out from between his. "Let me go. I am leaving."

The next thing she knew, she was on her back. His strong grip held her hands stretched over her head. She squirmed and he tightened his grip, trapping her.

A heavy frown settled over his countenance and he growled, "No, you are not. You, my lady, aren't going anywhere until we settle this matter."

She moved, and John's lower body rested lightly on hers. Horatia suspected that if she tried to escape he could easily stop her. She raised her chin and used the coldest tone she could muster under the circumstances. "It *is* settled. You need a wife who can bear you children, and I will not be your mistress."

"*Mistress?* Dratted, stubborn, obdurate woman." He blew out a puff of air. "You're right. You will not be my mistress. You will be my *wife*." His eyes narrowed to green slits. "What do you think you've been playing at these last weeks, gracing my bed?"

That was a question she didn't want to answer. Her cheeks burned, but how she felt did not matter. She had to stop him from making a grave mistake. One he'd grow to regret.

"You are impossible." She tried to sit up and his body, all of it hard muscle, lowered onto her. He must be made to listen to reason. "You need at least an opportunity to have an heir. I want you to have that chance."

John glared at her and said in a hard voice, "Tell me, Horatia. If you didn't plan to marry me, why did you accept me, and why are you here now?"

That must be the tone he used with his crew. Well, the plaguy man did not rule her. Doing her best to be indignant, which was really very hard to do lying naked beneath him, his nether parts touching her, she raised her chin. "I did it for your own good. So that you could see how wrong I am for the position."

John almost laughed out loud and struggled to keep his lips firm. He could already feel the heat from between her thighs. All he'd have to do is bend his head, take one of her luscious pink-tipped mounds in his mouth, and the conversation would end. But that wouldn't solve the problem. "This is one hell of a way to show me. Allowing me to take you anytime I wished."

She huffed. "You did not. I took you just as often."

Damn her for looking so adorable, and for being so mulish. He had to make her see what she was doing. He changed his tone from firm to an insulting drawl. "But why, Horatia? To act as my whore?"

"How dare you?" This time she struggled against him in earnest. Tears filled her eyes.

Finally, a reaction he could deal with. Kissing her eyelids, tasting the salty tears seeping from beneath them, he softened his voice. "Why?"

She turned her head and sobbed. "Because I love you, and I wanted just a little of you before you found a suitable bride."

His heart ached for her. She needed to see her own worth.

He moved off her, drawing Horatia to him. "My poor love. Do you think I could ever marry someone else after knowing you?" He stroked her long curls falling around them. "I need you. Where would I find another woman who has the strength and intelligence to help me undo the damage my father and brother did to the estates and dependents?"

She shook her head and stared at him. "But, John, you *must* have an heir. I do not—"

He captured her lips, setting siege to her mouth. Ripping

her breath and arguments from her. Horatia clung to him, voraciously returning his kisses and demanding more.

When he finally lifted his head, her lips followed. "My love, the truth is, I don't know, and neither do you, if you can have children or not. All I know is George never did."

Horatia's eyes opened and seemed to gaze at nothing. "But he said he . . ."

"He did support some children, but they were not his."

Frowning, she pushed back her hair and took a breath. "You mean all this time I might have been able to become pregnant and—and he allowed me to think I could not?" She sat up and rubbed her face. "Why? Why would he do that?"

"I've asked myself that same question since you first told me you were unable to conceive. Perhaps he needed to believe it wasn't him. Or that you'd think you had been cheated out of children by marrying him." John caressed her back. "The truth is, I just don't know."

She was still for several moments before her eyes grew wide. "This means I could be—I could be *breeding*?"

He laughed and drew her down against him. "It's only been a couple of weeks. Though I suppose there's a possibility."

"No, you don't understand. The old healers say there is a certain time a woman can conceive, and this past week was during that time."

His breath left him like he'd been punched. "You mean you really might be with child?"

Horatia shrugged. "If they're correct."

A baby? They could be having a child. "We need to find a vicar or a reverend or some sort of English clergyman now. The sooner we're married the better."

Laughing, she snuggled down on top of him. "It does take some time for the whole process to be complete. *If* I'm increasing, that is."

"I am well aware of that, but I'm not giving you any chance of escape."

She walked her fingers up his chest. "I think we should wait to marry until I know I am able to give you an heir."

Horatia was out of her mind if she thought he'd let her go. "No."

"What do you mean?" She frowned. "It's a perfectly reasonable suggestion."

Enough was enough. What would it take to get through to her? He flipped her on her back and drew her under him. "I mean, no. My love, if I don't marry you, I will not marry anyone. I was perfectly truthful when I told you my other brothers have done their duty. In fact, they're probably hoping I will not sire children."

Her chin firmed and it was clear she wasn't done with her arguments. "But would you not like one of your own?"

He searched for something to say and touched her stomach. "My love, the only one I want will come from here."

Her eyes misted. "I—"

He touched a finger to her lips, stopping her. "Only you."

Finally all the tension seemed to leave her body. She nodded and smiled. "In that case, I will marry you, my lord."

Thank God. This time she was telling the truth. "I'll start sending out inquiries concerning a cleric, but first, since you want me to have an heir so badly, we should probably practice some more."

Horatia's arms came around his neck. "You'll need to tell everyone you are an earl."

"It will make Smyth very happy. I'll have him attend to it."

He lowered his head to kiss her.

"I love you, John, but I've never been in love before, and I don't know exactly how to go on."

He kissed her lightly. "Nor have I. We'll figure it out to-gether. I'm sure it can't be that complicated."

He was determined to find someone to marry them as soon as possible. Who knew how long she'd be in this con-veniently docile frame of mind? If he left it too long, she was sure to find some other reason she wasn't worthy to be his wife. It was a good thing George was dead. Right now, John would kill him for allowing her to think she should never wed again. *The bloody bugger*.

Later that afternoon, John inquired of the innkeeper if there were any English clergy in the area. He also wrote the embassy in Paris. After having sent the dispatch off by spe-cial messenger, he returned to his chamber. Unfortunately, Horatia was gone, and his valet was laying out his evening kit. "Smyth, you may now tell the rest of our group I'm an earl."

It was below Smyth's dignity to smile, but John thought he detected a movement in his valet's lips as he bowed.

"Yes, my lord. I take it her ladyship is fully apprised of your situation."

John couldn't keep the grin off his face. "She is indeed, and I'm in desperate need of a vicar, or rector, or something like that." He stripped down to his pantaloons before wash-ing his face and neck. "I want to have this wedding over and done with before her nephew shows up. I know nothing about him, but if he's anything like his grand sire . . . And with my brother and father's reputations, suffice it to say, I don't want any trouble."

His valet nodded. "Yes, my lord. There are other English travelers in the town. Mr. La Valle and I will do our best to endeavor to discover their haunts."

John drew his shirt over his head. "Thank you."

If there was a person able to marry them between here and Paris, Smyth would find him and drag him back.

The next day after luncheon, while his betrothed was resting, John was summoned downstairs. A short, slender, neatly dressed gentleman waited for him in a parlor. John held out his hand. "Good day to you, sir. How may I help you?"

The gentleman bowed and gave a slight smile. "I believe it is I who can assist you."

John raised a brow. Could this be a clergyman? "Indeed, how is that?"

"I have been informed, my lord," the man said, "by a few different sources, that you wish to marry."

John gave thanks to the Deity and smiled. "That's correct, and as soon as possible."

The other man nodded. "In that case, as soon as I have determined your affianced bride is of the same mind, we can make the arrangements."

John stepped to the door and caught one of the maids. "Please bring refreshments and have her ladyship attend me."

The maid bobbed a curtsy, and left.

He left the door open and motioned the cleric to sit. "I'm afraid you have the advantage of me, sir. May I know your name?"

"Indeed, I am the Right Reverend Hubert Weston. I have had some acquaintance with your brother." John frowned, and Weston hurried to say, "I've been given to understand you are a much different sort of gentleman than he was."

"I would hope." John tried to keep from scowling. "If I were of the same ilk, you'd refuse to perform the ceremony. There will be nothing harum-scarum about this marriage. I've already drawn up the settlements."

When Horatia entered the room, he went to her and took her hand. "My love, this is Mr. Weston, who will be able to perform the wedding ceremony."

Thankfully, she beamed. "How wonderful. What do we need to do?"

The only difficulty was John wanted to wait until the next morning and Horatia wanted to be married that afternoon. The contretemps was solved by Mr. Weston.

"My lord, my lady, this afternoon would suit me better. I am to leave to-morrow after luncheon. I do hope you understand."

"Perfectly," she replied and smiled at John. "You see, my love, we cannot wait."

John glanced up at the ceiling. "Very well, we shall have Smyth and La Valle sort it all out. Mr. Weston, I hope you will be able to join us for a small celebration after the wedding."

He bowed. "I would be delighted, my lord."

"Right, then," Horatia said and walked to the door to call their servants. When Smyth and La Valle arrived, she glanced at Weston. "In two hours?"

"Yes, my lady, if you wish."

Horatia nodded briskly at La Valle. "Have Risher attend me in my chamber and gather everyone else. I would like to marry on the terrace."

La Valle bowed. "My lady. Everything will be ready."

Horatia felt like a giddy girl again. She was getting married and this time to someone she was in love with. Nothing could be better. If only she could wrap her arms around him and kiss him. Unfortunately, the vicar was still in the room. Instead she took John's hand. "I shall see you soon."

He raised her fingers to his lips, and the tingles ran through her. His gaze, warm with desire, was enough.

"Mr. Weston. Thank you."

It was all she could do to walk sedately up the stairs. Risher was there when Horatia arrived. "The wedding is in two hours. Find something appropriate."

John sent the settlement agreement he'd drawn up. Horatia read the document carefully. He had been adamant that none of her money would go to the property his father and brother had so badly dissipated. Tears filled her eyes and she blinked them away. If she'd had any doubts at all, the agreement banished them.

Two hours later, she was dressed in a Pomona-green silk day gown. One of the servants' children brought flowers for her hair, and she wore a long strand of perfectly matched pearls looped twice around her neck. Risher and La Valle accompanied her down the stairs and out onto the terrace, where all the others were gathered. It was good to be married among the people who had become her family. *If only Huntley and Caro were here.*

John looked particularly handsome in a dark blue jacket of Bath coating, and breeches.

"Right," Mr. Weston said, "I see we are all present. Shall we begin?"

For the second time, and hopefully the last, Horatia said her vows. This time, rather than staring at the floor, she gazed into her soon-to-be-husband's eyes. When it was John's turn, his gaze captured hers. In all her life, she'd never felt so loved.

Not many minutes later, it was over, and she was now the Countess of Devon. Horatia wondered how that fact alone would change her life. She'd left England after a different sort of hasty marriage and under a cloud. She'd spent years re-building her reputation, and now she would return with a husband who was determined to repair his family's name.

John handed her a glass of champagne. "To us, my lady."

"To us, my lord." Tears misted her vision, but she would not cry.

She had never been happier. They had a lot of work to do, and possibly a baby on the way, and finally, finally, her life had meaning again.

Huntley handed Caro down in the yard of the Hôtel de l'Europe on the edge of Strasbourg's old town.

"I refuse," Caro announced, "to travel another foot until I've had at least two days to walk around."

Hoping to mollify her, he agreed. "I think we all need a pause in our journey. Will a full day suit you? We're only three more days from Nancy."

"Very well, one day." She glanced up at him and heaved a sigh. "I am so tired of this constant traveling."

"I know, my love. Yet the roads aren't good enough to allow us to go faster. You'd be bounced to death." He wanted so badly to tell her he loved her, but the last time he'd approached the subject of the permanency of their marriage, she'd looked afraid. Though lately, he was almost positive she loved him as well. Perhaps now she'd tell him how she felt.

"I know you're right." She shook her head. "I feel like I've been jostled to death already."

Maufe came out to announce their chambers had been arranged and led them in. Rather than take her hand, Huntley put his arm around her. "You'll feel better after you've had a bath."

She leaned closer to him. "I'm sorry I'm being pettish."

Perhaps if he found some chocolate for her she'd feel better. "You have a right to be."

"May we take a short walk before dinner? I know it's late."

"If you wish." He brought one of her hands up to kiss it. "I'd like one as well."

While Caro washed the dust of travel off, he found Maufe. "Ask the landlord if there is some sort of café with chocolate desserts."

"Yes, my lord."

The sun hung on the horizon, streaking the clouds with pink against the deepening blue sky as they strolled down to the canal surrounding Strasbourg. Seeing another couple walking arm in arm, Huntley placed his around Caro.

She smiled at him, her earlier tension gone from her lovely face. "It's so peaceful here."

"Yes, it's a good place to stop for a pause. I'll be very happy to arrive in Nancy. I know it's not the end of our journey, but we will all be together again. I'm worried about Horatia."

Caro's voice was soft. "You worry about everyone you care for. It is your nature."

He raised a brow. He'd always thought of his father as the one who fretted about his family. Yet now that Huntley had a wife . . . "I suppose it is. I've never thought about it before."

She turned them up a street leading back to the hotel. "What are we having for dinner?"

"Since we want to try the local dishes, the chef suggested *choucroute garnie*. Ham, sausage, and sauerkraut."

"It sounds interesting. That is the one thing I have enjoyed, tasting all the different dishes."

Shortly after they'd returned to the private parlor at the hotel and begun dinner, Maufe came in with a small box. It wasn't large enough to hold even a piece of torte. Huntley took the package. "What is it?"

Maufe grinned. "Something very special."

After dinner, Huntley ordered champagne and set the box

before Caro. While he filled their glasses, she opened it. Several round chocolate disks were wrapped in tissue paper. He'd never seen anything like it before.

"What is it?" she asked.

"Chocolate, though I've never seen it in that form before."

Caro picked one up and took a bite. "Mmm. Heavenly."

He looked at the card inside the box. "Debauve and Gallais. Chocolate *pistoles*." He took one from the box and tasted. "Whoever brings these to England will make a fortune."

Caro took a second one. "I agree. We should visit their shop before we leave."

He gave a bark of laughter. "Knowing you, you'll buy out their whole stock."

Smiling, Caro nodded. It seemed to take so little to make her happy. God, how he loved her. Just the thought she might still be thinking about leaving him drove him mad.

That night in bed, he noticed her breasts were a little larger and there was a hint of a soft swell to her stomach. He was glad she'd finally recovered from her illness and gained some weight. She gave a high, breathy sigh as he caressed her. Once they arrived in Nancy and he'd assured himself his aunt was well, he'd have a serious discussion with Caro. He'd tell her how much he loved her and pray she could love him in return, after which they'd have to thrash out where to live until they returned to England. Huntley needed to know if the blackguard who raped her was the reason she did not wish to go back home. If so, he'd find a way to remove what frightened her.

She rolled over and frowned sleepily. "Why did you stop?"

Smiling, he stroked her again. "I got distracted. I'm happy you are completely well again."

A small line appeared between her brows. "I still feel fatigued though."

He kissed her neck and took one tightly budded nipple in his mouth. "How tired are you?"

"Mmm, not that tired."

Huntley kissed her lips, then licked and kissed his way down over her stomach until he reached the nest of soft, light wheaten curls between her legs. He stroked her center with his tongue and she arched up, urging him on. When he circled her small pearl and sucked, she cried out, her fingers tangling in his hair.

Soon she was thrashing wildly and sobbing his name.

"Are you ready, my love?"

"Yes, yes, please. Gervais, now!"

He entered her slowly, making every stroke, every touch drive her higher. His, she was his, and if she had any thoughts of leaving him, she'd have to reconsider because he would not let her go.

Caro encouraged Gervais's thrusts. Her breasts rubbed against his chest and the feel of his curls abrading her bosom was more intense. Wrapping her legs around him, she tried to make him hurry, but he'd not be rushed. Flames coursed through her, driving her into a frenzy. Why was he taking so long?

He held her close and filled her like he never had before, as if to show her she was his. If he only knew she already belonged to him, body, soul, and heart. She cried out, and he took her mouth, ripping away her wits. The fire between them burned brighter, and just when she couldn't stand the tension anymore, he shuddered and pumped deeper. Light exploded around her as she came around him harder than she ever had before.

Their hearts beat together as he lay on top of her, kissed her lips and neck, and nipped her ear.

"My wife," he whispered fiercely.

Caro held on to him with as much strength as she could, and whispered back, "My husband."

She thought then that he'd tell her he loved her, but the next sound she heard was his soft snoring. A tear slipped down the side of her face. She refused to let him go. When they got to Nancy, Godmamma would help her.

She and Huntley slept late the next morning. Though they made love again, neither of them brought up what had happened the night before. It was as if it were a raw wound that could not be touched.

As they explored the city, her nerves tightened. "I'll be happy to get to Nancy."

He glanced at her. "As will I."

Oh God, did he plan to leave her there? Andrew had told her he loved her, and he left. Gervais hadn't even promised that.

When they left the next morning, the tension was still thick between them, and Caro didn't know how to change it.

Their little group arrived in Nancy mid-afternoon of the third day to find the hotel strangely deserted.

Huntley jumped down from the coach. "Stay here. I'll see what is going on."

She nodded. It was almost a relief to be alone for a little while.

He strode back, his face all hard angles and grim, holding a letter. "We are instructed to go to Dijon. It's another four and a half days."

Despite trying not to, Caro burst into tears. She was so tired of traveling. Come to think of it, she was just tired lately.

She quickly found herself in his arms, and he was kissing her. "I know, my love, this is disappointing. They have no other guests. We can spend the night here, or go on. The landlord knows of a hotel he can recommend a few hours away."

When she lifted her head, his damp cravat fixed her attention. "Oh, Gervais, I've ruined your neckcloth."

He chuckled and held her tighter. "I'll tell Maufe to procure an oilcloth for the next time. What do you wish to do?"

She took a breath. "Go on. I just want to get there."

"Very well," Huntley said, "I'll tell the others."

Once they were back on the road, the enormity of what this could mean hit Caro. Was Godmamma all right? "Gervais, who sent the missive? Is Godmamma ill or injured?"

He shook his head. "She sent it but gave no reason for the change in plans." He took Caro's hand. "I share your concerns and want to arrive there as soon as we are able."

"Don't worry about jolting me around, then. It is more important to reach Dijon."

He nodded. "Raphael and Collins know."

She held on to Huntley's hand and worried about what disaster could have struck her godmother.

Chapter 23

Four days later, and only ten miles or so from Dijon, Caro pressed her hand to her mouth, and Huntley knew she was going to cast up her accounts. He banged on the roof. "Stop the coach. Now."

He bundled her out and held her as she bent over and lost her lunch. Her forehead was cold and clammy. She shivered in his arms. His poor love. He prayed her illness wasn't serious but braced himself if it was. "We must find an inn." Drawing out a flask with brandy, he held it to her lips. "Drink some of this. It should settle you."

Obediently, she tilted back her head and then sputtered. "Oh, that's horrible."

Maufe came running up. "What is it, my lord?"

"Her ladyship's not well. Go on ahead and find us someplace she can rest. We'll try to finish the trip to Dijon in the morning."

"Yes, my lord. Straight-away."

After Maufe jumped up beside Collins and they left, Huntley picked his wife up. Maneuvering his way into the coach, he sat down with her on his lap. "We'll wait here for a few minutes."

Caro nodded. "I do not know what happened. It was so sudden."

"Nor do I." Unlike before when she was sick, the pulse in her wrist was strong. "If it occurs again, I'll call in a doctor."

Tears started in her eyes. "Oh, Gervais, I so hope I'm not going to be ill again."

He dabbed her eyes with his handkerchief. "I'm here for you. Just rest against me, my love."

He cradled her in his arms. Everything had been going so well. What had happened? About a half hour later, the sound of hooves beating a tattoo on the road roused him from thought. Caro was sleeping. He heard Collins hail them. "My lord. We've found a place not far from here."

"Let's go then." Huntley hoped the movement of the carriage didn't set her off again.

In the few minutes it took to arrive, the color had drained from her face. "It won't be long now. Try to hold on."

She nodded, but it was a close call. The minute he lifted her from the coach, she bent over again.

Caro wiped her mouth with the handkerchief he handed her. "Whatever this is, I hope I do not have it for long."

He picked her up again. "I'm calling a doctor." Catching sight of Maufe, he asked, "Where are our chambers?"

Maufe ran ahead of him. "Chamber, my lord. The inn is very small and not someplace we want to remain for a long time."

"Have them send a message to the nearest doctor."

Maufe opened the door to a small room at the back of the inn.

Viewing the dingy chamber with disapproval, Huntley asked, "Is this the largest one they have?"

"Yes, my lord. It has a small room with a bed through this door."

Though the bed in his room looked barely large enough for two, he supposed it was better than the alternative of traveling onward. "It will have to do. Have Nugent attend me."

Nugent appeared as he was trying to remove Caro's pelisse. "If you hold her, my lord, I'll get that."

"Thank you."

His wife's face was so pale, and she looked as if she was going to be sick again. "I need a basin."

Maufe shoved it in front of Caro before she threw up again. This time there was nothing left. He and Nugent got his wife into the bed a few minutes before Mrs. Collins entered accompanied by an old woman.

Huntley frowned. "Who are you?"

Her dialect was so strong he had trouble understanding her. Though he was sure he'd heard "healer." Well, she looked clean enough. "No doctor here, then?"

The woman shook her head and asked a question.

"I don't understand her." He called to Maufe standing in the corridor. "Get the landlady."

While they waited, the woman pointed to Caro. He nodded. He supposed it wouldn't hurt to allow her to examine his wife. Soon the woman smiled and made a motion with her hand indicating a large belly. "*Enceinte.*"

With child? His child. Something must be wrong. His mother was as healthy as a horse when she was breeding. "Why is she so ill?"

The landlady appeared. "Many women are ill during the early months. *Milord.*"

Her French was much easier to understand. "How long before she is well?"

The women shrugged and the healer answered, "Maybe only a week, maybe four."

Four weeks? They were not remaining here four weeks, not even one. He needed to get Caro to Dijon, to his aunt, and a doctor. He glanced at Nugent, Mrs. Collins, and the two Frenchwomen speaking. "What did you say?"

"She says," Mrs. Collins replied, indicating the healer, "that you should not share a bed with your wife. The motion can make her even more unwell."

Glancing down at Caro, now sleeping peacefully, he growled, "I need a walk."

He left the room. Not sleep with her? Were they mad? But if it would cause her to feel even worse, then maybe he should sleep elsewhere. He strode around the village, and when he made his way back to their chambers he was told that Caro had eaten some broth and drank a tisane made with ginger.

"She's resting again, my lord," Nugent said. "Your dinner is about to be served."

After dinner, he was again distracted from seeing his wife, this time by a problem with one of the horses. When he finally made it to their chambers, she was sleeping again. Huntley sat in a chair beside her and held her hand. Finally, he sought the bed in the small room.

He awoke tired, his back hurt, and his mood was foul.

He missed his wife. Yet buoyed by the thought of a child, Huntley approached the door to their chamber and heard Caro cry, "No, I don't want him."

He felt ill, as if someone had punched him in the stomach. She didn't want him? Why? His mind turned to some of

their earlier conversations. The heir, she said she owed him
an heir. That was the reason she never said she loved him.
She enjoyed being with him but never intended to have her
affections engaged. He called for Maufe, and when he'd
dressed, left the inn. His throat tightened. If that was how
she felt, he'd stay away from her until she asked for him.

Caro woke up feeling worse than the night before. Even
with the window open, the inn smelled of cabbage and fried
foods. Nugent offered to have Dalle, whose French was
passable, find a doctor. "No, I don't want him and I don't
want that either." She made a face at the bowl containing the
thin gruel. "I want his lordship."

Nugent left the room and came back a few moments later,
her expression grim. "He's gone out, my lady."

That was it. He didn't love her. He just wanted a child,
and now that she was breeding, he had no more time for her.
Caro burst into tears.

Nugent patted her hand. "I'll tell his lordship you want
him, as soon as he returns."

"No." She wouldn't beg him to be with her. "He knows
the way to this chamber."

Her spirits sank lower as the day went on and Gervais
didn't come to her. By the time Nugent blew out her candle,
Caro was the most miserable woman alive. Even the news
that they were leaving in the morning failed to rouse her.
Her life couldn't possibly get any worse.

The next day, she smiled at Gervais when he helped her
into the coach, but instead of getting in next to her, Nugent
climbed in. Caro bit her lips and stared out the opposite window.

He closed the door. "If you need me, I shall be on horseback."

She'd had a salty broth and tea made of ginger that morning. With any luck at all, she'd be able to keep it down. Whatever the case, she refused to be ill in front of him. He wouldn't care how she felt. She hastily wiped her tears away.

The trip to Dijon passed without too much of a problem. The times she'd felt nauseous, she chewed the dry bread the innkeeper had given her and sipped ginger tea.

Finally the coach pulled into an inn. Gervais pulled open the door, then handed her down. The first person she saw was Horatia. "Godmamma!"

She folded Caro into an embrace. The tears she'd held back escaped, and she hugged her godmother back. "Godmamma, I'm so glad to see you."

"Caro, my love," Horatia said, handing Caro a lace-trimmed handkerchief. "Huntley tells me you are unwell. Let's get you to your chamber."

She nodded. "I'm so ill."

A tall, rangy man with sandy hair accompanied them into the inn.

Caro frowned. "Who is that?"

"John. I'll tell you about it later. Right now, you need to have a bath and rest."

Caro allowed herself to be ushered up the stairs and into a large, airy bedchamber. A bathtub stood by the fireplace, which had already been lit. "Thank you. I'll feel better shortly."

Horatia gave her a wry smile. "You won't. Your mother was always ill when she was breeding."

Taking a chair, Caro nodded. "I'd forgotten."

Her godmother's sharp eyes studied her. "If you want to discuss it, I'm just down the corridor."

After her bath, Caro sat staring out the window, waiting for her husband. The door opened part way then stopped.

"John," Gervais said from the corridor, "I'll meet you downstairs to discuss what we should do."

He'd made love to her, but he didn't love her. Caro's heart cracked. She couldn't go on like this. What a fool she'd been, thinking she could live with him, love him, and not care if he returned her love. *Idiot, if you hadn't fallen in love with him it wouldn't matter*. Yet she had, and more than anything, she wanted him to love her in return. And now instead of comforting her, he was down with John, planning the next part of their journey, and he hadn't even included her.

Caro's stomach churned and she dashed for the basin. What's more, he'd left her at the other inn when she was sick. Gervais really didn't care about her at all. He just wanted his heir. If only she had somewhere to go, she'd leave. After rinsing her mouth and taking a piece of the candied ginger she'd been given, she sat on the bed.

Gervais strode in. Fine lines of concern creased his brow, but it wasn't for her.

"Are you feeling better?"

"No." She blinked back the tears that pricked her lids. If only he loved her, everything would be all right again.

Much to her dismay, instead of taking her in his arms, Gervais paced the room. His face showed no emotion and his voice was flat, as if her being ill was business to resolve. "Horatia has sent for a doctor. We'll see what can be done."

Caro wanted to yell and scream. She wanted him to hold her, but it would never happen again. Her heart sank. She couldn't live with him like this. She wrapped herself in what was left of her dignity. "I think it's best if we separate."

He stopped moving, his face darkened in anger. "*What?*"

She firmed her chin. "This, our marriage, isn't working."

"I don't care if you think it's working or not," he bellowed so loudly she winced. "*You* are mine. The child is mine, and you're not going anyplace. Is that clear, *my lady*?" He turned and stalked out, slamming the door behind him.

Caro fell back on the bed and wept. Steps echoed in the corridor, and she hastily wiped her cheeks before the door opened again.

"Caro, my love." Horatia hurried toward Caro and wrapped her arms around her. "I heard Huntley. Tell me what is wrong. What has happened between you?"

"I love him, and he doesn't love me. All he wants is his heir. I thought I could live with him even if he just liked me, but I cannot."

Horatia stroked her hair and made shushing noises. "There, there, my dear. I'm sure you are mistaken. I think he's very much in love with you."

"But he's never said it, and now all he cares about is the baby."

"Sometimes men can be very foolish. Wash your face and go take a turn in the garden out back. Let me see what I can do to help straighten this all out."

Nothing would help. Still, Caro nodded and rose to splash her face. "You're right. Maybe the fresh air will make me feel better."

After giving her a kiss on the cheek, Horatia left the room and hurried down the corridor into her own chamber. "Risher, I need to see Nugent and Maufe."

"What is it, my lady?"

"I'll explain it all when they get here." She paced until Risher returned with the other two. She thought briefly about telling John her idea, but he'd be on Huntley's side. Really, how could someone of her blood be so stupid? A soft knock came at the door. "Come."

"My lady, you wished to see us?" Maufe asked.

"Yes, I would not involve you, but your master and mistress need our help."

Nugent's lips formed a thin line. "We heard the shouting."

Closing her eyes, Horatia shook her head. "The entire hotel no doubt heard him. Maufe, I want you to find out who from the hotel is leaving in the next hour or so and at what time. Several minutes before the departure, find Lord Huntley and ask if he's seen Nugent or her ladyship."

When he nodded, Horatia turned to Caro's dresser. "Nugent, I've sent Caro out for a walk in the garden. Keep her out of Lord Huntley's sight until you hear him bellowing again. Then I want you to bring her to the front of the hotel and leave her there." Horatia clapped her hands together several times. "Come, come. There is no time to lose."

Once the servants left, she turned to Risher. "Get me a wrapper and take out something for me to wear so it will appear as if I'm dressing. Go to Caro's room and put away everything on her dressing table. He won't notice more than that."

Risher narrowed her eyes. "What are you planning?"

"I'm going to make him think Caro's run away."

Shaking her head, Risher went to the wardrobe. "I hope you know what you're doing, my lady. He's got a temper like the old lord."

Horatia smiled wryly. "So do I. Yet it's clear Caro and Huntley are in love, else they'd not be acting like this. I'm just helping them resolve their problem."

A few minutes later, there was a knock on the door. "My lady?" Maufe said.

"Come in."

He opened the door. "There is a coach leaving in the next fifteen minutes or so. It's being loaded as we speak."

"That cuts it close, but it might do. Job well done, Mr. Maufe. Carry on."

He shut the door.

About ten minutes later, a door down the corridor opened and closed. Booted feet pounded down the stairs and the muted sounds of people getting out of the way drifted up. Risher glanced at Horatia. She nodded. "It won't be long now."

Taking a seat at her dressing table, she waited. Soon there was a loud and insistent banging on her parlor door. She raised a brow at Risher and tried to keep her lips from twitching.

"Where is my wife?" Huntley roared.

Good Lord, he sounded just like his grandfather. She faced the door and in her most imperious tone said, "You may as well come in. I have no intention of holding a conversation with you through the door."

The door slammed open and bounced against the wall. He stood in the entrance. Anger and concern warred in his darkened face. "Where's Caro? I searched all over the inn. She wouldn't go anyplace without telling you."

Horatia calmly raised her chin. "Caro has left."

His jaw clenched. "When?"

"A few moments ago." Turning away from him and back into the mirror, Horatia signaled Risher to continue dressing her hair.

He gave an anguished groan and the sound of his boots echoed in the corridor.

Horatia met her dresser's gaze in the mirror. "Well, maybe he'll finally realize what he needs to do."

"I certainly hope so, my lady," Risher agreed. "I would like to see them settled before we leave for Paris."

Nugent and Maufe entered Horatia's parlor.

"It went against the grain for me to deceive him," Maufe said.

Nugent took his hand in hers and nodded sagely. "But it's for the best. Both of them needed a little push."

"Collins!" Huntley roared as he raced down the stairs.

"He's gone to see about some horses," John said. "What is it?"

Huntley couldn't let her go. Somehow he had to make it right between them. He responded without stopping. "Caro, she's leaving. I have to stop her."

"I'll come." Whitton fell in behind him. "Do you know where she's gone?"

"No." A coach with a team of six just started out of the yard. "There." Huntley pointed. "See if you can stop the horses."

John raced out and, ignoring the coachman's protests, grabbed the leader's harness. Huntley jerked the door open and reached inside. "Caro!" Something hard hit his hand. He jerked it back and glanced up. Two elderly ladies scowled at him. "I'm sorry, I—I thought you were my wife."

"Well," one of the ladies said, "if that's the way you treat her, no wonder she doesn't want you."

"Ain't no one been out here for the last twenty minutes or so," the coachman added.

Huntley closed the door and backed up as the coach lurched forward. Vanished. She'd left, and it was his fault. Where would she go, and how was he going to find her?

"Gervais?" a small, tentative voice asked.

Caro. He swung around and almost before it registered that it was her, he crushed her to him. "Thank God. Caro, Caro. I can't live without you. Please don't go."

"You don't want me just because of the baby?"

"God, no. Is that what you thought?" He kissed her hair and her temple. "I'm such a fool. Caro, I love you. I've loved you for weeks now."

She stared up at him, all the pain she'd been feeling in her beautiful blue gaze.

"Then I don't understand why you didn't come to me when I was so ill."

"Oh, my darling." He kissed her eyes, tasting her salty tears. "I thought you didn't want me."

Her chin quivered. "Not want you? I was never so lonely and miserable."

"My love, I'm so sorry. I'll never spend another night away from you." He'd never let go of her again. Why had he listened to that old woman?

He captured her lips and plundered. He finally released her enough to speak, but not to leave.

Tears stained her cheeks, but she was smiling again. "I love you too. I couldn't live with the thought you didn't return my feelings."

John cleared his throat. "You two might want to consider taking this inside. You're creating quite a stir out here."

Huntley glanced up at the growing crowd. "Yes, of course." He reached down, swooping Caro up into his arms.

"*Gervais!* You can't just carry me with all these people here."

"You're in a delicate condition and you're not well."

Her light giggle tinkled musically in his ears. "I feel much better now. Even ladies who are breeding can walk. I'm sure your mother did."

"You're not my mother. You're my wife, and I love you."

Laughter mingled with tears as she pressed her face into his neck. "Yes, my lord husband."

Others around them laughed as well, before suddenly becoming silent.

Caro glanced up and froze.

Di Venier, mounted on a black horse, stared at her and Gervais as if he'd like to murder someone. Probably her husband. A large traveling coach loomed behind him. Were they never going to be rid of him?

He dismounted and bowed. "Lord Huntley, I will take your burden."

Gervais pulled her closer. She wondered if he had his pistol. Yet even if he did, with her in his arms, he couldn't get to it.

Rage burbled up in her. She trembled slightly. One hand held tightly onto Gervais, the other formed a fist. How dare di Venier threaten her husband and her child? She would not allow him to ruin her life. "You arrogant, insufferable, perfidious popinjay. I demand you leave my husband and me alone."

Di Venier, who'd been swaggering forward, stopped. "I would give you a better life, a—"

"You lecherous murderer," Caro spat at him. "I would rather end my life than allow you to touch me."

Gervais's grip on her tightened again. "My love," he whispered, cautioning her.

She shook her head. "No. I will have my say. This cannot go on. I'll not be frightened any longer, and I won't let this toad destroy what we have."

The marchese stared as if he couldn't believe what he was hearing. "But you, a woman of passion, with *him*, an *Englishman*?"

Did the stupid man assume only Venetians could be passionate? She fixed di Venier with a cold look. "I am carrying my husband's child."

His eyes grew wide. "No, this cannot be happening. God is not so cruel. You are lying!"

"How stupid you are," she sneered. "Why do you think we married so quickly?" Right now, she'd do or say anything to stop di Venier. If she had a pistol, she'd shoot the marchese herself for keeping her out here when all she wanted was to be alone with Gervais and not feel sick anymore.

For just a moment, an anguished, haunted look appeared in di Venier's eyes, then they hardened and he withdrew a gun from the pocket of his greatcoat. "I think not."

In her ear, Gervais whispered, "No matter what happens, don't move. I'll try not to ruin your gown."

His arm shifted under her, moving her skirts aside. She tightened her grip on him.

"If you value your life, Lord Huntley, put her down," di Venier demanded.

"Go, now," Gervais said. "If you try to take my wife, you'll not leave here alive."

The air crackled between the two of them.

"I'd listen to Huntley, if I were you." John's laconic voice disturbed the tension.

Di Venier's gaze went back and forth between John and Gervais. Di Venier raised a hand and another man, armed with a musket, came forward. "I think not."

Why would the man not believe her? "I'm not going anyplace with you."

His lips curled. "Not even to protect your husband?"

Part of her couldn't believe he'd kill Gervais, but another part of her knew di Venier would at least try. Her life wouldn't be worth living if anything happened to Gervais.

As if he could read her mind, her husband said, "Stay."

The yard was so still, but blood rushed in her ears. A

large red traveling coach trimmed in gold with an ornate crest on the door pulled into the yard behind di Venier, yet no one seemed to notice.

The Duca di Venier descended, and in a strong voice said, "Antonio."

The marchese's eyes slanted toward the duke. "What are you doing here?"

"Did you think you could hide your plans from me? I am here for you. To stop you from making a grave mistake."

"Nonno. I will come as soon as Lady Caro joins me."

"Have done with this foolishness. I have arranged a marriage for you and the contract is signed. Will you disgrace the name of di Venier with this childish behavior?"

"She is the one I want."

The older man's tone gentled but was still full of command. "Yes, yes, I know, but this one is already taken and does not appear to want to leave her husband." He made a signal and two servants stood on either side of the marchese.

The duke addressed her. "My lady. I apologize for my grandson. I beg you will forgive him."

Before she could even think of an answer, di Venier lunged. Gervais shifted her in his arms and a shot rang out, and the pistol the marchese had held fell to the ground. Blood flowed from his hand, making Caro's stomach lurch.

Gervais turned her head to his chest. "Don't look."

One of the duke's servants took hold of the marchese, escorting him to the red carriage. The other took his horse and tied it to the back of the coach the marchese had brought. In a matter of moments, both carriages were gone.

She rested her head against Gervais's shoulder. "Do you think it's truly over this time?"

"Yes. He won't bother us again." He kissed her. "We have some making up to do."

Caro grinned. "Yes, I think you're right. You may let me down now."

He turned toward the inn.

"Gervais—"

How he managed to kiss her and at the same time carry her up to their chamber, she'd never know. Yet by the time he placed her gently on the bed, most of her laces were undone. She had no idea he was so talented.

Chapter 24

Satisfied, Horatia smiled as she watched Huntley carrying her formerly staid goddaughter, elbowing his way through the crowd of interested on-lookers that had formed at the inn's door. That was a job well done.

Her back prickled as a large male body stood behind her. "You are sure," John commented dryly, "you could not have got the same results without all the drama? Before the marchese showed up, it was like watching a Drury Lane farce."

She glanced up at her handsome husband. "We probably could have got them in the same room without their shouting at each other, but there was too much pent-up energy that needed to be released."

"Termagant." He put his arms around her. "Who were the old ladies leaving in the carriage?"

"The Misses Berry. Two redoubtable spinsters well able to look after themselves."

As he led Horatia back into the inn, he said, "Shall we expect the young couple to join us for dinner?"

"Hmm." She gave him a sidelong glance. "It would not surprise me if we didn't see them until breakfast. Though they do have to eat. Which reminds me, I must try to discover a remedy for Caro's morning sickness, the poor thing."

They reached their chamber door and John opened it. "The next time you decide to plan one of your little events, please let me know in advance."

Horatia turned and kissed him. "I do expect a couple of people to arrive, but not for a few days at the soonest."

"Who would that be?" he asked as he nipped her ear.

"Caro's and Huntley's parents." She sighed with contentment. She had only been married for a few days, but so far, it was turning into the most enjoyable thing she'd ever done.

John stopped for a moment. "I wonder if your nephew and goddaughter will thank you for that. I had no idea you were such a meddler."

Horatia drew her brows together. "No, neither did I. It seems now that I am deliriously happy, I want the rest of the world to be, as well."

Trying to fix John's life for him had been her first attempt at it, and to-day it had come naturally. Perhaps it was a latent talent.

The first of her gown's ties loosened.

"Deliriously happy, is it?" He kissed her neck. "Not just amazingly?"

Her mouth dried in anticipation as his hands traveled up from her waist to her breasts. "No, definitely . . ."

"My lady," Risher called in a low but urgent voice from the corridor, "you must come straight away. Both the Marchioness of Huntingdon and the Marchioness of Broadhurst have arrived, and they—"

John opened the door. "Please come in."

Risher ignored him. "And they want to know where Lord and Lady Huntley are."

"Oh dear," Horatia said as she started toward the door. "I don't think this is a good time to interrupt them."

John held her back, fastening her laces again. "Hold still," he ordered. "It won't do for you to run around the hotel with your gown falling down. Risher, see if you can stop the mothers from making any forward progress. They might have a shock if they disrupt their lord and ladyship."

"Yes, my lord." Risher rushed out of the room.

"There you go, my love." He held his arm out to her. "I think you miscalculated."

They hurried out the door. "I think I did. How did they get here so soon?"

Horatia didn't even want to think what her sister-in-law's and friend's responses would be if they entered Caro and Huntley's chamber.

When Horatia and John reached the other end of the corridor, Caro's mother, with Huntley's right behind her, over Maufe and Nugent's objections, had reached out and grasped the door latch.

"*No, don't!*" Horatia yelled, too late.

Caro's legs were wrapped tightly around Huntley as he thrust one last time. He swallowed her cry with a kiss and emptied his heart and soul into her. "I love you."

"I love—"

"*Caro!*" a woman cried from the door.

He quickly dragged the cover up and roared, "Who the devil are you, madam, and what are *you* doing in *my* chamber?"

Beneath him, his wife's eyes were like saucers, and she turned the brightest shade of red he'd ever seen. He glanced at the door. A woman standing stock still, slapped her hand over her mouth.

"*Out. Now.* Maufe, remove that person, or I'll do it." He made as if to throw off the cover.

"Huntley, you stay right where you are."

"Mama?"

"Yes, my lord, right away." Maufe bowed. "My lady, you must leave now."

"Oh dear," Horatia said, ushering the two women out of the room. "Sally, perhaps you and Emily should wash and rest from your journey."

"Who is Emily?" Huntley asked. How many women were out there?

Caro was making some kind of noise, and he thought at first that she was crying, but when he looked, she was laughing so hard, tears were in her eyes.

"What is going on?"

She tried to speak and went into whoops again. "Oh my," she said and got no further.

He disengaged himself and rolled so that she was now on top. Bringing her down to him he kissed her through her giggles.

Finally, she was able to bring herself under control. "That was my mother."

He closed his eyes and groaned. "But what was she doing entering our room like that?"

Caro shook her head. "I have no idea. I suppose we shall have to join both of our mothers later."

"If she hasn't fled the hotel in shock." He reached out, tugged the bell-pull and closed the bed hangings. Soon the sound of a tub being brought into the room and water being poured could be heard. "I wrote your father that we'd wed, and I am sure that my cousin, Everard, did as well."

Caro chuckled. "So they know we're not living in sin."

He smiled. "I hope this cures your mother of pushing her

way into a person's chamber uninvited." The door shut. "But what the deuce are they doing here?"

His wife shrugged. "I suppose we will find out later."

Placing his hand lightly on her stomach, he asked, "How are you feeling?"

"Much better than I have been," she replied. "Perhaps it was all the travel."

"I am sorry for not staying with you, my love. I should never have listened to the old hag."

"No, no," she said, placing her fingers on his lips. "I was just as much at fault. I should have called for you. Nugent did ask if she should bring you to me. Yet . . . oh, it doesn't matter anymore."

"It does matter." He captured her gaze. He needed to know everything that had happened. "No more secrets. I think it's time you told me everything about what happened before you left England."

She nodded and slipped off him. Running a hand over his chest, she wondered where to begin. "When I was sixteen, I fell in love. My father said I was much too young, but the young man said he would wait. Though when he went to Town for the Season, he found another lady and married her." Gervais stroked her hair. "Later, I was told he'd had no choice but to marry money, and soon, because of his father's and grandfather's gambling."

He kissed her temple. "Go on."

"The Season after that, I was seventeen, and Mama decided to bring me out, but I was still pining for Andrew."

"Andrew?"

"The young man, Andrew Seaton."

Gervais nodded. "I've met him and the lady he married. It's clear it was not a love match."

She knew he said it to make her feel better, and it did.

Though she was glad now she'd not married Andrew. Gervais was all she wanted. "I had a number of offers, but could not find anyone I truly wanted to wed. When my father proposed a match, I accepted. At the time it didn't matter to me who I married, if it wasn't Andrew."

Huntley rubbed her back and cuddled her closer to him. She had started to tense, but he always seemed to know exactly what to do to calm her. "Yet when I came to know my betrothed better, I knew I could not go through with it." She tried to keep her voice from hitching. It had been weeks since she'd even thought about all of it.

"Who was it, my love?"

She thought only briefly about keeping the name to herself. Yet Gervais was her husband and had a right to know. "He is now the Earl of Thornbridge."

Huntley sucked in a breath and growled, "Thornbridge. I have an old score to settle with him."

That was not welcome news. Gervais had been so good about not fighting the marchese, until he had to shoot him, that she hadn't thought he might fight someone else. She clutched him and held on as if he were ready to leave now, and said as fiercely as she could, "No, if anything were to happen to you, I would die."

He kissed her again and stroked down her back and around to her stomach. "He doesn't have the skill to hurt me. I should have killed him the first time."

"The tweenie you told Nugent about?" she asked.

"Yes."

Caro breathed in deeply. "I knew he was evil. I just didn't know that he would . . ."

His grip on her tightened. "I'll not allow the rascal anyplace near you again. Not even in the same town."

That she knew. Gervais would never allow anyone to

harm her, but neither would she allow him to be hurt. "It's over. You healed me."

He shook his head. "What about all the other women and girls he has and will hurt?"

Caro's stomach turned. "Gervais, I don't feel well."

He sprang from the bed, grabbed a basin, then held her hair back. When she was done, he handed her a cup of weak tea, donned his dressing gown, and tugged the bell-pull.

Nugent appeared in the doorway.

"We need some of the ginger tea," he said. "Her ladyship has been ill again."

"I'll get a bowl of salty broth as well, and some dried bread."

Gervais came back to Caro, sitting down next to her. "We are not going anywhere until you've recovered from this malady."

"Thank you." She cast around for something to keep her mind off her stomach and realized that they'd both forgotten their mothers. "I wonder why Mama is here."

He sat up, bringing her with him, and said, "I wonder what both our mamas are doing here and if our fathers are far behind."

Her eyes widened. "You don't think they will object to our marrying, do you?"

He laughed. "It really doesn't matter if they do. Neither of us are minors, and we are both eligible. Though I did promise my father I'd not bring home a wife. I'm going to assume he meant a foreign bride."

How strange everything had turned out, Caro thought. Her husband had been escaping the match-making mamas, and she had resolved never to marry. And now they were both happy, in love, and wed. Not to mention the baby. She chuckled. "Not just a wife, but also a child on the way."

Gervais's lips curved up and his eyes were almost green as he gazed at her. "And I wouldn't give up either of you."

She was so happy her heart ached. "No, neither would I."

Horatia and John were in a parlor overlooking the courtyard terrace, enjoying the local wine. "It appears that everything is working out," she said. "Though I knew both their fathers would be happy with the match."

He covered her hand with his. "We need to make some decisions of our own."

She nodded. "Yes. I suppose we shall have to travel to your estates and decide what must be done."

"We will, but what about your servants?"

Horatia took a sip of wine. "I am still of a mind to buy a house in Paris."

He stroked her hand, and a shiver ran up her arm. John's deep voice washed over her. "We'll find an agent when we arrive in Paris, but right now I'd like some more of your time."

How was it he could discuss buying property and make it sound like he was undressing her?

He rose just as her dear friend, Emily, Marchioness of Broadhurst, and her sister-in-law, Sally, Marchioness of Huntingdon, joined them. Both ladies turned curious gazes on Horatia and John.

Horatia stifled a sigh, motioned them to take their seats, and called for more wine to be served. "Please allow me to present my husband, John, Earl of Devon."

Strange how much she enjoyed saying that.

Both ladies hugged her, and Sally said, "My dear, I thought you had decided not to marry again."

What a thing to say in front of John. Though she probably should have expected it. Her sister-in-law had always been extremely forthright. Horatia fought the blush rising in her neck. "I said I would not wed again unless a man caught my attention." She glanced briefly at John; he grinned. "He certainly did that."

"Well," Sally said, "I am very pleased for you and wish you both happy." She looked at John and then to Horatia. "When did you marry?"

"About a week ago," John replied.

She told them how the flight from Venice and meeting John had come about.

Emily grinned. "I can tell you my girls will think it very romantic. I cannot say I would disagree with them." She paused for a moment. "Thank you for protecting my daughter so well."

Sally frowned a bit. "I'll be interested to know how it was everything was settled between Huntley and Caro."

Emily nodded. "Yes indeed."

"Not that it matters," Sally said, "but what did the children say?"

Horatia shook her head. "We haven't had an opportunity to discuss it yet. They arrived perhaps an hour ago, and we'd just gotten things sorted out when you arrived."

Emily blushed. "Yes, well. I can see they are getting along."

Horatia drew her brows together. "How did you get here so quickly? I sent the letter less than a week ago."

Sally settled back and took a sip of wine. "We were all still in London when the notes from Huntley, Caro, and Everard arrived. Although we were all extremely satisfied with the news, it did take us by surprise. Of course, there was nothing for it but for Huntingdon and Broadhurst to begin working on the marriage settlements." She glanced at John. "No offense intended, but you know what men are when they start to bicker."

He laughed. "I am sure they would refer to it as discussing the finer points of the contracts."

She smiled. "Indeed. Well, be that as it may, Emily thought Caro would not be in a hurry to return to England, and we decided to travel to Nancy and join you. Fortunately, Horatia, the missive you wrote from here arrived at the embassy before we started out."

Emily took up the thread. "We've hired a large house in Paris and intend for everyone to spend Christmas together there." She glanced at Horatia and John. "You two are, naturally, expected to join us. Our families have been friends for an age, but to have our children married is something special indeed."

Sally leaned forward and took Horatia's hand. "And to have you back among us"—tears started in her eyes—"Huntingdon will be so happy."

"Yes," Emily said. "We told them we'd return as soon as possible, so we should leave in a day or two."

"My lady," Huntley said from the door where he stood with his arm around Caro, "we thank you very much, but Caro will not travel again until she is feeling better. If you knew how ill she has been, you would not ask it of her."

"What is the matter with her?" his mother-in-law asked.

Caro blushed. He drew her a little closer. "She is in a, um, delicate condition."

The Marchioness of Broadhurst glowered at him as if Caro had had nothing to do with it. Silk skirts flew as her ladyship rushed to her chick and took one of Caro's hands. "You poor girl, come sit down."

With the look the marchioness had just given him, Huntley knew better than to relinquish his wife to her; he might never get Caro back again. He tightened his grip on her waist and led her to a chair. "Here, my love."

Fortunately, she appeared as if she'd rather stay with him than be borne off by her mother.

"Thank you." Caro turned to face the rest of the ladies. "My husband is right. I cannot travel any more for a while. We have been bumped and jolted from Ulm to here, over some of the worst roads I've ever been on. Just the thought of getting into a coach again makes me quite queasy."

As her mother chafed Caro's hands and exclaimed how horrible the early months of pregnancy were, his mother interrupted. "Black horehound."

They all stopped talking.

"What?" he asked.

"Black horehound," his mother repeated. "It works every time."

"But, Mama, how would you know? You were never ill."

Just for a moment, he knew where his youngest sister got her look of disgust. "Because I drank a tisane of the root every morning before I rose."

Anything was worth a try, and if his mother swore by it, then . . . He motioned for one of the inn's servants to ask Maufe to attend him. Once his valet arrived and had been given instructions to find an apothecary, Huntley turned back to the ladies, who'd settled into a comfortable coze.

Keeping a possessive hand on Caro, he turned to John. "I don't believe we have been properly introduced."

The man grinned. "It has been rather hectic. I am John, Earl of Devon. Your aunt and I married a week ago."

Huntley grinned. Well, well, it appeared as if Horatia had an interesting journey as well. "You work quickly."

John flushed. "I suppose I did, but it didn't seem like it at the time."

John glanced at Horatia, and Huntley knew he had the same look on his face when he gazed at Caro. "Welcome to the family."

"Thank you."

"I think we have a mutual friend in Lord Evesham," Huntley said. "He was Lord Marcus Finley."

John grinned. "Yes indeed. Marcus and I crossed paths many times. Fortunately, we were always on the same side."

"He was very favorably impressed by you as well," Huntley said.

Caro's hand tightened on his, and she glanced at her mother.

"I can tell," the lady said, "you are enjoying married life, but, my dear, in the afternoon and in your condition."

Caro gave her mother the most facetiously innocent look he'd ever seen on her face, and replied sweetly, "But, Mama, you always said that my husband would tell me how to go on."

Huntley choked on a laugh. Caro would never have responded like that before their marriage. Her mother blushed.

He took a drink of wine and almost spewed it out when his mother said, "There you go, Emily. That's what you get for putting your nose where it doesn't belong." His mother patted Lady Broadhurst's hand. "It's hard to let go, particularly when you haven't seen your child for such a long time. Unless, of course"—his mother gave him a sharp-eyed look—"he doesn't behave himself."

He almost rolled his eyes. Still, he was happy to see everyone getting along so well.

"Yes," Lady Broadhurst said, "I suppose you're right. Tell me, Caro, when is the child due?"

"The best we can figure out, it will be sometime in late July."

"When do you and Huntley plan to return to England?" her mother asked.

"We have not yet decided," he said. "There are some details we need to work out."

Lady Broadhurst glanced piercingly at Caro, before saying, "If it's Thornbridge you're worrying about, my dear, he's dead."

Her eyes flew wide, and he narrowed his and asked, "How?"

"He was at a house party and got separated from the group he was riding with. Apparently, he ran across a young woman. Fortunately, both the girl's father and betrothed arrived in time and killed him."

"What happened to the man who killed him?" Huntley said.

"There was an inquest," Lady Broadhurst said. "It was found to be done in defense of the man's daughter."

Caro slumped back in her chair like she'd had the wind knocked out of her. "It's over then."

Huntley had been toying with the light curls at the back of her neck and moved his hand to her shoulder. "Yes, it is over."

For both of them. Now it was time to get on with the rest of their lives.

Epilogue

When Caro, Gervais, and their families arrived in Paris, they learned some of their friends were there as well.

Phoebe, Countess of Evesham, greeted Caro as if five years hadn't passed and introduced her to Anna, Baroness Rutherford, and Serena, Viscountess Beaumont. Lord Beaumont, who'd had a horrible reputation and was now reformed, greeted Gervais.

They gathered in the drawing room of Phoebe's Paris residence. Horatia and John were present as well. Even though they were still in France, it felt like home.

Caro held up a glass of wine. "It is so nice to have old and new friends together."

Gervais took a drink of brandy. "Indeed." He glanced at Marcus and Rutherford. "Do you always spend Christmas in Paris?"

"No, we received a letter asking for our presence."

Caro raised a brow. "My mother?"

Phoebe laughed. "Both your mothers."

Rutherford cleared his throat. "So tell us, how did your marriage come about? I distinctly remember you leaving Yorkshire vowing not to marry."

Gervais drew Caro closer and told the story. At the end, he asked, "Has anyone heard from Wively?"

The men all shook their heads.

He raised his glass. "Here's to Wively's successful return from the West Indies. I wonder if he'll find a wife as well. If he does, then he'll be as lucky as I've been."

Please turn the page for an exciting sneak peek
of the next historical romance in
Ella Quinn's
Marriage Game series
ENTICING MISS EUGÉNIE VILLARET
Now on sale wherever
print and ebooks are sold.

Chapter 1

Miss Eugénie Villaret de Joyeuse followed Gunna, an old black slave, down a narrow back street lined with long houses in Crown Prince's Quarter. Her maid, Marisole, stood watch as Eugénie and the woman entered the building.

"He here, miss."

A baby, not older than one year, sat in the corner of the room playing with a rag doll. His only clothing was a clout, which, by the strong scent of urine, needed to be changed.

Other than the boy and the old woman, they were alone in the cramped dark room. Eugénie crouched down next to the child. "What happened to his mother?"

"Sold."

Naturally, why did she even bother to ask? It was cruel to separate a mother and child, but there was no law against it here.

"When?"

"A few days ago." Gunna glanced at the child. "He gone to plantation soon."

Even worse. He'd likely die before he was grown. Eugénie placed the small bag she carried on the floor. "Help me change him. He can't go outside like this."

A few minutes later the baby's face and hands were clean, his linen was changed, and he wore a clean gown.

She handed the woman two gold coins. "Thank you for calling me." The Gunna tried to give the money back, but Eugénie shook her head. "Use it to help someone else. Our fight is not finished until everyone is free."

One tear made its way down the woman's withered cheek. "You go now, before the wrong person sees you."

Eugénie pulled a thin blanket around the babe's head, thankful her wide-brimmed hat would help hide his face as well as hers, and stepped out into the bright sunshine.

"That's her!" a male voice shouted.

She shoved the babe at Marisole. "Take him and run! I'll catch up."

Eugénie quickly drew out her dagger, concealing it in the shadows of her skirts, and turned, crouching. A large man stood hidden in the shadow of a building, while a wiry boy she guessed to be in his late teens, came at her. She waited until he reached out to grab her arm, then sliced the blade across his hands. Before he started to scream, she dashed down an alley between the long houses. Doors swung open, and several women stepped into the street behind her. That wouldn't help for long, but it would delay the pursuit.

Perspiration poured down her face as Eugénie pounded up the hill, using the step streets to cross over to Queen's quarter. Ducking behind a large flamboyant tree, she waited for several moments, listening for the sound of men running, but there was nothing.

She took a scrap of cloth and cleaned the blade before returning it to her leg sheath. Then Eugénie removed her bonnet and turned toward the breeze, drawing in great gulps of air as she fanned herself with the hat.

A few minutes later she caught up to her maid. "How is the babe?"

Marisole smiled. "Look for yourself. He is fine."

Wide green eyes stared up at Eugénie, and the child blew a bubble and smiled. "Come, *mon petit*. Not long now and you will have a family."

The front door of a well-kept house in Queen's quarter opened as they approached.

Once in the short hall, she smiled. "Mrs. Rordan, thank you for agreeing to care for him. It will only be for a few days."

"As if I wouldn't." Mrs. Rordan grinned as she took the babe. "Captain Henriksen's already been in touch. There is a good family on Tortola who will adopt him." She handed Eugénie a bouquet of flowers. "For your mother; perhaps they'll help cheer her. You'd better get home, now."

"*Merci beaucoup*. She will love them." She kissed the little boy on the cheek. "Safe passage and a good life."

As Eugénie and her maid walked back to Wivenly House, Marisole said, "You were almost captured."

That was the closest she had ever been to getting caught. She drew her brows together. If they were after the child, why didn't the men follow? Did they know who she was? Even if they did, even with Papa gone, she had to continue. "Yes," she told Marisole, "but it is better not to question fate."

July, 1816, England

William, Viscount Wively, caught a glimpse of sprigged muslin through a thinly leafed part of the tall hedge behind which he'd taken refuge.

"Are you sure he came this way?" an excited female voice whispered.

Damn. He didn't like the sound of that. Will always found himself in sympathy with the fox at a hunt.

"Quite sure," came the hushed response. "You must be careful, Cressida. If I reveal to you what Miss Stavely told me in the *strictest* confidence, you must vow *never* to repeat what I'm about to say. I swore I'd never breathe a word."

"Yes, yes," Miss Cressida Hawthorne replied urgently, "I promise."

He'd been dodging the Hawthorne chit for two days now, and unfortunately she wasn't the only one. The other woman sounded like the newly betrothed Miss Blakely.

"Well then," Miss Blakely paused. "I really shouldn't. If it got out, she'd be ruined!"

"I already promised," Miss Hawthorne wheedled.

After a few moments, the other girl continued. "Miss Stavely said she followed Lord Wively to the library so that they'd be alone and he'd have to marry her."

"What an excellent plan." Miss Hawthorne's tone fell somewhere between admiring and wishful.

"Well it wasn't."

Even thinking about the incident with Miss Stavely made Will shudder. There were few worse fates he could imagine than being married to her in particular. Fortunately, the lady was not as intelligent as she was crafty. The minute she'd turned the lock, she announced he'd have to marry her. However, she'd failed to take into account the French windows through which Will had made his escape.

"What do you mean it wasn't?" Miss Hawthorne asked.

"Have you heard a betrothal announcement?"

Their footsteps stopped. Drat it all, there must be another way out of here. He surveyed the privet hedge, which boarded three sides of this part of the garden. Across from him was a wooden rail fence about five feet high. Large rambling roses in pale pink and yellow sprawled along it, completing the enclosure. Whoever designed this spot had wanted privacy. Will's attention was once again captured by the voices.

"No." Miss Hawthorne said slowly, as if working out a puzzle. "So it didn't work."

"Do you know what Miss Stavely failed to take into account?"

When Miss Hawthorne didn't reply, Miss Blakely continued. "She didn't bother to ensure she had a witness at hand. Miss Stavely said Lord Wively looked her up and down like she was a beefsteak and told her he'd ruin her if she wished, but not to think he'd take her to wife."

Perhaps not his finest moment, though Will had only wanted to scare the chit. Not that it had worked. She had practically launched herself at him.

"Oooh, how wicked." Miss Hawthorne giggled. "He's so handsome, and has such nice brown hair. I'd love to be compromised by him." She paused. "But only if he had to marry me, so you must make sure to bear witness."

Will had no intention of marrying Miss Hawthorne, or any other fair English maiden. Harpies in disguise, all of them. More interested in being Viscountess Wively and the future Countess of Watford than in their duties as a wife. From what he knew of her, Miss Hawthorne would probably only allow him in her bed for the purpose of getting with child. Surely he could do better than her.

When it came time for him to be leg shackled, he'd be the

one choosing. Yet even that would not be for at least another year or two. In the meantime, Will would be damned if he'd allow himself to be trapped into marriage. Thank God he'd already made plans to leave England for a while.

The sounds of the ladies' shod feet came closer.

Damnation. Will glanced around. The only escape was a large mulberry tree in full fruit. His valet, Tidwell, would have a fit about the stains, but needs must. As quickly and quietly as possible, he ascended the tree, careful not to let the slick leather soles of his boots slide off the branches.

"I am sure I saw him go this way," Miss Blakely said.

From his perch in the tree, Will had a view of the tops of their ridiculous bonnets. Why women had to use all those ribbons and furbelows on their hats defied logic.

"As did I," Miss Hawthorne replied. "I wonder where he could have got to."

"Do not worry. I shall be vigilant. We will find a way to ensure you are Lady Wively."

The hell she would. Will scowled. Did a lady exist who would not be impressed with his title, and would allow him to do the hunting? Probably not.

"Oh, look." Miss Hawthorne exclaimed. "A mulberry tree. We must pick some, perhaps the cook will make tarts, or I can have them with cream."

Will stifled a groan. Featherheaded females. Why had he ever allowed his mother to talk him into this house party on the eve of his departure for the West Indies?

Her friend linked an arm in Miss Hawthorne's. "Perhaps it might be better to send a servant. You wouldn't want to ruin your gown."

"You are correct." Linking arms, the two headed back to the formal garden, then she added, "but let us find someone straight away. Lord Wively must be around somewhere."

Will tipped his hat. *Sorry ladies, this fox is going Halloo and Away.*

He waited until they were half-way to the lake before climbing out of the tree. Upon regaining the house, he sneaked up a back staircase and strode to his bedchamber. "Tidwell!"

"I'm right here, my lord." The valet poked his head out from the dressing room. "No reason to shout. I'm getting your evening kit ready." He held up two waistcoats. "Would you prefer the green on cream or the gold?"

"I'd prefer to leave. Get everything packed. You've got an hour."

Tidwell bowed. "As you wish, my lord." His eyes narrowed as he took a sharper look at Will. "If I do not treat those stains, they'll never come out."

He glanced down. Not only mulberry juice, but leaf stains as well. "You'll just have to make do. It's not safe for me here."

"Another ruined suit." His valet sighed. "More problems with the ladies, I presume."

Taking pity on Tidwell, Will said, "Pack me a bag. You remain here until the toggery is cleaned. I'll take my curricle and meet you back at Watford Hall."

Tidwell immediately brightened. "Yes, my lord."

Changed into fresh clothing, Will donned his caped coat and hat, then found his host and made his excuses. By the time he stepped out into the stable yard, his carriage was ready, and his groom, Griff, was holding the horses' heads.

Will climbed into his curricle. "Good job."

"Thought it might be gettin' a bit hot for you hereabouts, my lord."

"Right as usual. Let their heads go."

Griff jumped onto the back as Will maneuvered the carriage out of the yard and onto the gravel drive. He caught a glimpse of Miss Hawthorne. She smiled at him, but when he smiled then inclined his head and sprung the horses, her jaw dropped.

Another close escape.

Five days later, Dover, England

The docks bustled with activity as ships prepared to sail with the tide. Will had met his friend Gervais, Earl of Huntley, in London, traveling down to the port city with him.

The early morning sky was about to lighten when they reached the packet on which Huntley was booked setting sail for France. "Godspeed in your travels."

He clasped Will's hand. "Good luck to you sorting out the problem in St. Thomas. I'll see you in the spring."

"Only if I can't think of a good excuse to remain abroad." Will grimaced. "Before I left, my father made me promise I'd marry next year."

"My father said the same to me. We'll lend each other support." Huntley's grim countenance reminded Will of a man going to trial. "Perhaps you'll be lucky enough to fall in love."

He almost choked. "You think that's lucky? I'd have to completely rearrange my life. No thank you. I'll probably end up picking one of the ladies my mother parades before me. At least then I'll know what to expect."

And he wouldn't risk living under the cat's paw because of a woman.

"My lord, the ship's about to depart," Huntley's groom called from the packet.

"You'll do as you think best." Huntley slapped Will's back.

"You as well." Will strode down the street to a Dutch Flyboat, one of the smaller sailing ships plying their trade ferrying passengers and goods to the many ports scattered up and down England's far Western coast.

Griff sat on a piling at the head of the pier. "'Bout time you got here. Tidwell's got the cabins all arranged, and the captain's just waitin' on you."

"Let's get onboard then. I can't miss the tide, or we'll be late for our rendezvous with Mr. Grayson." Will drew in a deep breath, savoring the air's briny scent. At one and thirty, Will hadn't had his blood rush with excitement of a new challenge for years. "Is there anything else you'd like to tell me?"

A large smile cracked Griff's weathered face. "Mr. Tidwell turned a nice shade of green when he got on the ship." He scratched his head as if he was giving the occurrence some thought. "Don't suppose he'll like the trip overmuch."

"Unless *you*," Will paused letting the word sink in, "wish to learn how to take care of my kit, you'd better hope Tidwell doesn't become too ill."

Griff, who'd been with Will since he'd sat his first pony, had carried on a good-natured feud with Tidwell since the valet had joined their household over eleven years ago. Will softened his voice. "Come now, I can't go about looking like a shagbag, and I daren't go without you. Who'd have my back when I get into trouble?"

"Well ye're in the right of it there." Griff nodded. "That peacock sure ain't goin' to haul you out o' some of the fixes you get yerself into. Why I recollect when—"

"Ho, Lord Wivenly is that you?" A short, middle-aged man with salt and pepper hair strode toward him. "I'm Captain Jones."

"Yes, sir. Are we ready to cast off?"

The captain directed an eye toward the water. "Just waiting for you, my lord."

Shortly after noon the following day, the boat docked at Plymouth's bustling port. Will descended to the pier wondering how, in all the hubbub, he'd find Andrew Grayson, an old friend who'd agreed to accompany Will, only to spy Andrew leaning up against a piling near the midsection of the ship.

"Handsomely done, Captain." Andrew straightened and inclined his head to Jones. "You've arrived in good time. We've a change in our travel plans. Lord Wively will need his baggage transferred to the *Sarah Anne* as soon as may be."

"Aha," the captain called out in a satisfied tone, "so Captain Black's going back again." Jones grinned. "I win my wager. I'll have it done straight away, Mr. Grayson."

Will furrowed his brow. "How do you know Jones?"

Andrew cast a glance at the sky as if searching for patience. "My maternal grandfather's in shipping, remember? I've spent time learning the business, as it will be mine."

That was one of the main reasons Will had asked Andrew to accompany him to St. Thomas. They walked in the direction of the main dock area. "I didn't know you planned on actually running the business. I thought you only wanted to be knowledgeable. Didn't some aunt leave you a snug little property with an independence?"

"Yes," Andrew nodded, "but my grandfather's bound by the settlement agreements to leave the shipping line to me as the second son, and I like knowing how to control what I'm going to own." He glanced back at Will with a raised brow. "Don't tell me you're worried I'll smell of the shop? Shipping is as respectable as banking, and look at Lady Jersey. She spends a good amount of time at the bank her father left her."

They reached another pier, where Andrew hailed a tall

man with broad shoulders, who'd clearly been at sea for a while. "That's Captain Black. His ship is one of the fastest you'll find, even with cargo."

"Mr. Grayson," the captain grinned, "I see you've found his lordship, and in good time."

"His gear will be here directly," Andrew said, "Captain Jones is seeing to it."

Captain Black turned his attention to Will. "Welcome aboard the *Sarah Anne*, my lord. I'll have you in St. Thomas in no time at all."

An hour later, Will stood near the bow of the ship, looking out over the water and trying to decided how to approach the problem his father had asked him to look into in St. Thomas. Though it would delay his exploration of the other islands, he knew that Watford's protective arms encircled all of their family, no matter where they were located, and Will felt the same way. Anyone in the Wivenly family was his to care for.

Andrew joined him. "Have you decided how you will approach the problem yet?"

Will wished he had; the whole thing was deuced strange. He shook his head. "My original intent was to pay my respects to my great-uncle Nathan's widow—funny that, Nathan was only a few years younger than my father—then meet with the manager, Mr. Howden. Yet after receiving the last letter from her, telling my father the business was failing, right on the heels of a report from Howden, showing it was as prosperous as ever, I don't know what to think, or whom to trust."

Andrew leaned against the rail. "Someone is being economical with the truth."

An understatement if Will had ever heard one. "The question is, who? I can't think of a reason my aunt would be dishonest. Her distress was clear from her letter. However, Howden has an impeccable reputation."

Andrew frowned. "Could there be another actor?"

Now *that* was something Will hadn't considered. "It's possible. I'll take great joy in making sure whoever is causing the problems will pay for their transgressions."

He'd make sure of it.

When it comes to love, there's never a dull moment in the Worthingtons' extended family circle . . .

Gerald, Earl Elliott, has finally decided to marry. Unfortunately, he seems only to fall for a lady once she is engaged to another. When his close friend, the Duke of Rothwell, asks him to look out for his sister, Lady Lucinda Hughlot, during her first London Season, Gerald is happy to oblige. After all, it will put him even more conveniently in the way of eligible ladies. Yet he's completely oblivious to Lucinda's growing attraction to him . . .

Lucinda is thrilled to finally be having her Season. Her mother would be thrilled as well except for the scandal the late duke caused before his death. To avoid gossip, the dowager duchess has decided an arranged match will cover her chaperoning duties. Lucinda, however, is far from pleased with her mother's choice of the Marquis of Quorndon—especially with her heart set on Lord Elliott. There is only one solution: Lucinda will find a lady for Quorndon. Then she will convince Lord Elliott of their love—and together they will convince her mother. All it will require are good theatrical skills—and a very genuine kiss . . .

**Please turn the page to begin
reading Ella Quinn's bonus novella
in her Worthington series,
I'LL ALWAYS LOVE YOU**

For my wonderful granddaughters, Josephine and Vivianne. May you find someone you'll always love.

Acknowledgments

Anyone involved in publishing knows it takes a team effort to get a book from that inkling in an author's head to the printed or digital page. I'd like to thank my beta readers, Jenna, Doreen, and Margaret, for their comments and suggestions. To my agents, Deidre Knight and Janna Bonikowski, for helping me think through parts of this book.

To my wonderful editor, John Scognamiglio, who loves my books enough to contract them for Kensington. To the Kensington team, Vida, Jane, and Lauren, who do such a tremendous job of publicity. And to the copy editors who find all the niggling mistakes I never am able to see.

Last, but certainly not least, to my readers. Without you, none of this would be worth it. Thank you from the bottom of my heart for loving my stories!

I love to hear from my readers, so feel free to contact me on my website and on Facebook. I also have a Facebook group for The Worthingtons. Please feel free to contact me if you have questions. My social media links and my newsletter link can be found at www.ellaquinnauthor.com.

On to the next book!

Ella

Chapter 1

Late March 1816
Rothwell Abbey

Lady Lucinda Hughlot, daughter of the former Duke of Rothwell and sister of the current duke, listened at the not-quite-closed door to her brother's study.

"Really, Rothwell." Her mother's exasperation resonated in every word. "I do not understand why Louisa cannot simply sponsor Lucinda herself."

"Mother, we have had this discussion before." Silence fell, and Lucinda knew he was trying to find another way of making the argument. "As you are well aware, Louisa gave birth not a month ago." Well, that wasn't new. Of course Mama knew. She'd been there. "I will not have her fagged to death trotting all over Town escorting Lucinda to entertainments. You will have to do your bit as well."

"Aside from that," Louisa said in a weary tone, "it would appear odd if you did not."

"I agree with Louisa," Rothwell said. "You are not at death's door, or even slightly ill."

"I could become so." Mama's dry tone would have been funny if Lucinda's Season were not at stake.

"In that event, *we* would not be able to go to Town,"— Louisa was beginning to sound as frustrated as Rothwell— "and that would end this argument about Lucinda's Season."

Lucinda bit down hard on her lip. Her mother had not been in society of any sort since Papa died. Although she had not been told the whole story—of that she was certain—there appeared to have been a scandal of some sort.

Unfortunately, there was little she could do about the decision. Rothwell was right. It was not fair for his wife to do everything for her when Mama was perfectly capable of doing her share.

"Are they still at it?" Her brother Anthony whispered, making Lucinda jump.

"Yes. Mama is still refusing to go to Town, and Rothwell is refusing to allow Louisa to be dragged all around chaperoning me."

Tony put a hand on her shoulder. "It will come out all right in the end. Rothwell and Louisa will get their way. But if you don't want to get in trouble for eavesdropping, you'd better come away from here."

Lucinda did not understand what made Tony so sure. Neither of them had had an opportunity to come to know their sister-in-law well. Shortly after Rothwell's marriage, Mama had insisted they repair to The Roses, her dower property, about a day's drive away. The whole family had spent Christmas at the abbey, and Lucinda had enjoyed seeing Louisa and her brother together, but there was not much time to actually speak with her.

Naturally, Mama had come for the birth of Rothwell and Louisa's daughter, Lady Alexandria Charlotte Hughlot, but

Lucinda had been left at The Roses. Yet despite not having spent much time with Louisa, Lucinda thought her sister-in-law had a great deal of sense. And even though she and Louisa were the same age, she seemed much more mature—that might have come from having had a Season—and was a force to be reckoned with. She had even saved hers and Rothwell's lives.

"You would deny your sister a Season?" Mama asked.

"No, *you* would deny her a Season." Rothwell's hard tone made Lucinda's heart drop. "What is it to be?"

The silence seemed to stretch into hours. "Very well. I shall go, but if the gossip starts up again because I am present, it will be on your head."

Lucinda glanced at Tony. "Gossip? Because of the scandal?"

"Go." He turned her around and gave her a push. "They are coming out."

She dashed off to the morning room. By the time the sound of padding feet could be heard down the corridor, and her brother and sister-in-law entered the room, she had an open book in her hands. Not that she had read any of it. At least her breathing had stilled.

Rothwell stood in the doorway. "It's done. Mama is not happy about it, but she will accompany us to Town."

"Thank you." Lucinda set the book aside, then rushed to her brother and hugged him. "There are two things I do not understand. Why is Mama so reluctant to go to London? And is the Season truly that busy?"

"To one who has not had a Season, it does not seem possible, but yes." Louisa pulled a face. "Balls, dinners, breakfasts, morning visits, picnics, the theater and opera, Almack's . . . and those are just the most common entertainments. When I came out last year, it took me more than two weeks to get used to it all."

"Not only that." Rothwell led Louisa to the sofa. "Worthington"—Louisa's brother—"insisted that she and her sister leave after supper because the younger children rose early in the morning. So, they weren't even up all night."

"Very true. I am not sure I could stay up all night. Especially now."

Her brother grinned. "In any event, we leave in a few days."

"But how will we manage it all? There is packing to do, and the servants to arrange, and—"

"Done, all of it." Rothwell patted his wife's knee. "Louisa was convinced Mama would change her mind. She put it all in motion over a week ago."

"Your mother does not know," Louisa said. "And please do not tell her."

"That brings me back to my first question. Why does Mama not wish to go to London? She used to like it a great deal."

Rothwell glanced at Louisa, who nodded. "When I returned last year, I discovered Father had suffered from dementia. Consequently, he forgot he had a wife and family. That not only embarrassed our mother—she didn't even tell me until I had started asking questions about the finances—but it caused her to feel ashamed that she'd done nothing." He shrugged. "Not that there was much she could have done with me in Canada."

"Your brother and I feel that she needs to go back into Polite Society, and the only way we could think of doing it was to insist she be present for your Season. It is also true that I *cannot*, with a new baby, do all the entertaining and gadding about that will be required to fire you off successfully. Aside from that, she loves you and wants to see you settled. That said, she does not understand—or, rather, agree—with my decision to nurse Alexandria. She would much rather I hand my child over to Nurse." Louisa chuckled. "In some ways, Nurse would like that as well. But I was not raised that way, and neither will my children be."

Well, that was more than anyone had told Lucinda before. "She almost never mentions Papa anymore. Do you think there will be gossip?"

Louisa exchanged a glance with Rothwell, then said, "No. There have been other events that have overshadowed your father's behavior before he died."

"His friends," Rothwell said, taking up the story, "know what happened, and they do not blame him for excesses over which he had no control. I think all will be fine, and Mama will enjoy being back in London."

"What would you have done if she had not agreed?"

"I had one more card to play." Her brother's lips twisted into a grim smile. "I would have told her Louisa was not up to holding a ball in your honor if she had to escort you everywhere."

Louisa's eyes widened in shock. "I can see how that would work. Although, I never actually had a ball in my honor. None of us did. Grace had no time to plan one because of all the weddings."

"Just as well." Rothwell put his arm around Louisa and pulled her closer. "Some other gentleman might have found you."

She smiled lovingly at him. "I think I was waiting for you and did not know it."

Love was grand, but they seemed to have forgotten Lucinda was in the room. She cleared her throat. "Should I go to Mama?"

Rothwell gave a start, which, for some reason, pleased Lucinda to no end. "I did not know you were still here."

Obviously, otherwise he would not have kissed his wife. "I was able to work that out all on my own."

He flushed, and his voice was gruffer when he said, "Yes, well. I would not go to her now, but you may tell your maid to begin packing."

Lucinda had to stop herself from skipping out of the room. She hadn't engaged in such behavior in years, but if she were to do it, now would be the perfect time. Instead, she strode as swiftly as she could, almost racing up the stairs to her chamber.

"Greene, come quickly." Lucinda opened the door to the dressing room. Empty. *Where could she be?* She reached for the bellpull and tugged it.

Several moments later, her maid entered the room. "My lady?"

"Not a word to anyone yet. The matter has finally been settled. We are going to London in a few days."

"That's what the senior staff thought would happen." Greene nodded. "And a good thing it is too. You deserve to have your come out, and no one could expect her grace to chaperone you all by herself. I'll make sure all the clothes you're taking are ready, then have the trunks brought down."

The clothes I'm taking? "Why wouldn't I bring everything?"

"You'll have new gowns waiting for a final fitting once we get to London." Greene went into the dressing room, as if that answered Lucinda's question.

Not willing to let the comment go, she followed on her maid's heels. "How would I have new garments waiting?"

"I gave her grace's maid your measurements when we were here at Christmas. She sent them to her grace's modiste."

Christmas! Louisa had been that sure Lucinda would have her Season. Her good opinion of her sister-in-law rose even higher. Since Lucinda did not have to worry about garments, she could begin gathering the other things she wished to take. After all, she might not return at the end of the Season.

Early April 1816
Mayfair, London, England

Gerald, Earl Elliott, strode out of his mother's parlor, up the corridor, into the hall, and out the front door of *his* house on Mount Street, almost forgetting to take his hat and cane from *his* butler.

The woman was going to drive him mad with her demands to redecorate every public room in the house. Not that he liked the Egyptian furniture that was there now. But it was *his* house, and he wished to redecorate it as he liked. And who knew what Mother would select this time. After all, she was the one who chose that horrible Egyptian stuff in the first place. Unfortunately, his mother—as she frequently reminded him—had possession of the town house until he married.

He should have stayed in the country, but Parliament had been called into session last month, and Gerald did not like to be absent in the event something momentous occurred. Yet at this time of year, the Lords mostly dealt with accounts and divorces. Although, if something crucial did happen, he had a list of peers to whom he'd promised to send urgent messages. Those lucky fellows had stayed at home with their families. Perhaps when he wed, he'd remain in the country as well.

Mayhap this was the year he'd find himself enthralled enough by a lady to propose marriage. The problem was, no matter how beautiful, or talented, or desirable a lady was, he never seemed to discover he was intrigued by her until she was betrothed to another.

Was fate playing tricks on him, or was it just poor luck that he had not noticed Ladies Charlotte and Louisa, now the Marchioness of Kenilworth and the Duchess of Rothwell, respectively, until it was too late? Not that he would let anyone know about his lack of perspicacity. Not only was he friends with both of their husbands, he'd seen them spar at Jackson's and had no desire to be on the receiving end of any punishment they might decide was right and honorable. It had also happened with Miss Turley, now the Countess of Harrington. How could Gerald be so blind to a lady's attributes?

Perhaps he simply hadn't met the right woman. That must be it. When the lady he was meant to wed came along, he'd know it immediately. Just as his friends had. He wished his mother could understand that.

He turned onto Carlos Place and skirted Berkeley Square as he headed to Jermyn Street, where his rooms were located. Once he wed, he'd move into his house and send his mother to her dower property, or wherever she decided to go. He could even buy her a house in Mayfair. The only time they didn't rub on well together was during spring and autumn, when the *ton* was in Town and the young ladies were having their Seasons.

When he reached the corner of Piccadilly and Saint James Street, he decided to go to his club instead of his rooms. Someone must have come to the metropolis in preparation of the Season. He mounted the steps to Brooks in anticipation.

After being greeted by a footman and ordering a glass of claret, Gerald strolled into the morning room to find the Marquis of Quorndon with his nose in a newssheet. Gerald had known Quorndon since Eton, and, although they were not close, they were on good terms.

"Quorndon, what brings you to Town?" Gerald took a seat on a leather chair next to the other man. Light green walls made the room look larger than it was. Various seating areas, all with comfortable dark leather chairs, were grouped around the room.

Lowering his paper, Quorndon replied, "Several things. The Lords." He gave Gerald a slight smile. "I depend on you to tell me what has been going on, if anything. Mainly, I came at my mother's behest. She has found me a lady she believes I would like to marry."

That was not surprising. Mothers always seemed to be finding ladies they would like their sons to wed. "Is she anyone I know?"

"I doubt it." Quorndon flicked open an elegant enameled and jeweled snuff box, took a pinch, and sniffed. Nasty habit, that. "She was meant to come out last year, but her father died. She is the elder of Rothwell's sisters. I believe her name is Lady Lucinda. Yes, I'm certain that must be it. My mother has mentioned it enough for me to remember."

If one were looking strictly at bloodlines, it was an excellent match. "What does Rothwell have to say about it?"

"Why, nothing at all. If he even knows." One of Quorndon's dark blond brows rose. "Strangely enough, the dowager duchess is the lady's sole guardian."

How had that come about? Normally, a lady would have two guardians, and one of them would be her brother. At least in this case. Still, there was nothing objectionable about Quorndon, after all. "I wish you luck."

"Thank you." Quorndon inclined his head. "However, I doubt luck will have anything to do with it. I shall meet the lady to establish if we would get on well enough to produce heirs. If that is determined to my satisfaction, we shall wed." He settled back into the chair. "Now, about the Lords."

Gerald studied the other man as he briefly reviewed what had or had not occurred over the past several weeks; Quorndon didn't appear to care about any of it. His snuff seemed to hold more interest for him than bills that would change the lives of the common people of England. In fact, just about everything seemed to bore him. Gerald hoped Quorndon had more interest in the lady he might be marrying, but even that was doubtful.

Perhaps he might benefit from a change. "Why don't you travel the Continent now that Bony is secured again?"

Quorndon gave an elegant shudder. "My dear Elliott, no thank you. I enjoy my creature-comforts. I have been told the highways in France are worse than our country lanes. Once they have been repaired and the French court has regained its former elegance, I may visit."

Well, there was no pleasing some people. Particularly when they did not wish to be pleased.

When Gerald married, he was determined to take an extended wedding trip to France, and Italy as well. He gave himself a shake. Until recently, he'd not given marriage much thought, but it seemed to be cropping up in his mind a great deal lately. If that was what he wanted, he'd better make sure the lady would like to travel as well. He'd also better hope he recognized the lady. This becoming attracted to ladies who were already attached really wasn't doing him any good.

A breeze moved the air, and he glanced up. Rothwell. Gerald's friend grinned at him, but merely nodded to Quorndon. If that was the way the wind blew, the marquis would have a harder time courting Lady Lucinda than he'd thought. Rothwell might not be his sister's guardian, but Gerald would bet his purse that he had a great deal of influence, and so would the new Duchess of Rothwell.

"Quorndon, I see you made it to Town," Rothwell said rather impatiently as he strode into the morning room.

With a sardonic smile, Quorndon spread out his arms theatrically. "As you see. My mother informed me that my presence is required."

"Matchmaking, is she?" Rothwell signaled to a waiter.

Quorndon's brows snapped together. "You don't know then?"

Shaking his head, Rothwell asked, "Know what?"

"It appears our mothers have decided your sister and I would make a good match." Quorndon took another pinch of snuff.

"Hell and damnation!" Several heads in the room turned toward them, and Quorndon's visage became a mask of barely suppressed fury. "Forgive me." Rothwell rubbed one temple. "It has nothing to do with you in particular."

"Indeed?" The marquis's tone could have frozen a pond.

"Don't fly up into the boughs. I would simply like my sister to find her own husband."

"Ah, yes. I had forgotten that you have a love match." Quorndon brushed a non-existent speck of lint from his jacket. "Not all of us are so lucky as to find a suitable lady with whom to fall in love."

Rothwell looked as if he would say something more, but instead turned to Gerald. "Elliott, well met. I'd like a word, if you have time."

"Certainly." He turned to Quorndon. "I shall see you again, I'm sure."

"I rather expect you will." They had both risen when Rothwell addressed them, and Quorndon resumed his seat.

Gerald motioned Rothwell to the other end of the room. The thick carpet muffled their footsteps, and they took chairs next to each other.

Once Rothwell had been served a glass of wine, he said, "Drat my mother. I wish she would leave well enough alone. I want my sister to be happy. If Quorndon and she decide they would suit, I will be glad." He shrugged. "If not, I'll have yet one more problem with which to deal."

"Truth be told,"—Gerald hesitated, debating whether he should involve himself or not—"Quorndon is not looking for a love match. If Lady Lucinda pleases him, he will do as his mother wishes."

Rothwell scowled. "Bloody hell. He won't be the only gentleman who won't care what she wants or thinks. I can tell you, I am not looking forward to this Season." He took a long draw from his wine. "Normally, I wouldn't ask a favor such as this, but I have no experience chaperoning a young lady." He swirled the claret, the liquid coating the sides of the glass. "I was gone so long I am not even sure who is on the hunt for an heiress and who isn't. Quite frankly, I don't see how Worthington managed three young ladies. If you could help me keep an eye on my sister, I'd be grateful. I will not have her forced into anything she does not wish to do. Especially marriage."

"Certainly, I'll help you." Not that Gerald knew quite what he should do. He was not a member of the family, and therefore had no real authority. Yet he could warn the duke or duchess if he thought there was a potential problem.

"Thank you." Rothwell heaved a sigh. "I should go home now. The ladies will be done shopping." He rose from his seat. "I'd like to invite you to drink tea with us later this afternoon. You can meet my sister, so that you'll recognize her at the events."

"My pleasure." Gerald felt sorry for his friend, and more than glad that his sisters were already married. All he had to do was pull his younger brother out of trouble every once in a while.

He was glad to do Rothwell a good turn; helping him watch out for Lady Lucinda would also put Gerald in the way of ladies wishing to wed. This Season, he would keep his eyes open.

Chapter 2

"You want me to marry the Marquis of Quorndon?" Lucinda echoed her mother's sudden suggestion. "I haven't even been to my first ball yet."

"Indeed." Mama's hands fluttered nervously. "His mother and I have been friends for ages. Since we were mere girls." She avoided Louisa and Lucinda's astonished gazes. At least, Lucinda thought her sister-in-law had the same look on her face as she did. "His title is not as old as ours, but it does date back to the fourteenth century. That is something, I suppose." As if Lucinda cared how old a peer's title was. If she fell in love, she wasn't even sure she would care if the gentleman was a peer. Mama gave Lucinda a polished smile, and immediately the back of her neck prickled. What was her mother up to? "His mother and I have been corresponding, and she happened to mention that Quorndon should wed soon. After all, the succession has not been secured. A peer must look to filling his nursery. And I . . . Well, with you coming out, you will, naturally, be looking for a husband."

Her mother glanced at her hopefully. There was more to this than Mama was saying. "Naturally."

She took a sip of her tea. "You can see how we thought a match between our houses would be extremely desirable."

"I can?" Lucinda cut a look at Louisa, who had a dubious expression on her face.

"Yes. It is entirely sensible. It will also take the burden off you to find a husband, as I have done the work and found one for you." Her mother smiled again, and this time Lucinda saw the desperation in Mama's face.

Lucinda was quite sure finding a husband would be a great deal of fun. She had to tell her mother how she felt, yet she hated to disappoint Mama. Still, this would not do. Lucinda might end up marrying the marquis—if she found herself in love with him—but she wanted to have a full Season. And she wanted to pick her own husband. From beneath her lashes, she peeked up at her mother, but Mama's face had hardened. She was truly serious about this match!

If only Louisa had had the baby earlier. Although, Lucinda did not know how that could have happened. They had been married a mere nine months when the baby came.

"When was the last time you met Quorndon?" Louisa asked in a deceptively soft voice, drawing Lucinda out of her thoughts.

"Not long ago at all," Mama said, drawing a raised brow from Louisa. "Well, perhaps it *has* been some time." Mama huffed. "A number of years, if you must know. Still, he was a very engaging little boy. Surely he is not much different now."

"I suppose it would depend on your perception." Lucinda waited for her sister-in-law to elaborate, but Louisa returned her attention to a piece of embroidery. That was disappointing.

The conversation seemed to be over, but Mama smiled again. "All one must do is simply compare Rothwell now to the way he was as a child." Mama's lips turned down at the corners. "Come to think of it, he was much more obliging as a boy than he is now, and not nearly as dirty."

The last time Lucinda had seen her brother he was wearing a cravat so white it blinded one. "I do not find Rothwell at all dirty."

Louisa's lips twitched.

"No, no, my dear. Not now. When he was a little boy. He was always tearing something. I despaired keeping him in clothes. Quorndon was never dirty, as I recall."

"Now, that does not surprise me at all," Louisa pronounced.

"In any event. We have been invited to Quorndon's house for dinner in two days' time." Mama quickly glanced at Louisa, smiled at Lucinda, and left the room.

"That is the evening of Lady Bellamny's party for the young ladies." Louisa had raised her voice enough to be heard, but Mama did not reenter the room. "She must find another evening. I cannot be made responsible for deciding which events you are to attend and have her making other arrangements."

The moment Lucinda could no longer hear the soft padding of her mother's slippers, she turned to Louisa. "What about the Marquis of Quorndon do you dislike?"

"I shall not tell you." She put her embroidery aside. "It is for you to decide if you like him or not."

That was not fair. If Louisa—who had a great deal of good sense—did not like the man, she should tell Lucinda the reason. "But why?"

"My very good friend, Dotty, now the Marchioness of Merton found something to like in my cousin, Merton, when the rest of us despised him. He has changed a great deal since he met her. Therefore, I shall not attempt to influence you. You will see if you like him." Louisa rose. "I must see to Alexandria."

A few moments later, one of the nursery maids came running into the room. "Her grace?"

It was amazing how Louisa always seemed to know to attend to the baby just before she was called. "On her way to the nursery. She should almost be there."

"Thank you, my lady." The maid bobbed a curtsey and dashed out again.

If the servant had taken the main staircase—an unlikely event—she would have met Louisa and saved herself the errand. On the other hand, having servants running up and down the main staircase would create a problem. Mama, for example, would not like it at all.

The low rumble of male voices filtered from the hall. *Rothwell must be back.* Maybe she could get her brother to tell her what her sister-in-law would not.

Lucinda hurried up the corridor to meet him as he started to climb the stairs. "A word with you, please."

"Of course." He turned to her.

"In the morning room." It was the room farthest from the hall, and they were less likely to be heard.

Moments later, they entered the room. "Shall I ring for tea?"

Her brother studied her for a moment, then frowned. "Mama told you about Quorndon."

"Er, yes." Rothwell did not respond at first, so Lucinda waited. She never knew him that well, by the time she was out of the nursery, he was at school, but in her limited experience, men would speak if given an opportunity.

"I've known him for years, and have nothing against the man. I do not like that Mama has decided to arrange a match. However, she is your guardian, and I cannot go against her

wishes unless the gentleman she chooses would be a danger
to you."

So, there was not anything wrong with the marquis. If there
were, her brother would know. She supposed anyone could take
anyone else into dislike. That must be what Louisa had done.
"Thank you."

He nodded and strode toward the door. Probably headed
to the nursery to be with his wife and child. Hopefully, by this
time next year, she too would have a husband and child.

Her brother reached the door and paused. "Lucinda, I have
invited a friend, Lord Elliott, to drink tea with us. Elliott is
someone you can depend upon if you require help."

What a strange thing to say. "Thank you. I shall strive to
do you credit."

Rothwell grinned, stepped toward her, then tapped her
nose as he used to do when she was a child. "I never thought
otherwise. I'll see you later. Louisa will be waiting for me."

How in the world did he know that? They must have
developed a secret form of communication. Or did all married
couples know what the other one wanted?

Lucinda glanced at the gilt-edged, alabaster mantel clock.
She had enough time to discover more about both Lord
Elliott—it would have been helpful if her brother had
mentioned his title—and Lord Quorndon before she dressed
for tea.

She entered the library and was surprised to find a box of
new books being shelved by the under-housekeeper, Mrs.
Reid. "Good day. I wanted to find a copy of *Debrett's*, but I
do not wish to interrupt your work."

A quick smile came from the woman. "I haven't seen it,
my lady, but you're welcome to look through these boxes.
Her grace sent us a list, and I know *Debrett's* was on it. There
is an older copy on the shelf to the right of that window." She
pointed to the north side of the room.

"Thank you." Lucinda glanced at the boxes. It would take longer than she had to go through them all. "I'll see what I can find in the old copy."

"As you wish." Reid turned back to her chore, and Louisa found the book.

As luck would have it, it was only four years old. Finding Quorndon was easy, and told her very little she had not already surmised. His bloodlines were desirable, as was the title. The current Lady Quorndon was the daughter of the Duke of Melbrough, and she was the same age as Lucinda's mother. They had probably come out together.

Finding Lord Elliott was a bit more difficult. In fact, the only one who matched—a gentleman of an age near her brother's and who was not married—was one of the rare earls who was not an earl of somewhere. The titles included the Baron Elliott of Bittlesbrough, Viscount Elliott of Bittlesbrough, and Earl Elliott.

Bittlesbrough must be his main estate. Possibly his only estate. The title was relatively new, having been created less than a hundred years ago, making the current Earl Elliott the Third Earl Elliott. Even though his line was not ancient, the first Earl Elliott had been a younger son of the Duke of Suffolk, and that title went back to the fourteenth century.

She shut the book. It would be more helpful if *Debrett's* included information as to hair color, or eye color, or how tall a man was. Although she knew more than she had before, it still was not enough.

For goodness' sake. He is only coming to tea. Rothwell specifically said he was not matchmaking, only introducing me to other gentlemen. Not only that, but he said I should make up my own mind.

Lucinda straightened her shoulders. There was no reason to rush into marriage, or an attachment. After all, marriage was for life.

The clock struck the hour, and she realized she had stayed in the library too long. Her maid would be looking for her.

When she got to her room, Greene had laid out three gowns. "These are the ones that arrived while you were out. I think the blue and cream would be nice, but the green almost matches your eyes. The yellow will brighten things up a bit."

"It has been dreary." In fact, the weather had been worse than dreary. It was too cold for the beginning of April. At this rate, Lucinda would be wearing heavy cloaks all spring. "I shall wear the yellow."

Her maid quickly helped her out of her day dress and into the yellow gown, which was embroidered with violets and vines. Once her hair had been redone into a softer style, she put on her pearl earrings. "I do not think I shall need a necklace. I shall want my Norwich silk shawl with the large flowers on it."

It was pretty, and she wanted to make an impression on Lord Elliott, even if her brother was not matchmaking.

Chapter 3

Louisa, Rothwell, and Mama were already in the drawing room when Lucinda entered.

"You look lovely." Her mother beamed with delight. "I must say, Louisa, that the modiste you chose is extremely talented."

Louisa caught Lucinda's eye and grinned. "Thank you, but I cannot take any credit at all for finding her. Lady Rutherford gave my brother the recommendation. Madam Lisette has become quite popular in the past few years."

"With her way of making a lady look her best, I can understand the reason why." Mama beamed at Lucinda again. Probably thinking about her upcoming betrothal.

Rothwell was standing by the fireplace, leaving the seat next to his wife empty, so Lucinda sat on the sofa next to Louisa.

Keeping her voice low, Lucinda asked, "Have you told my mother about Lady Bellamny's party?"

"I have." Her sister-in-law nodded. "The dinner shall be held at another time. I also suggested that meeting Quorndon at tea might not be as awkward."

At least tea did not last as long as a dinner would. "I assume you attended Lady Bellamny's party last year. What was it like?"

Before Louisa could answer, her brother's butler, Fredericks, announced Earl Elliott. The name still sounded strange to Lucinda, but the gentleman did not look odd at all. He was as tall as her brother and broad shouldered. His rich mahogany hair was fashionably styled, curling a little at the ends, and his deep blue eyes twinkled with good humor.

He was dressed in the same mode as Rothwell, in a well-cut dark blue jacket and snowy cravat, but unlike her brother, who preferred dark waistcoats, Lord Elliott's white and yellow striped waistcoat was embroidered with flowers, giving him a less serious demeanor. His pantaloons molded to his legs, and one could see one's reflection in his boots.

Clearly the man engaged in enough exercise to not require padding. But what drew her eye was the indentation in his cheek when he smiled. It enthralled her, and it made him look . . . adorable.

"Elliott." Her brother strode forward to greet the man. "Welcome."

"Thank you for inviting me. London has been thin of company until this week." He shook Rothwell's hand before turning to Louisa, who had risen, stepped forward, and held out her hand. "Your grace." He bowed and touched her fingers. "I hope I find you in good health."

"You do, Elliott. It is good to see you."

"And your daughter?"

"She is in what I can only call rude, good health." Louisa

motioned to Mama. "Your grace, may I introduce Lord El-liott to you? Elliott, my mother-in-law."

The tight smile from earlier appeared on Mama's mien. "A pleasure to meet you, my lord. I believe I met your father several years ago."

"Very possible, ma'am. He was in Town a great deal." He bowed, but she did not offer her hand. Had she taken him in dislike? And if so, why? He seemed perfectly presentable.

Louisa turned to Lucinda. "Lady Lucinda, may I introduce Lord Elliott to you? He has been a friend of Rothwell's for many years, and has been a friend to me and my sisters as well. Elliott, my sister, Lady Lucinda Hughlot."

She dipped a shallow curtsey and held out her hand. "It is a pleasure to meet you, my lord."

He bowed, and when he took her fingers his touch warmed them, even through his gloves. "It is a great honor, my lady. I hope you enjoy your Season."

"I intend to do just that, my lord." She smiled at him, and when he smiled back, the dimple appeared again. How very handsome he was.

Fredericks supervised the footmen, who brought in the tea trays. Unlike tea at home, this one included both small and larger sandwiches, as well as biscuits and cream tarts. Louisa poured, and Lucinda handed out the tea-cups. When she glanced at Mama, her lips were as pursed as if she had sucked on a lemon.

Rothwell took two of the larger sandwiches, prompting Lucinda to ask, "Would you prefer the beef and cheddar, or the egg salad, my lord?"

"Beef and cheddar, please." She placed two biscuits and a tart on Earl Elliott's plate.

"My lord," Louisa said. "Please tell me what has been going on in Parliament."

He cast a swift look at Lucinda. "We are mainly dealing with the accounts, and some personal bills. The real work will start next week, after Easter."

She had the feeling that something was not being discussed because she was present. What a bother it was to be an unmarried young lady. "How long have you been in Town, my lord?"

"Since this session started, about two months ago." He grinned. He seemed to smile easily. "Someone must keep up with it. Although, I suppose once I have a family I shall be like Rothwell and come to Town in my own good time."

Her brother sputtered and objected, and Louisa laughed. Even Mama seemed to relax.

Despite what Rothwell had said, Lucinda saw no reason to ignore Lord Elliott as a prospect. He had made a good first impression. She wondered what Lord Quorndon would be like.

Lady Lucinda was . . . beautiful. Glossy, chestnut curls framed her oval face, but what drew Gerald were her sea green eyes. They reminded him of the ocean in autumn. Not only was she much lovelier than he had expected, but when her grace turned the conversation to politics, she was knowledgeable, and interested in what was going on, and warm. Even the touch of her fingers seemed to please him.

The dowager duchess looked none too happy about the conversation, but that was most likely because young ladies were often told not to let a gentleman know how bright they truly were.

Gerald had always thought that was ridiculous. Gentlemen who wanted a stupid or only moderately clever lady would be unhappy when, after they wed, they discovered they had been deceived by a female who was more intelligent than they thought she was . . . Likewise, a lady should not have to suffer a man who could not appreciate her talents.

Rothwell was wise to watch carefully any gentleman who expressed an interest in her. Especially a man such as Quorndon, who did not appear to care very much who he married.

Gerald brought his thoughts back to the conversation that the new Duchess of Rothwell—he'd almost called her Lady Louisa—was most defiantly directing.

"Your grace, will we see your sisters and mother here this Season?"

"I assume you mean will Merton, Kenilworth, Worthington, and Wolverton be in Town to take up their duties in the Lords." She smiled. "Yes. Fortunately, my brother's house is ready for the children, which will allow my mother and Wolverton to move into Stanwood House. Do not look to the ladies to be gadding about Town very much." She shrugged one shoulder. "We all have new babies to care for. I shall be delighted to see my family again."

The dowager duchess's expression tightened even more. Was her grace not supposed to have mentioned the new additions to the families, or did she not approve of ladies caring for their children?

"I shall be happy to see all of them as well." The duchess's sister, and her friend, Lady Merton, livened up any event they attended. "When do they arrive?"

"Tomorrow and the day after. I have planned a family dinner. You are most welcome to take your potluck with us, if you would like."

Gerald had begun to decline when Rothwell said, "Yes, that would be perfect. You are a good friend to us all and can round out the numbers."

"Not to mention bring everyone up to date on Parliament." Louisa cast a teasing look at Rothwell.

The dowager duchess's mien turned to stone. Lady Lucinda's head swiveled between her brother, her sister-in-law, and her mother as if she expected something to happen.

If the dowager duchess wanted Quorndon for her daughter, Gerald was never going to be a favorite with the woman. But Lucinda promised to be an interesting young lady. Not only that, but he had vowed to her brother that he would befriend her and help take care of her. What better way to begin than by joining a family event. "I'd be delighted. Thank you for inviting me."

A few minutes later, Rothwell and her grace exchanged glances, and Gerald decided it was time to take his leave. He rose and bowed. "Your graces, again, welcome back to Town. Your grace,"—he bowed to the dowager duchess—"a pleasure. Lady Lucinda, it was delightful meeting you. I hope your Season is everything you wish it to be."

"I'll walk you out," Rothwell said, rising. He shut the door behind him. "Thank you for coming."

They were almost to the hall when Gerald said, "Your mother did not appear at all happy to see me."

"She will not be happy to see any gentleman who pays attention to Lucinda. Except for Quorndon, of course." When they reached the hall, he waved the butler away. "Mama did not wish to come to Town, and I believe she has seized onto an old friend's son—whom the old friend wishes to see wed— as a way of quickly dispatching her duties."

"That's not very fair to your sister." In fact, it was a deemed shabby thing to do.

"I agree." Rothwell gave a frustrated sigh. "Unfortunately, I do not see how I can stop my mother from making the match."

Gerald wasn't about to put himself in the middle of a family situation. "Thank you, again, for tea. I look forward to dinner. At some point, I would like to make the acquaintance of your daughter."

Rothwell's worried expression relaxed. "She is beautiful. I am told it's too early to know, but I believe she will favor Louisa."

"In that case, I do not envy you in another eighteen years."

Rothwell barked a laugh. "I suppose I shall be as bad—or worse—with her than I am with my sister, or Worthington was with his."

"No doubt you will." Gerald would make sure he was present, if only for the entertainment.

Rothwell shook Gerald's hand. "Louisa will send an invitation once everything has been set."

He walked down the steps, intending to go back to his rooms, but took a hackney to Covent Garden, where he spent several minutes selecting a posy of flowers. Once he was satisfied, he took another hackney to his house on Mount Street.

The door opened as he walked up the steps, and his butler bowed. "My lord."

"Good day, Collins. Is her ladyship at home?"

"No, my lord. She is drinking tea with Mrs. Millcombe."

Gerald held out the flowers. "Put these in water, and give her these when she returns, with my regards."

"May I ask what the occasion is, my lord?" Collins took the flowers and handed them to a footman.

"Tell her they are from her dutiful son." After their last argument, Gerald would let her ponder that puzzle.

The door closed behind him as he walked down the steps. His mother might aggravate him about the house—although that was most likely because she wanted to see him married—but she had never attempted to match make, and for that he was grateful to her.

The more he thought about it, the sorrier he felt for Lady

Lucinda. There was nothing unusual about an arranged marriage, but to allow a young lady to look forward to her coming out and then take the pleasure of a Season away from her was mean spirited. Not only that, but Quorndon was much too sure of himself if he thought Lady Lucinda would have nothing to say about the proposed match.

Gerald laughed to himself. He would do his best to make sure the lady had plenty of choice.

He tried to shrug off the little voice inside of him saying that he must keep his eyes open. He had already decided to do that. This year, he would recognize the lady immediately.

Still, he should most likely think about what he would like in a wife. All the ladies he had been attracted to were intelligent. Late last year, he'd visited Harrington and his wife in Paris and been told how she had successfully kept their horses from being stolen. Lady Charlotte, now Lady Kenilworth, and her friend, Lady Merton, ran a charity for children who had been abducted and searched for their families. Rothwell's duchess had helped him turn his finances around.

Yes, his future wife must be intelligent and strong-willed. He would like help running his estates. She should be able to discuss politics, and literature, and all matter of other things.

Gerald would like her to be well-looking, but what was more important was passion. He couldn't marry a lady for whom he felt nothing. Was that the problem? He had admired his friends' wives—belatedly—and wished he'd chosen them, but had he felt any passion for them?

He was almost to Jermyn Street when he finally decided he had not. They were all beautiful, but he had not wanted to bed one of them. That was disconcerting. He'd been sure he would know the lady he was meant to wed when he saw her. But what if he didn't?

A hand grabbed his shoulder, jerking him back. "Elliott, watch where you're going. You almost stepped in front of that carriage."

He glanced at his old friend. "Featherton, thank you. I must have been deep in thought."

"Well, you need to keep some wits about you if you're going to walk the streets." His hand dropped. "Are you going to your rooms?"

"Yes." Gerald glanced around, seeing that he was only one street over from where he resided. "Yes, I am."

"I'll accompany you, shall I? I must attend to some business before I drive my sister around the Park."

Featherton lived in the building next to Gerald's, and they frequently came across each other. "Is she just out?"

A hackney rattled by, splashing mud that nearly hit his boots. Even though it rained a great deal in England, he'd never seen it so wet. The only good thing to say about it was that the rain washed away the soot and dirt.

"No, it's her second Season. No rush about marrying though. My parents want her to choose wisely." His friend grinned. "By next week, she won't have time for her poor brother."

He wished Lady Lucinda's mother wanted the same for her. "Have you given any thought to marrying?"

"I am not yet ready, and my father is not pressing me. However, I do not expect that to last much longer. Are you thinking of finding a wife?"

He and Featherton were of an age, but his friend had a healthy father and would not assume the title for many years. "Yes. I promised myself I would find a bride this Season."

"I understand. You hold the title and need an heir." They reached the corner of Jermyn Street and turned. "And so many of our friends have married."

That was an understatement. "Huntley and Wively are the only ones, aside from us, who are not wed."

Featherton laughed. "I think they will be the last of us to wear a leg-shackle."

"I wouldn't be at all surprised. One does wonder what type of lady would entice either of them to the altar."

Gerald wondered what type of woman would make him decide to start a family. Whoever she was, he needed to meet her soon.

Chapter 4

"Well, I think Lord Elliott was delightful, and very witty." From the drawing room window seat, Lucinda met her mother's scowl with an innocent smile. Mama was being vastly unfair to poor Lord Elliott.

"He may be as witty as he likes," Mama said in an austere tone, "but, unlike Lord Quorndon, he has nothing to recommend him. His title is not even a hundred years old."

"He has a personality." Her brother's tone was so dry, Lucinda almost burst into whoops. "And he is wealthier than Quorndon."

That did not appear to impress her mother at all. What it did do was make Mama turn her sour look at Rothwell.

"No one is suggesting that Lucinda marry Elliott," Louisa said. "Quite the opposite. He was invited because he is a friend of Rothwell's and mine. In fact, no one should be trying to match her with anyone. It should be her decision." Mama opened her mouth, and Louisa hurried on. "Please feel free to invite Quorndon to drink tea with us, if you like."

As long as Louisa did not object to Lucinda finding out if she would like to wed Lord Elliott, she was perfectly willing to meet Lord Quorndon.

"I believe I shall." Mama rose regally from her wide, French, cane-backed chair. "I will see you at dinner."

Rothwell closed the door behind her and pulled a face. "I wonder how long this is going to last."

Lucinda was confused. "Has she not already invited Lord Quorndon and his mother to tea?"

Louisa nodded her answer before looking at Rothwell. "I expect it will last until she finds her way forward to rejoin the rest of Polite Society." She sighed. "I also think she is trying to protect Lucinda, much as my mother attempted to protect me from you. She was mistaken in you, and I firmly believe your mother is mistaken in her beliefs as well. The important thing is that you"—she glanced at Lucinda—"have a good time."

"Indeed. Do not allow this match to spoil your fun," her brother said.

"Yes." Her sister-in-law smiled. "Take the time to form friendships with the other ladies you will meet at Lady Bellamny's soirée."

That was exactly what Lucinda would do. For her mother's sake, she would give Lord Quorndon an opportunity to engage her affections. That was the least a dutiful daughter should do. If she found he was not for her, she would cross that bridge when she came to it. "Thank you."

The next morning, Rothwell and Louisa went to Worthington House to visit her family, leaving word that they would not return until after dinner. Lucinda wished she could have gone with them, but her mother had invited Lord Quorndon and his mother for tea that afternoon and required her company that evening. She suspected it was most likely her mother's way to keep her from meeting Lord Elliott again. Mama really had taken him into dislike, and for no good reason at all.

Instead, she went shopping with her mother for stockings, handkerchiefs, gloves, and other items that one tended to need in abundance.

A lady hailed her mother in front of Hatchards bookstore. "If you do not mind, I would like to see if there are any new books that would interest me," Lucinda said.

"Not at all, my dear." Mama glanced at the fashionable lady coming toward her in a Pomona green walking gown. "I shall meet you inside."

"Thank you." As Lucinda entered the store, her mother said, "Minerva, I did not expect to see you in Town." At least Mama sounded happy to see the lady.

Lucinda stopped to breathe in the smell of new books and leather before making her way to the shelves. She could happily remain here for hours if her mother would allow it.

She hated being at odds with her mother. They had always been close, but all the to-do about the Season seemed to be pulling them apart. Perhaps if her mother met enough of her old friends here, and there was no gossip about Papa, Mama would not focus so much on Lucinda finding a husband so quickly.

She had been absently looking at the books when she found herself in the exact place she wished to be. Unfortunately, the book she wanted was not within an easy reach. She stood on her toes and held on to one of the shelves, trying to be careful not to topple it over onto her.

As she stretched her arm up, another arm, this one covered in fine, Prussian blue Bath coating, reached from behind her. "Is it *Emma* you desire?"

Lord Elliott! How perceptive of him. Glancing back over her shoulder, she smiled at him. "Yes, please. It is just out of my reach. How did you know?"

He pulled out the volume. "I wondered if you would have had a chance to read it while you were in the country. My mother and sisters raved over it."

"No, I have not had an opportunity, but I am quite fond of all the books I have read by this author."

"I do not think you will be disappointed." He grinned at her. "I liked it. She has a way of peeling back the layers of society, which I enjoy."

"I agree." She found her cheeks had grown warm. Why did he have this effect on her? "Do you come here often?"

"Whenever I get word of new books that might interest me." His lordship placed the book in her hands.

"I am not so spoiled for choice. We do not have a bookstore near us at home. I have been indulging myself as often as I am able."

"When I'm home, I have Hatchards send me a list of their new books. Then I order what I think I might like."

"What a clever idea." Lucinda wondered if she could do something like that when she returned to The Roses—if she returned at all. She might marry. In that case, she would have to wed a gentleman who was as fond of reading as she was. And who would not attempt to control what she read.

"Lucinda." Mama came up to them. "What are you doing?"

"I was attempting to reach this book"—she pointed to the empty space—"but his lordship very kindly got it down for me. Was that not well done of him?"

"Yes. It was," her mother replied. Then again, there really was not anything else she could say and remain polite.

"Thank you, my lord." Lucinda slid a look at him, and the dimple was there. "I believe my mother wishes to return to Rothwell House."

"My pleasure, my lady." Lord Elliott bowed. "Your grace, very nice to see you again."

"Thank you for assisting my daughter." Mama inclined her head and took Lucinda by the arm. "We must be on our way."

She glanced back briefly at his lordship, but he was looking at a book.

Once she and her mother were in the carriage on the way to Grosvenor Square, she considered saying something to Mama about her attitude toward Lord Elliott. Yet it would not do any good, and might cause another disagreement. Amazingly, he did not appear to care at all what Mama thought or how she behaved toward him. Was it simply that he had excellent manners, or did he simply not value her opinion? Either way, Lucinda admired his sangfroid.

Once again, she dressed carefully for tea. This time she wore a blue muslin gown embroidered with yellow flowers. As before, her mother was in the drawing room when she arrived. Yet the atmosphere was different. Tenser.

"Another lovely gown," Mama said. "There is no reason for you to be nervous. You are beautiful, and I am certain Lord Quorndon will think so as well."

Perhaps the problem was that Lucinda did not know if she wanted him to think she was beautiful. "Thank you, Mama."

"They should be here at any moment." She patted the sofa next to her. "Come, sit with me. You shall pour the tea, and I will hand out the cups."

In other words, Lucinda was to show the marquis how graceful and accomplished she was. Would she be required to play the piano for him as well?

Taking a deep breath, she let it out slowly. Her mother

might think it was for Lord Quordon to approve of her, yet Lucinda knew it was equally important that she approve of him. And his looks would have very little to do with her opinion.

A light knock came on the door before it opened. "Your grace. Lord and Lady Quorndon."

Lady Quorndon floated into the room, followed by her son. Both had curling blond hair, blue eyes, and reminded Lucinda strongly of porcelain dolls. Where the lady was small and slight, the gentleman was larger, though not greatly so. He was slender, but not skinny. He definitely did not have Lord Elliott's broad shoulders.

Her ladyship wore a Celestial blue silk gown, embroidered at the hem, and a spencer of the same color, with embroidery at the cuffs to match the hem.

Instead of the darker colors worn by her brother and Lord Elliott, Lord Quorndon wore a jacket of Aethereal blue and a heavily embroidered yellow waistcoat. The points of his collar were so high they almost touched his cheek bones.

"Judith." Smiling, Mama rose, and Lucinda followed suit. "How delightful to see you again."

"Madeline." The lady held out her arms as they kissed the air next to each other's cheeks. "I am thrilled to see you." Lady Quorndon rapped her son's arm with her fan. "Surely you remember Quorndon?"

"Of course, my lord." Mama inclined her head.

"Your grace." Lord Quorndon's bow was the most elegant gesture Lucinda had ever seen a gentleman make. "It is a great pleasure to see you again. Although my memory is faint, I recall that we met several times when I was a scrubby brat."

"I do not believe I—or anyone else, for that matter—ever called you 'scrubby.'" Mama laughed lightly.

"Quite right. I do not suppose they did." Lord Quorndon smiled, but it did not reach his eyes.

Nor could Lucinda imagine him as a grubby child. A point that was not in his lordship's favor. From the tip of his perfectly arranged hair to his highly polished boots with gold tassels, the man looked as if he had never engaged in anything more strenuous than lifting a tea-cup. No wonder her sister-in-law had not been impressed.

She pasted a polite smile on her lips, strolled forward, and dipped a slight curtsey.

"And this must be Lady Lucinda!" the marchioness exclaimed. "The last time I saw you, you were in a cradle."

"A pleasure to meet you, my lady."

"I suppose you have guessed that this is Quorndon?" his mother said proudly.

"I did, indeed, make that assumption." Lucinda held out her hand to his lordship. Fortunately, he did nothing more than bow and kiss the air above her fingers.

Fredericks cleared his throat, and Mama ushered Lucinda to the sofa. The Quorndons took seats on the opposite sofa. Soon afterward, the tea service and plates of small tarts and biscuits were set on the low table between the sofas.

"My lady," Lucinda asked. "How do you prefer your tea?"

Once everyone had a cup of tea and a plate of biscuits— the Quorndons having eschewed tarts—the conversation turned to the upcoming Season. An hour later, two things were perfectly clear: Politics would not be discussed, and Lucinda had very little in common with Lord Quorndon.

Despite their apparent inability to find anything upon which to agree, she decided to take a more direct approach, one that her mother could not avoid noticing. "I have become very fond of early morning rides. Do you ride in Town, my lord?"

"At home I will take my hack out when necessary. But in Town I only ride if there has been a party got up to Richmond, or some such place, and the other gentlemen are riding.

Generally, I prefer a carriage. I find the aroma of the horse, no matter how clean the beast is, lingers."

She stifled a sigh and tried again. "I love picnics. We go on them quite a bit during the summer." Before he became ill, her father used to take them in the spring and summer. She would always have fond memories of their picnics.

"Unfortunately, so do the ants." Lucinda could have sworn his lordship shuddered. "I much prefer to take my meals at a table."

No horses, no picnics. She wondered if he liked the same books she did. "Have you read the latest novel by the author A Lady?"

Lord Quorndon flicked an imaginary piece of lint off his jacket. "No, I much prefer Byron. I find him much superior to any female author."

Lucinda clamped her mouth shut. How dare he? Not only did he deride an excellent lady author, but he preferred a male author whose excesses were scandalous. She, for one, could not bring herself to separate Byron's life from his work. "What of Shakespeare? I do love his comedies."

"I suppose one must at least pretend to be interested," his lordship drawled.

Their mothers exchanged glances, and Lady Quorndon said, "I propose we attend the theater next week. I have been told there is an excellent comedy playing at the Theater Royal."

Lucinda waited for his lordship to say he was not fond of comedy. Instead, he smiled at her. "That sounds like a wonderful idea. What think you, my lady? Do you have a taste for the theater?"

"I do, my lord. Or at least, I enjoy our Christmas panto-mimes. I have not yet been to a real theater."

"Perfect. My mother shall arrange it." He leaned back against the cushions, appearing very proud of himself.

Was it usual for a gentleman to leave arrangements like that to his mother? If she married Quorndon, what part would his mother play in their lives? These were questions to which she needed answers. "I look forward to the evening, my lord, my lady."

"Well, then." Lord Quorndon rose. "I believe it is time for us to depart." He assisted his mother to rise, then bowed to her and her mother. "Your grace, my lady. It has been a pleasure."

"Yes, indeed," Mama said, relieving Lucinda of crafting a response. She could merely smile and curtsey. "Judith, I look forward to hearing from you about the theater."

"I shall ensure it does not interfere with any of the important entertainments." Lady Quorndon gave Mama a significant look. "We cannot have Lady Lucinda miss any essential events."

Lucinda's smile almost faltered. If her ladyship wanted Quorndon to marry her, why, then, would Lady Quorndon encourage her to attend events? This was all very confusing, and she daren't ask her mother.

They accompanied Lord and Lady Quorndon to the front door, bid them farewell, then strolled back to the morning room. Mama took the same seat she had before and picked up a cream tart. "I think that went well. Do you not agree?"

Lucinda's jaw dropped, but she quickly snapped it shut. She could either agree with her mother, or tell her the truth: that Quorndon and she were unlikely to make a match.

"Naturally, today was a little stilted. It is difficult to meet the person your parent has decided you should wed." A little stilted? Could Mama not see that a match would be close to impossible? "I think he is a perfect gentleman, and very much like he was as a child."

The conversation between her mother and sister-in-law came rushing back to Lucinda.

Quorndon was never dirty, as I recall.
Now, that does not surprise me at all.

Lucinda had not understood it at the time, but she did now. How could anyone imagine Lord Quorndon being anything other than a perfect porcelain figure? His mother as well. The thought that Lady Quorndon could live with them if he and Lucinda married was not to be thought of.

His mother wanted this match as much as her mother did. The question was why was it so important, and what could she do to stop her mother from pursuing this match?

Chapter 5

The next morning, Lucinda awoke to the sound of a bird singing in the lilac tree next to her window. Unfortunately, it would be another month before she could enjoy the tree. If she hurried, she could be out of the house before anyone who could stop her was awake.

Reaching out, she tugged the bellpull, and a half an hour later her groom, Kerr, helped her mount Nan, her gray mare.

Kerr swung onto his hack. "Where are we going, my lady?"

Prancing beneath her, Nan was fresh, and clearly wanted some exercise. There was only one place in Mayfair Lucinda knew she could ride at good pace without causing talk. "The Park. I understand that my sister-in-law was allowed to ride there with a groom." Kerr closed one eye and drew up the edge of his mouth, giving her a skeptical look. "Follow me, I know where it is."

Soon they were trotting out of Grosvenor Square, headed toward Rotten Row. The air was fresh for London, and puffy clouds dotted the sky. Now if only the weather would become warmer. Seeing only one rider in the distance, she urged Nan into an easy gallop, giving the horse an opportunity to run.

"Well met, my lady," Lord Elliott said as he rode up and doffed his hat. His eyes sparkled, giving him a slightly roguish appearance. His mussed hair made her want to run her fingers through it, putting it in order again. He seemed more handsome this morning than he had before. "I didn't know you enjoyed early morning rides."

His large roan stallion eyed Nan, who playfully tossed her head. Not only was Lord Elliott handsome, but it seemed they both liked morning rides. That was more than she could say for Lord Quorndon. "It is my first opportunity since arriving in Town. It is peaceful here at this time of day."

"Much more so than during the Grand Strut. Have you experienced the *ton* at its afternoon finest?"

No, but she had heard it was the place to be seen in the afternoon. Would his lordship ask her to accompany him? "I have not yet had that pleasure."

Lord Elliott grinned. "In that case, please allow me to take you for a carriage ride today."

"I would be delighted." Lucinda returned his smile. She would have to convince Louisa to support the outing in the event Mama objected.

"Excellent. I shall come for you at five." His grin widened, the dimple making a showing.

"I look forward to it, my lord."

"As will I." He bowed and trotted off in the direction he had been headed before he'd stopped to speak with her.

Lucinda didn't even bother to hide her sigh. The man could certainly sit a horse. She hoped he was similarly skillful with the ribbons. That must be on her list of requirements for a husband. Books as well. Which made the marquis quite ineligible for the position.

She nudged Nan forward. Lucinda could not imagine being wed to Lord Quorndon. Yet if he were to find a lady that would capture his interest—she was positive that he had not—perhaps she would be allowed to marry where she wished. Well, there was no time like the present. If such a lady existed, she would most likely be at Lady Bellamny's soirée this evening.

Even if Lucinda failed to find a husband for herself this Season, perhaps she could find a wife for Lord Quorndon. Even *her* mother could not possibly expect Lucinda to wed a gentleman who was in love with another woman.

When she came down for breakfast after washing and dressing, Lucinda was pleased to find only her brother and sister-in-law in the breakfast room. Rothwell was seated at the end of the table, with Louisa on his right side. Both of them were reading newssheets. Athena, their eight-month-old Great Dane, lay between them, her head on her paws. She glanced up, then resumed her position.

Lucinda smiled brightly. "Good morning."

Rothwell raised his head slightly and nodded, but Louisa lowered her paper. "Good morning to you. Have you been out riding?"

"Yes." When she approached the covered dishes on the sideboard, Athena ambled over to greet Lucinda and be stroked. "Are you not normally in the nursery?"

"She is," Louisa said. "But Nurse took exception to her attempting to save Alexandria from a bath."

Ever since the baby had been born, Athena had appointed herself guardian of the child. "It amazes me how afraid she is of water."

"If it cannot be consumed, the Danes have no use for it." Louisa took a sip of tea. "Join us. Would you like a section of the newssheet?"

"Please. I'll read what you have finished." Mama did not approve of reading at the table, but Rothwell and Louisa insisted on being current. After one of the footmen placed fresh toast on the table, her sister-in-law motioned for another pot of tea. "I saw Lord Elliott this morning." Lucinda strove to speak casually as she made her selection, a baked egg and ham. "He invited me for a carriage ride this afternoon."

"Excellent." Her brother looked up. "He will be able to tell you who everyone is."

"Indeed." Louisa handed the part of the newspaper she was reading to a footman, who placed it next to Lucinda's place setting. "I received the vouchers for Almack's."

She had heard about Almack's but did not know much about it, other than not everyone was allowed and birth was more of a recommendation than wealth. "That is good."

"It's a dead bore," her brother growled. "But don't repeat me."

"It is not that bad." Louisa patted Rothwell's hand. "The worst part will be waiting for approval to dance the waltz."

"If Quorndon is there, that will be a problem," Rothwell grumbled before going back to his reading.

Lucinda set her plate on the table and looked over at her brother. "Why are you so out of sorts this morning?"

Folding his newssheet, he put it aside. "I received news that it is too wet to start planting. If this weather doesn't improve soon, we will have problems getting a full season in."

No wonder he was in such a foul mood. "We do seem to be having more rain than usual."

"We do, indeed." He grimaced before swallowing the rest of his tea. "I'm sure Elliott will be at Almack's. Featherton as well. I shall ask one of them to receive permission to waltz with you."

That would solve the embarrassment of having to wait. Before Lucinda could answer, her sister-in-law said, "You cannot smother her with your friends."

"Of course I can." Her brother's eyes widened. "What's the point in having them if I can't make use of them?"

When Louisa closed her eyes, Lucinda quickly said, "I do not mind at all. It is not as if there is a gentleman I wish to dance with." The image of Lord Elliott on horseback floated through her mind. "I would be perfectly happy for one of Rothwell's friends to ask me."

"Aside from that, my love." Rothwell captured his wife's hand. "You cannot tell me that Worthington did not help you on occasion."

A slow blush rose in Louisa's cheeks. "No, I cannot. Very well. Arrange for Lucinda to be asked to waltz. I am going to look in on our daughter." Rising from the table, she glanced at the dog. "Come, Athena. The torture by water will be over now."

Once her sister-in-law left the room, Rothwell bussed Lucinda's cheek. "I shall probably ask Featherton. We do not want to abuse Elliott's kindness. Especially as he is taking you out this afternoon."

Lucinda pulled over the rest of the newssheet as she tucked into her breakfast. Was Lord Elliott only taking an interest in her because of his friendship with her brother, or could he actually like her for herself? Before her interest grew, she would have to find out. The only question was how should she go about it?

Gerald found himself grinning at the prospect of taking Lady Lucinda out that afternoon. Not that he was interested in her as a prospective mate. Although, she did have an excellent seat. One of the best he'd seen on a female. And he enjoyed listening to her lyrical voice. It was like hearing a melody.

He gave himself a shake. No, no. His only role was to assist Rothwell in keeping an eye on her. Helping him would serve Gerald as well. Attending the same events as Lady Lucinda would give him the opportunity to look over the ladies and choose a wife. It wasn't as if he'd spend all his time looking after Lady Lucinda.

His duties would begin with the Promenade. Would she be impressed, or think it a great waste of time? Then again, she could be nervous. In that case, he'd be there to assist in becoming familiar with the *ton*. All in all, it should be an interesting occasion.

Just as he had finished tying his cravat, his valet, Rouse, brought in a missive. "It is from her ladyship, my lord."

The only "her ladyship" was his mother. "Very well."

He plucked the letter from the tray, opened it, and sighed. "I am to escort her to Almack's next Wednesday."

"Very good, my lord. I shall enter it into your diary." Rouse bowed and began picking up discarded neck cloths.

"Thank you." There was no being late to Almack's. They'd lock one out.

At least it wouldn't be a complete waste of time this year. After all, it was the prime place to look for a spouse. Gerald had no doubt Lady Louisa would be there. Thus enabling him to, as the saying went, kill two birds with one stone.

The rest of the day he attended to estate business and had a meeting with one of his committees for the House of Lords. When he arrived at Rothwell House, he was pleasantly surprised not to be kept waiting.

Lady Lucinda descended the steps as Gerald was admitted to the hall. "Good afternoon, my lady."

She glanced up from pulling on a light, tawny-brown leather glove. Her jonquille yellow carriage gown, topped by a paisley spencer in spring colors, hugged her bosom. For a moment, he had trouble dragging his gaze upward. She wore a high-peaked hat lined with cream-colored silk. The whole effect made what he could see of her brown hair richer than before. Her green eyes reminded him of the color of new leaves. And there was an energy in her that had not been there before. It was as if she had emerged from a cocoon.

How had he not noticed how beautiful she was before? If she wished, she could do much better than Quorndon.

Lady Lucinda reached the bottom step, and Gerald offered her his arm. "Shall we depart?"

The hand she placed on his arm was as light as a feather. Then she smiled so brightly he had to blink. If that was the look she gave gentlemen, he and her brother would have their work cut out for them. "Yes, I believe we should."

They had no sooner reached the pavement when she stopped, almost jerking him to a halt. Dropping her arm, she made her way from the side of his phaeton to his horses. "What a beautiful carriage, and your horses! They look perfectly matched." Standing in front of the pair, she rubbed their noses. "I wish I had a carrot or an apple to give them."

"I keep apples in the carriage, if you would like to reward them when we return."

Eyes sparkling, she glanced at him. "Yes, indeed." She turned back to the horses. "You are such handsome gentlemen." The dammed beasts actually puffed out their chests for her, and he found himself feeling a bit left out. "I shall give you something later." She strode back to him and grinned. "I like your carriage as well. Maroon is one of my favorite colors, and the gold piping sets it off nicely." She slowly walked to the back of the carriage, nodded, then glanced at him. "Now, my lord, I am ready to see what awaits us at the Park."

He felt like preening. She was definitely not nervous. He

pulled down the steps and handed her up. "I look forward to hearing your opinion."

Even though the Season did not start in earnest until after Easter next week, Polite Society was out in force. A glossy display of carriages, from sporting vehicles to landaus, filled the carriageway. Young gentlemen on horses walked beside some of the carriages, while others led their horses to stroll beside young ladies in an array of pale muslin gowns and fashionable hats.

After threading his phaeton into the carriageway, he settled the horses down to a slow walk. A little distance down the path, a bright yellow landau had pulled to the verge. "I think you will shortly meet Lady Jersey."

Lady Lucinda's eyes widened. "The one who is called 'Silence'?"

"The very one, but do not repeat that to her. It is not meant as a compliment. She's also one of the Patronesses of Almack's."

She tilted her head slightly to one side. "Yes, I believe either my mother or sister-in-law mentioned that." Lady Lucinda straightened her shoulders and assumed a more demure look. Still, her eyes sparkled with joy. "I shall be on my best behavior."

Gerald wanted to laugh out loud. The rider who had stopped at Lady Jersey's carriage moved on. He pulled up and inclined his head. "Good afternoon, my lady."

"Indeed it is, Elliott." The sound of the voice answering almost made him wince, as his mother gazed at him from the other side of Lady Jersey. "Mother, I didn't see you."

"You see, I said this bonnet was too large." As Lady Jersey glanced from him to Lady Lucinda, her brows rose slightly. "My lord, good afternoon to you. I trust I will see you on Wednesday."

"You will, my lady. I would not miss an evening at Almack's." When her ladyship's eyes focused on Lady Lucinda, he said, "Lady Jersey, Mother, may I introduce you to Lady Lucinda Hughlot, Rothwell's sister."

"A pleasure to meet you, my lady." Lady Jersey smiled reassuringly. "I look forward to seeing you on Wednesday as well."

"Thank you, ma'am." Lady Lucinda gave her ladyship a polite smile. "I also look forward to Wednesday."

"Lady Lucinda." His mother's tight smile did not bode well for him. Whatever was amiss, he'd hear about it soon. "A pleasure."

"Thank you, ma'am," Lady Lucinda replied evenly.

Either he was too much attuned to his mother's moods, or she had a good deal more countenance than most young ladies he'd met. "Well, then. We shall be on our way." He inclined his head again. "My lady, Mother, have a pleasant outing."

A few moments later, the Earl of Huntley and Viscount Wively, two friends of his and Rothwell's, rode up, demanding an introduction.

"Lady Lucinda, I am devastated that I did not meet you before Elliott." Wively, a confirmed rogue, bowed. "It is entirely unfair that I should not be the first gentleman to tool you around."

She grinned and held out her hand. "But how did you know it is my first time in the Park?"

Taking her fingers, he kissed the air above her hand. "I make a point of always noticing the most beautiful ladies, and I have not seen you before. Ergo, it is your first time."

Gerald wanted to snatch her hand back and tell Wively to move on when Lady Lucinda said, "Will I see you at Almack's next week?"

"Ah, no." Most of the color drained from Wively's face, and Gerald barked a laugh. "I do not attend Almack's."

"Why not?" Lady Lucinda asked.

The man's mouth opened and closed, but he was unable to speak.

"Wivenly is avoiding the Marriage Mart until he is a little older," Huntley replied.

A faint line formed between her eyes. "I do not understand. If you are friends of my brother, you must be around the same age."

"A direct hit." Huntley laughed, and Gerald took perverse enjoyment in seeing Wivenly squirm. "But not in his mind, dear lady." Huntley executed a short bow. "Allow me to take him off before he swoons from fright. Delightful meeting you, my lady. I hope you enjoy your Season. Elliott, see you around."

Once they'd ridden away, she turned to Gerald. "Why does Lord Wivenly not wish to wed? My brother has been much happier since he married."

"Some gentlemen mature much more slowly than others." Or, in Wivenly's case, were unwilling to give up whoring. Huntley was more stable, but still marriage shy. "When he does get around to marrying, I pity his wife." She opened her mouth and Gerald rushed on. "And no, I am not going to explain the reason."

"That," she said sternly, "is one of the reasons I wish to wed. No one explains anything to single ladies."

"I have no doubt you will achieve your goal." But not to Quorndon, or Huntley, or any other gentleman Gerald knew.

He'd have to keep a close eye on her to ensure no unsuitable gentleman came near her.

In an attempt to avoid any summons his mother intended to send, Gerald decided to dine at Brooks. When he entered the dining room, he was surprised to see most of his married friends.

He shook hands with Rothwell and nodded to Merton, who

had married Miss Dorothea Stern, and to Kenilworth, who had wed Lady Charlotte Carpenter. "Where is Worthington?"

"He's with his wife and children," Rothwell grumbled.

"I thought you'd be with your wives as well." Gerald didn't understand. Had they all had arguments with their ladies?

"Lady Bellamny's party for young ladies is this evening," Kenilworth informed Gerald. "Our wives are there to show support for Lady Lucinda."

"Gentlemen are not allowed until it is time to fetch our ladies," Merton added.

"Not exactly correct." Kenilworth sipped his claret. "We are allowed entrance toward the end of supper."

Supper? A vague memory concerning Worthington, his wife, and Lady Bellamny came to Gerald. "Is that not where Worthington met his wife?"

"I believe it might have been," Merton said. "They married shortly thereafter."

"If you're all going there, do you mind if I accompany you?" It appeared as if Rothwell was more interested in finding his wife than protecting his sister. Once the gentlemen arrived, Gerald wanted to make sure Lady Lucinda did not meet anyone she should. Naturally, Worthington had not been in any way unsuitable, but one never knew who had a sister coming out.

"Not at all." Rothwell motioned to a chair. "Have a seat. I'll tell the servant to order another beefsteak."

Chapter 6

Later that evening, Mama and Louisa accompanied Lucinda to Lady Bellamny's elegant town house near St. James Square.

After greeting Louisa warmly, Lady Bellamny, a plump lady swathed in a purple gown, with gold feathers in her hair, leaned forward and kissed Mama on her cheek. "Madeline, I am so happy to see you in Town. It has been far too long."

Lucinda had to keep her jaw from dropping. She had never heard anyone speak to her mother with such familiarity. Despite Mama's misgivings, she had friends here that she did not have at home.

"Thank you, Almeria. I have missed you as well." Mama smiled happily, making Lucinda blink. "Perhaps I shall spend more time in Town." Mama drew Lucinda forward. "Almeria, this is my eldest daughter, Lady Lucinda. Lucinda, please meet an old and dear friend, Lady Bellamny."

Lucinda curtseyed. "My lady. It is a pleasure to meet you."

For a moment, she felt as if she were being inspected, then her ladyship nodded. "You'll do well. Not a diamond of the first water, but very pretty and unaffected."

Pasting a polite smile on her lips, she said, "Thank you, my lady."

"And intelligent." Lady Bellamny's feathers waved as she nodded again. "No girl likes to hear that she is not the most beautiful lady of the Season, but you'll be better for it."

Louisa took Lucinda's arm. "Come, you should meet some of the other ladies."

Once they were out of Lady Bellamny's hearing, and she was greeting a new arrival, Lucinda asked, "Is she always like that?"

"If you mean straight to the point, even if you do not wish to hear what she has to say?" Lucinda inclined her head. "Yes. She told me being beautiful was as much a curse as a blessing."

That was hard to believe. "Was she right?"

Louisa tilted her head to one side, and her eyes narrowed slightly. "Yes. There are too many gentlemen who fail to look beyond a pleasing face and form." With her dark hair and lapis-blue eyes, Louisa must have been one of the most beautiful ladies of last Season. "I will tell you one thing I have observed. When you find the right gentleman, he will believe you are the most beautiful woman in the world."

That did not make any sense at all. One's looks did not change. "How do you know?"

Louisa smiled. "I have seen the way a man in love looks at his lady. Even when others have decided she is only passably pretty, she will be beautiful to him."

"Your grace?" a fashionably dressed lady with blond hair addressed Louisa.

"Lady St. Claire." Louisa smiled, holding out her hands. "How are you this evening?"

"Quite well." The lady took Louisa's hands, leaned forward, and kissed her cheek. "I wish to introduce my niece, Miss Marlow. She is my brother's daughter. I am sponsoring her this Season."

Louisa introduced Lucinda. After she greeted Lady St. Claire, Lucinda held out her hand to Miss Marlow. She was one of the most perfectly featured ladies she had ever seen. Glossy, golden curls framed her oval face. Her eyes were cornflower blue, and the faintest of blushes colored her perfect complexion. She looked almost like a porcelain doll.

An image came into Lucinda's mind of Miss Marlow and Lord Quorndon as figurines placed side by side on a fireplace mantel or in a highly polished cabinet.

Could it be that she was the answer to Lucinda's problem with his lordship? Indeed, as fastidious as the man was about his clothing and person, Lucinda could imagine he would like a wife whose looks complemented him.

She could not have stopped the smile from forming on her lips if she had wanted to. "I am very pleased to meet you, Miss Marlow."

"Thank you," the lady replied. "I am happy to meet you. I think coming to know other young ladies will be of help to us all." Lucinda could not agree more. Miss Marlow glanced at her mother and Louisa. "Would you mind if I take Lady Lucinda to meet some of the other ladies?"

"Not at all," her sister-in-law responded. "That is, after all, the purpose of the soirée."

Miss Marlow introduced Lucinda to Lady Alice Wexford, the daughter of the Marquis of Grantham. Lady Alice was above average height with a serious demeanor.

Holding out her hand, Lucinda smiled. "It is a pleasure to meet you, Lady Alice."

"And you as well, Lady Lucinda." Lady Alice glanced around the room and sighed. "Is this your first time in Town?"

"Yes. I was to have come out last year, but we were in mourning for my father." Lucinda held her breath, waiting to see if the other lady would comment on her father.

Instead, a sympathetic look entered her gray eyes. "I am sorry for your loss. Did you wish for a Season?"

That was an odd question. Did not every young lady want a London Season? "I have been looking forward to it for a few years now."

"Oh." Lady Alice looked at a loss for words. Then she leaned closer. "I did not want one at all. I would have been happier to have remained in Lincolnshire with my books and attended the local assemblies. I am only here to please my father."

"Perhaps you will have a better time than you think." Lucinda made a mental note to invite Lady Alice to go walking or for tea.

Miss Marlow once again took Lucinda's arm. "Please excuse us, my lady. I have promised to introduce Lady Lucinda to some other ladies I have recently met. Shall I see you next week at Almack's?"

"My mother received the vouchers yesterday." Lady Alice imparted the news with so much dread that Lucinda almost put her arms around the lady to comfort her.

"I am positive everything will be fine." As Lucinda patted the young woman's shoulder, she caught Miss Marlow struggling not to grin. "We shall see each other after Easter."

Next, Lucinda met Miss Tice and her good friend Miss Martindale. The two ladies had been friends since infancy and appeared to be inseparable.

"We have decided," Miss Tice said, "that we must find husbands whose estates run together."

Miss Martindale nodded vigorously. "That way, we will not be forced to live far from each other."

"I wish you luck." Lucinda exchanged a look with Miss Marlow, whose lips were twitching so much she had to put her hand over her mouth. Had they pored over *Debrett's* and a map of England to make a list?

Once Lucinda and Miss Marlow were far enough away from the ladies that they wouldn't be overheard, Lucinda commented, "I feel sorry for Lady Alice."

"I think she is making a great deal over nothing," Miss Marlow said indignantly. "I cannot imagine *not* wanting to marry."

"To be fair, she did not say she had no wish to wed. She just did not want to come to Town." That begged the question of whether there was a gentleman at home Lady Alice liked.

Miss Marlow linked her arm with Lucinda's as they strolled around the room. "What are you looking for in a husband?"

"I have decided I want a love match." She glanced at her new friend. "As for requirements, he must be a gentleman, able to support a wife,"—she could not imagine being allowed to marry anyone who could not afford a family—"and he must like horses as much as I do, and not keep me from reading what I want. What do you wish for?"

Miss Marlow pulled a face. "I would have to say that I agree with your first two requirements, but I would ask that he not make me ride a horse. I have been afraid of them since I was a child. My father would like me to wed a peer, or a man who will become a peer. I have not decided if that is so important."

Lucinda remembered that her sister-in-law had found a match for a suitor she had not wanted. Could she do the same thing? Lucinda was hard pressed to keep her smile to herself. It appeared that Miss Marlow would be perfect for Lord Quorndon. Somehow, Lucinda would have to arrange an introduction.

Fortunately, the opportunity came much sooner than she thought it would. Just as they were finishing supper, there was a small commotion at the entrance to the supper room.

Miss Marlow, as did everyone else, glanced in that direction. Her eyes widened. "Who is that?"

Lucinda looked at the door as several gentlemen strolled in. Among them were her brother and Lord Elliott, who looked extremely elegant in a black jacket, striped waist coat, and a perfectly tied cravat. Not to mention shirt points that were not so high he couldn't see. "Which one?"

"No, over there, bowing to the lady with the blond hair sitting next to the older lady."

The older lady was Lucinda's mother. But the man—resplendent in a Prussian blue jacket and matching satin breeches—bowing to his mother was *Quorndon*!

A slow smile drew her lips up. "The Marquis of Quorndon. Please allow me to introduce you."

"How kind of you." Miss Marlow's bow lips curved into a satisfied smile.

Lucinda linked her arm with her new friend's and led her across the room. "My lady, I did not see you earlier."

Lady Quorndon fluttered her hand. "I did not wish to interrupt you. Fortunately, there is no need to chaperone you young ladies at this event, so we older ladies may chat all we wish."

"Good evening, my lord."

Lord Quorndon smiled politely and bowed. "My lady."

Lucinda curtseyed before turning her attention to Miss Marlow. "Mother, Lady Quorndon, I'd like to introduce you to Miss Marlow, Lady St. Claire's niece." Lucinda waited until the ladies had greeted her friend. "Miss Marlow, may I introduce Lord Quorndon to you?"

She performed an elegant curtsey and held out her hand. "A pleasure to meet you, my lord."

Lord Quorndon's eyes widened and his cheeks flushed slightly as he bowed over her fingers, taking them in his hand. "The pleasure is mine, Miss Marlow."

Lucinda was glad to see that he held her friend's fingers a little longer than necessary.

She cut a look at her mother, but the older ladies had gone back to their comfortable coze. Miss Marlow and Lord Quorndon's reactions to each other were promising. Lucinda must find some way to arrange another meeting between them before they left the soirée. And—before Mama and Lady Quorndon noticed the looks of interest on the couple's faces.

But where? Not the Park. It was too crowded during the Fashionable Hour.

Think, think, think. There must be somewhere . . . "Miss Marlow, have you been to the British Museum yet?"

She glanced at Lucinda. "I have not, but I have heard I should attend while in Town."

"I would be delighted to escort you ladies." Lord Quorndon made the offer so quickly, Lucinda's head spun.

Yet they must attend early in the day. Did his lordship arise before noon? Well, if he was interested in Miss Marlow, he would. "Perfect." She kept her smile to herself. "Would tomorrow at eleven suit?"

"What a wonderful idea." Miss Marlow clapped her hands lightly.

Lucinda thought she saw a slight grimace on his face, but he bowed. "Ladies, I am at your disposal."

This might be easier than Lucinda had thought. She glanced around and saw her brother making his way through the crowd. "Miss Marlow, we should look for your aunt and my sister-in-law."

As they strolled away, Lucinda saw Lord Elliott still standing near the door. What would it take to convince him to join them at the museum tomorrow? Perhaps she could mention it if she saw him riding in the morning. At least he would be awake long before eleven. Or perhaps she need not wait that long.

Gerald and his friends were ushered into Lady Bellamny's elegant supper room. Potted plants lined the walls, and round tables were scattered around the room. It seemed as if they were not the first gentlemen to arrive.

Quorndon was on one side of the room, greeting his mother and the dowager duchess. Gerald scanned the gathering until his eyes rested on Lady Lucinda sitting next to another lady. She glanced toward the door, and, for a brief moment, their eyes met.

Then the other lady claimed her attention by pointing toward Quorndon. A sly smile appeared on her face. She took the lady by the arm and led her across the room.

"What the devil is my sister up to?" Rothwell's low growl sounded behind Gerald, who had not taken his eyes off Lady Lucinda.

"She appears to be introducing Quorndon to her friend."

"If she's scheming, I hope she doesn't catch cold at it," Rothwell responded. "I'm going to look for my wife."

"We'll come with you." Kenilworth surveyed the room. "Where your wife is, ours will be as well."

Merton nodded as he and Kenilworth followed Rothwell.

"I'll just remain here a moment." Gerald glanced at Lady Lucinda again.

What scheme could her brother mean, and was it something about which he should be concerned?

This looking after a young lady was much more involved than he'd originally thought. Not only that, but if he spent all his time chaperoning her, he'd have no time to look for a wife of his own.

The lady with Lady Lucinda curtseyed, and Quorndon

bowed. The tableau reminded him of one of his mother's Meissen porcelain figures, albeit not in last century's clothing.

Devil a bit!

Gerald would bet his last groat she was matchmaking.

The next thing he knew, she was headed directly for him. Now what was she up to?

"Good evening, my lord." Her eyes sparkled with the look of a cat who'd got into the cream.

"My lady, good evening. Are you looking for your brother?"

"Not yet." She addressed the other lady. "Miss Marlow, may I make Lord Elliott known to you?"

Gerald did the pretty and waited for Lady Lucinda to tell him what she wanted.

She glanced at him hopefully. "Miss Marlow, Lord Quorndon, and I are visiting the British Museum tomorrow. I wonder if you would like to join us."

"It has been a long time since I have been there. I should be delighted to accompany you." It would also give him a chance to find out if she really was scheming.

"Excellent." Once again, she gave him a brilliant smile. "We shall meet there at eleven."

"In the morning?" He couldn't believe she had convinced Quorndon to rise before noon.

Her brows drew together, and she gave Gerald a stern look. "Of course in the morning."

"Naturally. I was just surprised that . . . It doesn't matter. Eleven is a perfectly good time of day to visit the museum. I shall see you then. It should not be too crowded."

"My thoughts exactly." She reassumed her sunny demeanor. "We should find my brother and Miss Marlow's aunt."

The two ladies ambled off, and Gerald wondered if he'd see Lady Lucinda riding in the morning. If he did, he intended to ask her some pointed questions about her plans for Miss Marlow and Lord Quorndon.

Chapter 7

Early the next morning, Lady Lucinda, her cheeks infused with color after a gallop, reined in next to Gerald. The weather was still cool, but the sky was clear, promising a lovely day. "Good morning."

"My lady. I hoped you would be here." Ever since last night he'd been trying to think of a way to address her mechanisms of the previous evening.

Her head swung around, and she met his gaze, holding it for a moment. "What a very nice thing to say."

Heat traveled up his neck, although he had no reason to feel flushed. Nevertheless, he refused to be distracted from his intent. "Are you by any chance attempting to make a match between your friend and Quorndon?"

"Oh, dear." She pulled her plump bottom lip—he had never before noticed how enticing her lips were—between white teeth. "I do hope no one else noticed. At least, until they fall in love."

Quorndon in love? Not likely. "Ah. What, exactly makes you think they will . . . er . . . fall in love?"

"Surely you saw them together. They are a matched pair."

"If you were putting together a team, I'd agree. Still, there is more to a marriage than the way a couple looks together—"

Lady Lucinda shrugged and took off at a gallop.

Drat the woman! She's not going to get out of this conversation that easily.

A minute or so later, Gerald caught up with the minx. "And if Miss Marlow does not engage his affection?"

"I'll find someone else. *I* do not wish to marry him, and the easiest way out of the match our mothers are attempting to make is to give him an alternative." Lady Lucinda's chin took on a mulish cast that reminded him of the duchess. Although, he didn't think she would take a gentleman out of a ballroom by his ear. At least, he hoped she wouldn't. "I will never be able to wed the gentleman I wish to marry if I do not find a match for Lord Quorndon."

Gerald fought to keep his jaw from dropping. She'd only been in Town for a little over a week. "*Have* you found a gentleman you wish to wed?"

Lady Lucinda glanced at him out of the corner of her eye, then gazed straight ahead. "I might have."

He wanted to run his finger under his collar. How could this have happened? He had been watching her so carefully. Well, when he was with her, that was. Had she met this gentleman when she'd been with the duchess or Rothwell?

It behooved Gerald to find out as much about her mystery man as possible. "Is he eligible?"

She stared at him, as if startled. "As eligible as you are."

That was a relief. He had heard of some young ladies who formed attachments with grooms, and footmen, and dancing masters. Still, he should have known Lady Lucinda would not do anything that would create a scandal. "Well then, I wish you luck in your endeavor."

Her lips curved in a small smile as she regarded him for a long moment. "Thank you." The next instant, her expression had vanished completely. "I am looking forward to seeing the museum."

"I believe you are more interested in how Lord Quorndon and Miss Marlow get on," Gerald retorted dryly, attempting to bring the discussion back to Lady Lucinda's matchmaking.

His tone didn't appear to bother Lady Lucinda at all. She urged her mare to a trot. He was going to drag her off that horse if she didn't stop riding away from him.

"You must admit that they fit together perfectly," she called over her shoulder.

"If one was only interested in physical appearances, yes. But there is much more to a marriage than that." At least, there ought to be. Though he had a feeling that for Quorndon, the way a lady looked on his arm might carry a great deal of weight.

"Oh, they have more in common than that," she said. "Neither of them likes to ride."

"That must be an important consideration." Gerald thought he'd kept his tone grave, but she must have heard his doubt.

"Well, I think it is." She brought her mare to a halt, and he pulled up beside her. "If Miss Marlow was to marry a gentleman who was an excellent rider, he would wish her to ride as well." Lady Lucinda pulled her lower lip between her teeth again, and Gerald had to take a breath. He shouldn't be reacting to her at all. "What I do not understand is why his lordship doesn't enjoy riding."

"He won't do anything that makes him appear at a disadvantage, and he's got the worst seat I've ever seen. Doesn't tool a carriage either." Lady Lucinda glanced at him with her brows raised. "Ham handed."

She nodded thoughtfully. "I can see him not wishing to make himself look bad. What does he do well?"

"He's the very devil with a rapier, and no one would ever fault his dancing. He's extremely particular with his clothing—"

"He is a dandy," she said, cutting him off. "I prefer your style over his."

Now what was Gerald to say to that? He had never had a lady compliment him in that manner. Heat rose in his neck. Good Lord, he was blushing.

She laughed lightly. "Do not tell me I have put you to the blush!"

"It appears that is exactly what you have done, my lady." He wished he could tamp down the heat in his face.

"I shall not apologize. What I said was the perfect truth. I will, however, change the subject. What shall we look at in the museum?"

In other words, what would they view while Quorndon and Miss Marlow got to know each other. "There are many fine paintings, as well as the Rosetta Stone, and the Parthenon sculptures. I'm quite sure there is enough to keep us busy for a few hours."

"Splendid." She glanced at the broach watch on her bodice. "I must go home. I shall see you later."

"I look forward to it." Gerald watched her ride off down the path toward the Grosvenor gate. What an amazing young lady.

Lucinda glanced back and gave a little wave. He returned her salute. Who in perdition had she decided on? Did the gentleman even know she was interested in him? Perhaps he should warn Rothwell, or his duchess.

Gerald arrived at his rooms to find a note from his mother asking him to join her for tea that afternoon. Based on her reaction yesterday, he'd expected to be summoned. He might as well hear what she had to say. She was like a dog with a bone when she wanted something.

First though, he would enjoy watching Lady Lucinda try to make a match between Quorndon and Miss Marlow.

Gerald scribbled a hasty reply to his mother accepting her invitation to tea, and went into break his fast. He finished dressing and answered correspondence until it was time to depart.

Just as he arrived at the museum, a landau carrying Lady Lucinda; Miss Marlow; her aunt, Lady St. Claire; another lady; and Quorndon pulled up to the pavement in front of the stairs leading to the entrance.

He reached the carriage in time to assist Lady Lucinda and the older lady from the vehicle.

"Mrs. Smithson," Lady Lucinda said. "May I introduce Lord Elliott? My lord, Mrs. Smithson, Lady St. Claire's cousin who is visiting for several weeks."

"I'm pleased to meet you, my lord." The lady curtseyed as he bowed.

"As I am to meet you." "Relieved" was a better word. Gerald was pleased that Lady St. Claire and her cousin had come to chaperone.

He held out his arms to escort both ladies, but Mrs. Smithson laughed. "You may accompany Lady Lucinda. I shall remain with my cousin."

Looking past Mrs. Smithson, he noticed Quorndon mounting the steps with Miss Marlow. Lady St. Claire waited at the bottom of the stairs.

Obviously, her ladyship was wasting no time in allowing Quorndon to come to know her niece.

"Excellent." Lady Lucinda slipped her hand in Gerald's arm, and a feeling of pride surged through him, which confused him. Granted, she was extremely lovely in a pink muslin gown embroidered with flowers and birds, but he . . . had no time to think about his reaction now. The rest of their party was making their way up the stairs.

"I am very excited," Lady Lucinda confided in a low, musical tone. "I have never been to a museum before."

He liked her enthusiasm and found himself drawing her a bit closer, most likely to get through the door. "Do you have any idea what you would like to see first?"

She grinned at him. "You have been here before, so I will allow you to choose."

Now his chest was puffing out. "I would be delighted." They had entered the hall. It was still early, but in one of the rooms a few older children were drawing in front of paintings. "Let us go upstairs first. You will be able to see the giraffes."

The moment she saw them, he was glad he'd suggested it. "How beautiful they are." She stood staring at them, as if mesmerized. "They look like a family."

Gerald had never noticed it before, but there were two larger animals and a smaller one. "Yes, they do. The animal next to them is a rhinoceros. Have you heard of them?"

Lady Lucinda flashed him a smile, and he found himself flushing. He was only supposed to be taking care of her, not having reactions to one of his best friend's sisters. "I have. They are supposed to be quite ferocious. I do wish they had brought the giraffes back alive."

"Indeed. A pity, that. I believe they were part of the collection bequeathed by Sir Hans Sloane and have been here for a very long time." Gerald sounded pompous, and he didn't like it.

"I am glad to have seen them, even if they are not living. Although, if they were alive and had been here for many years, they most likely would be dead by now." Her tone was wistful, and if he could have brought the beasts back to life, he would have. "Shall we find the Rosetta Stone? I am told it is quite impressive."

She had let go of him to walk around the front of the animals, but now returned her hand to the crook of his arm. He'd not known he had felt the loss so keenly until then.

Gerald tried to shrug off the way his senses seemed to notice everything about Lady Lucinda, including the light scent of lemons and lavender that wafted through the air when she moved.

Nothing seemed to bore her. She inspected everything she saw as thoroughly as she had his cattle and the giraffes.

Two hours later, they met the rest of their party in the main hall.

"Have you been waiting long?" Lady Lucinda looked abashed.

Miss Marlow giggled. "Not *that* long."

Her aunt chuckled. "Well, not long enough to have sent someone to look for you." Lady St. Claire glanced from Lady Lucinda to Gerald. "I take it you found much to interest you."

"We did." She turned to her friend. "Did you see the giraffes?"

Miss Marlow and Quorndon gave identical shudders as she said, "And the other beast. They all looked fearsome. I am glad they were not alive."

"Truly?" Lady Lucinda, a wicked mirth in her eyes, said, "I told Lord Elliott I would have loved to see them alive."

Miss Marlow edged closer to Quorndon, who appeared pleased that she had.

"If we are all ready to depart,"—Lady St. Claire motioned to the door—"I propose we retire to my house and have a light luncheon."

To Gerald's surprise, they all fit easily into the landau. He, Quorndon, and Mrs. Smithson took the back-facing seat while Miss Marlow, her aunt, and Lady Lucinda took the one facing toward the front. Naturally, the conversation revolved around what they had seen.

Lady Lucinda had been struck by the importance of the Rosetta Stone, but Miss Marlow and Quorndon had not seen its magnificence. They all agreed that the ceiling paintings above the staircase were beautiful and exquisitely done. Gerald and Lady Lucinda differed with Miss Marlow and Quorndon as to the Roman antiquities; The other couple had found the landscape paintings more to their taste.

As Gerald escorted Lady Lucinda into St. Claire House on South Audley Street, she whispered, "I think today has been a resounding success."

"I thought you might say that." She wrinkled her nose at him, and he couldn't help but to respond to the grin. "I agree. Quorndon and Miss Marlow seem to have much in common."

If the outing was to be declared a success based solely upon Lady Lucinda's matchmaking, then yes. Yet for Gerald, the day had been one of continuing consternation. The more he came to know Lady Lucinda, the more he liked her. Yet given the way her mother had reacted to him, that would only cause her problems. He was not even certain what Rothwell would say. From now on, he must keep his distance and intensify his search for a wife.

"I wonder how long it will be before he proposes," she mused.

Gerald shook his head. "He only met her last night. Aside from that, the expectation is that he will wed you."

"Oh, pooh." She fluttered her fingers. "I shall gladly tell him and Miss Marlow to follow their hearts. Aside from that, she need never know our mothers tried to arrange a marriage. I do not think he will tell her."

"You have a point." Lady Lucinda was almost as frightening as the new Duchess of Rothwell. "I'd almost forgotten that you have your mind set on another gentleman." Another reason it did him no good at all to be attracted to Lady Lucinda.

She slid him the same slightly devious look she had that

morning. But what the devil did it mean? "Indeed, I do. Come, I am a bit peckish." They entered the hall behind the others. "Will you be at Almack's this week?"

Did her question have something to do with the look she'd given him? "As a matter of fact, I shall."

"Wonderful!" Lady Lucinda faced him, appearing perfectly delighted. "Do you think you can arrange for me to be approved to waltz? I am told that a gentleman must be recommended by one of the Patronesses as a suitable dance partner."

Apparently, she did not want Quorndon or her mother to know who her mystery gentleman was. But should Gerald perform the service? He'd better speak to Rothwell first. "I shall try."

"Thank you." She tightened her hand on his arm. "I knew I could depend upon you."

Good God! What have I got myself into?

He should tell her brother, but that would be a betrayal of the worst sort, and she would never trust him again. And if he continued to be a friend to her, he might be able to put a stop to any plans she had to marry anyone unsuitable. Still, she'd said her gentleman was as eligible as he. Ergo, he was making a mountain out of a molehill and would look like an idiot if he started running off about mystery men.

He and Lucinda entered the room only to find the elder ladies engaged in a comfortable coze, and Quorndon and Miss Marlow ensconced in one of the two window seats, their heads together.

Lady St. Claire raised her head. "Luncheon will be served shortly. I have ordered tea while we wait."

"Thank you, my lady," he and Lucinda answered at the same time.

Drat, he should not think of her by her first name. Perhaps if he only did so in his head it would be all right. As long as he didn't make a blunder and say it to her, or in public. Yes, that would be fine.

"Let us sit in the other window seat. They are so comfortable." She led the way, and Gerald could do nothing but follow. It would have been rude to interrupt Lady St. Claire, and he was not about to interfere with Lucinda's plans for Quorndon and Miss Marlow.

Lucinda patted the place next to her on the wide seat, but Gerald grabbed a nearby chair. "This will be more comfortable for me. I like to look at the person with whom I am conversing."

She smiled brightly. "Do you enjoy being in Town, or would you rather be in the country?"

"I do not think I would choose one over the other. I enjoy the Lords." He grimaced. "Most of the time. I would ask you the same question, but you have not been in Town long enough to know."

Her plump, rosy lips formed a moue. "Very true. I shall answer that question at the end of the Season."

If she hadn't married and left Town by then. Gerald again had the feeling that he should do whatever he could to discover which gentleman had captured her interest. After all, mere rank did not make a man eligible.

Chapter 8

Lucinda walked through the door of Rothwell House. "Is the duchess at home?"

"Yes, my lady." Fredericks bowed. "She is in her parlor."

"And my brother?" She almost crossed her fingers, hoping he was gone.

"Out, my lady." Perfect. She would be able to have a conversation without Rothwell's interference.

"Thank you, Fredericks." She went to her room, giving her spencer, hat, gloves, and reticule to her maid.

"Her grace, your mother asked where you were," Greene said. "I told her with Lord Quorndon and Miss Marlow, just like you asked me to, my lady."

"Thank you. I would not have wanted her to worry." It wouldn't do to tell anyone, other than Louisa, that Lord Elliott had accompanied them.

"Yes, my lady." Greene removed Lucinda's gown and

shook it out, then slipped a day dress over her head, fastened the gown, and draped a shawl over her shoulders.

"I will be with my sister-in-law."

"Yes, my lady." Her maid turned toward the dressing room.

A few moments later, Lucinda scratched on Louisa's door. "It is Lucinda."

"Come, but do not speak. I must finish this column."

She entered the parlor to find her sister-in-law's head bent over a journal. Sinking into a wide, cane-backed chair, she waited, taking the time to look at the new wall coverings and curtains in pale yellows and creams. The new chair fabrics were various patterns consisting of flowers, vines, and birds.

After several moments, Louisa pushed the ledger aside and looked at Lucinda. "Thank you for being patient. Now, what can I do for you?"

Lucinda clasped her hands together to keep from fidgeting with her gown. "I would like to know what you can tell me about Lord Elliott."

"Earl Elliott?" Lucinda nodded. Her sister-in-law picked up a pencil and tapped it on her blotter.

"Rothwell considers him a good enough friend to trust him with you. That alone tells me that he has no serious vices."

Shrugging, Lucinda shook her head.

"He does not engage in excessive gambling, or erratic behavior. He is a good dancer. I do not recall that he courted anyone last year."

That was surprising. "But he must wish to wed."

She caught herself leaning forward in the chair and resumed her previous position. She had done exactly what she had not wanted to do and given away the depth of her interest.

"I imagine he will." Louisa tapped her pencil again, then pulled a sheet of paper toward her. "I understand that you do not want Quorndon. Frankly, although you must not say a word to your mother, I cannot see the two of you together. Yet the Season has just begun. Do you not wish to meet more gentlemen before you form an attachment?"

Lucinda hid her grimace. "I suppose I should tell you that I have seen Lord Elliott in the Park during my morning rides, and he joined my outing with Lord Quorndon, Miss Marlow, her aunt, and cousin at Montague House." When Louisa's lips began to flatten, Lucinda rushed on. "They were not clandestine meetings. Indeed, as far as he was concerned, the meetings in the Park were accidental, and I needed him to be at the museum so that Lord Quorndon and Miss Marlow could come to know each other. That is all." Louisa raised her brows. How was it that she seemed so much more mature than Lucinda? "I asked him to help me be approved to waltz. Rothwell said he planned to ask Lord Elliott, or another of his friends."

"That is true," her sister-in-law commented as she tapped her pencil again.

This was not going well. "We have so much in common, and he does not treat me as if I do not have a brain." Lucinda gave up not fidgeting and wrapped her necklace around one finger. "But I think he only considers me as his friend's sister."

"Let us assume that he does begin to court you." Louisa began to write. "Your mother is not going to like it at all."

"No. Although, if Lord Quorndon proposes to Miss Marlow, it might be easier to talk her round."

"You have a point." Louisa drew her brows together. "She does want you to marry. If only so that she may return to the country."

If Lucinda knew her brother better she would approach him, but she did not. Or rather she knew him as a big brother who had played with her and fixed her toys when she was little and he was home from school. He probably still thought of her as a child. "Will you talk to Rothwell?"

"I must," her sister-in-law said firmly. "We do not keep secrets. That will also give me the opportunity to discover how he feels about a possible match. I do think you would benefit from meeting other gentlemen."

"Did you?" Lucinda knew that it was not until late in the Season that Rothwell had met his wife.

Louisa sat for a few long moments in silence before answering, "Truthfully, I cannot say that I did. I would have had the same reaction to him if I had met him the first day of the Season." She set aside her pencil and smiled. "I do like your idea about finding a match for Quorndon."

"I thought you might." Lucinda grinned. "When you see them together you will understand why I thought they would be perfect for each other. And neither of them likes to ride horses."

"Whereas you and Elliott do." Her sister-in-law pulled a face. "Horses are not everything, you know."

"No, they are not." She kept her excitement to herself. Louisa was coming around, and she could convince Rothwell. "Yet if one person does like them and the other person does not, it could become a large problem."

"They will have to have more in common than that," she prodded.

Really, people need to have more faith in me. "I believe they do have a great deal in common. At the museum they agreed on which sites they liked best. In any event, she has a great deal more in common with Lord Quorndon than I will ever have, which is to say absolutely nothing at all."

Louisa's lips pressed together as one side of her mouth quirked up. "That was fairly obvious to me."

"Mama will have to come around." Lucinda's tone sounded more convinced than she felt.

"Promise me one thing." Louisa waited for Lucinda to nod. "You will not elope. It would harm both your reputations."

She stared at her sister-in-law, shocked that she would think Lucinda would be so reckless. Still, considering her mother, it was a fair request. "I would never do anything so scandalous."

"Thank you." Louisa rose from her chair. "I'm going to the nursery. I shall see you at tea."

Not more than two minutes after she left the room, a cry sounded from the nursery above.

"I wish I knew how she did that." Then again, with luck, by this time next year Lucinda might find out for herself. What would it be like to have a child with Elliott's curls and blue eyes?

Gerald handed his hat and cane to his butler. "Her ladyship is expecting me. Is she in the back parlor or the drawing room?"

"The back parlor, my lord, but—" The butler quickly shoved his hat and cane into a nearby footman's hands.

"Collins." Gerald used his I-am-the-master tone. "You will not announce me in my own house."

"Yes, my lord. May I say that we shall be happy to see you in residence?"

"Soon, Collins. Soon. With any luck at all, I shall wed this Season." At least, that was the plan.

His butler bowed. "Her ladyship will be pleased as well."

"So she says." He glanced around the hall and into the parlor reserved for people who would not be asked to drink tea. That room was not used very often. Still, everything had his mother's mark. The blue floral print fabrics she liked were particularly abhorrent. "She won't like leaving this house."

"As you say, my lord."

Gerald could not tell whether his butler agreed or not. But the truth was he would most likely have a devil of a time getting his mother out of it. It would behoove him to start looking for a town house for her before he married. He'd have to have Rouse look into suitable properties for her.

The door to the back parlor was partially open, giving him a view of his mother with her companion, Cousin Anne.

He knocked lightly before entering. "Good afternoon, Mother, Cousin Anne."

"Ah, Elliott. Here you are. Anne and I were just discussing the importance of ensuring that the family of your future bride has no history of mental disorders."

"Yes, indeed." Anne nodded vigorously, picking up the cue. "One would not wish to be concerned that one's spouse or children would suffer any future disabilities."

What the devil were they getting at? Gerald bowed before strolling into the room. "You mean such as the one from which our king suffers?"

His mother frowned. "Well, naturally, but one cannot wish the children of our king to be unmarriageable. The line must continue."

"Of course." He gestured toward the chair at the end of the table between two sofas. "May I sit?"

"Oh, yes." Mother smiled. "We were so involved in our conversation I quite forgot you were standing."

He lowered himself into the chair, still wondering where this discussion was going and what it had to do with him. He had not heard that any of the young ladies making their come out this Season had madness in their family lines.

Before his mother could continue, Collins and one of the footmen entered, carrying two trays: one with the tea, and the other bearing biscuits, cake, and the sandwiches Mother knew Gerald liked.

She handed him a cup of tea and a plate of sandwiches and seed cake. "As we were saying, you must be careful which lady you choose to wed."

He picked up a lemon biscuit and took a bite, waiting for her to get to the point.

"Even very prominent families can suffer from mad family members," Anne added, shooting a look at his mother. They were definitely up to something.

His mother nodded. "Very true. For example, poor Lady Lucinda's father—"

"Suffered from dementia." He cut her off. This is what the look she'd given him in the Park was about. "Which is very common in older people." He took a sip of tea. "I seem to remember that your own grandmother forgot who just about everyone was."

Mother's face fell, but she recovered quickly. "Indeed she did, but we were able to stop her from the outrageous behavior exhibited by the previous duke."

"Only because she was an old woman. Had it been my great-grandfather, the solution would not have been as easy." He drained his cup and set it down. "I am assisting Rothwell in watching after his sister. That is all."

"It is?" She refilled his cup. "Are you sure?"

"Mother. I will not have this conversation. You will welcome whichever lady I choose to marry." Her eyes widened for the beat of a heart. Not surprising, considering he rarely took a firm tone with her. "Now, I have something I would like to discuss."

"Of course, dear. Have some sandwiches." She offered him another plate.

Ever since he had moved into his own rooms, she'd decided he did not get enough to eat. "Thank you."

She changed the subject, to the balls and other events taking place over the next several days, until he'd finished off the food. "As I will wed before the Season is out, you should consider where you will live while in Town. If you would like, I can have Rouse assist you in searching for a house."

"There is no need for that." She waved her hand. "I have a lovely town house on Half Moon Street I shall move into once your betrothal is announced."

Of course she did. She was his mother. She never did anything he expected her to do. "Very well, then. I shall inform you as soon as I have become affianced. Thank you for tea."

He rose, bowed, and left the parlor as quickly as he could. Gerald damn sure did not want to listen to any more nonsense about Lucinda's father. Whatever made Mother think he was going to court Lucinda, he couldn't guess. Not that he would, but if he decided to turn his attentions to her, it was none of his mother's business. He was an adult, a peer, and he would make his own decisions as to whom he'd marry.

Lucinda was beautiful, intelligent, graceful—and his best friend's little sister. Which reminded him. He really should see Rothwell about dancing with Lucinda at Almack's. The sooner Gerald spoke with her friend, the sooner he could mark it off his list of errands.

Gerald turned left on Carlos Place, and a minute or so later saw the man he was looking for headed in his direction. "Rothwell, well met."

"Elliott, I wanted to speak with you. I was going to go to Brooks, but if you'll agree to help me, or, rather, my sister, I can return home."

He didn't know what helping his sister had to do with Brooks, but . . . "I wished to speak with you as well. You first."

"Well, you see, my wife explained how agonizing it was not knowing if a gentleman would be introduced to her for the waltz the first time she attended Almack's, and I thought you would be amenable to finding a way to be recommended to Lucinda."

That was easier than Gerald had thought it would be. "Of course. I'll speak with Lady Jersey. I believe she'll agree." He still didn't understand why Rothwell was headed to Brooks, unless he was going to ask someone else. For some reason Gerald couldn't put his finger on, he didn't like that idea. "Why Brooks?"

"If I didn't find you, I thought I'd find Kit Featherton there. He is always willing to help a lady."

Like hell Featherton would. Gerald had to stop himself from clenching his jaw. "Well, you found me, and I shall be happy to dance with Lady Lucinda."

"Thank you." Rothwell took Gerald's hand and shook it as if he was relieved. "I want to make sure she has a good Season. But this is a lot more work than I thought it would be. To be honest, I would've been happy to have remained in the country until the baby was older."

"I take it you're not letting the nurse tend to her?" One of his own sisters insisted on spending a great deal of time with her children.

"She does, as do the nursemaids, all three of them, but Louisa insists on nursing Alexandria herself, and it's interrupting our sleep. Not that she is alone in her decision. Her sister and Lady Merton nurse their children as well. It has become fairly common, from what I've been led to understand."

"I believe that is correct." Gerald wondered if the lady he chose for his wife would wish to eschew a wet nurse. If so, they'd definitely remain in the country. "I look forward to tomorrow evening."

"I as well. Thank God there's nothing tonight other than dinner at Worthington House. It's good to be able to talk to men going through the same thing."

He'd almost forgotten that not only had Lady Merton and Lady Kenilworth given birth not long ago, but Lady Worthington and Lady Wolverton, the mother of Worthington's sisters, had as well. What would it be like to be part of a large family? "Have a good evening."

"Thank you, you as well." Rothwell headed home, and Gerald turned toward Brooks.

Chapter 9

Gerald entered the morning room off to one side of the main corridor in Brooks. Once again, he found Quorndon sitting in the same leather chair he had been before, holding a glass of wine between two fingers and staring into the fire. An empty decanter of claret sat on the table.

"Good afternoon," Gerald greeted him.

"Good afternoon, Elliott." Quorndon took a sip of wine. "Have a seat if you wish."

He motioned for the servant to bring another bottle before sitting in the chair next to Quorndon. "You look to be in a brown study."

He glanced at Gerald, and seemed to be having a hard time focusing. "I think I may have to disappoint my mother, and I dislike doing that in the extreme."

"I'm afraid I can't help you there. I am a constant disappointment to my mother."

"Pity. She is usually my closest confidante." The man switched his gaze back to the fire.

Gerald had never seen Quorndon so blue-deviled. "And you cannot speak to her about this . . . problem?"

"No. It seems we may want different results." He drained his glass just as the waiter brought a fresh decanter.

Was he speaking of marriage with Lucinda? He'd been so sure of her before. Or was her matchmaking bearing fruit? And how was Gerald to find out? "I am held to be a fairly good listener."

"I fear I am becoming quite attached to Miss Marlow." The man actually sighed.

"Correct me if I'm wrong, but did you not meet her only last evening?" Gerald wished Lady Lucinda could be here to hear his lordship. On second thought, no he didn't. She'd take great joy in pointing out that she was right.

"Indeed." The man lifted his head. "Yet it feels as if I have known her forever."

Despite the drubbing Gerald would receive from her, this was good news for Lucinda. "But your mother still wishes you to marry Lady Lucinda?"

"It is her fondest desire." He'd never heard Quorndon sound so low, nor seen him becoming quite so foxed.

"Yes. Still, you are the one who will have to live with the lady." Gerald could absolutely not envision Lucinda and Quorndon being anything close to happy. "You do require children. One must want to take ones wife to bed to do that."

Quorndon's slightly blurred gaze focused on Gerald. "By God, you're right." The man stood. "Thank you, Elliott."

With overly precise steps, his lordship made his way out of the room. He signaled to the footman. "Call his lordship a hackney."

"Yes, my lord."

Gerald was reaching for a discarded newssheet when Ned Carver, grandson of Viscount Carver, dropped into the seat Quorndon had vacated. "Mind if I join you?"

"Not at all." Gerald set the paper back down. "When did you get to Town?"

"A few days ago." His friend took the glass a servant handed him, and Gerald filled it with claret. "Thank you. One of my sisters is coming out, and we had to be here for Lady Bellamny's party."

"I didn't see you when the gentlemen were allowed in."

Carver coughed, then doubled over, holding a handkerchief to his nose. "For God's sake. Don't say things like that when a fellow has just taken a sip of wine." He wiped his nose, straightened, and took a breath. "I'm not getting any closer to her ladyship than I have to." Folding the linen, he put it back in his pocket. "Do you have plans for the Season?"

Gerald waited until his friend swallowed before speaking. "I am looking for a wife." A groan greeted this declaration. "Now what?"

"M'father is after me to marry. It did not help that my sister met a number of young ladies and offered to introduce me to them." Carver took another drink of wine. "It seems all of my friends are wearing a leg-shackle. Now you're going to join them. It's the love matches that are the problem. Makes a man want to stay home with his wife. It's getting to the point that a gentleman won't have anyone left with whom to drink."

Or go whoring or gambling with. "Featherton's still holding out."

Carver brightened. "As long as he's not married, I can convince Father that putting a Parson's noose around my neck is not that urgent." He downed the rest of his glass. "I always say talking with a friend can put things into perspective. Thank you."

It occurred to Gerald that Lady Lucinda was correct. They were all of an age where they should be thinking about setting up their nurseries.

"On the other hand,"—Carver refilled his glass—"if I were to meet a lady with whom I became enamored, I might consider marriage."

He made less than no sense. "I thought you just said you did *not* want a love-match."

"I don't. But even Merton fell in love. If it happens, there's no point fighting it. I have been told Lady St. Eth is sponsoring her niece, and Rothwell's sister is coming out as well."

A sudden pain stabbed Gerald's jaw, and he had to force himself to loosen it. *Damn the man! How the hell am I going to protect Lucinda if everyone and their brother goes after her?*

There was only one thing to do. "A shame that Rothwell's mother already has a match planned for Lady Lucinda."

"Her mother?" Carver took a long draw from his glass. "I suppose she'll be looking higher than a mere mister."

It was all Gerald could do to hide his grin. "So I have been told."

"Almack's," Lucinda said yet again. She could not believe she was finally attending one of the famous assemblies. Closing her eyes, she said a short prayer that Lord Elliott would be allowed to waltz with her.

"You won't be going anywhere if you don't sit still so I can finish your hair." Greene's nonsensical tone broke through Lucinda's thoughts. She held her head still as her maid threaded a pink ribbon with seed pearls through her hair. She wished she had curls, but her hair just waved.

Her maid stepped back. "There."

She stared at her reflection. Lucinda had never had her hair so elaborately dressed. A braid looping from one side of her head around to the top was held in place by a pearl-tipped hair pin and the ribbon. Small curls framed her face. "*My* hair did that?"

"Yes, my lady. All we needed was the right cut."

What would Lord Elliott think? "And your skill. Thank you."

Greene added a pearl necklace and earrings before putting a spangled shawl around Lucinda's shoulders and giving her a silk reticule that matched her gown. "All ready."

"Thank you again. I have never felt so beautiful." Would Lord Elliott think she was the most beautiful woman he had ever seen?

Was she asking too much?

Lucinda, her sister-in-law, and brother arrived at Almack's at nine-thirty. She was amazed at how plain the outside of the building looked. Built of plain white stone, it had large windows with little in the way of ornamentation. "Is it grander inside?"

"No," Louisa answered as they waited for the carriage to reach the front door. "It is large, but as plain as the outside. Supper consists of stale bread and butter, weak tea, lemonade, and ratafia. It is not the elegance of the place that makes it important; it is the elegance of those allowed to enter."

There had been so much to do to prepare for her first real public event that Lucinda forgot to be nervous. Until, that was, she, accompanied by her sister-in-law and brother, was just about to enter the hallowed assembly room of Almack's.

Suddenly, her stomach lurched into her throat. She clutched Louisa's hand. "I think I'm going to be ill."

"You and every other young lady here. Charlotte and I felt the same way. Only Dotty did not suffer from nervousness."

That was a relief. Lucinda concentrated on looking around until her stomach calmed.

They passed the massive supper room on the ground floor and made their way to the ballroom. It was huge, with chairs and small sofas lining the walls—many of them already occupied. An orchestra played from a small balcony that jutted out over the dance floor halfway down the room. Blue curtains adorned the windows.

Rothwell led them to three chairs not far from the middle of the room. "This gives me a good view."

"When will the waltz be played?" Lucinda asked.

"Not until after a country dance and the quadrille." Louisa sank into a chair.

A tall gentleman with brown hair strode up to them and bowed. "Rothwell, your grace."

"Featherton." Rothwell grinned. "Good evening." Her brother turned to her. "Lucinda, allow me to introduce a friend of mine, Mr. Featherton. Featherton, my sister, Lady Lucinda Hughlot."

"A pleasure, my lady. May I be the first to ask you to dance?"

That was very kind of him. Other than Lord Elliott and Lord Quorndon, she had not met any gentlemen. "Thank you, sir. I would be delighted."

"Your servant." Mr. Featherton bowed again. "I shall return to claim my set."

"I'll look forward to it." Where was Lord Elliott?

She glanced toward the entrance and saw Lord Quorndon and his mother enter, followed by Miss Marlow, her aunt, and a gentleman who, by the silver in his dark hair, was around forty. He must have been Lord St. Claire. Had Miss Marlow and Quorndon come together, or was it serendipity that they had arrived at the same time?

There was a stir as a group of two gentlemen and several ladies, one an extremely beautiful woman with auburn hair, entered. As Lucinda turned to ask who they were, she spotted Lord Elliott headed toward them from across the room. He must have already been present.

"Rothwell, duchess, Lady Lucinda." Lord Elliott bowed to Louisa before taking Lucinda's fingers in his large hand. His dimple peeped out, and even through their gloves she began to tingle.

It was a good thing her mother had remained at home— Lucinda could not seem to hide her reaction to him. "My lord. How nice it is to see you."

"I'll wager you'll think it's even nicer in an hour or so," he murmured as he straightened. "In the meantime, do you have a partner for the quadrille?"

"No. So far, only Mr. Featherton has requested a set." That should have made her sad, but the only gentleman she really wished to dance with was Lord Elliott.

"I would be happy to stand up with you." Did he realize he was asking for two sets? She glanced at her brother, but he was busy returning the salute from one of the men who had just arrived. "Thank you."

"Never thank a gentleman for the honor of dancing with you." He grinned at her before strolling away.

For the next hour, one of the Patronesses or another brought gentlemen to be introduced—and that was in addition to the men who already knew her brother or sister-in-law. It was not long before the only set left was the waltz.

"I didn't realize there were so many men I didn't know," her brother grumbled.

"You were gone for three years." Louisa patted his arm reassuringly. "I promise you will make it through this evening."

Rothwell scanned the ballroom. "We leave after supper." He sounded so distraught that Lucinda's lips began to twitch. She covered her mouth when he glanced toward her. "I want no arguments."

"None at all. I made sure I did not accept any requests to dance after supper." By then she would have had two dances with Lord Elliott, and thus far, none of the other men had stirred her at all.

The music began as Mr. Featherton came to collect her. He was an excellent dancer, and he set about attempting to calm her nerves. Not that she had any after her initial reaction. Louisa had done an excellent job of preparing Lucinda. Still, she made all the appropriate responses. She did not want him to think he was wasting his time.

Finally, Lord Elliott approached them with Lady Jersey on his arm. She greeted Rothwell and Louisa before saying, "Lady Lucinda, may I recommend Lord Elliott to you as a suitable partner for the waltz?"

Her heart took flight. She had been expecting it. Hoping, praying would be more accurate. Still, he had done what he'd promised to do.

Lucinda almost forgot to curtsey. "Thank you, my lady."

A few minutes later, she was in his arms, twirling around the floor. His hand engulfed her smaller one, and his palm seemed to burn through her silk evening gown. She could not help but notice how firm his waist was. Yet it was not just that. She felt as if she were floating. Surely no one danced as well as he did.

Lucinda hoped he had not wished to stand up with a different lady. "Was it very hard to get Lady Jersey to agree to recommend you?"

"Not at all." He smiled. "I think she was relieved that I wasn't asking to dance with Lady Serena."

Not understanding, Lucinda asked, "The lady with the auburn hair?"

"Indeed." They'd changed positions and were skipping around.

"I saw her come in. She is very lovely." She waited to see if he would agree. Had he wanted to dance with the other lady?

"I suppose she is." He did not sound as if he had wanted to waltz with her. "How are you enjoying Almack's?"

"Very much, indeed." She lost her breath when he twirled her around.

Not that Lucinda had much experience, but Lord Elliott was definitely the best dance partner she had ever had. Her opinion was confirmed when they stood up for the quadrille. She had never seen a man so light on his feet, not even her brother.

"You dance very well," he said as he made his final bow. "These steps are not easy to master."

"Louisa taught me over Christmas." Lucinda placed her hand on his arm. "She and Rothwell had a small ball, and before that we had a dancing party so that those of us in the country could practice."

"That sounds like something the duchess would do."

"Now that I know her better, it does." Her sister-in-law was not only kind, but intelligent enough to know that having experience dancing could only help those who had previously lacked it.

When they approached Rothwell and Louisa, her brother looked at Lord Elliott, raised a brow, and said, "Two?"

"I knew how it would be with Lady Serena here. I did not wish Lady Lucinda to have to sit out a dance when I could stand up with her."

What did that mean? That he only danced twice with her because he did not want her to be embarrassed or feel slighted. Not that he had *wanted* to stand up with her twice? She glanced at Louisa, who gave an imperceptible shake of her head.

"Let us go down to supper, such as it is." Lord Elliott held his arm out to Lucinda.

"It's a shame we can't leave now." Her brother took his wife's arm.

"Never fear." Louisa grinned up at Rothwell. "I left orders for a small repast to be served when we arrive home. My brother was always hungry after returning from Almack's."

The supper conversation consisted of the problems the weather was causing with spring planting, and the possibility that the landowners would have to delve into their reserves to get themselves and their dependents through the next year, which unfortunately did nothing to answer Lucinda's questions about how Lord Elliott might feel about her. Still, she did learn that he had four other estates in addition to Bittlesbrough, and that he had invested in ventures that would not be harmed by this year's harvest. It did not matter to her how wealthy he was, but it was nice to know he was intelligent about not having all his funds in one place, and that he knew how to manage them. That should reassure her mother.

Chapter 10

Gerald escorted Lady Lucinda to Almack's entrance hall, where she and her family waited for their carriage. She danced so well, he could have happily danced another set with her. He had never had a partner so light and responsive in his arms that he did not even need to think about the dance. None of the other ladies with whom he'd stood up came close to her skill and grace. He tried not to think about how well she fitted him. As it was, he was lucky Rothwell had not made a fuss about the second set. Gerald wondered what the hell he'd been thinking to do such a thing at Almack's.

He would have liked to have departed when she had, but it would have appeared singular, especially after two dances, and he was still looking for a wife.

Lady Jersey caught Gerald's eye and raised a brow when he re-entered the ballroom. He had known her much of his life.

It would behoove him to explain that he was not in love with Lady Lucinda, nor she with him.

Yet where was her mystery gentleman?

None of the other gentlemen appeared to have met her before. He hadn't caught any of them gazing at her as she danced. Was it possible the man could not gain entrance to Almack's? Not everyone could. If so, what did that say about the man?

"Elliott." Lady Jersey's curious voice intruded on his thoughts. "Two dances? And on the opening night of the Season. What were you thinking?"

Hell and damnation! "Lady Evesham's cousin is gathering so much attention, I did not wish Lady Lucinda's feelings to be hurt."

This time Lady Jersey raised both brows. What was wrong with his reason? "Indeed?"

"Yes, of course. I promised Rothwell I would help look after her." His collar was suddenly tight. That had been happening a great deal lately. He'd have to speak to his valet.

She gazed at Gerald for several seconds, then heaved a breath. "I shall do my best to scotch any rumors. Do not let it happen again, unless you are serious about the young lady."

"Yes, ma'am." He would have to be more careful. He did not want to raise Lady Lucinda's expectations. "Are there any ladies to whom you would like to introduce me?"

"Yes. One young lady has not been able to waltz yet."

He followed her to a young woman who stammered through the introduction. Featherton would have been a better person to put the lady at her ease, but Gerald did his best. Fortunately, after the waltz, he saw Featherton making his way toward them.

He danced the next set with a Miss Martindale, who only appeared to be interested in where his estates were located, and the final set with Lady Alice, whose calm, gray eyes could not erase the image of sparkling green ones.

By the time the evening ended, he was no closer to finding the right woman than he had been yesterday. In fact, the only lady to remain in his thoughts was Lady Lucinda.

The next several weeks saw him attending almost every entertainment for which he had received a card. Many times he was in the company of Rothwell, his duchess, and sister. Gerald still had not figured out who Lady Lucinda's gentleman could be, but the more time he spent with her, each time he danced with her, and every conversation they had, the more he liked her.

She was not only beautiful and intelligent, but kind as well. He'd lost count of how many times she'd asked him to dance with a young lady who had no partner. Not only that, but Rothwell told Gerald she'd decided to join the charity his duchess, her sister, and her friend had formed.

What unsettled him even more was that he had started to compare every other woman he'd met to Lucinda. Could she be the lady he wanted? How would he know?

The next morning, he once again met Lucinda riding. He had grown used to speaking with her each day, and he would miss their meetings once the Season ended. "Good morning, my lady."

"Good morning." She smiled cheerfully. "Did you enjoy Lady Rutherford's ball last night?"

What he'd enjoyed was dancing with Lucinda. "I did indeed."

"It certainly showed that there is life after one's baby is older. I know my sister-in-law and brother will be happy to have more sleep and not be at an infant's beck and call."

Gerald choked. He didn't know whether to be appalled or laugh. He rarely met a young lady so direct. It must come from spending time with her sister-in-law. He couldn't think her mother would approve. "I suppose they might. Would you like to go riding with me this afternoon?"

Tilting her head, she gave him a slightly sly smile. "Yes, I would."

What the devil was she up to? She had not mentioned her mystery gentleman in a while. Was she attempting to make the man jealous?

Later that afternoon, in his high-perched phaeton they came upon Lady Evesham, accompanied by Lady Serena in the former's famous high-perched phaeton. Gerald doffed his hat. "Good afternoon."

The ladies greeted them. "We had to take advantage of one of the few nice days we've had."

"It has been a trifle rainy," Lucinda commented. "I must compliment you on your carriage, my lady. It is my dearest wish to be able to drive one."

"You see, Serena?" Lady Evesham laughed. "I am not the only lady who likes the high-perched phaetons." She turned back to Lucinda. "You should ask Elliott if you can drive his. Then he can convince your brother that you should have one of your own."

Gerald didn't even want to hear Rothwell's response to that suggestion. Still, it was a shame that Lucinda did not have her own carriage.

She turned to him. "May I please drive your phaeton? I do know how. My father taught me."

He was not proof against her bright, pleading eyes. "Yes. Do you think you can handle the pair now, or would you rather take the ribbons when there is not so much traffic?"

"Now will do." She threw a look at Lady Evesham. "Thank you for the suggestion, my lady."

"My pleasure." Her ladyship grinned. "Please give my best to your brother and sister-in-law."

The ladies drove off, and Gerald handed the reins to Lucinda. "Here you are."

"Thank you." She expertly threaded the ribbons through her fingers and gave the pair their office.

For the first several moments he kept himself ready to grab the reins, but it soon became clear that she was an excellent whip. He settled back to enjoy the novelty of a female handling his cattle.

It was too bad her brother couldn't afford to buy her a carriage and pair. Lucinda would have to marry a gentleman wealthy enough to give her the things she deserved.

I could afford to set up her stable.

Where in perdition had that thought come from?

As they neared the gate, she glanced at him. "May I drive them to Rothwell House?"

"If you wish." Her broad smile made him want to puff out his chest. The question was why was she the only woman who affected him that way?

A few minutes later, she expertly feathered the corner into Grosvenor Square, pulled up in front of her house, and handed him back the ribbons. "Thank you. I cannot tell you how grateful I am that you trusted me with your carriage and pair."

"You drive extremely well." Gerald jumped down, went around the phaeton, and handed her down. "Shall I see you this evening at Miss Martindale's come out ball?"

"Yes, you will." Lucinda met his gaze directly. "Shall I save you a waltz?"

That was a pleasure not to be missed. "If you please."

The door opened, and the butler stood waiting. "I shall see you later."

"Until then." Gerald climbed back into his carriage and drove to the stable.

After he handed his pair to a groom, he headed toward Piccadilly. He should have been considering his meeting tomorrow with his solicitor, but his thoughts kept coming back to Lucinda.

"Elliott, you'd better move off to the side." Carver grabbed Gerald's shoulder. "Stopping in the middle of the street could get you killed."

Blinking, Gerald looked around. Damn, he'd done it again. He was on Jermyn Street, but didn't even remember crossing Piccadilly Street. At this rate, he was going to get himself run over.

"You don't look to be in your altitudes." His friend peered at him. "Are you ill?"

"No. Not at all." In fact, if Lucinda was the lady he'd been looking for, then . . . "On the contrary. Things are going along nicely."

The only problem was how to find out if she was the one without unfairly raising her expectations if he discovered she was not meant for him?

The next day, Lucinda hoped Lord Elliott would invite her to drive with him again. Yet when the invitation did not appear, she agreed to go walking during the fashionable hour with Arabella Marlow. Not that she wasn't a good companion— Lucinda would just rather be with Lord Elliott.

"Have you heard the news?" Arabella nodded to a lady in a curricle.

"Which news?" The *ton* was rife with gossip.

She leaned close to Lucinda, keeping her voice low. "Lady Alice has accepted a proposal of marriage from the Marquis of Harwich."

"When did that happen?" Not that it was unexpected. The two had been spending a great deal of time in each other's company. "And how did you find out?"

"My aunt is a good friend of the dowager Lady Harwich." Arabella smiled.

"I am happy for her. She was so sure she would not have a good time this Season." Lucinda thought back to the night she first met Alice.

"I said then that she was being silly." Arabella's head swiveled in the direction of the carriageway. "There is Lady Quorndon."

Unlike his mother, Lord Quorndon was seldom to be found during the Grand Strut. The one or two times he had gone out he was in his landau, accompanied by Arabella and her aunt. "Speaking of his lordship,"—Lucinda wasn't quite sure how to ask the question—"are there any developments?"

Her friend sighed deeply. "We have become much closer." Arabella angled her parasol so that she did not have to see Lady Quorndon. "But there is a problem with his mother. She wishes him to wed another lady. He has asked me to be patient for a little while longer."

Lucinda knew the other marriage was not going to happen. "I think you should both follow your hearts." When her friend did not answer, she continued, "I realize that one's family is an important consideration, but it is not as if you are not perfectly eligible. I," she said in a firm tone, "would tell him he must make a decision. After all, you do not wish to waste time on him if he cannot bring himself to be his own man."

Lady Quorndon waved at Lucinda, and she returned the greeting. After the carriage passed, Arabella nodded. "That is exactly what I shall do. Have you made any progress with Lord Elliott?"

"I wish I knew." Other than Louisa, and possibly Rothwell, only Arabella knew that Lucinda had fallen in love with Elliott. "We go on together so well, yet I have the feeling that he thinks of me as his friend's little sister. I can assure you it is extremely lowering not to be seen as a woman by the gentleman one wishes to wed."

Arabella harrumphed. "I do not know which is more frustrating: knowing a gentleman loves you but does not want to face his mother, or not knowing if he loves you at all."

"I think that if Lady Quorndon knew her son loved you, she would wish him to wed you. Lord Elliott wanting to marry me is only half my battle. My mother does not like that his title is so new." There was no way Lucinda would tell her friend that the match Quorndon's mother wanted was with her.

"Obviously it is no use at all waiting for our gentlemen to act." Arabella's normally soft chin firmed. "We shall have to come up with a plan."

They could come up with all the schemes they liked, but would they be able to put them forward? On the other hand, nothing ventured, nothing gained. "What do you suggest?"

"I shall tell Quorndon that he will either inform his mother he wishes to marry me, or I will have to look for another husband." She glanced at Lucinda. "Naturally, I will not be that straightforward. My mother always said it is better to allow a gentleman to think your suggestion is his idea."

She wished her mother had given her advice. "That still leaves Elliott."

"You will have to tell him how you feel." Lucinda stopped walking and opened her mouth, but nothing came out. Her friend shrugged. "It may be that he simply does not realize you are interested in him."

"What if he does not love me?" Lucinda didn't know why she asked the question when she was quite sure she did not wish to hear the answer.

"In that case, you have lost nothing but a fanciful dream." Arabella started to stroll again.

It took a moment for Lucinda to convince her feet to move. "I am not sure I have the courage to ask him."

"I do not think I can help you with that. If you do decide to act boldly, we will have to figure out when to execute our plans."

They left the Park. When they reached the corner of Grosvenor Square and South Audley Street, said their farewells.

Lucinda had a great deal of thinking to do about Elliott— she liked calling him that. Was she daring enough to actually confront him about his feelings? Was she a mouse, or a lioness like her sister-in-law?

She handed her bonnet to Fredericks. "I shall be in the library."

"My lady, her grace, your mother wishes to see you in her parlor."

Mama's parlor was now attached to her bedchamber. Lucinda held out her hand for her bonnet. "I may as well take that to Greene myself."

"As you wish, my lady." Fredericks bowed and gave her back the hat.

A short time later, she knocked on her mother's door and was given leave to enter. Tea and biscuits were on the low table in front of the sofa Mama liked. Somehow, she had managed to avoid most of the events Lucinda had attended, ergo, it had been two days since she had last seen her mother.

Lucinda sat on the chair across from her mother. "You wished to speak with me?"

"Yes, dear." Her mother poured the tea and handed her a cup. "I understand from Rothwell that your Season is going well."

"It is." She sipped her tea. Strange. Mama did not normally like blend bergamot, but it was Lucinda's favorite afternoon beverage. "I am having a great deal of fun. Although I can see how it could become tiring if one did too much." Some ladies were made to attend up to three events an evening. She was glad she only had to attend one.

"That is excellent. Lady Quorndon and I have decided that a ball would be the perfect occasion to announce your betrothal to Quorndon."

Chapter 11

Thank the heavens Lucinda had not just taken a sip of tea. She would have spit it out. "What?"

"I agreed that you would have a Season." A frown appeared on her mother's face. "It has been over a month. I should think that would be time enough."

It would never be time to wed Quorndon. "I thought you were enjoying seeing your old friends again."

"That has nothing to do with it," Mama said, her tone tight. Taking a sip of tea, her mother made a face. "I want to see you settled."

Someone must have said or done something to make her mother want the betrothal to take place so soon. Anger warred with the sense of dread that she would be stuck in a horrible marriage. She had to do something. Lucinda set her cup down and rose. "I have no desire to wed Lord Quorndon. In fact, I cannot think of a worse match for either of us."

Her mother's eyes widened before she assumed a cold mask through which Lucinda could see nothing. The only sign of Mama's anger was the sound of the fine bone china cup clinking as her mother put it down.

"You have one week before I make the betrothal public."

"Good day, Mother." Lucinda curtseyed and strode toward the door.

"Lucinda,"—her mother's voice stopped her—"I will not have you driving with Lord Elliott. He is not for you. In the future, I shall expect you to accompany Lord and Lady Quorndon if you wish for a carriage ride."

There it was. The catalyst Lucinda needed.

She would not lie to her mother, and therefore chose not to respond.

Straightening her shoulders, she left the parlor and headed straight to the desk in her bedchamber. Pulling out a sheet of fine pressed paper, she made sure her pen was sharpened, dipped it into the standish, and began to write.

My dear Arabella,

I will do as you suggest. I propose that we attend Lady Talgath's party tomorrow. I shall speak with my brother and sister-in-law about taking the duchess's landau. I am sure she will not object.

Yr friend,

Lucinda

Less than an hour later, Louisa had agreed to not only allow Lucinda the use of her carriage, but to accompany her as well.

"I'll have Rothwell invite Elliott and Quorndon to come with us." Louisa put her arm around Lucinda, hugging her. "You know that I wish you good luck in this venture. However, you must be prepared if it does not turn out as you desire."

"I know." She had hung all her hopes on Lord Elliott. Yet she had the sinking feeling she might be disappointed.

The only comforting thought was that she was fairly sure her friend would succeed with Quorndon, so she would not have to marry him.

Gerald frowned. Lucinda looked miserable. Not that anyone else would notice. She had a polite expression on her face, but her eyes lacked their sparkle, and her usual *joie de vivre* was missing.

Over the past few weeks, they had become friends, his feeling that she could be the lady for him had grown stronger. In fact, he was quite sure he had fallen in love with her. When they were apart, not an hour went by that he didn't think of her and what she'd be doing. Therefore, he noticed what others did not. He'd do anything to make her happy again.

They were attending an event at Lady Talgath's estate outside of Town, which was famed for her bluebell meadow. Massive trees dotted the grounds, benches had been placed to provide shade and a small amount of privacy, and a path wound around an ornamental lake. The sounds of birds mingled with the laughter of young ladies.

He had ridden with her brother and Quorndon—they had given him the option of traveling in the carriage, but he chose to ride. At least he kept his seat. She had driven in the landau with her sister-in-law and Miss Marlow. Thankfully, neither of their mothers were present.

Once they arrived, Quorndon had gone off with Miss Marlow to stroll around the lake. Unfortunately, Gerald did not know if his lordship intended to ask for the lady's hand in marriage. Was that why Lucinda was so upset? Did she believe Quorndon would not ask Miss Marlow to marry him? Or was it another gentleman? Her mystery gentleman?

He led Lucinda toward one of the many wrought iron benches placed to encourage one to enjoy the plantings. It was next to a tree with wide branches, offering some seclusion. "I've never seen you look so blue-deviled. Tell me what is wrong."

A slight frown turned down the corners of her rosy lips as she glanced at him. "If I cannot confide in you, there is no one." She heaved an unhappy sigh. "I am determined not to marry Quorndon. But my mother is pressuring me to allow her to announce our betrothal and making me feel like the most horrible, ungrateful daughter that she ever had the misfortune to bear. I thought she had married for love, but it was an arranged match that turned into love." She threw one hand in the air. "She does not understand that I do not wish for her to select my husband."

It wasn't surprising that the dowager duchess would use guilt where a more forceful method would not suffice. Did Lucinda feel the same for him as he did for her? Was now the time to find out?

After all, she had not mentioned her mystery gentleman in quite a while. Had she changed her mind about the man? Could she now be in love with him?

Gerald paused beneath the lower branches of the tree and took a breath. "Is there anyone you would like to marry?"

She gazed at him, staring into his eyes as if she could find the answer in them. "There might be."

A spark of hope ignited in him. *Is it I?* Taking her hand, he drew her around the trunk of the tree where no one could see them. "Might be?"

"Yes." She nodded slowly and their eyes met and locked. The yearning in hers threatened to unman him. "He has become a trusted friend, and I very much enjoy spending time with him. Yet I do not know if he feels the same way about me. That we could, perhaps, have something deeper than friendship. I do not know if there is that sort of passion between us, or if it could develop."

Was it, indeed, him? Had he been blind for weeks? His boots brushed her skirts as he stepped closer. "How do you propose to discover if this friend wants something more?"

"I do not know." Her head tilted slightly, but her gaze never left his. "I am leaving it to him to inform me."

Gerald's gaze dropped to her lips as she licked them. He wanted to draw her into his arms. "And the passion." More than anything else in the world, he wanted to taste her. "Do you think a kiss would be enough for you to know?"

"I think it might be. I have never been kissed."

"Lucinda,"—he placed his hands on her waist, savoring the soft swell of her hips—"kiss me." Not giving her a chance to answer, he pressed his lips to hers, feathering lightly, willing her to respond. To his immense relief, she threw her arms around his neck and pressed her body against his. Slanting his head, he trailed his tongue along the seam of her lips, begging her to open for him. On a soft sigh, their tongues met and danced together as flames of passion licked his skin, making him want more.

If only he could take her somewhere more private. He drew her firmly into his arms.

Mine.

The word echoed in his brain. No matter what battles they had to fight, they would be together. He would do whatever he had to do to ensure their future.

Their kiss turned heated, searing every fiber of his being. Never had he experienced anything like it—the need for her was more vital than his next breath. He couldn't stop his hands from moving closer to her breasts, just enough that he was able to cup them, caress them with his thumbs, and feel her nipples harden under his touch. Finally, he'd come home.

Frissons of pleasure coursed through Lucinda as Elliott stroked her back before sliding his hand over her derrière. Heat coalesced between her legs. She had hoped she would enjoy kissing, but she never guessed it could be so wonderful, stealing her every thought until everything faded but him, and the pleasure of his touch.

Thank the Fates that Gerald's feelings for her matched hers for him. She had been afraid that she would have to initiate their first kiss. That would have been awkward. Especially if he had not responded. Yet not only had he initiated the kiss, but his every taste, touch, took her beyond any sensation she could have imagined.

They were so close his heart and hers beat together as one. His light touch on her breasts made her moan with pleasure. One of his large, strong hands pressed her into him.

Giving into her desire, she rose onto her tiptoes.

He groaned, then broke their kiss.

"What is it? Did I do something I should not have?"

"No, you did nothing wrong." His voice was low, harsh. "Someone is coming."

After all the time Lucinda had waited, this was not at all fair. "Well . . . well, drat."

His laugh was short and harsh, and she smiled. "Drat indeed." He stepped back and studied her. "You'll do. Is my cravat a mess?"

"Slightly crushed, but I think I can fix it." As she smoothed the wrinkled part, she thought how intimate the gesture was. And how much she liked making it.

The voices of a couple strolling nearby caused them to glance at each other. When the voices faded, his hands returned to her waist. "Lucinda?"

Like him, she kept her voice to a whisper. "Yes, Gerald?"

With her hand in his, he dropped to one knee, his gaze holding hers. "I love you. I know we will face difficulties with your mother, but would you make me the happiest man in England and the whole world and marry me?"

Simple and direct, just like the man himself. There would be no games between them. "Yes. I will marry you. I love you too; I'll love you always."

"And I'll always love you." Rising, he drew her into his arms and kissed her. Once again, their passion flared. "Now we need to find a way to bring our marriage about."

"Where there is a will, there is a way." No matter what, she would not allow her mother to keep them apart.

"Lucinda, are you under there?"

"Arabella." Quorndon admonished her. "It could be anyone."

"I recognize the trim on her skirts." Arabella peeked under the wide branches of the tree, a broad smile on her face. "We wanted to tell you first."

"Good Lord, I cannot believe I'm doing this." Lord Quorndon ducked in after her. "I have asked Miss Marlow to marry me."

"One problem down," Gerald muttered into Lucinda's ear.

"Congratulations to you both!" Lucinda hugged her friend. "I knew you would be perfect for each other."

"Yes, indeed." Gerald shook Lord Quorndon's hand. "I am very pleased for you."

Her brows raised in inquiry, Arabella glanced from Lucinda to Gerald.

"Yes, Lord Elliott has just proposed, and I have accepted." She heaved a sigh. "We just have to gain my mother's approval."

"That should not be a problem once we announce our betrothal," Lord Quorndon said.

Lucinda glanced quickly at Arabella, who grinned. "Yes, he told me."

"Naturally," Quorndon continued, "we must speak to Lord St. Claire, but we expect no difficulty from that quarter."

Her mother would not be pleased. "And I will have to listen to my mother complain about how I failed."

"Oh, dear." Arabella pressed her lips together. "Will she go on and on? Is there another way to tell her?"

"Yes. There is." Gerald's tone was so commanding they all looked at him. "We will bring Lady Quorndon and your mother together and make the announcements at the same time."

"Are you having a meeting under here?" Rothwell and Louisa ducked under the branches and joined them. He glanced at Lucinda. "We've been looking for you."

There was no time like the present to find out if her brother would support her. "Lord Quorndon and Miss Marlow have become affianced, and I have accepted Lord Elliott's proposal of marriage." Lucinda waited for a show of surprise from her brother, instead a slow smile curved his lips.

Rothwell nodded. "Well, first, allow me to congratulate all of you. I believe the matches you have arranged for yourselves are much better than those my mother attempted to make."

"Thank you." Relief washed over Lucinda. Perhaps his support would make Mama change her mind.

"Yes, indeed. I wish you all very happy," Louisa added. "What have you decided to do, or have you?"

"We have discussed the matter"—Lucinda gestured to the other three—"and have decided to make our announcements to the mothers jointly. After Quorndon speaks with Miss Marlow's uncle, that is."

"That will take the wind out of Mama's sails," Rothwell commented. "Yet do not expect her to simply give up."

"I suppose that would be too much to ask." Louisa pursed her lips.

"There must be options." Lucinda looked from her brother to her sister-in-law. "Something I can do to force her to allow me to wed Elliott." *Think, think, think.* "Rothwell, you and Louisa could accompany us to Scotland. It would not be scandalous if we had you as chaperones."

"No, my love." Gerald tightened his arm around her. "The journey would still have to be clandestine, and it would harm not only Rothwell's reputation, but ours as well."

Well, drat. "I suppose you are correct." Lucinda thought some more. "I could refuse to wed another gentleman and wait until I was of age, or until she gave in."

"Not that I wouldn't wait for you," Gerald said, "but I'd prefer to marry sooner rather than later." He drew his brows together. "I thought she did not like me because she wanted Lucinda to marry a marquis." He focused on Rothwell. "But that's not it at all, is it?"

"No." Lucinda huffed. "She objects to the newness of your title."

"That makes no sense." He huffed as if offended. As he should be. "My breeding and bloodlines are as good as yours."

"As I have tried to explain to her," Rothwell grumbled. "If this meeting is at an end, shall we head back to Town? The sooner this is resolved, the happier I'll be."

"You're not the only one." Gerald led Lucinda out from under the tree's canopy, squinting at the bright sunshine.

"I am extremely pleased that I shall not have these problems with my mother," Lord Quorndon said. Rothwell gave him a dubious look. "I'm of age. Even if she doesn't like it, there is nothing she can do."

"There is that." Lucinda wished she was of age—or that her mother was not so difficult.

A group of young ladies and gentlemen were passing by on the path when the six of them emerged from under the tree canopy. If Rothwell and Louisa had not been present, Lucinda knew there would have been talk.

As it was, Miss Martindale giggled, and Miss Tice said, "You missed the announcement."

Lucinda shook her head, not understanding. Mr. Camp, who was escorting Miss Tice, explained. "Lord Beaumont and Lady Serena are betrothed."

"It must be the bluebells," Lord Quorndon murmured.

Miss Martindale's eyes rounded. "I beg your pardon?"

"Nothing." Arabella pinched his arm. "It was nothing worth repeating."

Lucinda threw her friend a grateful look. None of them could announce their betrothals until later. It would not do for the news to precede them.

Their group lost no time hurrying back to the house and sending for the horses and carriage. Unfortunately, they also had to find Lady Talgath, thank her for the lovely time, and bid her adieu.

"The rest of you can go to the carriage," Louisa offered. "Rothwell and I will speak with her ladyship. It will be faster."

Lucinda was in the process of nodding her head when Lady Talgath appeared.

"Must you depart as well? Lord Beaumont and Lady Serena rushed back to Town to tell their families they are betrothed."

Lucinda smiled politely, but had to fight down the heat growing in her chest and neck. "How delightful for them!"

"It is indeed." Lady Talgath gazed at Lucinda more closely. "You would not have similar news, would you?" Before she could deny it, the lady cut a look at Arabella, whose face had turned a lovely shade of rose pink. "Oh! Upon my word! Both of you! Who would have guessed that I would have three betrothals at my little party!" In a flutter of shawls and scent, her ladyship embraced both Arabella and Lucinda. "My lords, you are very lucky gentlemen. I wish you all happy." She ushered them out the door. "Lose no time informing your families. Although I see that Rothwell already knows."

"If only it were that simple," he muttered.

"What did you say, your grace?" Lady Talgath asked.

"Nothing at all." He bowed. "Thank you for inviting us. We enjoyed your party immensely."

Once they reached the road, Rothwell motioned to the outrider he'd insisted upon having. "Go to Lord Quorndon's house, and mine. Inform Lady Quorndon and her grace that we will be arriving within the hour and wish to speak with them both at Rothwell House. Tell Fredericks to serve tea when we arrive, and to ready two bottles of champagne to bring at my order, but not before."

"Yes, your grace." The footman rode off at spanking pace, dust rising from his horse's hooves.

"Do you think we will talk Mama around that quickly?" Lucinda asked.

Rothwell grimaced. "She will not have a choice."

Chapter 12

Lucinda exhaled slowly. The last time she had seen her brother so resolute was when he had declared their mother would help bring her out.

"The betrothals will be all over Town by dinner," Rothwell said. "To withhold her consent after it's known that I approve would be to publicly set her will against mine. Also, Quorndon is no longer available."

"We've taken care of my mother and your mother," Lord Quorndon said. "But I must still speak with Lord St. Claire. I propose I ride ahead and formally ask for Miss Marlow's hand."

"I suppose you must," Rothwell said. "But be quick about it. Your presence is required for the meeting with our mothers."

Lord Quorndon galloped off. "Arabella," Lucinda said. "I must thank you for your blush. It has, apparently, eased the way for Lord Elliott and me."

"I am happy that for once it has done some good." She twisted her lips into a grimace. "Usually it only gets me into trouble."

To ensure the footman and Lord Quorndon were able to complete their tasks before the rest of them arrived in Town, Rothwell ordered that the carriage be kept to a sedate pace on the way back to Mayfair. By the time they arrived, Lord and Lady Quorndon were drinking tea with Lucinda's mother.

Mama smiled brightly when Lucinda entered the room with her sister-in-law. "I hear there is to be an announcement?"

Lord Quorndon stood and crossed the parlor to Arabella. Lucinda placed her hand on Gerald's arm, and Rothwell and Louisa stood next to them. Short work was made of the formalities.

"What is this?" Mama asked.

Lord Quorndon drew Arabella forward. "We have two betrothals to announce. Miss Marlow has graciously agreed to become my wife."

Mama sucked in a breath, and her face paled to a chalky white. For a moment, Lucinda thought she would swoon.

"You and Miss Marlow?" Mama held one hand to her breast, and her voice was thready.

"Yes, your grace." Lord Quorndon bowed. "Something occurred that I never expected or, indeed, believed could happen." His gaze softened as he glanced at Arabella. "I fell in love."

"Thank God!" His mother flew forward, hugging them both.

Mama's glance went from Lucinda to Gerald. "And?"

Lucinda straightened her shoulders. Now was not the time to falter. "Lord Elliott and I fell in love as well. He proposed, and I have agreed to marry him."

Her mother's face twisted into an angry mask. "Yet I have not agreed to allow it."

"If you do not want to appear at odds with me,"—Rothwell used his I-am-the-duke-tone—"you will accept that they will marry."

"No one need know about a proposal that you have no authority to approve." Mama's hard tone matched his.

"That, however, is precisely the problem. Lady Talgath knows," Rothwell said. "By this evening, half of the *ton* will know." He raised one brow. "You are, of course, free to continue to withhold your consent. However, everyone will know that I approve of the match."

As the moment stretched, Lucinda tightened her grip on Gerald's arm. He covered her cold fingers with his warm hand, and they waited for her mother's decision.

"It seems you leave me little choice." Eyes cold, her mother rose and left the room.

Lucinda let out the breath she had been holding. "It is not perfect, but it is good enough. I doubt she will ever forgive me."

"Dear child." Lady Quorndon touched Lucinda's cheek. "She will come around. I shall talk to her."

"Thank you." Lucinda placed her hand on her ladyship's. "I hope you are happy with the way things turned out."

"My dear, I could not be more delighted." Lady Quorndon glanced fondly at her son and Arabella. "Look at the two of them. It is as if they were created for each other."

Lucinda took a moment to congratulate herself on a match well made. "I could not agree more."

Fredericks came in with the champagne and began to pour. "May I say, my lady, that I and the staff wish you very happy."

"Thank you, Fredericks." Now if only Mama would agree, Lucinda's life would be perfect.

"When would you like to wed?" Louisa asked.

"As soon as I can procure a special license," Gerald responded.

Rothwell barked a laugh. "I wish you luck with that."

"You will want to have a trousseau made," Louisa added.

"Not if I take her to Paris on our wedding trip." Gerald slipped his arm around Lucinda's waist. He wanted them married and away from here. "Would you like that, my love?"

"I have never thought of such a thing, but yes." She gazed up at him, her green eyes shining with happiness. "Going to Paris with you is a perfect idea."

"It's settled then." He grinned. "Lucinda can buy a new wardrobe in France. One week?"

"Sooner, if we can manage it." She returned his smile.

"You cannot complain," the duchess said to Rothwell.

"No, I suppose I can't. Elliott, my office at nine in the morning. We will discuss the settlement agreements."

"I'll be there."

A few minutes later, he set his glass down. His mother wouldn't be any happier than the dowager duchess, but he must tell her before she heard about their engagement from another source. "Lucinda and I must inform my mother."

The door to Gerald's soon-to-be-residence opened before he and Lucinda placed one foot on the front steps.

"My lord, my lady." Collins bowed. "Welcome."

"Why do I get the feeling we are expected?" Gerald mused, more to himself than anyone else. "My dear, this is Collins. Collins, meet Lady Lucinda Hughlot, soon to be your new mistress."

Gerald could have sworn that for a fleeting moment, his butler smiled.

"My lady." The butler bowed. "It is an honor."

Lucinda inclined her head, looking more like a duchess than a future countess. "I am very glad to meet you as well, Collins."

He bowed again. "Her ladyship is in the back parlor."

"I think you're right," Lucinda said after they'd gone halfway down the corridor. "I wonder if your mother is aware of our betrothal."

"But how?" Their houses were not so close together that regular servants' gossip would account for it.

"I do not know."

"We'll find out in a minute."

The door to the parlor was open. His mother and cousin sat together on one of two sofas, staring expectantly in his and Lucinda's direction. The strange thing was Mother didn't seem to be upset. "She knows."

"Elliott, Lady Lucinda." His mother came forward holding out her hands. "We have been waiting for you to arrive."

"So it appears," Gerald said, "but *why* have you been waiting?"

His mother glanced briefly at his cousin. "Anne was performing a service for me earlier today, and she happened to see Lady Berryfield, who had heard from her daughter, Lady Manners, who had been at Lady Talgath's event earlier, that she had every expectation of hearing you and Lady Lucinda were betrothed."

"Naturally," Anne said, taking up the story, "I said that I could not discuss it at the moment, and as soon as I finished my commission I came straight home to tell dear Edith the news."

"So you see, we knew you would be here as soon as you were able." His mother drew Lucinda into her arms. "I cannot tell you how happy I am that you are joining the family."

He narrowed his eyes at his mother. "You are?"

"Oh, you are thinking of our earlier discussion." A slow smile formed on Mother's face. "It was Sally Jersey's idea. You have been so slow in finding a bride that we thought a little well-timed opposition would help you along. I know how much you dislike my interference."

He was going to strangle her—or at the very least lecture her. As soon as he could think of exactly what to say.

Lucinda covered her lips with one hand, but not before a laugh slipped out. "I wonder if it worked."

He thought about it for a few seconds. It might have. He had started noticing her more after his mother's comments. "I hate to admit it, but I think it did."

"There!" His mother practically crowed.

There was nothing else to do but shake his head.

"Excuse me, my lord, my ladies," Collins said. "I have brought champagne and tea."

They spent the next hour discussing the upcoming nuptials and the house.

"Mother, if you have your own house, why did you insist on keeping mine?"

"My thinking was really very simple. As a single gentleman, you could not entertain ladies. Therefore, you had no need of it. But, more importantly, I hoped that at some point you would comply with the terms of your father's will and marry."

"I can assure you I would not have wed merely because I wished to have possession of the house."

"No." She heaved a sigh. "That soon became obvious. Thus the reason for my scheme." A moment later, the smile returned to her face. "I envy you your trip to Paris. I have not been since before you were born."

She wasn't going now either. "We shall write you and tell you what you need to know in order to make a trip in the summer or next year."

"Thank you, dear. That is an excellent idea." She took a sip of champagne. "I shall be busy at my house tomorrow, but Lucinda, you should lose no time in meeting with Mrs. Roswell, our housekeeper. She will be able to oversee any changes you plan to make so that it can all be done while you and Elliott are on your wedding trip."

He took Lucinda's hand. "Are you available tomorrow?"

Her dark brows drew together, then she replied, "I am going with my sister-in-law to Madam Lisette's directly after breakfast to order clothing for the journey. She has some sort of relative who is a modiste in Paris; I shall wish to visit when we arrive. I should be free by noon."

Which meant he'd have to discover a way to spend some time alone with Lucinda after she met with his housekeeper.

The next afternoon, Gerald still hadn't worked out a way to get Lucinda to himself. Ever since he'd discovered he loved her—indeed, even before that—he needed to make her his. Granted, the wedding was only days away, but he did not want to wait.

When he arrived at Rothwell House, she was waiting for him, wearing a walking gown that matched her beautiful green eyes. His heart squeezed. How had he not recognized that she was the lady for him when he'd first seen her?

She put her fingers on his arm. "Meeting with your housekeeper is making this all seem so real."

His stomach dropped. What would he do if she decided she didn't what him after all? "Are you regretting promising to marry me?"

She stared at him, her eyes wide. "No. Why would you think such a thing?"

"Nerves. It's taken me so long to find the right lady."

"I, on the other hand, was fortunate to find the right gentleman almost straightaway." Taking his hand, she raised it to her lips. "Let us go and see how much work there is to be done."

As soon as they arrived, his mother greeted them, then called for her bonnet. "I would love to show you the house." Mother kissed Lucinda's cheek. "But Mrs. Roswell will do a much better job. You will be able to talk to her about what you would like to change without fear of hurting my feelings." His mother placed one finger to her lips. "I do hope you replace this dreadful Egyptian style furniture."

He couldn't believe what he was hearing. "You chose that furniture."

"Yes, dear. It was another attempt to convince you to marry. I thought if you hated the furnishings and decoration you would find a wife to change it."

Lucinda went off into a peal of laughter, while he fought to keep from gaping. Did he even know his mother?

"Oh, there you are, Mrs. Roswell." His mother grinned at Lucinda. "This is our—now your—housekeeper, Mrs. Roswell. Mrs. Roswell, Lady Lucinda, soon to be your new mistress."

His housekeeper bobbed a curtsey. "Welcome, my lady. Her ladyship said I was to show you and his lordship the house."

"Thank you, Rosy." Gerald took Lucinda's arm. "We're ready."

An hour later, Rosy had made several pages of notes, and they hadn't even got to the master's and mistress's bed-chambers. He wondered what horrors he'd find there. It would probably be horrible. He and Lucinda would have to spend their wedding night at a hotel.

Rosy opened the door. The walnut furniture, darkened by age, was the same, but the hangings and coverings were all new and tastefully done. Cream and gold stripes covered the walls. The bed hangings were cream, embroidered in maroon and gold. Two chairs next to the fireplace were covered in maroon velvet.

"It is beautiful!" Lucinda exclaimed, walking into the chamber.

"I couldn't agree more." He glanced at his housekeeper. "When was this done?"

"In the past few weeks." Rosy opened the door to the connecting bedroom. "My lady, I hope you like your chamber as well."

Lucinda entered the room and clapped her hands over her mouth. "I love it! Yellow is my favorite color."

A knock sounded on the door, and a maid came in. "I'm sorry to interrupt, but we need Mrs. Roswell below stairs."

"I'm coming." She glanced at Gerald and Lucinda. "I am sorry, my lord, my lady. It must be important. I left instructions that I was not to be bothered."

"Not at all. I can take it from here." This was his chance to finally be alone with Lucinda. "The rooms do not appear to need anything."

"Thank you for understanding." He thought he saw a sly gleam in Rosy's eyes, but she left the room too quickly for him to be sure.

"Well." Lucinda strolled around the chamber, running her fingers over the back of the sofa, caressing it. "What shall we do?"

He knew what he wanted to do. Taking her in his arms, he kissed her. "My love, do you know what goes on between a husband and wife?"

A blush colored her cheeks. "Louisa told me this morning."

Gerald's mouth dried. He placed his hands on her shoulders, stroking her neck. They had barely had time to kiss—was he rushing her? "What did she say?"

"She said that if you were anything like Rothwell, you would find a way to take advantage of the house inspection to make me yours. There is to be kissing." She put her hands on his chest, sliding them up around his neck. "We have not had much time for kissing."

Bending his head, he pressed his lips to hers, running his tongue along the seam of her mouth. There was no need to coax her. She opened her mouth, and on a soft moan allowed him in. He slanted his head and their tongues danced. God, she tasted good, like a lemon tart.

He pressed kisses along her jaw and throat. "What else did she say?"

"She said you would touch and kiss me everywhere, and that I would enjoy the feelings." She drew a sharp breath when he rubbed his thumbs over her hard nipples. Reaching up, Lucinda kissed him. "Yes."

She was going to be the death of him. "Was there anything else?"

"That you would want to see me naked, but I would be able to see you as well, and touch and kiss you." Copying what he'd done, she fluttered kisses on his jaw. "Your neckcloth is in my way."

He held his breath, then let it out. There was one more question he must ask: "Did she tell you it would be painful?"

"Yes." His cravat slid to the floor. "But only the first time." Lucinda pushed at his jacket. "She said you would make sure I enjoyed most of it, and that it would be the most wonderful experience, and I must not be afraid."

Thank God for helpful sisters-in-law. "I will make it as perfect for you as I am able."

He helped her remove his jacket. Unfastening her gown was surprisingly easy. Their clothes slipped to the carpet. At first he was careful about removing her hair pins, but soon they were dropping to the carpet, and her long tresses fell over her shoulders and down her back. "You're beautiful. The most beautiful woman I've ever seen."

Good Lord, Louisa had been right. A man in love always thought his woman was beautiful.

Lucinda stared at Gerald's chest. A sprinkling of dark hair on his muscular chest. He was a work of art. He drew one of Lucinda's nipples into his mouth and the place between her legs began to throb. His hard shaft rose between them. He groaned when she touched it. It was as soft as she'd been told it would be.

He lifted her up, holding her against him as he carried her to the bedchamber and crawled onto the mattress, taking her mouth again as his hands caressed her body. Soon his lips were where his hands had been. His teeth lightly grazed one already hard nipple before he moved to the other. Her hips bucked when he slid his fingers between her legs. "More."

"Are you sure?" Gerald's worried gaze captured her.

"Absolutely sure." Tension built as he stroked between her legs and entered her with his fingers. She cried out as the tremors engulfed her. He held her gently, kissing her face and lips. "Now it's time for the rest."

Though he was as gentle as he could be, and she tried to relax, knowing it was going to hurt made it difficult. A sharp pain pierced her as he filled her, stretching her until she didn't think she could meet his needs.

He stopped. His gaze filled with love, concern lining his forehead. "How do you feel?"

"I'm fine." Or she would be.

Gerald withdrew, and when he entered her again there was soreness, but not the pain she had felt before. With his every stroke, her apprehension fell away as need consumed her and she rose to meet his thrusts. Soon the tension exploded within, and she gasped as a wave of convulsions left her sated. Moments later, he shouted her name and fell off to his side, cuddling her next to him. "I love you."

"I love you too." Lucinda nestled her head on his chest. She had never felt this close to another person. "Will we sleep together after we marry?"

"Yes." He rolled her over so that her body covered his. "I want to wake up to you every morning."

"I want that too." She cupped his cheek. "I shall always love you."

"I'll always love you." He wove his fingers through her hair. "I can't believe it took me so long to figure it out."

A clock struck the hour. "What time is it?"

Gerald grinned. "I don't think we need to worry about that."

She meant to kiss him lightly, playfully, but the moment her lips touched his, passion shot through her body. It was several moments before he spoke again. "When our"—she relished that he'd said "our"—"housekeeper left, my only thought was that I would finally have you alone."

"You think she did it on purpose?" After all, what could have been so important that the woman wouldn't return?

"I do. I also think my mother left the house as soon as she could."

She bent her head and kissed him softly. This cuddling was very nice, and Lucinda hoped they would do it often. "I wondered about that." She was playing with his chest hair again when an uncomfortable thought occurred to her. "If they left us alone on purpose, they all know what we're doing."

Gerald's chest began to shake with laughter. "To be precise, they don't know what is going on, they are probably hoping something is going on. It will depend upon how disheveled you look."

The rest of Louisa's advice now made sense. "That was the reason my sister-in-law told me to wear something that would not wrinkle easily, and to bring extra hair pins."

Epilogue

Three days later, Lucinda watched in the mirror as Greene put up her hair into a knot. "What did you think of the staff at our new home?"

"They were all very nice and helpful when I was preparing your bedchamber." Greene held up a strand of pearls, then put it down. "I'll wait until you return from the church. You'll have your bonnet on in any event."

"I think the pearl necklace and earrings will be enough for the service." She was already wearing a turquoise and diamond bracelet from Louisa. Rothwell had given her a beautiful gold butterfly broach set with emeralds and diamonds that had been in their family for centuries.

Greene took a pearl and emerald necklace Lucinda had never seen before from her jewel box. "Where did that come from?" she asked.

"Lord Elliott, my lady. He brought it earlier this morning and gave it to his grace."

She fought back the tears of joy that threatened to spill over. She would not cry today, no matter what kind of tears they were. "I cannot imagine anything lovelier."

Just as her maid had clasped the necklace around her neck, a knock sounded on the door. Greene opened it, and Arabella floated into the bedchamber. "I shall not hug you; you look too beautiful, and I would not wish to muss you." She handed Greene a small package. "Something borrowed."

Lucinda and Arabella had decided to support each other at their weddings. Yet due to Gerald's plan to leave for Dover early the next morning, Arabella and Quorndon would wed directly after Lucinda and Gerald. Louisa had suggested a joint wedding breakfast be held at Rothwell House.

Once Greene had affixed three pearl-tipped pins into Lucinda's hair, she handed her friend a cameo broach. "Something new."

"Oh, this is perfect!" Arabella leaned over carefully and bussed Lucinda's cheek before pinning it on her bodice.

Louisa entered the room and smiled. "You both look beautiful. However, if you wish to be married today, we must leave. Miss Marlow, could you give us a moment?"

"Yes, your grace." Arabella floated back out of the room.

There was only one dark cloud on the extremely sunny day: Lucinda's mother hadn't spoken to her since the betrothal. "Mama?"

"She has accepted the marriage and will be present."

"How did you do it?"

"We discovered that Quorndon is not in as good financial condition as she had believed. In fact, even if he had not fallen in love with Miss Marlow, she is a much better choice for him. Her father is extremely wealthy, and her dowry is equally large. Not only that, but Lady Quorndon let it slip that Miss Marlow has a head for figures that Quorndon does not." Louisa raised one brow. "Your mother did not at all like the idea that she had been so deceived in the man." This last part was said so exactly like Mama would have said it that Lucinda could not stop herself from laughing.

Her sister-in-law slipped an arm through hers. "I would let the matter go. By the time you return from your wedding trip, all will be well again."

Lucinda entered the side door of the church followed by Arabella. Gerald was dressed in a dark blue jacket and breeches, but his waistcoat was embroidered with flowers and vines that matched the trim on her gown. Clever man. He was the most handsome gentleman she had ever seen. And he was hers.

Gerald stood with Quorndon and the young clergyman in front of the altar at St. George's church as Lucinda made her way to the altar. Sun filled the large windows lining the walls, illuminating her as she strolled toward him. Or was it that she sparkled so brilliantly that she would have brightened the church had it been raining? "She is exquisite."

"Yes, indeed," Quorndon breathed.

Only then did Gerald notice Miss Marlow. The lady could not hold a candle to his Lucinda, whose yellow silk gown trimmed with embroidered flowers hugged her legs as she walked toward him—legs that had been wrapped around him and would be again.

Rothwell slapped Gerald on the back as he went to Lucinda. "Not long now."

Only a minute later, they were saying their vows. Her voice was firm and strong as she promised herself to him. Finally, the clergyman pronounced them man and wife.

Joy filled his heart as, finally, she was his.

AUTHOR NOTES

The Regency was a time of great change in attitudes about marriage. Many in both the older generation and the younger believed love matches were messy and undignified. Still, there were those who yearned for love in their marriages. It was a conflict that would continue for another century.

Not much was known about dementia or other mental disorders. Therefore, they were considered embarrassments to families at best and to be avoided at worst. It would not have been unusual for a parent or guardian to object to marriage if one party had mental problems in the family.

About Gerald Elliott's title: I didn't plan for him to be Earl Elliott. In fact, it was a bit of a shock when I realized what I'd done. Calling him Lord Elliott in one book and then mentioning that he was an earl in another . . . these things happen when one is not paying good attention to secondary characters. There are very few earls who are not "Earl of Placename," yet there are some. The most famous is Earl Spencer. The title was first Baron Althorp, then Viscount Althorp, and finally Earl Spencer.

I hope you loved Lucinda and Gerald's story. Those of you who read The Marriage Game series will have recognized the mention of Lady Serena and Lord Beaumont from *The Seduction of Lady Serena*. Also Lords Huntley and Wively and Mr. Kit Featherton are still running around as bachelors. For those of you who haven't read The Marriage Game, all the books can be found on my website, www.ellaquinn author.com.